# Murder Mystery
## A Blizzard Rages. A Killer Strikes.
### Ely North

Red Handed Print

Copyright © 2024 by Ely North

All rights reserved. This book or parts thereof may not be reproduced
in any form, distributed, stored in any retrieval system, or transmitted in
any form by any means—electronic, mechanical, photocopy, recording, or
otherwise—without prior written permission of the author, except in the case of
brief quotations embodied in critical reviews and certain other non-commercial
uses permitted by copyright law.

Website: https://elynorthcrimefiction.com

To contact ely@elynorthcrimefiction.com

https://www.facebook.com/elynorthcrimefictionUK

Cover design by Cherie Chapman/Chapman & Wilder

Cover images © Paul / Liam Grant Photography / Dimitri Bodski / Adobe Stock
Photos

Disclaimer: This is a work of fiction. Names, characters, businesses, places,
events, locales, and incidents are either the products of the author's imagination
or used in a fictitious manner. Any resemblance to actual persons, living or dead,
or actual events is purely coincidental.

Published by Red Handed Print

First Edition

Kindle e-book ISBN-13: 978-0-6459958-6-2

Paperback ISBN-13: 978-0-6459958-7-9

# Also By Ely North - DCI Finnegan Series

Book 1: **Black Nab**

Book 2: **Jawbone Walk**

Book 3: **Vertigo Alley**

Book 4: **Whitby Toll**

Book 5: **House Arrest**

Book 6: **Gothic Fog**

Book 7: **Happy Camp**

Book 8: **Harbour Secrets**

Book 9: **Murder Mystery**

**Book 10: Wicker Girl (Pre-order)**

DCI Finnegan Series Boxset #1: **Books 1 – 3**

DCI Finnegan Series Boxset #2: **Books 4 – 6**

Prequel: **Aquaphobia** (Free ebook for newsletter subscribers)

*Note: All books are available from Amazon in ebook, paperback, and in **Kindle Unlimited** (excluding Aquaphobia). Paperbacks can be ordered from all good bookshops. **Boxset print editions are one book compiled from three books. They do not come in a box. *** Pre-orders only apply to ebooks.

# Character List

**Kindlewood Hall Country Hotel** – A North Yorkshire Victorian country manor converted many years ago into an upmarket hotel.

**Virgil Langley** – Current proprietor (husband to Penelope, brother to Murdoch)

**Penelope Langley** – Current proprietor (wife to Virgil, sister-in-law to Murdoch)

**Ethan Langley** – Adopted son of Virgil and Penelope

**Murdoch Langley** – Investment banker (younger brother to Virgil)

**Lucy Hargreaves** – Front of house receptionist at Kindlewood Hall

**Chef Antoine Galois** – Esteemed international chef at Kindlewood Hall

**Logan Fitch** – Local accountant to various businesses

**Hugh Foster** – Local cattle farmer

**Maggie Thornton** – Owner of a bed-and-breakfast in the nearby village

**Amy Holland** – A guest passing through

**Dr Pierre Quint** and **Madame Edith Quint** – Mother and son on holiday

**Imogen Sato** – Renowned brutal food critique

**Eve Sinclair** – Investigative journalist

**Podger** – Stray cat that calls Kindlewood Hall, home

# 1

# Kindlewood Hall Country Hotel – North Yorkshire

**Monday 16th December**

The hum of a vacuum cleaner drifts down from the first-floor landing as the last guest drives away, the car wheels scrunching over a thick layer of gravel. The grandfather clock from the drawing room awakens and tolls ten times.

Lucy Hargreaves returns from the kitchen with a strong brew of Americano coffee and takes her seat behind the reception counter.

She enjoys Mondays. It's peaceful, and she doesn't see much of the owners, Virgil and Penelope Langley.

The hotel is open seven days a week, serving breakfast daily. Lunch and evening meals are served six days a week—but never on Mondays, which is another reason she enjoys them. No chef with his beady-eyed, salacious gaze brushing up against her at every opportunity.

Tapping at the laptop, she pulls up the email from her best friend Violet, and re-reads it for the third time, unconsciously smiling, as the rich, comforting aroma of coffee mingles with the intoxicating fresh scent of pine from the Christmas tree, infusing the air with an almost festive calm. A cough followed by soft singing drifts from the office behind her. Tapping at the keyboard, she switches from her personal email to Kindlewood Hall's Gmail account, then turns around as Virgil Langley bangs and clatters from the doorway, golf clubs slung over his shoulder. He leans them up against the counter and ponders, rubbing his chin.

'Now, did I feed the fish?' he asks himself, staring back into the office at the tropical fish tank. In a eureka moment, he lifts a finger in the air. 'Yes, I did. I remember now.'

Lucy, unseen, rolls her eyes. The same routine plays out at least three times a week with Virgil Langley and his precious tropical fish.

'Lucy, I'll be out until late afternoon. I'm playing nine holes with Hugh Foster this morning, then lunching with Logan Fitch.'

She raises an eyebrow, surprised. 'Oh. I take it the ice has thawed?'

Virgil smiles and straightens, puffing out his chest. 'I doubt this was covered in your Business Management degree, but it's always wise to oil the wheels of industry. Friends are better than enemies, Lucy. When disputes arise and harsh words are spoken, you let the dust settle... then you hold out an olive branch.'

Mentally, she tries to count the number of cliches in his statement but abandons it. Virgil Langley may be a bit of an old soak, occasionally lose his short temper, and be scatterbrained, and a panic merchant to boot, but out of all the people that work at the hotel, she has a little soft spot for him. He hasn't a bad bone in his body. He's simply a little... eccentric and hopeless.

Two rapid mews are followed by a dirty white cat jumping onto the counter. With tail erect, it paces back and forth, meowing sharply.

'Ah, Podger,' Virgil declares, picking the cat up and stroking it lovingly. 'Where have you been, eh? Out all night, no doubt up to mischief.' He walks back to the office and places the cat on the office chair. 'You wait here until the evil witch has gone out—yes?' The cat purrs contentedly and sits on its back legs, staring at the fish swimming back and forth. 'He's amazing, you know. He can sit there for hours watching the fish. They fascinate him. Never tries to get at them, though. Right, where was I?'

'Golf with Hugh Foster. Lunch with Logan Fitch,' Lucy prompts, wishing he'd hurry up and leave.

He closes the office door, winks at her, and taps his nose. 'Not a word to you know who, about Podger, eh?'

'I'll not say a word, Mr Langley.'

He slings the clubs over his shoulder. 'Good. I know I can depend on you.'

Lucy smiles benignly and watches as he strides briskly down the long hallway to the entrance. One of the golf clubs rubs up against the tall Christmas tree and dislodges a bauble. It clatters to the floor and rolls under a radiator.

'Damn and blast! Pick that up, would you, Lucy? There's a good girl.'

'Sir.'

'Oh, and can you feed Podger once Mrs Langley has departed?'

'Yes, sir,' she replies as the front door slams shut.

Her eyes flick back onto the laptop as she takes a sip of coffee. A hundred thoughts dart around her mind as she mentally juggles what to put in her reply to Violet. They were never the sort of friends to waste words describing the minutia of life. No, when they talked, it was always high octane; rumours, facts, gossip, innuendo. Never a dull moment.

She switches back to her email account and types out a line, pauses, then deletes it.

'Boring,' she mutters to herself.

Her focus is again broken as the click clack of heels tap across the tiled floor. She adjusts her ponytail and rises as Penelope Langley approaches.

Lucy, although aged twenty-three, has a youthful demeanour, akin to an eighteen-year-old. Her face still parades a smattering of freckles, which she's slightly embarrassed about but refuses to cover up with makeup. Hazel eyes rest beneath auburn hair. A Yorkshire lass through and through, Lucy has a touch of the Irish about her—impish and quietly sharp, with a keen eye for human nature and its foibles.

'Good morning, Mrs Langley,' she says as Penelope enters the reception.

Penelope Langley, her ash-blonde hair styled to perfection and her piercing green eyes framed by the faintest of crow's feet, exudes polished authority in her tailored designer suit and ever-present pearl necklace. She stops, massages the pearls absentmindedly, and stares at the entrance before finally turning to address Lucy.

'Have you seen Mr Langley?' she asks.

'Yes. He left a few moments ago.'

'Where was he going?'

'He said he was playing golf with Hugh Foster, then having lunch with Logan Fitch.'

Penelope appears distracted. 'Good. He's finally done as I asked,' she mutters to herself. 'Did he say what time he would be back?'

'Late afternoon.'

She releases the pearls from her fingers. 'Hmm... I see.' Straightening, as if slapped awake, she fixes Lucy with a piercing stare. 'How many guests are booked in for tonight?'

'Fifteen.'

'Good, I suppose.' She turns as if to leave. 'Oh, by the way, we're expecting a few food deliveries today for the forthcoming Murder Mystery Christmas weekend. As you know, it's Chef Antoine and the kitchen staff's day off. Make sure you meet each delivery driver and double check the produce and reconcile it with the invoice before they drive off. We've been burnt before. Then transfer the vegetables into the cold room and the meat into the walk-in freezer. And one of the cleaners has not turned up today, so Mrs Baker may need some help. It's a relatively quiet day for you, so make yourself useful.'

'Yes, Mrs Langley.'

Penelope's attention drifts onto the reception countertop and the muddy paw prints.

'That damned cat,' she hisses. 'Have you seen it?'

Lucy manages not to blink. 'No, Mrs Langley.'

'I've told *you* and my *husband* a thousand times before, that damned feral cat is not allowed inside the hotel.'

'He's very crafty, Mrs Langley. He always manages to find a way in.'

'Hmm... well, if you come across him, shoo the fleabag outside. It's not a good look having a mangy old cat wandering around the place. And clean the counter. The reception area is your responsibility, Lucy. A vacuum, dust, and polish is in order.'

'Very good, Mrs Langley.'

'Right, I have a meeting at eleven with the Small Business Development Council, followed by a massage for my stiff neck. I'll be back around three-thirty. Please don't call me unless it's absolutely necessary. Oh, one more thing. I've told you this on at least a dozen occasions—when guests are in our presence, you address me as ma'am, and Mr Langley as sir. Yesterday, you erred once again.'

'Apologies, Mrs Langley.'

'Don't let it happen again. We receive three to four job applications per week begging to work in such an esteemed establishment as Kindlewood Hall. Don't forget, no one is irreplaceable, Lucy.'

'I won't, Mrs Langley.'

Penelope wheels around, her heels click-clacking sharply as she heads for the front door. The moment her back is turned, Lucy scowls and fires off a series of two-fingered salutes in rapid succession, unseen and full of resentment. She waits, listening, until the rumble of Penelope's Range Rover Vogue fades into the distance.

Finally, she sinks back into her chair, pulls up the email, and begins typing.

### Subject: Greetings from Munster Mansion!

Dear Violet,

I know you don't *do* social media, so what a wonderful surprise to receive an email from you this morning. To say we're best friends, we're pretty hopeless at keeping in touch (LOL).

Trust you to land a job in Bali as a tour guide for British tourists. You always were the lucky one. I'm green with envy.

As for me, I'm still here, stuck in the wilds of North Yorkshire, working as receptionist at Kindlewood Hall Country Hotel, or Munster Mansion as I call it. I say receptionist, but to be honest, I'm more of a dogsbody. Apart from greeting guests and booking reservations, I help out in the kitchen, serve meals, work behind the bar, clean, and tidy. They even had me helping the gardener mow the bloody lawns during the summer!

I shouldn't complain. I have free accommodation in the old gatekeeper's cottage. It's my own little refuge, far away from the madness of the hotel. I also have free meals, which means if I'm frugal, I can get by without spending a penny. Already have a ton of money saved for our Contiki Expedition together next summer. Believe you me, I'm counting down the days until Australia.

Working here is not too bad, I suppose. It's a magnificent early Victorian country manor house set in a beautiful landscape, even if the interior is starting to go to seed a little. I'm learning all about the hotel business, every aspect of it. And I can tell you one thing I have learned, it's how **not** to run a hotel. I'm not joking, this place is like a soap opera.

**Let me fill you in.**

Firstly, the place is owned and run (I use the term loosely) by the Langleys. They're both in their early sixties. They bought the place way back in the dark ages. I think they come from old money, as they say.

**Virgil Langley** is the Lord of the Manor—think Prince Charles, but with a much worse drinking problem, a temper that flares up like a match, and just enough charm when he's sober to make you forgive him. At this point, his blood's probably 50% single malt. He's all over the shop, with whisky bottles stashed in various hiding spots that he visits religiously throughout the day. By late afternoon, he's merry. By early evening, he's drunk. And by late evening, he's completely hammered. But he's harmless, really, and he puts up with a lot. I actually quite like him.

His wife, **Penelope Langley**, is the ultimate ice queen with a wandering eye. She treats the staff like we're invisible—until something goes wrong and she needs someone to blame. I swear she's got a secret room where she practises her disapproving gaze. Nothing's ever good enough for her. She's a total stickler for protocol, and don't even think about leaving a fingerprint on the silver.

And she's always disappearing... if you know what I mean. (Nudge, nudge, wink, wink.) I've got no proof, but I'd bet good money she's having an affair with Murdoch Langley, Virgil's younger brother. You should see them together. The sly little glances, the way they light up when they're around each other. She starts fiddling with her pearls like she's auditioning for Downton Abbey, and he flicks his hair back like he's in a shampoo ad.

To be fair, Murdoch is kind of handsome—in a George Clooney, silver fox sort of way—if that's your thing. But the aftershave... ugh. It's so cloying it could knock out a horse. Always a turn-off for me.

The problem with the Langleys is they are forever falling out and having petty disputes with people. (I have compiled a list below - ha, ha!) Apparently, they have an adopted son who they disowned some years ago. I've never seen him, and he's *never* talked about, but I've heard whispers about him. **Ethan Langley** used to work here until he blotted his copybook. A bit of a playboy, by all accounts. The archetypal prodigal son. I cannot confirm, nor deny the rumours, but he supposedly cooked the books and swindled the Langleys out of a large sum of money, which left them in a precarious financial situation.

So, let me give you the rundown. A who's who of people the Langleys have alienated at various times.

1. **Logan Fitch** – Semi-retired, ex-accountant to the Langleys. Picture a grumpy bulldog in a rumpled suit. He's still bitter about some fee dispute and knows where all the bodies are buried (metaphorically... I hope). He was the one who alerted the Langleys to the discrepancies in their accounts and pointed the finger at their wastrel son. You'd have thought they'd have thanked him for it, but oh no, not the Langleys. As it happens, Virgil is having lunch with Logan today, building bridges, as it were.

2. This one's funny. **Imogen Sato** – Food critic extraordinaire. Imagine the lovechild of Gordon Ramsay and Cruella de Vil. She wrote a review last year that nearly tanked us. I'll quote you the summary of her review.

"The food was as inspiring as a wet weekend in Grimsby. The service was slower than a snail on elephant tranquillisers, and the ambience at Kindlewood Hall was akin to a funeral parlour, but not as much fun, and as moribund as the food. As for the hosts, the less said the better—though I'm tempted to say it, anyway."

Pretty brutal, right? The Langleys threatened to sue the publisher for defamation, but the case was eventually dropped when they finally realised you cannot defame food. And after all, it was only one person's opinion. Since then, they've hired a new chef, which brings me on to...

3. **Chef Antoine Galois** – Our new culinary genius. Looks like a young Gérard Depardieu, temper like a volcano. He costs the Langleys a fortune. Once served dinner to Emmanuel Macron, Boris Johnson, and Joe Biden... or so he says. Anyway, he's not a happy bunny at the moment because he hasn't been paid for the last two months. He's one of those creepy, sleazy guys who stares at your tits and bum. Also has a nasty habit of brushing up against you, accidentally on purpose. Urgh!

4. **Maggie Thornton**—a late-middle-aged divorcee who runs a B&B in the village. Small but fierce, like a Yorkshire Terrier, except her hair's not as good. She and Mrs L have had more catfights than an alley full of strays. They're on a lot of committees together.

5. **Hugh Foster** – A local farmer built like a brick shithouse. He's in a dispute with the Langleys and swears the

drainage from Kindlewood Hall is poisoning his pastures. Honestly, the way he goes on, you'd think we were running a nuclear power plant, not a hotel.

6. **Murdoch Langley** – Mr L's brother and, as mentioned, I suspect, Mrs L's bit on the side! He's like a pound shop Richard Branson – all fly no trousers. Virgil and Murdoch are always having a go at one another. It doesn't last long before they kiss and make up. They're a bit like the Gallagher brothers, but not as entertaining.

And that's the tip of the iceberg!

I'm looking forward to this weekend in a ghoulish sort of way. The Langleys have organised a Christmas Murder Mystery weekend. You know the thing; a bunch of amateur actors disguised as guests commit murders and the real guests try to figure out whodunit!

I'm expecting a complete fiasco, especially if Virgil can't keep off the sauce. You probably think I'm being mean, but guess what the intrepid duo have done? They've only gone and invited all the above mentioned to the weekend, free of charge, in an arse-kissing exercise. I predict fireworks.

Now, this one is top secret, so hush-hush and stick it in the vault.

A few months back, an investigative freelance journalist called **Eve Sinclair** got in touch with me. She's working on an expose of the hospitality industry. Zero-hour contracts, low wages, ever-expanding job descriptions, sexual harassment - you know the sort of thing. She promised that when her piece is published, she'll use pseudonyms, not real names. And she isn't going to name and shame particular businesses. Anyway, believing her, I gave her a few titbits about the working practices here and the dysfunctional owners. And guess who I noticed as a confirmed guest for this weekend's shenanigans? Yep... Eve Sinclair.

Oh God, I hope she doesn't let anything slip to the Langleys. She wouldn't, would she? No, of course not. I'm being silly. Last thing she wants to do is blow her cover.

And one last thing before I go, and this is possibly the most bizarre. Another confirmed booking for the weekend is a local detective chief inspector and his wife. He's called **Frank Finnegan**. Quite well known around these parts, as he's solved some high-profile crimes. Why in hell's name would a police officer attend a murder mystery weekend? Isn't that like a busman's holiday?

Unless, of course, he knows something I don't (ha, ha).

Pray for me, Vi. If I survive this weekend without committing a murder myself, it'll be a miracle. The things I do to save up for our trip! You'd better have a cocktail waiting for me when I finally escape this madhouse and meet you in Brisbane.

Miss you tons! And let's please, both of us, write more often.

Love,

Lucy

XXX

P.S. If you don't hear from me after this weekend, organise a search party, or possibly a good lawyer!

Lucy re-reads the email, frowning slightly as she tweaks a word here and there. A low thrum outside catches her attention—the unmistakable growl of a diesel engine. She glances out the window, watching a truck rumble its way down the driveway. With a sigh, she snaps the laptop shut.

Opening the office door, she stops and fixes the cat with a look.

'Come along, Podger, brekky time.'

Podger mews in reply, leaps gracefully from the office chair, and pads along behind as Lucy heads for the kitchen to help with the food delivery.

# 2

# Somewhere in Whitby

**Thursday 19th December**

Frank is on his hands and knees, groaning and cursing as he struggles with the Christmas lights.

'Get in there, you recalcitrant little bleeder,' he encourages.

The bulb finally slots into its socket with a click.

'Got you. You pernicious sod.'

He navigates backwards, on all fours, from underneath the lower limbs of the Christmas tree, like a reversing robot dog, as he's pricked and poked by malevolent pine needles. He slumps onto his backside breathing heavily and reaches for the tot of whisky on the coffee table. Music fills the room as numerous stout and hearty fellows, resembling Dickens' Mr Bumble, belt out God Rest Ye Merry Gentlemen from the television set. He takes a sip of the single malt then thinks, *what the hell, it's Christmas,* and knocks the remaining fluid back in one shot. Crossing his fingers, and offering up a silent prayer, he clicks the power back on and squints through one eye at the lights.

'Damn and bugger the bastard things!' he bellows at the top of his lungs.

Meera, alarmed, rushes into the living room from the kitchen, her hands held high, sticky with dough.

'What the hell's the matter? Oh,' she says, well versed in Frank's yearly grapple with the Christmas lights. 'Another bulb gone, has it?' she asks, bearing a severe pout.

'No! I just enjoy sitting on the floor with pine needles stuck up my bloody backside.'

'I told you to buy a new set. They must be over fifteen years old. Sandra buys new lights every other year. They're that cheap these days. And the modern ones keep on even when a bulb blows.'

'You should have married Sandra then,' he grizzles.

'And you still haven't stuck the star on top of the tree. It doesn't feel like Christmas until the star's on.' Her voice trails off as she heads back into the kitchen.

'I'd like to stick you on top of the tree,' he mutters under his breath. Wearily, he lifts himself from the carpet and tops up his whisky glass as a news update flashes on the TV.

*"There could be disappointment for those dreaming of a white Christmas this year. The latest bulletin from the Met Office predicts the arctic storm, moving in a southerly direction across Northern Europe, is set to change course and veer eastwards, sparing most of Britain from an icy blast. The so-called Beast from the East is set to plunge much of Scandinavia into chaos over the festive season, with temperatures expected to drop to minus twenty-five degrees Celsius."*

Frank presses the remote control and flicks through the channels until he lands on a re-run of Fawlty Towers.

'What's minus twenty-five degrees Celsius in the old money?' he shouts through to Meera.

'How the hell would I know? Look it up on your phone.'

He taps at his mobile, and with clumsy fingers, eventually enters the correct request. 'Well, I'll be,' he murmurs to himself. 'It's minus thirteen degrees Fahrenheit, Meera!' he shouts.

'Then turn the heating up!'

Frank stares down at Foxtrot, who is contentedly performing cleaning duties on his genitals, in front of the gas fire.

'Give it a rest, lad. You must have the cleanest canine tackle in the whole of North Yorkshire.'

The aromas drifting from the kitchen are too much for Frank, and although he's had several stern warnings not to enter, he can't help himself. He gently pushes the door open and surveys the scene.

Bowls, plates, and wooden spoons clutter every surface, each bearing traces of flour, dough, and a rainbow of spices. Cooling racks groan under the weight of freshly baked mince pies, their flaky crusts filled with a rich mixture of raisins, sultanas, and a hint of rum. A fruitcake, dense with dried fruit, sits on the counter, having been baked weeks ago and regularly fed with whisky, awaits its marzipan and icing layers. The scent of gingerbread, cut into festive shapes and ready for decorating, mingles with the sweet aroma of cinnamon-spiced apple pie. A pot of mulled wine simmers on the hob, infusing the air with its warming fragrance of star anise, nutmeg, and citrus. The oven is on full blast, roasting a succulent ham, glazed with honey and cloves, while a tray of sausage rolls, the pastry crisp and golden, taunts Frank. Amidst the turmoil, jars of homemade chutney and cranberry sauce stand ready, alongside a bowl of bright red berry trifle, layers of custard and cream just beginning to set. The kitchen hums with the promise of Christmas, each chaotic detail a testament to the joy and tradition of the season.

'Something smells good.'

'Out!'

'Aw, come on, Meera, love. I'm fair famished. How about a couple of sausage rolls and a few mince pies?'

She glares at him. 'No!'

He saunters up behind her, places his hands around her waist, presses in and kisses the back of her neck. 'Not even for old Frank?'

Closing her eyes, she cannot but help enjoy the warmth and closeness. She stops kneading dough and turns to him. 'Two sausage rolls, two mince pies, and that's your lot,' she says with a mock scowl. 'I don't want this lot ravaged before Christmas Day.'

Frank beams and pecks her on the lips. 'No woman can resist the Finnegan charm for long.'

'Ha! As if. Oh, and on one condition,' she states as he collects a plate and hovers over the sausage rolls.

'What?'

'Go and buy a new set of lights before your treats.'

'Tonight?'

'Yes, tonight.'

'But it's nearly seven o'clock.'

'So what? The shops are open until ten.'

'It will be bloody heaving. I think you're being unreas...'

She slaps his hand away from the rolls. 'Tonight! I noticed they were selling lights at the chemist on Upgang Lane. It's only a five-minute stroll. You can take Foxtrot with you for his nightly walk. Kill two birds with one stone. And put the carols back on. I was listening to them.'

He reluctantly agrees. 'Okay.'

As Meera's attention returns to the mountain of dough on the counter, Frank craftily pinches a sausage roll and hides it behind his back, then swiftly exits the kitchen.

'Come on, Foxtrot, walkies!'

The dog whimpers and lifts one paw over his eyes.

'You've got a broken wire somewhere in that pea-sized brain of yours. I've never come across a dog that doesn't get excited about a walk.' He shows the dog the sausage roll, and whispers, 'If you're a good boy, I'll save you a bit.'

Foxtrot obediently sits up, awaiting his lead.

## 3

Frank exits the chemist shop with the box of Christmas lights tucked under his arm. He walks down White Point Road until it meets with North Promenade, then ambles across the frozen grass that crunches underfoot. Picking up the Cleveland Way, he takes a left turn in the direction of Sandsend, pulling his woollen hat further down as an icy breeze off the sea attacks his ears. He glances down at Foxtrot.

'Hellfire, lad, it's cold enough to freeze the barnacles off a choirboy.'

Lifting his pace, he strides briskly along until he comes to a small car park at the end of Upgang Lane. Looking up, he spots the comforting lights and warm glow emanating from inside the White House Inn.

'I think we're in need of sustenance, Foxtrot. I'm not sure we'd make it home alive without a little pick-me-up.' The dog whines and shivers. 'Come on, lad. Look lively.'

Like the lure of the promised land, man and dog march towards the pub.

———◆———

Frank tests the new Christmas lights, and nods, quietly impressed. Standing on a small stepladder, he reaches up and carefully positions the silver star on the tip of the tallest branch. Tentatively, he descends, fully aware of the statistics. Falls, even from a few feet, pose a serious threat to men over sixty, claiming more lives each year than one might expect. He has no desire to join that illustrious pantheon of the height-challenged fraternity.

A mental image flashes through his head, as if he's witnessing his own funeral.

*"Dearly beloved, we are gathered here today to mourn the tragic loss of Frank Finnegan, who failed to comply with the Work at Height Regulations 2005. As you all know, anyone ascending above 1.2 metres must be secured with a fall arrest harness attached to an approved anchor point. He wore no hard hat with chin strap, no safety goggles, no non-slip footwear—and most damning of all, no high-visibility vest. Had he donned that vest, his tragic fall while decorating the Christmas tree might well have been avoided."*

Switching the dining room lights off, he calls his wife.

'Meera, come and have a look.'

'What is it now? Can't you see I'm busy,' she replies, bustling into the room. She abruptly halts, then claps her hands together in glee. 'Oh, Frank, they're beautiful,' she murmurs.

Frank holds the controller in his hand and presses a button. 'Look at this—it's got six different settings. The lights can flash rapidly, fade in and out, or blink intermittently. And they come in red, green, blue, and white.'

'It's perfect and you've put the star on. Now it's Christmas,' she says, kissing him on the cheek.

'Flick the lights back on,' he says. 'I need to tidy up, then I can finally put my feet up.'

As the room floods with light, he picks up the old Christmas lights and stares at them. 'I wonder if I could get these fixed?' he ponders.

Meera scowls. 'Don't be bloody ridiculous. Throw them in the bin.'

'In the bin?' he queries, as if he's been asked to chop his arm off.

'Yes, in the bin. They probably cost you a fiver twenty years ago at the back of the market. They only had two positions—on and off.'

Frank glares back disapprovingly. 'You know, when I was a lad, my dad fixed things. If something broke, he didn't throw it away, he'd mend it. People were frugal and resourceful. That's the problem these days—we live in a disposable society. Built in obsolescence in everything we buy. It's a capitalist ploy to keep reaching into our wallets. Bastards.'

Meera winds the old lights into a ball and drops them in the bin. 'It's a set of ancient Christmas lights, Frank, not a global conspiracy by the Illuminati to squeeze ten quid out of you.'

'They cost fifteen, actually,' he replies, staring dolefully into the bin. 'Maybe I'll put them in the shed and take a look at them another day.'

'No you don't! That shed is already chock-a-block with broken kettles, microwaves, toasters, a vacuum cleaner, and a bloody video player. I mean, why in hell's name are you keeping a video player? Do you really think that one day there'll be a sudden resurgence in video? Even CDs and DVDs are ancient history. Everything is in the cloud now, streamed straight to our TVs, tablets, or phones.'

'Aye, well, I don't trust that bloody cloud. It's a disaster waiting to happen,' he grumbles. 'Mark my words.'

Meera's eyes narrow as she gazes at him dubiously. 'You do realise it's not a real cloud, don't you, Frank? It's not a big fluffy thing in the sky that contains the entire world's data, and those photos you once took of your foot when it got severely sunburnt.'

'Of course I realise it's not a real bloody cloud,' he huffs indignantly.

Truth is, the finer intricacies of cloud technology are a riddle, wrapped in a mystery, inside an enigma to Frank Finnegan. Zac once tried to explain it to him using a packet of Liquorice Allsorts and a bucket but gave up after ten minutes.

Meera changes the subject. 'Oh, time for your surprise,' she states, pulling open a drawer. 'An early Christmas present.'

'Oh, aye,' Frank says, his eyebrows arching in gleeful anticipation. 'Have you paid another visit to that lingerie shop in Scarborough?'

'No. I haven't.' Beaming, she hands him an envelope with *Surprise* written on the front.

Lifting the flap on the unsealed envelope, he slides the postcard out. A beautiful scenic photograph of an old country manor covered in snow is on the front. He opens the card and squints at the blurry words, then looks around.

'Where are my glasses?'

'On your head.'

'Oh, yes.' As he fumbles his spectacles on, the words come into sharp focus.

### *Welcome to Kindlewood Hall's Infamous Christmas Murder Mystery Whodunnit Weekend*

*We invite you to immerse yourself in a captivating weekend of intrigue, exceptional gourmet cuisine, and exclusive selections of fine wines, spirits, and beers—all within the historic grandeur of our Five-Star (pending) Victorian country hotel.*

### *Check-in: From 1:00 pm, Saturday, December 21st*

*Your ticket Includes Saturday evening meal, Sunday breakfast, and Sunday Christmas lunch*

*Prepare for an unforgettable experience at Kindlewood Hall, where mystery and luxury meet this festive season.*

'What in blue blazes! A bloody murder mystery weekend? What possessed you, woman! I spend my whole year arse deep in murder and mystery.'

Meera's face knots into a ball of fury. 'I knew it! I damn well knew it!' she explodes. 'When Prisha and Zac suggested it, I knew what your reaction would be.'

'Oh, this was their bright idea, was it?'

'Yes. They thought it would be a nice end to the year. You know, your close work colleagues and their partners relaxing, having a bit of fun—for a change,' she adds pointedly. 'God forbid we should ever enjoy ourselves.' She yanks the card from his hand and tosses it in the air. 'Forget it! I'll cancel. I doubt we'll get a refund at such short notice, but there's no point going if you're sporting a face like a spanked arse all weekend.' She storms into the kitchen.

Frank stares down at Foxtrot, who seems most perturbed at the angry voices. The dog blinks up at him, imploringly.

'Okay, okay, I get it, Foxtrot. I don't have any choice in the matter, do I? I'll go and patch things up. Happy wife—happy life.'

# 4

**Saturday 21st December**

Frank stuffs a toiletry bag into the small holdall and zips it up, then heads downstairs. The front door slams and Meera enters.

'How was he?' Frank asks.

'The dog?' she asks, taking her coat off and throwing it over the back of an armchair.

'Aye, of course, the bloody dog.'

'Foxtrot's fine. He likes it at Sandra's. She fusses over him. Are you packed?'

He holds the bag up. 'All done.'

'Is that all you're taking?'

'It's a two-night stay.'

'It's a posh hotel, Frank.'

'I know it's a posh hotel. We went there for Gordon Critchely's retirement do, not long ago.'

She raises an eyebrow. 'You need to be smart-causal.'

Deciphering her loaded comment, he replies in an affronted manner. 'I am smart-causal.'

She gives him a derisory once-over and throws him a fierce pout. 'Hmm... I'm going to make a cuppa, then we'll set off. Do you mind putting my suitcase in the boot?'

'Where is it?'

'In the hallway,' she states as she disappears into the kitchen.

Frank heads to the hallway and gazes down in disbelief at the luggage. 'Blood and sand!' He bellows back into the living room. 'They will have their own kitchen sink at the hotel, love! Not sure you need to bring ours along.'

'Ha, ha. Very funny.'

———◆———

The journey from Whitby to Kindlewood Hall, near Easington, usually takes around thirty minutes. Today, though, it feels much longer. As Meera sings along to Last Christmas by Wham, Frank grips the steering wheel and stares out of the windscreen, his apprehension rising with every passing second.

'This has to be the worst Christmas song ever written,' he grumbles.

Meera glances at him, mock-offended. 'What's wrong with it?'

'What's bloody right with it? It's the equivalent of a stick of wilted celery. About as welcome as a limp prick on a wedding night. No verve, no backbone. Sounds more like a requiem than a Christmas song. It's hardly full of Christmas cheer, is it? Makes me feel like sticking my head in the bloody oven.'

'Wouldn't do you much good, Frank. It's electric,' Meera snorts, swiping at the playlist on her phone. 'Okay, misery guts, what do you want to listen to?'

Frank doesn't hesitate. 'Slade—Merry Christmas Everybody. Or what about the Pogues—Fairytale of New York? Or Lennon—So This Is Christmas. Something with some bloody guts.'

Meera taps her phone screen, and the opening piano chords of Fairytale of New York spill from the car speakers. Shane MacGowan's slightly off-tune voice fills the car, followed by Kirsty MacColl's clear, lilting tones.

Frank and Meera belt out the lyrics, their voices a comical contrast—one with the soulful power of Aretha Franklin, the other sounding like a malfunctioning vacuum cleaner sucking up cat litter.

As the song ends, they laugh in unison. Meera reaches over and gives Frank's thigh a squeeze. 'Starting to relax?'

'Aye,' he admits with a grudging smile. 'Takes about a week before I properly unwind.'

'Good. Have you got any mints?'

'In the glove box.'

Meera flips open the glove box door and begins rummaging inside. A metallic clanking sound makes her pause. She pulls out two pairs of police-issue handcuffs, holding them aloft like a magician revealing a surprise. Her eyebrows shoot up.

'And what exactly were you planning to do with these?'

Frank performs a startled double-take. 'Ah, I've been wondering where they got to.'

'You weren't planning anything kinky, were you?' Meera teases, dangling the cuffs by one finger.

Frank chuckles. 'No, but I'm game if you are?'

Meera tosses the handcuffs back into the glove box with a loud clatter, pulling out a packet of Murray Mints instead. 'No, thanks. But I appreciate the offer.'

Frank shakes his head, grinning, as she pops a mint in his mouth.

As the car heads out of town, Frank notices a large convoy of trucks pulling out of an industrial estate.

'Looks like the gritters are setting out early. Snow must be on the way. Turn the radio on.'

'What for?'

He glances at the dash. 'Time for the Shipping Forecast.'

Meera winces. 'Oh no, really? Not the bloody Shipping Forecast again. Do we have to listen to it every time we go somewhere in the car? When was the last time you ever went out on a boat? Anyone would think you were Lord bloody Nelson.'

'I like to keep abreast of the weather.'

'You can see what the weather's like by looking out of the window,' she snaps, reluctantly tapping at the console.

'Shush.'

*"And now on BBC Radio Four it's time for the Shipping Forecast issued by the Met Office on behalf of the Maritime and Coastguard Agency on Saturday 21st December.*

*There are warnings of gales in all areas except for Trafalgar, Fitzroy, and Biscay. The general synopsis at 12—00. Viking, North Utsire, South Utsire, Forties, Cromarty, Forth: Easterly backing southeast 5 to 7. Storm 10, veering to violent storm 11 by the evening, thundery showers, possible snow, poor visibility."*

'Hell, I don't like the sound of this.'

'Join the club. We're listening to the Shipping Forecast whilst sitting in a car heading inland.'

'Shush.'

'Don't shush me.'

Frank gazes out at the morass of slate-grey bank of cloud hovering with malevolence in the distance. Glancing at the dials on the console, he notes the outside temperature, 2°C. Yet, strangely enough, there's barely a breeze.

He flicks from Radio Four to Radio Three and the midday news.

*"Good afternoon. And straight to our top, developing story today: the Arctic storm, dubbed the Beast from the East, which was originally forecast to miss the UK, has now veered westward from Scandinavia and is presently moving rapidly over the North Sea, heading towards Scotland and Northern England.*

*Meteorologists predict the storm will intensify as it approaches, bringing with it blizzard conditions and temperatures plummeting to as low as minus twenty degrees Celsius. Winds are expected to reach gusts of up to 100 miles per hour, causing significant damage and disruption. The storm could affect power supplies and communication networks in many areas.*

*Authorities are urging residents in the north to stay indoors, with severe weather warnings in place. They are also advising people to secure any loose objects outside, as the high winds could make these dangerous.*

*While the storm is set to hit land in the next eight hours, and possibly last for twenty-four hours, the good news is, it should have dissipated by early Sunday evening, leaving behind clearer skies and a return to more manageable winter conditions. However, the Met Office has predicted heavy snowfalls for much of the north. Stay safe, stay warm, and we'll keep you updated as the situation develops."*

Frank pulls over to the side of the road.

'What are you doing?' Meera quizzes.

'I think we should cancel and go home.'

'What! Don't talk daft. Those tickets cost a lot of money.'

'I know but...'

'It doesn't matter where we are—at home or the hotel—it's not going to stop the storm. You're being silly, Frank. Come on, let's get going. Another thirty minutes and we'll be in a nice, warm hotel with an open fire. I'll be sipping on a glass of bubbly, and you'll be guzzling a pint of bitter.'

Much to Meera's annoyance, Frank switches back to the Shipping Forecast.

*"Fair Isle, Faeroes, Southeast Iceland: Violent storm 11, temperatures below minus 6 degrees Celsius, visibility very poor. Mariners are urged to seek shelter immediately. That concludes the Shipping Forecast. Please take extreme care as the storm approaches the UK."*

Frank has a simple decision to make; face the wrath of the storm or the fury of his wife.

He puts the car into gear and sets off for Kindlewood Hall Country Hotel.

# Kindlewood Hall

Lucy Hargreaves looks up as the front door to the hotel opens. Murdoch Langley strides towards her, immaculately dressed as usual. Nothing but high-end designer fashion for this investment banker.

'Good afternoon, Lucy,' he says, dropping his small overnight suitcase onto the tiles of the reception area.

'Good afternoon, Mr Langley,' she replies, his overpowering aftershave already offensive.

He tut tuts. 'Now, now, Lucy, we've had this out before, haven't we? You know me well enough to call me Murdoch.' His smile is one step away from smarmy.

Lucy flushes slightly. 'Yes, but Mrs Langley insists I address all guests and visitors by their surname.'

He chuckles. 'Ah, of course. And who am I to usurp the boss's commands?'

Lucy is saved from any further interaction as Penelope Langley appears from nowhere.

'Murdoch, my dear, so good of you to come.'

'And why wouldn't I? Fine food, a luxurious bed for two nights, and charming company.'

They do the cheek-to-cheek kiss thing, and chuckle.

She takes him by the arm and leads him towards the drawing room. 'Murdoch, I still haven't quite finished the Christmas decorations. Would you mind giving me a hand? Lucy, take Mr Langley's suitcase to his room.'

Lucy, already rushed off her feet, scowls as the phone rings again. She lifts the receiver and recites the memorised introduction.

'Kindlewood Hall Country Hotel, this is Lucy speaking. How may I help you?'

As she deals with yet another cancellation, Virgil Langley emerges and hurries behind the counter.

Lucy continues. 'Oh, I see. No, of course, we fully understand, sir. You're not the first to cancel due to the weather, and I doubt you'll be the last. No, there'll be no charge for the cancellation.'

'What?' Virgil yells. 'Who's cancelling?' he demands.

Lucy puts her hand over the mouthpiece and turns to him. 'It's Mr Crossgate. He and his wife were booked in for the weekend but have cancelled due to the storm forecast.'

'Lucy, you know our policy. Forty-eight hours' notice must be given to avoid a cancellation fee.'

'But...'

He cuts her off and snatches the phone from her. 'Mr Crossgate, Virgil Langley here, the proprietor. I'm sorry but our receptionist misinformed you. There will be a cancellation fee. Fifty per cent of your total charge. What? I don't give a damn about the impending storm. You know how weather forecasts are unpredictable at the best of times. We have a strict cancellation policy that is on your confirmation booking. If you'd taken the trouble... What? How dare you! Don't take that tone with me.'

Penelope strides from the drawing room and hisses at Lucy. 'Whatever's going on?'

'Mr Langley is arguing with a guest who wishes to cancel due to the weather,' she replies rather meekly.

Penelope leans over the counter and yanks the phone from her husband's hand, glaring at him. 'Hello, Mrs Langley speaking. I apologise for any confusion, but there definitely will be no charge for your cancellation, Mr... ah, yes, Mr Crossgate. There seems to have been a breakdown in communication,' she adds, throwing daggers at Lucy. 'Yes, I fully understand. Have a very Merry Christmas and we hope to see you again soon at Kindlewood Hall. Yes, goodbye.' She slams the phone down and enters into a heated argument with her husband.

'What the devil's going on, Penny? We have a strict cancellation policy. We cannot be dictated to by the whims of our guests.'

'It's an unprecedented weather event, Virgil. We must show leniency in such extreme conditions.'

Virgil points outside. 'Weather conditions, look at it. Not a drop of snow or rain, not even a breeze. It's a little cold, that's all.'

'You know as well as I do, the full brunt of the storm is not expected to hit until early evening. You can hardly blame people for wishing to stay home, especially as the authorities are advising just that.' Penelope turns to Lucy. 'How many cancellations so far?'

Lucy glances at her notepad. 'Fifteen couples, so thirty in all.'

Virgil slaps his hand to his brow. 'Damn it! We'll lose a fortune.'

His wife glowers at him. 'Don't be so melodramatic, Virgil. We're not losing anything. It simply means we won't be receiving the money we anticipated.'

'What about all the extra food and drinks we've bought? I've stocked up on wine, spirits and an extra five barrels of beers.'

'You can take the drinks out of the equation. They won't spoil. As for the food, the meat will keep in the freezer. The vegetables we'll use next week, and we'll cancel our usual order.'

As they continue to bicker, the phone rings again.

'This is Kindlewood Hall, Lucy speaking. How may I help you?'

Murdoch Langley saunters through, holding a glass of sherry. 'Problem?' he asks, all suave shop front.

Virgil gazes at his brother. 'We have guests cancelling left, right and centre. What happened to the British Bulldog spirit, Murdoch? You know, shoulder to the wheel, grit and determination. It's the woke generation. Pampered and cosseted from cradle to grave.'

Lucy interrupts. 'Erm... Mr Langley, it's Colin McGuire on the phone. He wants to speak with you?'

Virgil pulls at his tie, his agitation apparent. 'Who?' he snaps.

'Colin McGuire, you know, from the acting troupe?'

'Ah yes.' He grabs the phone. 'Colin, Virgil here.' He falls silent, bearing a grave expression, occasionally nodding and offering a "yes, yes". He says goodbye and hangs up, ashen faced.

'What is it?' Penelope asks fearing the worst.

'The actors. They've cancelled. They were supposed to be travelling up from the Midlands but have decided it's not worth the risk. Don't want to get stuck in a logjam on the A1 should the snow arrive. It's a catastrophe. An unmitigated disaster.' He licks his lips, desperate for the first whisky of the day. 'We have guests arriving for a murder mystery weekend and we have no actors, no murder, and no mystery. Our reputation will be shot.'

'Don't be so bloody ridiculous,' Penelope says. 'Pull yourself together and lift your game. This is what's going to happen. Once all the guests have arrived, we'll muster in the drawing room and explain the situation and hand out free drinks. They will still be served an excellent three course dinner tonight and Christmas lunch tomorrow. We'll provide free drinks for the weekend and obviously reimburse them a portion of their bill in lieu of the cancelled event.'

'Free drinks?' Virgil repeats, alarmed. 'Beer, wine, and sherry only. I'm not handing out spirits,' he snaps indignantly.

Penelope purses her lips and shakes her head. 'Very well. After dinner, we'll move to the drawing room where a roaring log fire will be blazing. We'll sing Christmas carols for an hour or so. I'm a little rusty on the piano, but I'm sure it will come back. After, we'll play charades. For those who don't wish to participate, they can retire to the library where we'll have classical music playing.'

Virgil is not convinced. 'And what about tomorrow? Sunday was supposed to be the finale with the murderer unmasked.'

'Tomorrow's another day. I dare say some of the guests will have become acquainted with one another and will keep themselves amused. We have board games, the snooker room, the indoor pool, and sauna. We'll all work as a team to ensure the best experience we can offer to every one of our guests.'

'Bravo!' Murdoch Langley shouts. 'That's the spirit. Now, how can I help?'

Her smile at Murdoch lingers, sweet enough that even her husband can't help but notice. 'We need to stock up on firewood. There's a huge log pile around the back next to the barn. Virgil, get the fires going now so they have time to warm the rooms. Drawing room, dining room, and library. Understood?'

'Yes, dear.'

'Oh, and we have an artificial Christmas tree somewhere. Find it and erect it in the drawing room. Lucy, I want you to get onto the internet and download piano music for, say, fifteen of the most popular Christmas carols, then print them out and place them on the piano stool.'

Penelope Langley's Dunkirk style preparations are brought to an abrupt halt as Chef Antoine Galois appears, dishevelled, and world-weary.

'What's the matter, Antoine?' Penelope asks.

He drags a hand across his face, then erupts. 'Mon Dieu! C'est incroyable! Sixty guests! Soixante! And I am expected to create a masterpiece—a chef-d'œuvre—with no help? Merde! This is sabotage! Sabotage! My name—my reputation! Built on years of perfect presentation, will be dragged through the dirt like a filthy rag! Putain! How am I supposed to create a flawless trois plats Christmas dinner alone? The roast will be overcooked, the soufflé will collapse like my career, and the sauce will—oh là là—it will be a disaster! The patrons will whisper behind their hands—*"Chef Antoine, he's lost it!"* They will never understand the impossible circumstances I am forced to work under! And sacré bleu, I'm still owed two months' wages! Deux mois! I should walk out now, but no! My pride keeps me here.'

'What do you mean, with no help?' Penelope asks, deep furrows running across her brow.

He thrusts his mobile in front of her face, shaking it back and forth. 'Read, read!' he screeches. 'A text message received no more than two minutes ago from that little snake in the grass, Jaque. He did not have the balls to speak to me in person. No sous chef, no commis chef, no kitchen porter, and no plongeur? All of them have abandoned me. Scared of a little weather. I am alone.'

Penelope reads the message and hands the phone back. 'Hmm...'

'That's it, we're finished,' Virgil states, now pacing back and forth. 'We're doomed. It's over.'

'Can everyone please calm down?' Penelope shouts, raising her hands in the air.

'I can help out in the kitchen once all the guests have arrived, Mrs Langley,' Lucy offers.

'Thank you, Lucy. Yes. That will help.' She fixes Chef Antoine with her most steely gaze, usually reserved for her husband. 'Chef Antoine, you must simplify the menu. This is supposed to be a traditional British Christmas dinner, so that is what we will serve—agreed?'

He throws his hands up in the air in exaggerated, Gallic fashion. 'And what about vegans? Vegetarians? This is the twenty-first century. We must cater for all tastes.'

'Offer one alternative. A mushroom quiche with garden greens or something similar. We can't pander to the minority in a time of crisis. We'll all pitch in and help you in the kitchen. You can do this, Antoine, I have faith in you. You are a great chef, and great chefs can achieve anything, even the impossible. Oui?'

Having played her ace and pumped up his ego, his anger subsides. 'Oui, oui,' he mutters, contrite. 'Chef Antoine can overcome any adversity. With everyone's help, we can come through this.'

'And as for your back-pay, I can assure you it will be resolved next week. A minor cash flow inconvenience, that's all, as I explained to you last week.'

Antoine bows slightly, his tone softening as he says, 'Merci beaucoup, madame, your support means everything to me.' He marches back to the kitchen, head held high, his dignity intact.

Penelope claps her hands together. 'Come, come, everyone. Let's bend our backs and get to work. Everyone knows what they must do.'

As they scurry off, Lucy shakes her head in bemusement. 'What a set of drama queens,' she murmurs as the phone rings once more. 'Kindlewood Hall, Lucy speaking, how may I help you?' She pauses. 'Ah, I see. You wish to cancel your weekend booking. Bear with me a moment while I pull up your details.'

# 6

The car turns off the main road onto the long, winding driveway of Kindlewood Hall. It rattles and bumps its way along for a further mile until the hotel comes into view.

'I love this place,' Meera says, beaming. 'It's perfect. It's almost like being in the middle of...' she swipes at her phone. '... what's it called, the Christmas Carol about the holly and the ivy?'

'The Holly and the Ivy?' Frank replies drily.

'No. Not that one. The other one. Ah, here it is.'

After a brief prelude, the choral singers begin.

*"In the bleak midwinter, frosty wind made moan,*
*Earth stood hard as iron, water like a stone;*
*Snow had fallen, snow on snow, snow on snow,*
*In the bleak midwinter, long ago."*

As the car rumbles down the long driveway, Kindlewood Hall looms into view, dark and imposing against the pale winter sky. The early Victorian façade, with its grand design and turreted roof, carries the weight of another era—once proud, now softened by time. Streaks of damp mar the walls, while ivy creeps upward as if reclaiming its hold.

To the left, a lake glints like tarnished silver, its frozen surface smooth and unyielding. To the right, skeletal branches claw at the sky, their black shadows stretching long over the dormant earth. The hills surrounding the Hall roll gently into the distance, encircling the scene in a cold embrace.

The wooden gate at the entrance hangs open, leaning at a weary angle, its hinges stiff with rust. As the car slows to a crawl, Frank's gaze flicks to the crooked sign above it - Kindlewood Hall. The faded letters barely legible, their vibrancy long since eroded.

The air is unnervingly still. No birdsong, the silence heavy and unnatural. Even the faint hum of the car's engine feels intrusive, breaking the watchful quiet of the frozen grounds.

Frank checks the gauge again.

The temperature has plunged to minus five degrees Celsius.

The hotel, with its welcoming red-brick walls, slate covered turrets, and windows tinted in frost, exudes a subdued warmth, standing starkly against the leaden sky. There is no movement—no rustle of branches, no whisper of wind. It's unsettlingly peaceful, a stillness that feels unnatural, as if the world is poised for something—waiting.

Frank, ever attuned to danger and how appearances can be deceptive, is unnerved by Mother Nature's unusual behaviour, but says nothing.

'Hey, Frank, do you remember when we first started dating? Our first Christmas together, we hired that drafty caravan near Scalby Mills in Scarborough?'

'I remember it well. I've only just thawed out.'

She slaps him on the leg. 'You didn't need any thawing out from what I can recall. You could have done with a bucket of cold water throwing over you. We spent most of the time in bed trying to keep warm.'

'Is that what you call it?'

She pauses momentarily and stares wistfully out of the passenger window over a barren field.

'Where did the time go, Frank?' she asks, her voice cloaked in sorrow.

He sighs, and parks up outside the main entrance to the hotel, alongside four other cars, turns, and takes her hand.

'The same place where all time goes, love—it's sucked into the past.'

'It seems like only yesterday I was young, free, going to watch Madness and the Specials and Haircut 100. And now I'm old, overweight. I have wrinkles and crow's feet. Flecks of grey in my hair. In another thirty years, neither of us will be here. We'll have been sucked into the past along with time, forgotten we ever existed.'

He places his fingers under her chin and gently turns her head. 'Hey, come on, love. You're not old. They say sixty is the new middle-aged, and you're only fifty-six. And those aren't wrinkles, they're laughter lines. And the crow's feet accentuate those big brown beautiful eyes of yours. Like the bottom of two HP sauce bottles.'

'You have a way with words.'

'And as for being overweight... that's nonsense. You've got a bit of meat on you, that's all, lass. That's the way I like my women. Who wants to curl up next to a wishbone on a night? Not me, that's for sure.'

'You're not doing yourself any favours, Frank.'

He leans in and pecks her on the lips. 'Come on, stop maudlin. We're here now. Let's enjoy the time we do have left instead of navel-gazing.'

A faint smile visits her lips. 'Yes. Sorry.'

'You sign in at reception and I'll bring the luggage through. Oh, and ask the manager if he has a forklift handy.'

'Why?'

'To get your suitcase to the front door.'

She cannot resist a chuckle as they both exit the car.

He lifts the luggage from the boot, then pauses momentarily as he watches his wife climb the steps to the entrance, the freezing temperature already seeping through his clothes and biting at his face.

He ponders Meera's words.

But it is the words left unsaid that upset him the most.

He knows her too well.

Taking a deep breath, which stings his lungs, he plods towards the hotel steps, luggage in hand.

———◆———

Meera stands at the reception counter, watching as a young woman in a smart uniform, her name tag reading *Lucy*, busies herself on the phone. Frank trundles up beside her, dragging the large suitcase on its wheels, his small holdall slung over one shoulder.

'No, we fully understand, Mrs Simpson. Your deposit will definitely be reimbursed, but it may not be until next week due to the weekend and Christmas break. We look forward to welcoming you to Kindlewood Hall in the future. Yes, yes. Goodbye.' Lucy sets the receiver down with a sigh and scribbles something on a notepad before looking up to address a guest who has quietly approached the counter.

'Miss Holland, how can I help you?'

The petite, pretty woman smiles faintly. 'I can see you're busy, but I was hoping to get some fresh air. Is there a walking track around the grounds?'

'Yes, there is.' Lucy brightens. 'Head out of the main gate and, a few yards to your right, you'll see a path. It leads down to the lake, winds through the woods, and circles back around near the old barns at the back of the hotel.'

'How long does it take, roughly?'

'About forty minutes at a steady pace.'

'Perfect. Thank you, Lucy.'

'My pleasure, Miss Holland.'

As Miss Holland moves off, Lucy turns her attention to Frank and Meera, her expression warm and professional. 'Good afternoon. How may I help you?'

'We have a booking for the Murder Mystery Weekend,' Meera begins. 'Mr and Mrs Finnegan.'

Lucy smiles, her posture relaxing slightly, relieved that guests are finally arriving. 'Ah, yes, we've been expecting you. Welcome to Kindlewood Hall.'

Before she can finish, Virgil Langley bustles into view, pulling a wicker basket on wheels packed tightly with firewood. His usual air of local squire—a smart tweed suit, polished brogues, shirt, and tie—is partially hidden beneath a long woollen coat, a thick scarf, gloves, and a bobble hat.

'Good afternoon!' he calls in his cheery but slightly flustered voice, setting the basket down with a thud. 'I do hope Lucy's been taking good care of you, Frank,' he declares, holding out his hand.

Frank turns and grins. 'Ah, Virgil,' he says, shaking hands. 'You were here not long ago for Chief Constable Critchley's retirement do.'

'That's right. Late July, if memory serves.'

Meera nods, smiling warmly. 'We're really looking forward to the murder mystery, aren't we, Frank?'

*Like a hole in the bloody head.* 'Aye. Can't wait for the bodies to start piling up.'

Meera surreptitiously swats his arm. 'Shame about the weather, but as I said to Frank, what would you prefer? Hunker down at home—same old, same old—or batten down the hatches in a luxury three-star hotel?'

Virgil stiffens slightly. 'Four-star, with a five-star pending,' he corrects, straightening to his full height. 'But I know what you mean. Lucy, please upgrade Mr and Mrs Finnegan to the premium suite.' He smiles at Frank. 'No extra charge.'

'That's very generous of you,' Meera says, practically glowing as Lucy hands her the key.

'Room eighteen,' Lucy explains. 'Up the stairs, turn right, and follow the corridor to the end.'

An awkward silence follows as Virgil glances at the basket of firewood.

Frank breaks the impasse. 'I take it you're well prepared for the storm?'

Virgil nods, but a faint frown appears. 'Of course. But I'm sure it won't be as tumultuous as the nervous Nellies at the Met Office are predicting, but just in case, we're pulling out all the stops.'

'What contingencies have you in place if the power goes down?' Frank presses, earning a disapproving glance from Meera.

'Our central heating and hot water run on a biomass system. Renewable and organic,' Virgil says proudly, puffing out his chest. 'We like to do our bit for the environment. And we've enough provisions to sink a battleship.'

'What about lighting?'

Virgil blinks. 'Lighting?'

'Aye. If the power goes, you'll have no light.'

'Ah... well, I hadn't thought of that. We do have emergency lighting in case of a fire. Although, it is a rather subdued red light. It highlights the corridors and exits.'

'And how long does it last?'

Virgil pulls at his scarf. 'Ha, ha. Good question. I'd say three to four hours.'

Frank twists his neck—a characteristic tic when he knows he's right. 'If the forecast holds, I'd wager money you'll lose power. High-tensile cables don't like freezing temperatures. Causes brittle fractures. Have you got backup generators?'

'No.'

'Hmm.' Frank's voice is thick with barely disguised scepticism. 'What about torches and batteries?'

'I've a couple of torches somewhere.'

'I meant for the guests.'

Meera swivels her foot into Frank's ankle, hard. 'I'm sure Mr Langley has been through this before, Frank. He's an experienced hotelier. Don't teach your grandmother how to suck eggs.'

Frank ignores her. 'Still, it's prudent to be prepared. Plenty of candles, Virgil?'

Virgil tugs at his scarf again, clearly flustered. 'Yes, yes, plenty of candles. They're for the candelabras on the tables, but as some guests have already...' He falters, unwilling to voice the deluge of cancellations.

Lucy and Meera exchange embarrassed glances as Frank doggedly questions the hotelier as though he's a suspect in a murder investigation. The front door rattles distracting Frank for an instant.

Meera seizes the opportunity to grab him by the arm. 'Come along, Frank. Mr Langley has enough to do without being grilled.'

Virgil's relief is palpable. 'We'll catch up later, Frank. Have a wee snifter on the house. And don't forget, all guests are invited to the drawing room at six sharp for complimentary drinks.'

'Sounds like a plan,' Frank replies as Meera leads him away.

The suitcase ker-thunks up the steps as Meera carries Frank's holdall.

Her frustration boils over. 'That was embarrassing.'

'What was?'

'You. Interrogating Mr Langley.'

'I wasn't interrogating him. I was merely—'

She cuts him off sharply. 'Interfering. You're not at the station, Frank. I thought you said you'd switched off?'

As they reach the landing, Frank stops. Ahead, a sign on the wall reads Guest Bedrooms, with an arrow pointing right. To the left, another sign reads Private Residence, a red cord strung between two portable stanchions blocking the corridor. Anyone determined could easily step over it. Straight ahead, a large window overlooks the oval car park and the fountain at its centre.

Frank lingers, staring out as the first delicate snowflakes gyrate down from the bleak sky, resting briefly on the stone window ledge before melting away.

'This is the start,' he murmurs to himself, bracing himself for what the imminent storm may bring.

# 7

Prisha's car jolts and sways as it bumps up the gravel track towards Clegg Farm, perched high on the hill. She's already left three messages for Adam, but he hasn't called back. Increasingly concerned, her mind shifts into overdrive, spinning through a mental list of worst-case scenarios.

*Trapped under a tractor. Tractor rolled down an embankment. Electrocution. Frozen to death in one of the fields. Crushed by a bull.*

'Stop it,' she mutters, shaking off her spiralling thoughts. She cranks the heater up to full and tightens her coat, but the chill still seeps into her bones.

She stares out at the countryside, harsher and emptier than she's ever known it. The haggard trees, the drained grass, the seemingly abandoned stone buildings—all of it feels different today. The silence is unnerving. The sky, neither grey nor white but some dull in-between, deepens as if preparing for something.

Finally, the car rolls into the farmyard. Relief floods her as she spots Adam by the kennels, untying the sheepdogs. The bright orange quad bike is parked beside him, a welcome splash of colour in the bleak scene.

She parks, cuts the engine, and steps into the freezing air. 'Adam!' she calls, her voice slicing through the stillness.

Clearly distracted, with a deep frown etched across his face, Adam looks up as the dogs pace back and forth, tails wagging in restless excitement. He waves briefly before returning his focus to untying the last leash.

Prisha hurries over, adjusting her scarf against the biting air. 'I tried calling you. Is everything okay?' she asks, greeting him with a quick kiss.

'Yes... well, no.' He exhales, his breath clouding in the cold. 'You've heard about the storm heading our way?'

'Yes, of course.'

'I've been flat-out. I managed to get the cattle into one barn, but the sheep are still up on High Paddock. I need to round them up and get them into the other barn. If the forecast's right, they won't survive those temperatures overnight, especially with the wind chill.'

Prisha hesitates, her next words tasting shallow before she even speaks them.

'You haven't forgotten about our trip?' Instantly, guilt stirs. *Here he is, worrying about his animals and his livelihood, and I'm asking about a weekend away.* She berates herself silently.

Adam pauses, then smiles faintly, tugging his woollen hat further down over his ears. The tip of his nose glows red against the frost-bitten air.

'No, I haven't forgotten. I'll round up the sheep with the dogs and the quad, drop some hay into the feeders, then a quick wash and scrub—and I'll be good to go.'

'How can I help?'

He leans in and pecks her on the lips. 'You can't. It's a one-man, two dog job. There's no point you hanging around here. You may as well head off, and I'll see you at the hotel in about two hours. Depending on the severity of the storm, I may need to duck out tomorrow for a couple of hours, to check on everything. Lucky the hotel is only a thirty-minute drive away.'

Prisha frowns. 'I can't leave you with all this work.'

He strokes her cheek with a gloved hand, his voice soft but steady. 'You've got a heart of gold, but what do you think I did before you came along? This is my life—I've been doing it since I was a lad. I know what I'm doing.' His lips twitch into a teasing grin. 'And anyway, if you stayed, you'd only get under my feet.'

The two dogs let out impatient howls, eager to be off.

Prisha hesitates, then kisses him again. 'Okay. But be careful, and I'll see you at the hotel.' She gives him a playful wink. 'We can warm up in the shower together.'

He grins. 'Best offer I've had all day. Bye, love. See you soon.'

Jumping onto the quad bike, he twists the accelerator, the engine roaring to life. He speeds across the yard towards the open gate, the two sheepdogs racing ahead, tails wagging and barking in pure excitement as they vanish into the distance.

# 8

As Prisha parks outside Kindlewood Hall and exits the car, a familiar Scottish voice calls out.

'Funny seeing you here.'

She smiles and waves at Zac as he pulls his luggage from the boot of his car. She grabs her bag and hurries over to him.

'Hey, where's Kelly? Already inside?'

His features radiate disappointment. 'Can't come. Sam has come down with tonsillitis, or so we think. No doctor's surgeries are open, so she's taken him to the hospital to see if she can get him some antibiotics.'

'Oh, no.'

'I told her I'd stay back, but she insisted I come. Said there was no point us both missing out. Anyway, I may head off after breakfast tomorrow. Skip the lunch.'

'That's such a shame. I was looking forward to catching up with her.'

Zac peers at her car, puzzled. 'Where's Adam?'

'He's rounding up sheep. He'll be here later,' she replies, making her way to the entrance.

Zac shakes his head. 'I don't envy him, but that's farming for you. It's not a nine-to-five job. It's a lifestyle.'

Locking the car, he zips up his black parka and stares at the sky as the snow continues to drift down, unhurried, graceful. He peers out at the wide expanse of countryside, already carpeted with a dusting of white. 'Soon be a winter wonderland,' he murmurs.

---

In the reception area there's a flurry of activity as Lucy Hargreaves and Penelope Langley try to process the glut of guests who all turned up within a few minutes of each other.

Zac trudges in and surveys the scene and makes his way to the counter, wondering where Prisha has disappeared to. Unable to see her, his attention turns to an older, well-presented woman dealing with a guest.

'Here's your key, Ms Sato. Number twelve. Top of the steps. Turn right and follow the corridor.'

'Thank you, Penelope.' She stares at the key for a moment. 'How quaint. You don't often see real keys these days.' Her comment is wrapped in so many layers of ambiguity, it's hard to tell whether she's being sincere or facetious. She hesitates, her smile sharp. 'I'm hoping my visit will be more... hmm, how shall I put it? Pleasant... than last time.'

Penelope offers her a smile, practised over many years. It appears friendly enough, but one little slip and the facade could crack, to reveal a death stare that would freeze hell over.

'I can guarantee it, Ms Sato. As I explained a couple of weeks ago, when my husband and I invited you for the weekend, we have a top-class international chef, Antoine Galois, now running the kitchen.'

'Yes. I've heard of him. A step in the right direction. And with the Christmas ambience, a jolly time should be had by all.' Imogen Sato picks up her small holdall and slings it over her shoulder. 'By the way, at some point, I'd like to inspect the kitchen. For review purposes, of course.'

With her fixed smile still in place, Penelope replies, 'We are a little run off our feet today, but I'll have a word with chef and see what we can arrange.'

As Imogen Sato heads to the stairs, Zac spots his chance. 'Hello, I was supposed to be here with my wife. Mr and Mrs Stoker. Unfortunately, my wife couldn't make it.'

As the reception area fills with more guests arriving, Zac is fast-tracked and handed his key.

'There you go, Mr Stoker. Room six. Turn right at the top of the stairs.'

'Thank you.'

'We're inviting all our guests for a complimentary welcome drink at 6 pm in the drawing room,' she explains, nodding to the left at a large set of open doors, and a roaring log fire within.'

'That's very kind of you,' Zac replies.

'Due to the weather, there have been a few changes to the itinerary, and we thought it only fair to explain to all our guests.'

'No problem. I fully understand.'

As he turns away, eyes searching for Prisha, an older woman accompanied by a middle-aged man shuffle forward. 'Penelope,' they both say in unison, without much joy.

'Maggie, Hugh, so glad you could both make it,' she replies, clapping her hands together, as if overjoyed. 'I apologise for the chaos. It's this damned storm that's on its way, but we must soldier on. I have you in adjoining rooms. I know how close you two like to be.'

It's always in the final sentence where the barb lies hidden beneath a veneer of innocuity.

Prisha appears beside Zac as if she'd been teleported there.

'Where did you disappear to?' he asks.

'Just having a nosey. It's all very nice—a drawing room with a log fire, library, billiard room, and a large lap pool and sauna. All very cosy.'

The front door bangs shut, followed by the murmur of foreign voices.

'Tiens, Maman, laisse-moi t'aider avec ta valise.' A French accent drifts from the entrance.

'Nonsense, Pierre. I'm fine. I'm not in my coffin yet,' an elderly woman replies in perfect English, though her heavy French accent lingers. 'Stop fussing.'

Prisha and Zac turn to see an attractive man in his early forties, grey hair brushed back and his beard immaculately groomed, guiding an elderly woman along the hallway.

The pair amble forward, the man cradling her arm protectively.

'Good afternoon,' the man says with a courteous nod towards Lucy.

She glances down at her guest list. 'Ah, you must be Dr Pierre Quint?'

The man almost bows. 'Correct. And this is my mother, Edith Quint.'

'We've been expecting you,' Lucy replies with a warm smile. 'I'll check you in quickly and show you to your room.'

Zac smirks at Prisha and nods towards the counter and the cluster of guests. 'You should have got in early, sunshine. Quite a queue, now.'

Prisha grins and dangles a key under his nose. 'I checked in online this morning. The key was waiting for me,' she says, heading towards the wide staircase.

Zac frowns. 'No one likes a smartarse.'

# 9

The classic E-Type Jaguar meanders at a sedate pace up the steep, narrow country lane, some stretches barely wide enough to accommodate a single vehicle. Fortunately for the occupants, Mr and Mrs Whipple, the roads are deathly quiet, and they've yet to encounter another soul. They are returning from a pre-Christmas break where they toured the lowlands of Scotland, Bennet indulging in a few days of his newfound passion of fly-fishing.

'I appreciate the scenic route, Bennet,' Mrs Whipple remarks, peering through the misty haze, 'but there's not much to see but mist and a light sprinkling of snow.'

Dr Bennet Whipple, however, is utterly oblivious to her mild complaint, lost as he is in the haunting strains of Dvořák's Symphony No. 9 in E Minor, softly humming along. As the car glides around a bend, he spots a layby marked "Scenic View" and, without hesitation, pulls over. Turning to his wife with the air of a man announcing the arrival of tea at a country estate, he declares, 'I believe it is time for some refreshment, my most esteemed Dove.'

'Really? We're only an hour from home,' she replies, slightly incredulous.

'My dear, whilst it may appear we are but a mere hour from the comforts of our hearth, I must remind you that fatigue is the silent harbinger of catastrophe upon the highways. Many a tragedy has been borne from the foolish presumption that one's endurance is limitless. Thus, as any wise man would, I propose we partake in sustenance to ward off such peril.'

Reluctantly, she acquiesces, retrieving a backpack from the back seat. 'I suppose,' she sighs. 'There are still some Mowbray mini pork pies left,' she adds pulling out a thermos and two cups and the pies.

'Ah! The delight of such sustenance knows no bounds,' Bennet exclaims, his eyes lighting up as she hands him the box. 'A veritable feast fit for the gods, I daresay! These past days, basking in the scenic splendour of Scotland, have stirred within me an appetite that cannot be denied.'

As she pours the coffee, Bennet savours each bite of his pork pie, staring thoughtfully into the fog-shrouded valley. He is blissfully unaware of the impending storm set to ravage the countryside, having obstinately avoided any news broadcasts, preferring the serene company of classical compositions.

Finishing his last bite, he wipes his mouth with a contented sigh and leans back, casting a fond look at his wife. 'Ah, dearest Dove, what felicity this week has brought. A most splendid reprieve from the rigours of our daily existence. I dare say we should engage in such frivolities more often.'

She leans over and plants a brief kiss on his cheek. 'It's been... pleasant,' she replies, hesitating for a moment before settling on the most neutral of compliments.

Bennet, oblivious to her tepid response, beams with satisfaction. 'Pleasant, indeed! And most invigorating, I dare say. It has rekindled my faith in humanity and for the first time in years, I can actually declare that I am relaxed... somewhat,' he adds as an afterthought.

His reverie is interrupted as Mrs Whipple leans forward, her hand coming to rest gently on his thigh. 'I know how to relax you some more, Bennet,' she murmurs with a mischievous twinkle.

Bennet stiffens, his eyeballs widening in alarm. 'Surely, my dear, you do not imply that within the sacred confines of this motor vehicle, we should engage in—how shall I phrase this delicately—acts of a matrimonial nature? Actions more appropriately confined to the conjugal boudoir?'

'And why not?' she replies huskily.

Her hand inches upward, and Bennet swallows hard, his mind racing. 'I—I assure you, such... spousal communion, as you so coyly suggest, is not only improper but highly illegal within a moving contraption such as this!'

'The car isn't moving, Bennet,' she counters with a playful smirk, her fingers deftly seeking the fly of his trousers. 'Let your hair down for once,' she whispers, glancing pointedly at his shiny bald noggin, realising it was a poor turn of phrase.

His heart races, and not from excitement. The very thought of engaging in such an indecorous act, on a country lane, in broad daylight, no less, is enough to send his head spinning. 'I—I must insist, my dear, this is beyond scandalous! The impropriety! The moral ramifications! And—and what if a passing constable or a man of the cloth were to amble by and witness such—such licentiousness?'

She rolls her eyes. 'There's no one around, Bennet. It's perfectly safe.'

'Safe, perhaps, but what of propriety? What of my standing in the community? What if the Lord himself gazes upon this wanton display of debauchery?'

With a final, mischievous tug, she leans in close, her voice a soft purr. 'Damn propriety, husband. It's just us. And what's a little marital fun in the countryside?'

Bennet's breath hitches, his hand fumbling awkwardly for the seat belt release as if to escape. 'Sweet Jehovah,' he mutters, 'forgive me my sins...' He fumbles with a lever and reclines back in his seat.

Shivering and crestfallen, Bennet stares disconsolately at the crumpled bonnet on his precious classic E-Type Jaguar, and the slow gurgling hiss from the radiator. Mrs Whipple pulls her coat collar up, and her bobble hat down as the wind and snowfall intensify.

'That's bad, isn't it?' she states, her face creased with worry as mucky brown liquid carves a path through the snow before disappearing under the drystone wall which is now in a state of union with the front of the car.

Bennet miraculously focuses his left eye on his wife, whilst his right eye still mourns the damage to his prized asset.

'It's a calamitous travesty, wife,' he replies, his usual term of endearment—Dove, replaced by a more perfunctory title.

'I swear, Bennet, I didn't knock the handbrake. It must have been you as you reclined the seat. I've told you before, the car is way too small for a man of your size. I've been telling you for years to trade it in for a Range Rover.'

The fierce glare he throws his wife is negated by the rapid build-up of snowflakes on his bushy eyebrows. A deep, sonorous, 'Hmm...' is his only response. He pulls his phone out and swipes through the contacts, and jabs at a button.

'Who are you calling?'

'The Royal Automobile Club.'

'Roadside assistance?'

'That is what I said.' He frowns and holds his phone skywards, grimacing as Mrs Whipple pulls out her mobile and follows suit.

'We must be in a black spot,' she murmurs. 'What should we do?'

Bennet performs a three-sixty-degree turn so slowly that Mrs Whipple can feel herself ageing. 'It appears, wife,' he intones, his voice as frosty as the gathering storm, 'that we find ourselves in a most unfortunate predicament, bereft of modern communicative apparatuses, abandoned by the capricious whims of technology.'

Mrs Whipple stamps her feet, which are already beginning to go numb. 'As far as I can see, we have but three options: hunker down in the car; head back the way we came, or carry on, by foot.'

Bennet draws himself up to his full height, snowflakes adorning his pate like a dubious crown. 'Our choices are lamentable, each one cloaked in a veritable shroud of menacing conclusions. From memory I think we are betwixt Liverton and Easington. To remain with the vehicle would be folly in these conditions, the metal exterior acting as a conduit to the freezing temperature outside. And yet, to set off on a perambulation with little knowledge of the terrain, or future conditions, is an act of folly reserved specifically for those who, in times gone by, would have been labelled imbeciles.'

'Well, we can't do nothing, Bennet,' his wife pleads.

'Indeed, we cannot. Our only recourse, dire though it may be, is to undertake a pedestrian expedition through this inhospitable terrain towards Easington.' He exhales heavily, as though the weight of the world rests on his shoulders. 'We shall persevere until we either stumble upon a rustic domicile or ascend to an elevation sufficient for these infernal devices to capture a shred of signal.'

With a deep, exaggerated sigh, he gestures dramatically down the snow-laden road. 'Come, wife. Let us march forth with fortitude into the tempest—hapless victims of circumstance and your... ill-timed amorous proclivities.'

He retrieves a ushanka from inside his heavy overcoat, wrestles it over his rotund head with some difficulty, and pulls the ear flaps down. The resulting look is faintly ridiculous, but he carries it with all the dignity of a man braving the Arctic.

# 10

The snow lies deep and still, blanketing every inch of the landscape in an unbroken sheet of white. Trees, naked of their greenery, look like they've been dipped long and slow in icing sugar. Dark evergreens are laden under thick layers, bowing in submission to winter's weight. Gates and fences, barely visible beneath the accumulation, carve faint lines across the grounds, all leading to the hotel's shadowed form, its walls softened, muted beneath the snow's heavy embrace. The air is hushed, thick with a kind of sacred silence, as if the world is holding its breath. The modern world's mechanical heartbeat has ceased—no distant engines, no electronic hum, no industrial drone. Simply perfect, unadulterated stillness.

Frank and Zac stand together, a duo of dark figures against the vast, pale expanse. The scene before them is both magnificent and slightly disquieting, as though each snowflake has settled with purpose. There's a purity that wraps around them, accentuating their senses.

Beauty on eyes.

Silence on ears.

Chill on skin.

Scent of smoke.

Powder under foot.

And yet, another sense, a sixth sense perhaps, awakens. A creeping awareness that, for all the inherent perfection the vision holds, something darker is coiled and waiting in the wings. The Beast from the East has yet to unleash its full wrath. The absence of wind, the lack of any howl through the trees, only deepens their unease.

And little do they know... something else is coming.

Another beast with as much deadly intent as the unprecedented arctic storm.

Prisha ends her phone call, clearly disappointed. 'That was Adam,' she states sullenly.

'What's wrong?' Frank asks, concerned.

'He can't make it. Says it's a total white out where he is.'

Zac gazes up at the gentle falling snow. 'I'd hardly call it a white out,' he says. 'He's only thirty miles away. Can't be that much different from here.'

Prisha shrugs. 'He said the stormfront hit ten minutes ago. He'd already set off but hadn't even got to the end of the farm track when he had to turn back.'

Frank purses his lips.

'Hmm... won't be long before it hits us then.'

Prisha steps forward, mesmerised by the tranquillity. 'I've never witnessed such peace and quiet before,' she whispers in reverential tones.

Frank slowly spins around. 'Aye, I haven't seen anything like this since I was a kid.'

'Can you hear that?' Prisha says.

'What?' Zac asks as he slinks away.

'No birds. You can always hear a bird in the countryside. A blackbird, thrush, a crow, or raven. But it's complete and utter silence.'

Frank reflects. 'They do say animals, especially birds, have an early-warning system. They sense things, weather events, before we do.'

'But where do they go?' Prisha asks.

Frank shrugs. 'Not sure. The bush dwellers will be tucked up safely in their nests. As for the birds that live in trees, I'll be buggered what they do.'

'Maybe they hire an Air BnB,' Zac says as he bends and scoops up a ball of snow and moulds it into a ball.

'Daft bug...' The last syllable is aborted as a snowball slams into the back of Frank's head. He jolts forward as if lanced with a pike. He rubs snow from the back of his neck and turns to face Zac who is grinning like a village idiot who's found a comb.

'What a shot,' he laughs. 'Mind you, the target was pretty hard to miss.'

Frank rushes towards him. 'Right, you've asked for it this time.'

Zac breaks out into laughter. 'Oh, aye. And what are you going to do about it, old man?'

'You'll see,' Frank yells.

Zac's smile drops from his face as his boss nears. 'Now Frank, I'm warning you, don't try anything funny. I know you could handle yourself in your day, but that was thirty years ago. Don't go giving yourself a heart attack. I don't want to hurt you.'

'You're going to cop it lad,' Frank says grinning.

Zac puts his fists up and takes a swing, which Frank wheels out of the way of. As it passes him by, he grabs Zac's arm and violently twists it behind his back.

'Ouch!'

'Oh, shut up you big sugar plum fairy.' With his right foot he kicks Zac's legs from under him and he lands headfirst in the snow.

'Boys will be boys,' Prisha laments slowly, smiling.

Frank presses down on the back of Zac's head until it's buried a good twelve inches below the snow. He holds him there for a while, one knee pressing into the small of his back, as Zac's legs twitch and kick like a Wildebeest pinned down by a dozen lionesses.

Prisha wanders forward. 'How long are you going to keep him like that?'

Frank chuckles. 'Oh, I don't know. Another hour?' He relents and stands up.

Zac yanks his head from the snow and flips onto his backside, panting and wiping snow from his face and head. 'That was disproportionate,' he yells, incensed. 'Uncalled for!'

'You started it.'

'Christ! You could get a job as head of Mossad. Bloody nutcase.'

Frank reaches down, grabs Zac's hand, and yanks him to his feet. 'Who's too old, eh?'

'You were lucky I lost my footing as you approached. Otherwise, you'd have been dead meat.'

'Yeah, right. Your mother might believe you.'

They eyeball each other for a second before breaking out into peels of unbridled laughter.

'Are you children quite finished?' Prisha queries, looking at her watch. 'It's almost six. Time for our complimentary drinks in the drawing room.'

As they walk towards the hotel entrance, Frank knocks the snow from Zac's back.

'I can't remember the last time I had so much fun,' he says.

Zac throws him a cheeky grin. 'Aye. It was a bit of a laugh, no? I felt like a kid again.'

'Oh, the days,' Frank sighs.

As they all kick snow from their shoes, Prisha lifts her head.

'Wait, can you hear that?'

'What?' Zac asks not taking much notice.

'A distant rumble,' she says, frowning.

Frank slowly turns, taking in the barren countryside. 'It could a convoy of gritters,' he says not convinced by his own words.

'No,' Prisha replies. 'It's too loud. It's almost like continuous thunder.'

Zac stops kicking snow from his boots and gazes towards the northeast. 'Christ, look at that,' he says, extending an arm.

Frank and Prisha follow his gaze. A few miles away, at the brow of a hill, a white wall billows over the top. It obliterates everything behind it as the growling roar intensifies.

Frank rubs a gloved hand through his hair. 'It's the blizzard front,' he mutters. 'The leading edge, and it's heading this way at a rate of knots.'

## II

The drawing room is delicately lit, exuding an understated warmth. A row of candles flickers atop the mantelpiece over the fireplace, where a day's worth of embers glows faintly, offering radiant heat and a modicum of light. Three chandeliers hang overhead, their bulbs dimmed to a soft, golden hue. The faint strains of carols drift from the hidden speakers.

In the corner, a tall but somewhat tired-looking artificial Christmas tree stands proudly, adorned with twinkling white lights and an assortment of mismatched decorations—baubles in varying shades of red and gold, a few slightly frayed ribbons, and a lopsided star perched at its peak. Tinsel loops around the tree in uneven spirals, catching the dim light.

Virgil Langley stands behind a makeshift drinks table inside the entrance, fussing with his tie. He's dressed smartly as always—tweed jacket, pressed trousers, polished brogues—but as he straightens his tie, he fails to notice the faint smudge of gravy on the lapel of his jacket or the splash of red wine on his tie. He leans forward, peering into the reception area, his eyes scanning for any signs of arrivals—particularly his wife. A garland of holly and pinecones, dotted with tiny red berries, frames the doorway, but Virgil barely notices it.

Satisfied he's alone, he pulls a silver hip flask from the inside pocket of his jacket, glancing nervously towards the clock. Five minutes until the guests arrive for complimentary pre-dinner drinks. He unscrews the flask and takes a gulp, then another, savouring the burn as it slides down his throat. A fleeting wave of euphoria washes over him. For a moment, a brief moment, the world feels bearable. Yes, there are problems—financial troubles, marital tensions, lingering bad feelings—but here, now, in his ancestral home, with carols drifting in the background and festive decorations cloaking the room, he feels an ease he hasn't known in years. Soon, everything will be sorted. Murdoch's money will fix it all.

Footsteps echo in the hall, brisk and unmistakably feminine. Virgil snaps from his brief reprieve, takes one last shot of whisky, then slips the hip flask away.

He straightens, clearing his throat, as the mask of the gracious host falls back into place. The lopsided star atop the tree seems to tilt further.

Virgil hides his displeasure at the first arrival. 'Ah, Imogen Sato—food critic extraordinaire. First guest to arrive for the freebies, eh? What a surprise. Now, what can I get you? Bubbly, white wine, red, or perhaps a beer?'

Imogen returns a well-seasoned passive-aggressive stare, immediately noting, as she had on her first visit, that Virgil Langley is a little too fond of the drink.

'I'll have a cocktail, thank you. A boulevardier, please.'

Virgil twitches and takes a half step back. 'A boulevard deer? I'm afraid we're fresh out of deer, dear—they seem to have migrated north this year,' he replies with a raucous laugh.

Imogen glares at him. 'A shot of bourbon, a shot of vermouth, a shot of Campari, and orange peel garnish.'

'Ah, I see. A boulevardier.' He fidgets for a moment. 'If you want a cocktail, you'll have to visit the bar in the dining room.'

'Is someone manning the bar?'

Virgil hesitates, his composure fraying. 'Well, actually, no. Little short-staffed tonight, thanks to the imaginary storm that's failed to materialise. Would a glass of bubbly suffice for now?'

Without replying, she helps herself to a flute of champagne and wanders over to stand in front of the fire.

'Bitch,' Virgil murmurs to himself as more guests arrive. 'Ah, gentlemen, what can I get you?'

Logan Fitch and Hugh Foster survey the drinks on offer.

'I'll have a Heineken, please, Virgil,' Hugh says, rubbing his hands together.

Virgil plucks a chilled bottle from the ice bucket and hands it to Hugh before turning to Logan, squinting slightly. 'Logan?'

'Erm, actually, could I have a glass of sherry?'

Virgil nods as he retrieves a bottle. 'Certainly.'

Logan leans over the table and whispers. 'Virgil, I'd like to catch up with you later for ten minutes. Somewhere private.'

Virgil grimaces. 'Really Logan? Tonight, of all nights? You can see how busy we are,' he replies drizzling sherry into a glass.

Logan shoots a furtive glance at Hugh who is busy ogling Imogen Sato from afar.

'It's about the business plan you handed me the other day. I had a chance to go over it yesterday.'

Virgil passes him the sherry, suddenly interested in the rendezvous. 'Ah, I see. Very well. When I give you the nod, we'll meet in my office.' He hesitates as if a thought has just occurred. 'It's nothing *bad*, is it?'

'We'll talk later,' Logan replies as he follows Hugh who has wandered towards the fireplace.

New voices announce the arrival of more guests. Amy Holland, the lone traveller, enters alongside Eve Sinclair. Both women linger in front of the drinks table, engrossed in conversation.

'My, that's exquisite,' Eve says, leaning in closer as Amy lifts a pendant on a gold chain for her to examine. 'And you made this yourself?'

'Yes,' Amy replies, her tone soft but proud. 'I run a small fashion boutique where I also sell my jewellery. People can order bespoke pieces of whatever they wish. This, for example, is a single preserved red rose petal inside a vial.'

Eve turns the pendant gently in her fingers, admiring it under the chandelier's dim light. 'The attention to detail is breathtaking. It really is beautiful.'

Virgil clears his throat loudly, his impatience rising. 'Ladies. Drinks?'

Amy startles slightly. 'Oh, sorry. Bubbly is fine for me, thanks.'

'And me too,' Eve adds with a polite smile.

'Easily done,' Virgil mutters, handing them two flutes. Then, with a pointed glance across the room, he mutters under his breath but loud enough to be heard: 'Unlike some pretentious snobs who ask for ridiculous cocktails.'

The venom in his tone doesn't go unnoticed. Both women follow his gaze to the fireplace, where Imogen Sato stands serenely.

Amy and Eve exchange a glance, shrugging lightly before moving away to resume their conversation.

Virgil wiggles his shoulders up and down, trying to release the tension that's built up during the day as two more guests arrive.

Local bed-and-breakfast owner, Maggie Thornton, is escorted by the French doctor, Pierre Quint, again, both absorbed in conversation.

'Ah, Maggie, and Dr Quint. What can I get you?'

They initially ignore him as their conversation about the wonders of Paris continues.

Virgil shakes his head and quietly tuts. 'Some people,' he mutters under his breath. He coughs loudly. 'Ahem, drinks?'

'Oh, sorry, Virgil,' Maggie says. 'A glass of chardonnay, please.'

'Coming right up. And doctor?'

Dr Quint studies the assortment of bottles, sporting a frown. 'Do you have Burgundy?'

Virgil offers him a forced smile. 'No, sorry I don't.'

'Bordeaux, perhaps?'

Virgil shakes his head. 'Unfortunately, not. I find French wines rather on the expensive side. I can offer you a fine

Australian red,' he says, lifting up a bottle of Yellowtail Merlot.

Dr Quint grimaces as if he's been offered a glass of vomit. 'Erm, no thank you. I'll have a glass of bubbly. It is Champagne, I take it? Not sparkling wine.'

As Virgil hands Maggie her drink, his confusion spreads. 'They're one and the same, aren't they?'

'Bon sang! No, they are not the same. Authentic Champagne is grown in the Champagne region of France, hence the name. It is made using traditional methods and is a blend of three types of grape, fermented for a second time in the bottle. Sparkling wine is mass produced in tanks and is not fit for pig swill.'

Virgil, slightly embarrassed, looks at the bottle of Tesco Italian sparkling wine. 'I see. Would you prefer something else, Dr Quint?'

His eyes drift to the ice bucket containing beer. 'Very well, a Heineken, please.'

Virgil grabs a beer and flips the top off and hands it to the doctor. 'Is your mother not joining us, doctor?'

'No. She's rather worn out after the long trip from London and is taking a nap. She may join us for dinner if she feels fit enough, although she has the appetite of a sparrow.'

As they leave, Virgil mutters, 'Unbelievable. Anyone would think I was offering them Novichok.' He fingers the hip flask in his pocket, but the sight of Penelope and Murdoch striding through the reception makes him think twice.

As Penelope enters, she gazes around the room at the guests who are standing in small huddles around the glowing embers of the fire.

'How's it all going, Virgil?'

'Good, good. Apart from the poisoned dwarf.'

Penelope frowns. 'Who?'

'That cow, Imogen Sato. Asked for some bloody ridiculous cocktail.'

'I hope you weren't rude to her, Virgil? A good review from her will boost our reputation and future income.'

'No, of course I wasn't rude. I know how to play the game, Penny. Smile and be polite to the entitled, pernickety, pedants.'

'Virgil,' she hisses. 'Watch your mouth. Have you been drinking?'

'Only the one to ease my blood pressure, dear.'

Murdoch Langley pours himself a generous glass of red, as his brother obviously isn't going to.

'Right,' Penelope says, glancing at the grandfather clock and twiddling with the string of pearls around her neck. 'Most of the guests are here. Who are we missing?'

'Finnegan's mob.'

'Ah, yes. We'll wait until they arrive then make the announcements.'

'Would you like me to do it?'

'No, I would not. I want to smooth feathers, not ruffle them.' She grabs a flute of bubbly. 'Come, Murdoch. Let's mingle.'

The murmur of amiable chatter and occasional laughter fills the air, mingling with the warm crackle of the fire and the soft strains of Christmas carols.

Virgil watches the gathering with barely concealed contempt, his eyes narrowing at the mix of guests. 'More freeloaders than paying customers. This is an unmitigated disaster,' he mutters, helping himself to a glass of red. Consumed with indignation, he fails to notice the slight tremor that shakes the table, causing the glasses to clink softly. The other guests, too, remain oblivious to the subtle rattling of the windowpanes and the faint wisp of smoke curling out from the fireplace.

# 12

Frank, Prisha, and Zac enter the heated cloakroom off the hotel hallway, quickly removing their heavy coats and hanging them up. The noise from outside grows steadily, almost like a jumbo jet powering up its engines. Concerned but not yet alarmed, they walk briskly down the corridor and into the reception area as Meera descends the stairs.

'Ah, there you are, Frank,' she says, dressed in a stylish yet understated evening dress.

'You look lovely,' Prisha comments.

'Thank you. Thought I'd make an effort, even if others couldn't be bothered,' she replies, casting a disappointed glance at her husband.

'No time for that now,' Frank says, making a beeline for the drawing room.

The chandeliers hanging from the ceiling begin to rattle, sending a light sprinkle of dust downwards.

'What's wrong with him?' Meera asks.

'The full brunt of the storm is about to hit,' Zac explains as they follow Frank.

'Ah, Frank, what's your poison?' Virgil says.

'Not now, Virgil.' He claps his hands together. 'Ladies and gentlemen, your attention for a moment, please.'

The room falls silent as everyone turns to him.

'What's the problem, Mr Finnegan?' Penelope inquires.

'Any moment now, the storm will hit. There's no need to be—'

The building shudders as the storm front slams into Kindlewood Hall, like a battering ram pounding against an ancient fortress. Champagne glasses topple, smoke billows from the fireplace, and the ancient floorboards groan and creak beneath their feet as all hell breaks loose.

Cries of alarm and confusion fill the air. Virgil scrambles to save the remaining flutes, but they crash to the floor along with the cheap bottles of supermarket wine.

Outside, the picture-postcard scene of a winter wonderland is obliterated by a wall of white as snow and hail whip past in furious horizontal streaks. It doesn't last long—maybe twenty seconds—but it's enough to put the fear of God into everyone. Eventually, the earthquake-like tremor subsides, replaced by a howling wind that arrives in petulant fits and starts.

People cough and splutter in the smoke-filled room.

Frank spins around. 'Virgil, if I were you, I'd do a quick check of every room. Make sure no windows have blown out. Penelope, if you have a pedestal fan, then grab it. It will help to clear the smoke.' He turns to Zac. 'Check the rooms where fires are lit—the dining room and library. Make sure no embers are on the floor.'

'Boss.'

---

The small gathering huddles by the window, mesmerised by the storm raging outside. Snow has already piled up to the wheel arches of most of the vehicles parked in the circular drive. Inside though, they are cocooned in warmth, the treacherous elements without exaggerating the comfort within. A Christmas carol drifts softly from the speakers—not a lively one like Deck the Halls, nor even the gentle reflection of Silent Night. No, the hymn—I Wonder as I Wander—is closer to a dirge, almost a requiem. Its melancholic, mournful tone, and lyrics of loneliness and isolation do little to lift the mood.

'Christ,' Zac mutters in Prisha's ear. 'Who's the DJ? Count Dracula?'

Virgil Langley grumbles to himself as he swipes the mop across the polished floor of the drawing room, the faint scent of spilled wine still lingering in the air. Broken glass crunches underfoot, despite his earlier efforts with the dustpan. He straightens for a moment, adjusting his tie, then leans back into his work, muttering under his breath about things going from bad to worse.

The sound of footsteps draws his attention as Penelope Langley strides into the room, her heels clicking against the freshly cleaned floor. She casts a cursory glance at her husband, frowning slightly at the sight of him with a mop in hand, then moves to the centre of the room. The guests drift back from the window in clusters and circle the fireplace, chatting amiably with one another.

Penelope clasps her hands in front of her, her string of pearls reflecting the faint candlelight. 'Could I have everyone's attention, please,' she begins, her tone warm but firm, honed from years of hosting such gatherings. 'I hope you're all settling in despite the weather. As you may have guessed, the storm has caused some unforeseen challenges.' She pauses, the faint murmur of the guests quieting entirely.

'I must apologise,' she continues. 'The actors we booked for the murder mystery weekend have been unable to make the journey due to the conditions.'

A small ripple of surprised murmurs passes through the room. Most of the guests seem indifferent, shrugging or exchanging small smiles as though relieved to avoid the theatrics.

From her spot near the fire, Meera whispers into Frank's ear. 'Oh, that's a shame. I was looking forward to it.'

Penelope offers a conciliatory smile. 'I'm sure you're all disappointed, but it cannot be helped. But not to worry,' she says, her voice lifting slightly. 'Despite the weather, I can guarantee a wonderful evening. We've prepared an exceptional menu of fine food and wine—'

Dr Pierre Quint mumbles something unintelligible, though the faint curl of his lip suggests it isn't complimentary.

Penelope pauses briefly, staring at something slightly familiar about him, but the thought dissolves immediately. 'And after dinner,' she continues, 'we'll bring some festive cheer to the evening. We'll gather around the piano for Christmas carols, and then, for those who wish, we'll have some good, old-fashioned parlour games.' She gestures towards the glowing fire, the room now bathed in a soft amber glow. 'Just as things were done in the olden days before television sets made us all passive captives.'

A few chuckles ripple through the guests, though Meera still looks mildly disappointed.

'If you'd like to make your way into the dining room, dinner will be served in fifteen minutes.' As Penelope finishes her speech, Murdoch Langley sidles up to her, takes her gently by the arm and leads her to a corner of the room. It doesn't go unnoticed by Prisha. As she pretends to listen to Hugh Foster talk about the rigours of his farming life, she keeps one eye on Penelope and Murdoch.

Their body language is difficult to read. Murdoch's posture seems stiff, his hand gesturing sharply while Penelope keeps her arms folded across her chest. At one point, she looks away, her expression briefly clouded. Prisha tilts her head, trying to decipher whether the exchange is heated or merely serious, but the exact tone eludes her.

Before she can dwell further, the clink of glasses and rising chatter pulls her attention back to the group.

# 13

The dining room's warmth contrasts sharply with the storm's icy rage outside. Snow pelts the bay windows in waves, blotting out the grounds save for the occasional stab of light from the Victorian-style gas lamps that coral the now hidden driveway.

The long table stretches across the room, the soft flicker of candles dancing on its polished surface. Christmas lights strung along the bay windows and mantelpiece cast a faint glow, barely competing with the candlelight. The fire in the corner burner crackles and spits, its heat not quite managing to chase away the draughts that have crept into the room.

Frank sits along one side of the table, nursing a glass of red wine. Behind him, double doors lead to the reception area. To his right is a small bar and, further along, the kitchen door.

To his left, Meera is deep in conversation with Maggie Thornton, the local bed-and-breakfast owner—a short, plump woman with a genial manner. Maggie leans in slightly, gesturing animatedly as she describes her guesthouse.

'It's much grander than it sounds,' she says with a twinkle in her eye. 'People hear "bed-and-breakfast" and think of cramped rooms and shared bathrooms. But no, I've got en-suite facilities in every room and small, but fully equipped kitchens. I provide a full cooked breakfast that's better than anything you'll find in these big hotels. Not that I'm knocking Kindlewood Hall, of course,' she adds, clearly knocking Kindlewood Hall.

Meera nods, smiling politely. 'It sounds lovely. I imagine it's a lot of hard work, though?'

Maggie beams, leaning in conspiratorially. 'I won't lie—it keeps me busy, but I don't mind. I've had all sorts through my doors. Walkers, birdwatchers, even the odd celebrity. You'd be surprised.'

Frank tunes out their chatter, letting his gaze drift down the table. His eyes land on Logan Fitch, seated to Maggie's left, quietly sipping his sherry. Logan seems utterly self-contained, his wiry frame bent slightly forward, as if guarding himself. From the little Frank has heard, the man is an accountant—a semi-retired one at that—but something about him seems tightly wound, like he's nursing a grudge.

At the foot of the table, Dr Quint is engaged in conversation with Imogen Sato and Eve Sinclair. Frank catches occasional snippets and takes in the body language. Imogen, with her sharp features and even sharper voice, leans towards Quint, flicking her hair back.

'So, doctor, where in France are you from?' she asks, her tone polite but her eyes betraying her physical attraction for the doctor.

'Lyon,' he replies smoothly, lifting his glass of red, staring at it suspiciously. 'My private practice is based there. Although this past year, I took some time off to volunteer with Médecins Sans Frontières.'

'How noble,' Imogen comments, genuinely impressed. 'Was it a rewarding experience?'

Quint nods solemnly. 'Rewarding, yes, but also challenging. Somalia is not an easy place to work. But one does what one can.'

Frank shifts his attention to the opposite side of the table. Eve Sinclair, chatting with Amy Holland, listens intently as Amy describes her recent travels.

'I run a fashion boutique in the Midlands,' Amy says, her voice soft, almost hesitant. 'This trip was a bit of a break—recharging before heading to my parents in Fort William. Love them to bits, but they can be a bit... well, exhausting.'

'Fort William? Beautiful area, I've heard,' Eve says. 'I've always wanted to visit.'

'It is,' Amy agrees. 'Now, after a couple of days at Kindlewood Hall, I feel ready to face the madness.'

Frank's gaze finally drifts to Murdoch Langley and Hugh Foster, seated further down the table. Their voices are low, their conversation more intense.

'Tech stocks are looking shaky,' Murdoch murmurs, swirling his wine. 'I pulled out of a few this week. Always better to cut losses early.'

'Hmm,' Hugh replies. 'I stick to utilities—safe, stable. None of this flashy crypto nonsense.'

Frank's gaze finally comes full circle, where it lands on Prisha, seated beside Zac at the head of the table. He suppresses a smirk. Prisha's been doing the same as him—watching, listening, filing details away. Years of police work will do that to you. Zac, oblivious, tops up his wine and murmurs something to her.

The hum of conversation weaves in and out, punctuated by occasional laughter and the faint spit and hiss of the fire. Frank takes another sip of wine, leaning back in his chair. There's a strange energy in the room—nothing he can quite put his finger on. Maybe it's the storm outside, the relentless snow hammering against the windows like an impatient guest demanding entry. Or maybe it's the mix of personalities at the table—familiarity clashing with awkward politeness, old grudges brushing against fragile attempts at reconciliation.

'What do you think?' Meera whispers, nudging him gently with her elbow.

'Hmm?'

'The atmosphere,' she says, nodding towards the table.

Frank considers it for a moment, then shrugs. 'I think it's early days,' he murmurs, his eyes flitting back to Prisha, who's now watching Murdoch and Hugh with quiet curiosity.

In the corner of his mind, Frank feels a faint unease, like the first distant rumble of thunder before a storm.

Penelope and Lucy emerge from the kitchen carrying trays of starters.

'I do apologise for the delay,' Penelope announces. 'As I've explained, we're short-staffed due to the storm.'

'If she mentions how she's short-staffed one more time,' Maggie whispers in Logan Fitch's ear. He reciprocates with a wan smile.

Lucy and Penelope begin placing bowls down in front of the guests, their movements careful but unhurried. Frank's stomach churns impatiently as he watches them make their way around the room.

Lucy places a steaming bowl of mushroom soup in front of Amy Holland, who beams up at her.

'Thank you. It looks yummy,' Amy says, her voice bright and cheerful as she reaches for a slice of sourdough.

With the arrival of the food, the rather strained, overly polite atmosphere lifts a smidgen.

'What starter did you order?' Meera asks Frank.

'Mushroom. Just my luck, of course.'

'What do you mean?'

'They're serving the food up anti-clockwise, so I'll be bloody last,' he grumbles.

'Oh, stop being a grump. Have some bread.'

'Never fill up on the cheap stuff.'

Frank picks up his spoon and taps it against his palm, impatiently. The smell of pea and ham soup wafting from nearby bowls is torment. Finally, his soup arrives. He pushes a napkin down his shirt front and is about to dig in when Meera nudges him.

'What?' he asks, clearly irritated.

'That's a dessert spoon. The other one is your soup spoon.'

'Does it bloody matter?' he hisses under his breath.

'Yes, it does. At least try to show some decorum.'

Swapping spoons, he leans over the dish and inhales the aroma. He dips the spoon in and lifts it to his mouth but hesitates as he glances across the table at Amy Holland, who is experiencing a mild coughing fit.

'Oh, please excuse me,' she says, covering her mouth with a napkin.

'Are you all right, dear?' Murdoch Langley asks appearing concerned.

'Yes... it's just...' she taps at her chest.

All eyes turn to Amy as she rises, red-faced and gasping.

Meera tugs Frank's arm. 'She's choking.'

'Aye, she doesn't look too chipper.'

Eve rushes to her feet and pats Amy on the back. 'Did it go down the wrong hole?'

'No, I... can't... breathe,' she stammers, her breathing ragged.

Frank shoots a glance down the table.

'Dr Quint?' he shouts, nodding towards the stricken woman.

'Water! Water, someone pass her a glass of water,' Zac barks, scanning the table for a glass and jug.

Amy clutches at the edge of the table as more people rush to her aid. Her legs buckle and she collapses. Chaos erupts as chairs scrape back and guests crowd around her, their voices a jumble. Frank is already on his feet, pulse quickening.

'Dr Quint!' he barks.

The Frenchman rushes to Amy's side, dropping to his knees. 'Stand back, give her some air,' he yells.

Frank watches him place two fingers against her neck, then move to pump her chest with sharp, efficient compressions. The man knows what he's doing, but Frank can tell from the grim set of his jaw that it's bad.

'Heart attack?' Frank asks, stepping closer.

Quint glances up briefly, his face drawn. 'I don't know. Her pulse is almost gone. She's not breathing.'

He forces open her mouth, searching for an obstruction but sees none. Pulling her body into the sitting position, from behind, he wraps his arms around her chest and jerks her up and down, but it has no effect. Laying her flat he carries on with chest compressions, a bead of sweat forming on his brow, his face creased in anxiety.

Penelope rushes into the room from the kitchen.

'What's happening?' she cries.

'Medical emergency,' Prisha states, moving around the room desperately trying to pick up a signal on her mobile phone. 'Do you still have a landline?'

Penelope shakes her head. 'No. It went years ago.'

'Has anyone got a signal on their phone?' Prisha bellows. She's greeted with a shake of heads. 'Wonderful. Penelope, do you have a defibrillator?'

Penelope fiddles erratically with the pearls around her neck. 'Yes... no. It was stolen six months ago. I've been badgering Virgil to replace it, but he hasn't got around to it.'

The lights flicker once, twice, before going out altogether. The firelight and candles are all that remain, casting long shadows that dance eerily against the walls.

Dr Quint sits back on his heels, his shoulders slumping as the room falls silent.

'Mon Dieu,' he mutters, his accent thick with despair. 'She is... dead.'

Frank feels the room shrink around him. The storm outside louder, more oppressive.

'Dead?' Frank murmurs. 'Are you certain, doctor?'

The doctor nods, grim faced. 'Oui, c'est sûr. She is gone.'

Frank is baffled. 'But how?'

The doctor rises, brushing his knees then adjusting his tie. He meets Frank's gaze, his tone grave. 'Unless I am mistaken, inspector, this young woman has been poisoned.'

# 14

The hush in the room lingers, stretching seconds into what feels like minutes, time distorting under the weight of shock.

'Poisoned?' Frank questions, standing over the stricken body. His voice is calm, but his jaw aches as his sad gaze scans Amy Holland's lifeless face. 'How can you tell?'

Dr Quint pulls out a pristine white handkerchief and dabs at his forehead. In the dim light of the fire and candles, his movements seem sharper, more deliberate.

'Ah, c'est évident,' he says, gesturing towards Amy's face. 'Observe—slight frothing at the mouth. She could not breathe, yet there was no visible obstruction in the airways. The sudden onset is telling. She was perfectly fine, then one spoonful of mushroom soup, and she befalls a paroxysm. It is... suspicious, non?' He pauses, his brow furrowing deeply. 'Although, it is possible it was something else. It may have been, how you say, une réaction allergique.'

'Allergic reaction—anaphylactic shock?' Frank prompts.

'Oui, exactement.' Quint nods, his expression solemn. 'That is what I fear.'

Frank glances over at Lucy Hargreaves, who stands frozen by the table, her hands twisting nervously at her apron. 'Did Amy mention any allergies to you, Lucy?' he asks, his voice steady but probing.

Lucy blinks, her face pale, and shakes her head quickly. 'No, sir. I asked when she checked in. She said she was vegetarian, but she didn't mention any allergies. She said dairy was fine.'

Frank rises to his feet and turns to the table, his gaze locking onto Amy's bowl of mushroom soup. The faint smell of herbs still lingers in the air, mixing uneasily with the scent of wood smoke and melting wax.

He frowns. 'Did anyone else order the mushroom soup?'

The other guests glance at one another uneasily before shaking their heads.

'No,' Lucy says softly, her voice trembling. 'Just Miss Holland... and you, inspector.'

Frank pulls Prisha and Penelope Langley to one side. 'Prisha, get photos of the body and the bowl of soup,' he says in a hushed whisper. 'Mrs Langley, we'll need a room to place the body in for the moment.'

Her fingers roll over the pearls around her neck. 'Yes, of course. Erm... we have a number of spare bedrooms...'

Frank interjects. 'No. Not upstairs. It's only temporary while I think how to preserve the body. Even if we had mobile reception, the chances of getting anyone here tonight would be nigh on impossible with the weather and the state of the roads. And a chopper is out of the question.'

'I see. Well, you could lay her on the chaise longue in the library.'

'Good. Zac, you and the doctor relocate Miss Holland to the library.' He straightens and addresses the gobsmacked guests. 'Ladies and gentlemen, my name is Detective Chief Inspector Finnegan, and this is my colleague DI Kumar. As you are aware, we have a predicament on our hands. All deaths are treated as suspicious until proven otherwise. I ask you to resume your seats at the table and continue with your meals. At some point during the evening myself, DI Kumar, or DS Stoker, will take a statement from you regarding the incident tonight.'

The farmer, Hugh Foster, bristles at the news. 'Bloody steady on, inspector. You saw for yourself what happened. You're not suggesting one of us had anything to do with it, are you?'

Logan Fitch adjusts his tie. 'The inspector is not suggesting that for one moment, Hugh. It's merely protocol.'

'Is anyone under suspicion, inspector?' Maggie Thornton enquires as the tension ratchets up a level as everyone begins firing questions at Frank.

'Please! Quiet!' he bellows. 'No one is under suspicion of anything. It's merely a formality. Now, if you'll excuse me.' He turns to Mrs Langley. 'Penelope, I'd like a word with the chef and your husband, please.'

'Certainly. Follow me.'

As Prisha clicks away taking photos, the other guests reluctantly resume their seats.

'I'm not sure I can eat anything now,' Eve Sinclair states.

Imogen Sato chuckles. 'I'm sure the Langley's aren't intent on poisoning all their guests in one sitting.'

'That's in very poor taste,' Murdoch Langley snaps, as he picks up his soup spoon, then gingerly places it back down.

Imogen shrugs apologetically. 'It was too sudden for it to be anything to do with the food served tonight. The poor girl had barely taken a sip of the soup. If it is some sort of poisoning, then I'd suggest it was from earlier.'

———◦———

Penelope Langley leads Frank into the kitchen, which is illuminated with a number of torches and candles jammed into wine bottles. Despite the poor lighting, it's a hive of activity as French chef Antoine Galois, clearly agitated, barks orders at a rather flustered Virgil Langley. Both men are oblivious to the recent calamity in the dining room.

'Virgil, Antoine, I have bad news,' Penelope states solemnly.

'Bad news,' Virgil repeats, incredulous. 'Nearly all our guests cancelled along with the actors. We have no kitchen staff, and the bloody power has gone. I don't believe for one minute things could possibly get any worse.'

Antoine opens the oven and pulls out a huge tray of roast potatoes. Steam billows forth as he carefully places the roasting tray on the counter. 'Virgil, baste the potatoes then return them to the oven.'

'Yes, chef,' he says, half-mockingly. He picks up a spoon, tilts the tray and scoops up duck fat and douses the potatoes. Belatedly, he glances at his wife and Frank. 'Bad news, you say? Don't tell me one of the guests has pegged it already?' he adds with a raucous laugh.

Frank and Penny exchange an embarrassed glance. 'Actually, Virgil. Yes,' his wife replies quietly.

'Ha, ha, ha!' he guffaws as his eyes fall onto Frank. 'This is a joke, isn't it, Frank?'

'I'm afraid not. The young woman, Amy Holland, passed away a few moments ago. The French doctor, Pierre Quint, suspects poisoning, which may have precipitated an allergic reaction resulting in anaphylactic shock.'

Chef Antoine's jaw drops open. 'Sacré bleu!'

Virgil swallows hard, apparently in a state of shock. 'Good grief.' He pauses briefly. 'What do you mean—poisoning?'

'She'd just begun her starter, the mushroom soup,' Penelope replies.

Frank clears his throat. 'Antoine, the mushrooms in the soup—can you tell me about them?'

The French chef rubs a hand through his dense black, slicked-back hair. 'Yes. I picked them with my own hand only yesterday. They grow wild in the woods behind the hotel.'

Frank raises an eyebrow. 'Wild mushrooms?'

'Oui bien sûr.'

'If you could stick to English, it would be appreciated.'

'Apologies. Yes, wild mushrooms. But they are totally safe. I grew up picking wild mushrooms. I know what is safe to eat and what is not. There is no way my mushrooms had anything to do with the young woman's death.'

Frank wishes he had his notepad and pen with him. 'And exactly what species of mushrooms are in the soup?'

'They are called Paddy Straw Mushrooms. They are usually finished by this time of year, but the wood seems to have its own micro-climate, and I found a cluster growing beneath an old oak tree.'

'Could you have been mistaken? Could they have been poisonous mushrooms?'

He gesticulates in an agitated manner with his hands. 'No! I have cooked with them many times before.'

'Have you any left?'

Antoine storms into the cool room and returns a moment later with a small basket and plonks it down in front of Frank. 'Paddy Straw mushrooms,' he declares.

Frank pulls out a hanky and carefully picks one up. 'Hmm... I'm no expert, but to the layman's eye they appear very similar to Death Cap mushrooms.'

'You are correct, inspector. Similar, but only to the layman's eye.' He picks one up and opens his mouth.

Frank grabs Antoine's wrist. 'No. Let's play it safe. Put the mushrooms in a sealed container with a clear warning on the lid. Take a ladle of the soup, place it in another container, and freeze it. I know the power's off but it will still be cold for a while yet. Any surfaces the mushrooms touched need to be scrubbed with disinfectant. We can't risk cross-contamination, no matter how confident you are about their origin.'

Virgil picks up his wine glass and knocks the contents back in one swig as the full enormity dawns on him.

'My God, Penny, we're done for. It's one thing after another. We have the food critic here. And now we poison a bloody guest. It's the end for us. We can't come back from this one.'

Penny snaps. 'For Christ's sake, Virgil, pull yourself together! We don't know what caused the young woman's death. It could have been anything.'

The kitchen door creaks and groans as the howling wind picks up again. Frank glances out at the snow as it's carried horizontally in a westward direction.

'I suggest, for everyone's nerves and peace of mind, we carry on... not as normal, but as normal as can be under the circumstances. You have a dozen guests who are hungry and frightened. We are in the midst of a catastrophic storm, and isolated from civilisation until things calm down. Let's all try to keep a lid on things and show some semblance of control. Are you with me?'

Penny, Virgil, and even Antoine all nod, slightly ashamed of their reactions.

'You're right, inspector,' Penny concurs.

Virgil forces a smile, refills his wine glass and declares, 'Yes. I agree.'

Antoine curls his lips. 'Oui. Je suis d'accord.'

Frank pulls a double teapot—hands on hips. 'We obviously can't keep the young woman's body in the hotel. I noticed some outbuildings behind the hotel when I arrived. Do any of them have a raised platform?'

Virgil frowns. 'Yes. The large barn. We store hay in there.'

'Good. And are you in possession of a sleeping bag?'

Penelope's eyebrows arch. 'Yes, somewhere. But why?'

'Because it's the nearest thing we have to a body-bag. It will protect Miss Holland from vermin and insects. The temperature must be minus fifteen outside, maybe a little warmer in the barn, but still cold enough to preserve the body.'

# 15

The lights flicker on and off a dozen times before remaining on.

'Thank Christ for that,' Frank says as he finishes searching the body and comes up empty-handed.

With a certain degree of difficulty, Dr Quint holds the deceased upright, his arms thrust under the armpits as Frank shimmies the sleeping bag up and over the victim. He carefully zips it and pulls the cord tight, so the hood shrinks around the head, leaving nothing on show apart from the tip of the young woman's nose.

'Please forgive me, lass,' Frank whispers. 'It's not the most dignified of endings but it's the best I can do under the circumstances.' He glances at the doctor. 'I'll take the feet, you the top half. There's a barn around the back which will act as a temporary mortuary.'

'Ah, yes. It will slow down the decaying process. The quickest route is through the kitchen and out of the back door.'

Frank shakes his head. 'That would mean carrying the poor lass through the dining room and past the guests. Probably not a good idea. I suggest we take her through the front entrance.'

'Apologies, you're right. I wasn't thinking,' he replies as Zac enters the room.

He puffs out his cheeks and smirks. 'This reminds me of the Fawlty Tower episode where one of the guests died and Basil Fawlty and Manuel were trying to smuggle him out of his room.'

Frank scowls. 'Show some respect,' he huffs, wincing as he bends at the knees to grab the legs.

'Yeah, sorry. Poor taste. Prisha is getting details of all the guests and staff. Need a hand?'

'Aye. You can make sure the coast is clear. We're taking the body to the barn at the back of the hotel. Open the front door for us. Have you a torch?'

'No.'

'I take it you weren't in the boy scouts?'

'No. Girl Guides. Much more fun. One day I'll tell you how I achieved my bushcraft badge.'

'Very bloody funny. Come on, let's go.'

Zac pulls open the door and sticks his head out. 'All clear,' he says in a hushed tone.

They carry the body from the library, through the drawing room, out into reception and down the hallway to the front entrance.

The outside lights illuminate the heavy, swirling snow through the glass of the door.

'You okay Pierre?' Frank says, puffing slightly.

He nods, and adds with a wry smile, 'Yes, I am fine. Although, I didn't envisage this when I arrived today.'

'No, nor me.'

Zac swings open the door and tramps down the steps, his shoes disappearing into the thick powdery snow, the wind whipping at his hair.

'Christ, it's cold.' He turns right and is immediately scolded by Frank.

'Other bloody way. If we go right, we'll walk right past the dining room. Not a reassuring look for the other guests. We'd look like a trio of bloody body-snatchers.'

'Okay, okay,' he replies, clearly irritated as he turns around.

Although the ground is covered in a thick layer of snow, with the aid of the exterior security lights, they manage to navigate up the side of the house, then along the rear, warm magnolia lighting twinkling from the rooms inside the hotel.

They stumble past the kitchen door as Zac scurries ahead to the barn and pulls at the large wooden door.

Stepping inside from the icy blizzard, he rubs snow from his shoulders. He clicks a switch and a solitary light bulb high above offers a weak light, but enough to gather the layout of the interior. Frank and the doctor stumble in.

'She can't be that heavy,' Zac says noting the fatigue in Frank's features. 'She was only a slip of a lass.'

'She's not heavy. Just awkward to handle. Right, where's the best spot?'

Zac points at a low, slatted platform to the side of the shed. 'I reckon over there. Off the ground.'

They carefully place the body on the platform, then all three stand back.

'It's far from ideal, but it's the best we can do for the moment,' Frank notes.

Dr Quint tucks in the hood of the sleeping bag, which has come loose, until there's nothing but the tip of the woman's nose on show.

'As you said, inspector, the cold will preserve the body. Que Dieu repose son âme. God rest her soul.'

---

Prisha is in the back office, behind reception, with Lucy.

'When did Amy Holland arrive?' Prisha asks.

'Friday, about midday.'

'Alone?'

'Yes.'

'Did she say why she was here, where she came from?'

Lucy's brow creases. 'Um... I think she said she was on her way to visit her parents in Scotland. She stopped off in North Yorkshire for a couple of days walking.'

'Anything else?'

'She said she ran a small fashion boutique in the midlands, and also made bespoke jewellery that she also sold.'

'Did she mention the name of the shop?'

'No.'

'Did she complain of feeling unwell?'

'No. She appeared fit as a fiddle.'

'Can you remember her movements today?'

Lucy puffs out her cheeks and sighs. 'It's been a very chaotic day, inspector.' Her eyes roll upwards as she tries to think. 'I served her breakfast about eight-thirty. And this afternoon she enquired about a short walk around the grounds, which goes down to the lake and through the woods and circles back to the hotel.'

'And when was the next time you saw her?'

'Tonight, at dinner.' Lucy pouts. 'I'm sorry, inspector, but your questioning makes me think there's more to this than a medical episode.'

Prisha smiles. 'Simply being thorough. Is there anything else you can tell me about her? Her demeanour, her state of mind, anything she may have said?'

Lucy shakes her head. 'She appeared happy, content at least. Quiet. Oh, yes, there was one thing.'

'What?'

'When she first arrived and checked in, Podger came into the reception.'

'Podger?'

'He's the hotel cat. Well, a stray actually. Usually very friendly. Anyway, Miss Holland crouched and coaxed Podger over, saying how much she loved cats. She went to stroke him, and Podger hissed and took a swipe. He scratched her on the arm.'

'Which arm?'

Lucy points to her left arm and traces a finger along it. 'The left, and it was quite a long scratch right down to her hand.'

'Did it bleed?'

'A little. I got the first aid kit and wiped the scratch with antisep...' She halts abruptly and puts a hand over her mouth. 'Oh my God... you don't think she could have died from the scratch, do you? You know, septicaemia or tetanus?'

Prisha ponders the idea. 'I'm no medical expert, but I suppose it's possible. Although, from what I witnessed, Amy seemed to be having trouble breathing. Right, if you could give me a key for her room, I'll see if I can find any ID or contact details for family or friends.'

———◆———

As Prisha turns the key in the lock, the creak of a floorboard has her faltering. She's unsure whether it came from inside the room or from somewhere else. She glances around the deserted corridor and holds her gaze on the top of the stairs, but no one appears. Entering the room, she turns the light on and has a snoop around. It's neat and tidy. One small suitcase inside the wardrobe along with a pair of jeans, underwear, socks, T-shirts, and one jumper neatly stacked on a shelf. A thigh-length puffer jacket and a blouse dangle from coat hangers. Closing the door, she enters the en-suite and examines the toiletry bag. Nothing of any note. Back in the bedroom, she's puzzled. There's no purse or handbag and nothing with her ID on it. And if she was here for a couple of days walking why are there no walking boots or backpack?

She flicks the light off and pulls at the door as a tall figure blocks the way. She yelps and jumps back, clutching her chest.

'Zac! You bloody idiot. You scared me half to death.'

He shrugs apologetically. 'Sorry. Find any contact details?'

Shuffling into the corridor and locking the door behind her, she replies, 'No. Nothing. According to the receptionist, Amy Holland was here for a couple of days walking before heading to her parents' place in Scotland for Christmas. Yet, there's no walking boots or backpack. Did you search her pockets?'

'Frank did.'

'And?'

'Zilch. Nothing.'

'No bank cards, driver's licence?'

'No. One scrunched up tissue in her front pocket.'

'What was her footwear?'

'A pair of pink Nike trainers.'

Prisha holds out her hands in amazement. 'Hardly the sort of footwear for hiking,' she states as they amble along the corridor. 'And if she had no credit or debit cards on her, then how did she pay for the hotel, her transport here, and her proposed transport to Scotland? I suppose it is possible an unscrupulous opportunist entered her room and stole her cards,' she adds as an afterthought.

Zac grimaces. 'It is odd but before you go all Miss Marple on me, we both witnessed her demise, and it was definitely some sort of medical episode. Accidental poisoning or allergic reaction.'

—◦—

Frank holds court in the dining room, where hushed conversations and whispers ripple through the gloom. He taps a wine glass with a knife, the sharp ping cutting through the apprehension.

'Ladies and gentlemen,' he begins, his voice steady. 'The young lady who passed away was known as Amy Holland. She arrived at the hotel yesterday, intending to stay for two nights before travelling to Scotland to spend Christmas with her parents. Unfortunately, we haven't been able to find any identification—either on her person or in her room.' He glances towards Prisha and Zac, seated alongside Meera. 'Now, I realise most of you arrived at Kindlewood Hall earlier today, but did anyone happen to interact with Miss Holland? If you did, then come and see me or one of my officers later.'

The other guests exchange uneasy glances, but no one speaks.

Murdoch Langley pours more red wine into his glass, the glugging sound loud in the quiet. 'It's all a bit peculiar, isn't it, inspector? A woman with no ID suddenly drops dead and may or may not have been poisoned.'

Across the table, Hugh Foster pushes his chair back and stands, nodding courteously at Penelope and Virgil Langley. 'Thank you for your hospitality, but as things have gone a bit pear-shaped, I think I'll call it a night and head back to the farm.'

Frank puffs out his chest. 'I don't think that's a wise idea, Mr Foster,' he says firmly. 'Not only have you been drinking, but the snow's three feet deep. You'd get bogged—or worse.'

Hugh bristles. 'Are you saying I can't leave, inspector?'

'No,' Frank replies, his tone measured. 'I have no authority to make you stay, but I'm advising you—in the strongest possible terms—for your own safety—remain at the hotel.'

The lights flicker, dimming the room to shadows before plunging it into full darkness. Only the scattered candles on the table offer faint, murky illumination, their glow throwing jagged shapes against the walls.

'Christ,' Zac mutters. 'It goes from bad to worse.'

Dr Quint rises, pulling a small torch from his jacket. 'I must check on my aunt. I don't want her stumbling about in the dark.'

Before anyone can respond, a violent, strident scream splits the air, ricocheting around the room. Maggie Thornton claws at her face, her eyes wide with horror.

Prisha leaps to her feet, rushing to the end of the table. 'What is it?' she demands.

Maggie, trembling uncontrollably, points a shaking hand at the bay window overlooking the front driveway. 'I saw... s... saw someone... or something,' she cries. 'It was horrible. Staring through the window.'

Prisha and Zac hurry to the glass, peering out. Snow lashes the panes in chaotic, swirling gusts, obscuring the view.

'Are you certain?' Prisha asks, her voice sharp.

'Positive,' Maggie says, her voice quavering. 'It was grotesque. Huge, with evil eyes staring in at us.' Her breathing quickens. 'A monster! A beast!'

Imogen Sato presses a glass of wine into Maggie's trembling hands. 'I saw it too,' she says. 'Drink this. It will calm you.'

The table erupts into chaos, chairs scraping as guests speak over one another, their terror mounting.

Frank raises his hands. 'Can everyone please calm down?'

His plea is ignored, the tension mounting.

*Bang. Bang. Bang.*

The dull, measured thuds echo from the front door into the dining room, silencing everyone. Anxious eyes dart from face to face, A suffocating quiet descends, dark and heavy.

Clutching a candelabra, Frank stares down the hallway towards the entrance. Prisha and Zac flank him, with Penelope and Virgil hovering further back in reception.

'Is the door locked, Virgil?' Frank asks.

'Yes. I locked it after you'd returned from putting the body in the barn. With no one at reception, I thought it best.'

*Bang. Bang. Bang.*

The pounding makes them all twitch.

The corridor feels longer than Frank remembers. The darkened shape of the Christmas tree, no longer illuminated by the candles, appears as an interloper.

'Go on, Frank. See who it is,' Zac urges, nudging him forward.

Frank hesitates. 'Ahem, yes, right,' he mutters, trying to mask his unease.

Prisha groans, snatching the candelabra from him. 'Pathetic. I'll open the bloody door.'

Frank quickly grabs it back. 'No. Leave it to me and Zac.' He glances at Zac. 'Right?'

'Thanks a bunch, pal,' Zac grumbles.

*Bang. Bang. Bang.*

'Okay, hold your—' Frank's voice cracks into a squeak. He clears his throat, forcing out a steadier tone. 'Ahem, hold your bloody horses! I'm coming!'

He edges forward, Zac trailing close behind. The door looms larger as they near it. Frank thrusts the candelabra into Zac's hands.

'I'm sure it's simply a lost traveller or a motorist in trouble, but just in case it's a...'

'What?' Zac asks. 'A homicidal maniac gripping a bloodied axe and a severed head?'

Frank blinks. 'I was going to say, but in case it's not, that candelabra's heavy. Use it if you have to.'

'Don't worry, Frank. I've got your back. Honest.'

*Bang. Bang. Bang.*

The sound reverberates through both men.

'Get on with it!' Prisha shouts from behind, losing patience with her gallant knights in shining armour.

Frank swallows hard.

He places his hand on the key.

Twists.

Yanks open the door.

'Arrrrrrrgh!'

# 16

The colossal, menacing figure on the threshold towers over Frank, but there's no immediate sign of hostility—and, reassuringly, no axe nor severed head. The face is obscured by a thick scarf, dark eyes peering out from a narrow slit, the entire figure blanketed in snow and ice. Frank's gaze drifts to the stranger's headgear, which, to the untrained eye, looks alarmingly like roadkill—possibly a raccoon or a possum. Neither animal is native to North Yorkshire in the midst of winter... or at any time, for that matter.

Frank finally speaks. 'Ahem, lost your way, stranger?' he asks, his voice betraying a faint tremor.

'Indeed. Is there, by perchance, room at the inn for two, Detective Chief Inspector Finnegan?'

Frank lets out an almighty sigh, a grin spreading across his face. 'Bennet bloody Whipple!' he explodes, the tension draining from his shoulders. 'You scared seven bells of shite out of everyone. You daft bugger! Come inside.'

As the imposing figure steps over the threshold, shedding clumps of snow onto the floor, a diminutive woman sidles up beside him, shivering like a shitting dog on bonfire night.

'My wife—Mrs Whipple. Wife—Detective Chief Inspector Finnegan,' Whipple announces with barely restrained pride.

Mrs Whipple nods at Frank. 'Inspector, I've heard a lot about you,' she says, her teeth chattering like a set of castanets.

Frank grins. 'All good, I hope,' he replies cheerily.

'On the contrary. My husband finds you irritating and most vexatious. He says you're like an itch at the back of the brain that cannot be scratched.'

Whipple's eyes swivel onto his wife. 'Hmm...'

---

Frank enters the drawing room, where Bennet Whipple sits draped in a thick blanket like a beleaguered monarch, huddled as close to the roaring fire as humanly possible without igniting. His hands emerge from the folds of fabric, trembling, as though life itself had betrayed him.

'Here you go, Bennet. A cup of piping-hot drinking chocolate, as requested,' Frank says, handing him the steaming mug.

Whipple accepts it with the solemnity of a religious offering. 'My profound gratitude, inspector,' he intones. 'You are, as always, a beacon of dependability in an otherwise chaotic world.'

'Sure you don't want something a bit stronger? A whisky or a brandy? Warm the cockles?' Frank offers, dropping into the chair beside him.

Whipple fixes Frank with a look of such weary disdain it could curdle milk. 'Inspector, you are, no doubt, well acquainted with my views on alcohol. It is the great corrupter. The elixir of fools. A loathsome invention, distilled from misery and seasoned with the tears of humanity. It is the universal cancer. A pestilence. An abomination fermented in the deepest abyss of despair.'

Frank grimaces, leaning back in his chair. 'Fair enough. So, what happened, then? You had a bingle in your precious Jag?'

Whipple sighs, a sound like the collapse of a civilisation. 'Alas, a most lamentable calamity befell Mrs Whipple and I. We had parked the vehicle to partake of some modest victuals, and—well, as fate would have it...' He pauses, his brow furrowing as though selecting his next words were a matter of great constitutional import.

'As fate would have it, what?' Frank prompts, already feeling a twinge of regret for asking.

Whipple continues, raising a hand with theatrical gravity. 'When, I assume, Mrs Whipple, in a moment of unfortunate carelessness, knocked the handbrake.'

Frank rubs his chin thoughtfully. 'Hmm... why didn't you put your foot on the brake?'

Whipple takes a silent sip of his drinking chocolate, then clears his throat. 'Alas, I was—how shall I put this—engaged elsewhere at the time.'

Frank arches an eyebrow. 'Engaged in what, exactly?'

Whipple's eyes narrow, affronted. 'Inspector, does it matter? Must you pry into the particulars of every fleeting moment of my existence? There is no profit to be gained from revisiting the sordid minutiae of past events. None. It is as futile as pondering the nature of the universe itself. I beg you to show some discretion.'

Frank smirks and raises his hands in mock surrender, having possibly deduced what Mr and Mrs Whipple were up to in the classic E-Type Jaguar. 'All right, Bennet. Calm down. No need to shout.'

'Shout? Shout?' Whipple booms, his voice reverberating off the drawing room walls. 'Inspector, let me assure you this is not shouting. Were I shouting, the very foundations of this venerable establishment would quake beneath us.'

'Right. Duly noted,' Frank says, rolling his eyes. He leans forward, lowering his voice. 'Although, nice work if you can get it,' he adds with a chuckle.

Whipple slowly turns and glares at him. 'And what does that cryptic afterthought allude to, inspector?'

'Nothing. Just saying. Anyway,' Frank begins, changing the subject, 'we had a bit of misfortune here tonight, ourselves.'

'Oh?' Whipple peers at him over the rim of his mug, his interest momentarily piqued.

'Aye. A bonny young lass—early thirties, I'd say—died at the dinner table.'

Whipple lowers his mug very slowly. 'And what, pray, did this unfortunate young woman succumb to?'

'Not sure yet,' Frank replies. 'We've another doctor in the house—a French fella, Dr Pierre Quint. He reckons it could've been poisoning. Or maybe an allergic reaction. She was eating mushroom soup at the time. Chef said they were wild mushrooms he picked himself.'

Whipple's gaze returns to the fire, his expression as solemn as Whitby Abbey. 'Wild mushrooms...' he muses. 'Hmm... and did anyone else partake of this most perilous broth?'

'I nearly did, but no. Only her.'

Whipple strokes his stubbled chin, his fingers moving with the deliberation of a scholar unearthing a great revelation. 'Curious,' he murmurs. 'Most curious indeed.'

'Aye,' Frank agrees. 'That's what I thought. An accident? Or something more sinister at play?'

Whipple leans back in his chair, pulling the blanket tighter around his shoulders like a prophet in the wilderness. 'Inspector, as I sit here, swaddled in borrowed wool and stripped of all creature comforts, I am reminded of how man, so accustomed to luxury, so inured to the softness of modern life, reverts to his primal state with alarming alacrity when deprived of the barest essentials. It is a grim commentary on our species, is it not?'

Frank chuckles, shaking his head. 'Don't worry, Bennet. All's been taken care of. Your wife's been shown to her room by Prisha. She's taking a long, hot shower to thaw out—alone of course—not with Prisha,' he adds as a postscript. 'And Penelope—Mrs Langley, the proprietor—has a cupboard full of lost property. Deodorants, soaps, toothpaste, unopened toothbrush packets, and enough cast-off clothing to outfit a small militia. She's kitted out Mrs Whipple for bed. That's the British way, you see. Pull together in times of crisis. Strength in unity.'

Whipple raises an eyebrow. 'Inspector, you sound like a 19th-century unionist.'

Frank shrugs. 'Aye. Maybe I do. And nowt wrong in that. United we stand—divided we fall.'

# 17

The impromptu after-dinner activities Penelope Langley had planned fizzled out after twenty uninspired minutes of half-hearted carol singing. Though the drawing room was warm and inviting, its ambience created by the subdued red emergency lights, flickering candlelight, and the soft glow of the fire, the atmosphere was weighed down by the lingering shadow of tragedy and the relentless storm outside. Conversation among the guests remained muted, pockets of small talk unable to shake the unease. One by one, they excused themselves, retreating to their rooms, until the house was eerily quiet well before ten o'clock.

Meanwhile, Virgil Langley lingered in the library with his brother, Murdoch, nursing a bottle of whisky. As the clock ticked by, their conversation grew slurred and muddled, the level in the bottle dropping as Virgil methodically drank himself into a stupor.

In the drawing room, the last embers of the fire glow weakly as Frank, Meera, and Penelope Langley rise from their chairs, preparing to head to bed. Penelope stretches with a weary sigh, her pearl necklace catching the faint light.

'Well, I suppose that's it for me,' she says, brushing down her skirt and checking her phone yet again. 'Still no signal,' she mutters under her breath.

Frank frowns. 'One or more mobile towers must be out somewhere. Don't hold your breath on it being fixed anytime soon. They won't send maintenance crews out until the storm's abated and the roads are clear.'

'Yes, I suppose you're right.' Looking pale and drawn, Penelope musters a faint smile. 'I'll say goodnight. Let's hope tomorrow brings some peace and normality.' She pauses, her gaze drifting towards the library, where the low murmur of Virgil and Murdoch's voices filters through the door.

'Virgil, I'm heading up. Don't be too late and make sure everything's locked up and the fireguards are in place.'

'Righto. Be up soon dear,' comes the muffled response.

'Goodnight, Mrs Langley,' Meera says warmly, looping her arm through Frank's as they head towards the reception area.

As Penelope disappears up the staircase, Frank stops mid-stride. He notices Bennet Whipple loitering with intent like a virgin at a pornographic film-star convention, half-shrouded in the dim light, his expression unusually tense. Whipple catches Frank's eye, then glances around before beckoning him with an urgent flick of his fingers.

Frank frowns, gently detangling his arm from Meera's. 'You head up, love. The doctor wants a word.'

Meera hesitates. 'Okay. Don't be long.'

As Meera ascends the staircase, Frank steps towards Whipple, lowering his voice. 'What's wrong Bennet?'

Whipple leans in, his voice a low rumble. 'Inspector, we must engage in a matter of some delicacy—privately, if you will. The kitchen shall suffice as a sanctuary. We are unlikely to encounter disturbance therein.'

Frank follows him through the dining room and into the kitchen where a candle flickers from its perch inside a wine bottle.

'What daft bugger left a naked flame unattended?' Frank mutters.

'That would be me,' Whipple replies without shame. 'I employed it earlier to illuminate my examination.'

'Examination of what?' Frank asks, his patience fraying.

'Mushrooms,' Whipple replies gravely.

Frank scratches his head, frowning. 'Bennet, you're acting bloody peculiar. Now, what's all this about?'

Whipple straightens, his face solemn, his voice dipping into a theatrical register. 'I find myself inexorably compelled to inspect the corporeal vessel of the recently departed.'

Frank takes a moment to untangle the verbosity. 'You mean Amy Holland? The dead woman?'

Whipple nods. 'Precisely. The circumstances of her demise are vexing, and I can scarcely retire without first satisfying my inquiries.'

Frank pulls a face resembling badly laid crazy paving. 'Are you out of your mind?' he exclaims.

'I can assure you, inspector, my faculties remain as crystalline and pure as a mountain stream in springtime.'

'Dr Quint took the poor woman's vitals and pronounced her dead. Her body is in the barn. The temperature outside must be minus twenty. What good is going to be served by you visiting the body?'

'I am a Home Office pathologist. It is my sworn duty.'

'Duty? You're not at work now, Bennet. You're officially on holiday.'

'As indeed you are, inspector. And yet, it does not deter you from instinctively reverting to your professional expertise, for what it's worth, in suspecting this unfortunate incident may not merely be a case of accidental poisoning.

To wit—the attending physician postulated death by the consumption of noxious fungi. Yet I have meticulously examined every fungal specimen within this domicile and can categorically affirm, none bear the tincture of toxicity.'

Frank rubs his chin, agitated. 'The doctor wasn't certain of the true cause of death—granted. It was an educated guess. But he did say it could have been a reaction to something she ate.'

Whipple straightens to his full towering height. 'Very well. I shall circumvent your obstinacy and attend to the deceased alone.' Whipple picks up the candle and heads to the door.

Frank shakes his head in dismay. Whipple may have the most brilliant medical brain he's ever known, but when it comes down to common sense, it's a desert of tumbleweed rolling by.

'Bennet—the candle. Straight away you open the door, it will be snuffed out.'

Whipple gazes at the weak, flickering flame. 'Indeed... an astute observation, inspector.'

'Not really.' He relents. 'Okay, I'll come with you. But we'll need to get wrapped up first.'

'Indubitably.'

***Frank unbolts the kitchen door and steps out into the tempest, his super high-powered micro-LED torch cutting a piercing beam through the swirling snow. The Beast from the East greets him like a kick to the head—savage beyond belief.

Despite his heavy overcoat, jumper, shirt, T-shirt, vest, bobble hat, scarf, gloves, thick trousers, thermal leggings, Marks and Spencer underpants, woollen socks, and boots—he's immediately chilled to the bone.

Whipple fastens his duffle coat, wraps a scarf around his face, and pulls on his ushanka, then follows him outside, valiantly yanking the kitchen door shut with great effort.

'Sweet merciful shit on a stick!' Frank exclaims, fearing the tip of his nose could drop off at any moment. 'This could freeze the gumnuts off a hairy mammoth.'

Whipple mutters an incomprehensible reply in his native tongue, but to Frank it sounds like he's in agreement, for once.

Both men hurry like old men running—which is more of a shuffle—towards the barn. The beam from Frank's torch slices through the storm, illuminating a narrow path for them to follow. He pulls at the barn door and steps inside, the wind howling in protest behind him.

Whipple enters and manfully shuts the door with a resounding clank. The comparative silence, the faint warmth, and the sweet smell of stored hay offer a modicum of relief.

They stamp their feet and shake their bodies to rid themselves of snow and ice.

'Bet you don't get this in Nigeria,' Frank says, trying to sound casually amusing as he shines the torch in Whipple's direction.

'Jumping juniper berries, inspector! Kindly desist from directing that infernal torch into my face.'

Frank apologises. 'Sorry, Bennet. It's an Imalent MS03. Thirteen thousand lumens. You can start fires with this bugger.' He sweeps the beam around. 'Meera bought it for my birthday. Okay, over here, on the right. We put the body in a sleeping bag on that shelf.' The light lands on the wrapped corpse. 'See it?'

'Indeed. I am not an imbecile. Please keep the light steady on the cadaver while I conduct a secondary adjudication,' Whipple says, lumbering forward with a grumble. 'This accursed weather—I surmise it emanates from the bowels of Hades itself. I wouldn't be surprised if Beelzebub himself paid us a visit tonight.'

'I hope not. I'm not in the mood for conversation.'

Whipple gingerly fingers the sleeping bag. The sound of a zipper being pulled down fights with the howls from outside and the creaking and groaning of the old wooden barn as it bemoans another of Mother Nature's tantrums.

He leans in, hands probing the body. 'The light, inspector, the light!' he shouts. 'How, pray tell, can I be expected to perform my duties in the absence of adequate illumination?'

'All right, keep your wig on, Bennet,' Frank replies, angling the torch downwards.

Unfortunately, the thirteen thousand lumens strike Whipple squarely between the eyeballs, sending him staggering backwards, clutching his face.

'Sweet Jehovah and holy mother in the afterlife!' he yells, flailing like a drunken man at chucking-out time. 'You've excoriated my retinas, inspector! I am bereft of sight!'

'You need to take more care, Bennet.' Frank says as he grabs Whipple's arm to steady him. 'Ahem... when you're ready.'

Whipple groans, muttering under his breath as he straightens his posture. With great effort, he composes himself and steps back towards the body, squinting warily at the light glaring down on the wooden platform.

'I am utterly bedazzled by phosphorescence and may very well be suffering from photokeratitis. I shall now conduct my examination with my eyes closed.'

'Whatever.'

'Isaiah,' he mutters.

'Isaiah?'

'Indeed, inspector. This unfortunate young woman is as rigid as a board. Rigor Mortis has set in far too expeditiously, considering she expired mere hours ago.'

'It's minus twenty, Doc. She's probably frozen solid.'

'Hmm... plausible, but improbable in such a brief interval. The ambient temperature in this barn is perhaps minus five, and she is swathed in a sleeping bag. Odd. Very odd.'

Frank says nothing, holding the torch steady as Whipple continues his examination.

'No pulse. The flesh is cold and unyielding, devoid of plasticity. There's a rigidity to the skeletal structure that I have seldom encountered. It is a troubling and vexatious confoundment.'

'Your conclusion?'

'The young woman is deceased.'

'You don't say,' Frank mutters, rolling his eyes, which are still in good working order.

Whipple zips up the sleeping bag and turns to Frank. 'Let us brave the malevolent tempest once more, inspector, and return to sanctuary and warmth. My examination is complete.' He pauses. 'And please refrain from directing that malevolent beam anywhere near my personage.'

# 18

Frank and Whipple hang their coats and hats in the heated cloakroom before heading back to reception as the grandfather clock strikes ten.

'I believe it's time for my bed, inspector,' Whipple announces.

'Aye, sleep tight, Bennet, and make sure the bed bugs don't bite.'

Whipple pauses, his eyes narrowing as he studies Frank. 'Are you insinuating this establishment harbours cimex lectularius, inspector?'

Frank frowns. 'What?'

'Bed bugs,' Whipple replies with the look of a lecturer. 'These diminutive, blood-feeding parasites of nocturnal habits pierce the epidermis with a specialised proboscis, injecting an anticoagulant to facilitate their sanguineous feast. Once engorged, they retreat to the shadows, leaving behind itchy welts as evidence of their nocturnal malfeasance.'

Frank chuckles. 'No, Bennet. It's an old saying—wishing someone a good night's sleep.'

Whipple blinks rapidly, his eyeballs still scorched into his frontal lobe, then harrumphs, clearly unimpressed. 'I see. Yet another example of British irony. Goodnight, inspector.'

Frank watches him clomp up the stairs, shaking his head. 'Hell, they broke the mould when they made him.'

His thoughts about Whipple are interrupted by raised voices drifting through the hotel. He pauses, frowning, then moves quietly into the drawing room. The sound emanates from the adjoining study—sharp, angry tones disturbing the stillness.

He hovers out of sight, listening intently.

'Don't deny it, Murdoch! You're a crook and a charlatan,' Virgil shouts, his voice trembling with fury.

'Don't talk bloody rubbish, Virgil. You're drunk and incapable of rational thought,' comes Murdoch's clipped reply.

'Logan went over the figures, and he says you've grossly underestimated the costs. You've deliberately set us up for failure.'

'Logan Fitch is a two-bit bookkeeper,' Murdoch snaps. 'My people reviewed everything with a fine-toothed comb. The figures are spot on, or as near as damn it. Why the hell would I deliberately underestimate costs?'

'Because you're a slippery, two-faced cheat. You always were. Even as a child. I'm onto you, Murdoch.'

There's a beat of silence, then Murdoch's voice drops, colder now. 'I'm going to bed. I can't talk to you when you're sozzled.'

'That's right, walk away,' Virgil spits. His voice lowers but carries venom. 'And don't think I don't know about you and Penelope. You bastard!'

Frank's eyes narrow as he inches closer to the doorway.

Murdoch's voice remains measured, though Frank catches the strain. 'You need help, Virgil. Your drinking has become a real problem. It's making you delusional—and paranoid.'

A chair scrapes loudly against the floor, followed by heavy, brisk footsteps. Frank slinks further back into the drawing room as Murdoch storms out of the study, his face flushed with anger.

Frank steps into his path, playing nonchalant. 'Ah, I thought I heard voices.'

Murdoch's eyes narrow briefly before smoothing into a polite but curt expression. 'Inspector. Yes, just my brother and I having a little chat. Nothing to worry about. Goodnight.'

'Goodnight,' Frank replies, watching him disappear into the reception.

Once out of sight, Frank hesitates for a moment before stepping into the study. Virgil is standing by the window, silhouetted against the pale glass, nursing a tumbler of whisky. His shoulders are hunched, his posture heavy.

'Everything all right, Virgil?' Frank asks, keeping his tone casual.

Virgil doesn't turn around immediately. When he does, his face is worn and tired, his eyes bloodshot. 'Yes, fine. Thanks.'

'Sounded like quite a row,' Frank presses lightly.

Virgil lets out a brittle laugh and shrugs. 'That's brothers for you. We'll kiss and make up in the morning. A minor misunderstanding. That's all.'

Frank doesn't buy it, but lets it go. 'Hmm. Right. Well, I'm heading up. I had a quick check of the entrance door and the kitchen. Everything's locked and bolted.'

Virgil offers a thin, unconvincing smile. 'Thanks, Frank. I suppose I'd better head to bed as well.' He turns and stares out of the window into blackness, his voice barely above a whisper. 'Is it all worth it, Frank? All this—life, the struggles, trying to hold everything together. In the end, does it mean anything?'

Frank pauses in the doorway, his hand resting on the frame. He studies Virgil for a moment, noting the desperation in his voice.

'Life wearies all of us, Virgil. No matter how strong we think we are. One thing I've learnt over the years is that you can't win every fight. Even the greatest boxers eventually reach their sell-by date.' He takes a step closer. 'Pick your battles wisely and decide which hill you're willing to die on. Sometimes, walking away is the bravest thing you can do.'

Virgil lets out a soft, humourless chuckle. 'You make it sound so simple.'

'It isn't. But neither is staying stuck in the same scrap over and over again, forever picking yourself up off the canvas.' Frank offers him a small nod. 'Goodnight, Virgil.'

Virgil lifts his glass to the window, as if toasting some unseen figure beyond the storm. 'Goodnight, Frank.'

Frank turns and walks away, leaving Virgil to his whisky, his thoughts, and the unrelenting howl of the wind against the glass.

———◦———

Virgil teeters on the landing, the torchlight jerking wildly from carpet to ceiling as he wobbles from side to side. The faint hum of the blizzard presses against the old manor walls, the wind keening faintly through unseen cracks. He fumbles with the red cord barring entry to the private residence quarters, his hand-eye coordination ambushed by the day's alcohol consumption.

'Damn it,' he blusters, wrestling with the hook on the stanchion. After several failed attempts, he lifts one leg over the cord, but it snares his foot. There's a brief comic interlude as he performs a graceless dance, arms flailing, torchlight throwing erratic shapes across the ceiling, before he crashes to the ground. The torch rolls away, spinning, its beam cutting through the darkness in dizzying arcs.

'Bloody thing!' he shouts, his voice echoing indignantly. Muttering curses, he untangles himself, grabs the torch, then leans heavily against the wall, using it to haul himself upright. A belch escapes as he pulls the room key from his pocket, wiping his damp brow with the back of his hand.

'Damn them all,' he mutters as he staggers down the dim corridor, the torchlight bouncing ahead of him like an errant will-o'-the-wisp. 'I don't need any of them. Not her, not him, not anyone. Cheating bitch.' His muttering builds, punctuated by bursts of venom. 'It was I who built this hotel from nothing. It was my foresight, my risk-taking that got us where we are today. It was me that shed blood, sweat, and tears. And what thanks do I get? Nothing. A big fat zero. Bastards, every last man jack of them... and her most of all.'

His tirade continues under his breath as he finally reaches his door. Hands tremble as he fumbles the key into the lock, missing twice before it slides in with a grating metallic scrape.

He pushes the door open—and an icy blast of air hits him square in the face.

'What the bloody hell?' he exclaims, shining the torch into the room. The beam catches the open window, its curtains flapping madly in the wind. Papers skitter across the floor like restless ghosts, and the faint smell of snow hangs in the air. 'What was that stupid woman thinking?' he laments, immediately blaming his wife. 'She has her room. I have mine. Why she's got to interfere in mine is beyond me. Good job this side faces west or the whole bloody room would be full of snow!' He locks and chains the door.

The chill sobers him slightly as he staggers to the window, but a sharp gust billows the curtain, snapping it against his face. Startled, he drops the torch, which rolls under the bed. The beam casts a faint glow that stretches to the far side of the room that lights up a pair of shoes he fails to notice.

Grumbling, he slams the window shut with a bang that rattles the panes. He rubs his hands together briskly, warming his hands.

'Soldier on, Virgil, old boy,' he mutters, staggering towards the dresser. He yanks open the sock drawer, rummaging until his fingers curl around the cool neck of the whisky bottle hidden within. Spinning off the top, he takes a long swig, the fiery liquid momentarily dulling the ache of self-pity.

'How did it come to this?' he murmurs, slumping onto the edge of the bed. The bottle rests loosely in his lap as he stares blankly at the floor. 'Universally hated. My wife having an affair with my brother. My stepson estranged. And me... what of me? A drunken, broken-down old man, on the precipice of financial ruin. Humiliation and the poorhouse await unless I take the offer from that snake in the grass. Is this what I deserve after sixty-odd years on this godforsaken planet?' His voice cracks, and he takes another gulp, the burn almost comforting.

A faint noise distracts him. He turns his head sharply towards the wall, his bleary eyes narrowing at the timber panelling. The house feels alive tonight, its old bones creaking and groaning in protest against the storm. A shiver crawls down his spine, but he shakes it off and takes another drink. 'It's the bloody wind,' he mutters, his voice thick.

He sighs heavily, slumps onto his knees, and sticks one arm under the bed, his fingers groping blindly for the torch. It remains stubbornly out of reach, casting faint shadows that stretch and distort across the floor.

'Will this damned day never end?' he mutters. His voice sounds small, swallowed by the pressing silence of the room.

A floorboard creaks.

He cocks his head.

His bloodshot eyes lift slowly, darting towards the source of the sound. For a moment, there's nothing—only the low howl of the storm buffeting the windows.

Until... he notices something in the torchlight... silent, inching forward.

He swallows hard as the shadow resolves into a shape.

Shoes.

Legs.

'Penelope?' he slurs, confusion thickening his voice. His eyes struggle to focus, climbing upward. His heart lurches as his gaze rises higher, up to the figure standing motionless above him. A glint from something grasped in their hand.

Virgil tilts his head back... exactly what the intruder wished for.

'You? But what... how...'

For Virgil, he's finally found his hill to die on.

# 19

**Sunday 22nd December**

Penelope Langley, smartly dressed in a tailored navy skirt and a matching blouse, pulls the dish from the oven. Her pearl earrings catch the muted morning light through the back door. The neatly tied scarf is both practical and stylish, adding a touch of elegance to her otherwise no-nonsense demeanour. Discarding the oven gloves, she glances at the clock on the wall and tuts sharply.

Using tongs, she lifts three rashers of bacon and two pork sausages from the oven dish and carefully arranges them on a plate.

'It's eight-fifteen, Lucy,' she hisses.

Lucy rolls her eyes, like it's her fault Virgil has yet to surface. 'Yes, ma'am,' she replies meekly.

Chef Anton is quietly humming a tune to himself as he cracks another egg and drops it onto the hotplate with a sizzle.

'I think it will be a better day today, madame,' he states, full of quiet cheer and in far better spirits than any previous day recently.

Penelope snorts, turning to him with raised eyebrows. 'Better, Antoine? No power. No communications. A dead guest in the barn. Most of the vehicles are under snow. And we could be stranded for days. How exactly is today "better"?'

Antoine shrugs lightly, still humming. 'We have gas, food, and life, madame. C'est ça. It is enough.'

Lucy peers through the service hatch into the dining room. 'More guests have arrived for breakfast,' she announces.

'This is intolerable,' Penelope snaps. 'Lucy, go to Mr Langley's room and knock on the door. Tell him I expect him in the dining room in less than ten minutes. And tell him to make himself presentable, and to brush his teeth. I don't want him breathing whisky fumes all over the guests.'

Lucy stops whisking eggs and heads to the door. 'Yes, ma'am.'

'And Lucy, take the master key. If he pretends to play dead, then enter and give him a bloody good shake. Throw a glass of water over him if needs be.'

'Yes, ma'am,' she replies, with absolutely no intention of following the last order.

Penelope huffs. 'He gets worse, Antoine,' she murmurs sadly. 'This next year is a critical phase for Kindlewood Hall. If everything goes according to plan, it could be the making of us. But for that to happen, we need everyone pulling their weight. And Virgil... Virgil has gone completely off-piste.'

Antoine chuckles softly as he slices rounds of black pudding and lays them carefully onto the hotplate. 'Off-piste,' he repeats, a smile playing at his lips. 'Very funny, madame.'

'What's funny?' Penelope asks, her tone sharp but curious.

'Virgil—off-piste.' Antoine's grin widens. 'If only he really was off the piste, eh? Then maybe things would run more smoothly.'

A reluctant smile tugs at Penelope's mouth. 'Ah, I see. Very clever.'

Antoine's humour fades slightly, and his voice drops to a quieter register. 'But seriously, madame. Your husband... he has a drinking problem. And unless he gets help, it will not improve. It will only... how do you say?' He pauses, frowning slightly as he searches for the correct word. 'Exacerbate. Oui, exacerbate?'

'Close enough,' Penelope murmurs, her tone softening. She picks up two plates, heading for the door, but pauses mid-step.

'Antoine,' she says, glancing back at him. 'You performed admirably yesterday. Under the most trying of circumstances.'

'Thank you, madame. But I was only doing my job,' he replies with a slight swagger.

Her eyelashes imperceptibly flutter above a faint smile. 'I know, but still. It is deeply appreciated.'

Their eyes meet for the briefest of moments before Penelope turns and exits through the kitchen door, her heels clicking softly on the tiled floor. Antoine watches her go, a trace of satisfaction on his face as he turns back to the sizzling black pudding, humming his quiet tune once more.

---

In the dining room, Frank sits at the head of the table with Prisha and Zac to his left.

'Here we go,' he says, rubbing his hands together as Penelope enters, carrying two plates. 'I'm ready for a proper fry-up.'

'Where's Meera?' Prisha asks, glancing at the empty chair beside Frank.

'She's feeling a bit off-colour. Bit of a cough and sneezing. She'll be down shortly once she's feeling more human.'

Penelope sets a heaving plate in front of Frank. 'Full English for Mr Finnegan,' she announces.

'And who ordered poached eggs with smashed avocado on toast?'

Prisha raises her hand. 'That's mine, thanks. Do you think I could get another black coffee when you have a chance, please?'

Penelope forces a polite smile, silently cursing. 'Of course.'

'Oh, and me too,' Zac chimes in, his gaze lingering enviously on Frank's plate, loaded with bacon, sausage, fried eggs, roasted cherry tomatoes, baked beans, black pudding, fried bread, and a lone hash brown sitting defiantly in one corner.

Penelope hurries off as Frank tucks a napkin into the collar of his shirt like a seasoned diner. He eyes the hash brown suspiciously, prodding it with his fork.

'Since when did hash browns muscle their way onto the menu of a full English breakfast?' he grumbles.

'I'll have it if you don't want it,' Zac says, his hand darting towards Frank's plate.

Frank's knife slaps the back of Zac's hand with a dull thwack.

'Ow! That bloody hurt!' Zac yelps, clutching his knuckles.

'It was meant to. I didn't say I didn't want it,' Frank retorts. 'I was simply making a point about our American interloper on an otherwise sacred plate.'

Prisha smirks, taking a sip of her coffee. 'You two are like a pair of squabbling kids.'

Frank raises an eyebrow but doesn't argue as he saws into a sausage.

The brief banter fizzles as Lucy bursts back into the dining room, her pace hurried, face creased with concern.

Prisha sets her fork down, frowning. 'That doesn't look good.'

Frank and Zac both swivel casually in their seats, their gazes tracking Lucy as she moves briskly towards the kitchen.

'No,' Frank mutters, his voice low. 'She's in quite the hurry. I wonder what's the matter?' His eyes flick briefly to the other guests scattered across the room, most still waiting for their breakfasts, oblivious to Lucy's obvious agitation.

---

'Well?' Penelope barks as Lucy enters, appearing slightly frazzled.

'I can't wake him, Mrs Langley,' she stammers, her voice pitched higher than usual.

Penelope continues decorating another plate with a full English. 'What do you mean, you can't wake him? Did you enter his room and give him a shake? My husband could sleep through the eruption of Mount Krakatoa after a night on the sauce.'

Lucy's hands fidget. 'I... I couldn't get into the room.'

'I told you to take the blasted master key.' She picks the two breakfast plates up and thrusts them towards Lucy. 'Here, you serve these. One is for Hugh Foster, the other for Mr Stoker. Give me the key. Really, Lucy,' she adds with a fierce pout.

'No, Mrs Langley, you don't understand. I opened the door, but the chain was on. I shouted through the gap, but he didn't reply. You don't think...' She tails off, unwilling or unable to articulate her fears.

'Think what?'

'You know—that something may have happened to him?'

'Like what?' Penelope questions, for the first time unease overtaking her annoyance.

Lucy fumbles with her fingers and throws Antoine a sheepish glance, who merely shrugs. 'Like a heart attack, or something,' she whispers.

Penelope snatches the key from her. 'No. My husband may be a drunkard, but he's as fit as a lop. A severe hangover is all he'll be suffering from.' She sweeps out of the kitchen, her usual elegant gait traded for a hurried stride.

Antoine flips the black pudding with a twitch of his spatula, watching Penelope vanish through the doorway. 'On récolte ce que l'on sème.'

Lucy blinks at him. 'What does that mean?'

'You reap what you sow,' he replies with a heavy sigh.

---

The strip of bacon hovers between Frank's plate and mouth as he watches Penelope Langley dart out of the room.

'Oi, oi,' Zac mutters. 'Something's afoot.'

Prisha frowns, leaning forward. 'You two seen Virgil Langley this morning?'

'Not me,' Zac replies, shaking his head.

'Last time I saw him was last night, just after ten,' Frank says, setting the bacon down. 'Well sozzled, having a right go at his brother, Murdoch.'

'What about?' Prisha asks.

Frank's brow knits together. 'Not entirely sure. I came in near the end. Virgil was accusing Murdoch of being a cheat. Something about deliberately underestimating costs—a financial disagreement by the sound of it. He looked at the end of his tether, but people do get maudlin when they're drunk.' He turns to Zac. 'Pass the HP, will you?'

Zac hands him the bottle of brown sauce. Frank takes it, flips the plastic lid and squeezes a healthy dollop onto his plate.

'I prefer the old glass bottles, not these squeezy plastic things,' he moans.

Zac grins. 'You really don't belong in the twenty-first century, do you, Frank?'

'I barely belong in the twentieth century. I don't get it though. Isn't glass more eco-friendly than plastic?' He dips the impaled bacon into the sauce and raises it in front of his eyes as the staccato clack of feet distract all three of them as they turn towards the doorway. Penelope Langley hurries back into the dining room, her face pale, fingers massaging the pearls around her neck.

'Mr Finnegan! Mr Finnegan!' she cries, her voice strained.

Frank lowers his fork, his attention fixed on her. 'What is it, Mrs Langley?'

She gasps for breath, her voice breaking. 'It's my husband. I can't wake him.'

Frank's fork clatters onto the plate. 'Have you checked for a pulse?'

'No! I can't get into the room. The chain's on.'

The three officers exchange glances, their professional instincts kicking in. Without a word, they rise and follow Penelope out of the room.

As they scramble up the stairs, Frank peppers her with questions. 'He's in the bedroom, I take it?'

'Yes. We sleep separately. We have our main living quarters where my bedroom's located. And next door is Virgil's bedroom, but they're not connected. It used to belong to our son, but when he moved out a couple of years ago, Virgil decided to move in. The arrangement suits us both. He's a shocking snorer.'

'Has he complained of feeling unwell?'

'No.'

'And he's in good health? No underlying medical condition?'

'No. He had a check-up a month ago and was given a clean bill of health. His only issue is that he drinks to excess.'

They reach the landing, turn left, and hurry down the corridor to the private residence. Penelope stops abruptly, pointing at a door slightly ajar but secured with a chain.

'Here! Here!' she urges, her voice rising.

Frank steps forward, rapping hard on the door. 'Mr Langley! Virgil! It's Frank Finnegan—can you hear me?'

Silence.

'Dear Lord,' Penelope whispers, her hand covering her mouth.

The creak of floorboards interrupts the tension. 'What in the devil's name is this resounding tumult?' Bennet Whipple's booming voice rolls down the corridor.

Frank glances briefly over his shoulder. The doctor stands there in nothing but a fluffy dressing gown, absurdly short, his bulbous knees visible.

Frank turns back to the door, ignoring the interruption. 'I'll break the chain. Stand back.'

Without waiting for permission, he throws his shoulder into the door. The wood splinters, the chain rattles, and the door bursts open with a loud crack, slamming against the wall.

'Dear God,' Frank mutters on witnessing the sight.

Virgil Langley, fully dressed, is on his knees, arched backwards, buttocks resting on the back of his heels, head lolling forward, as if in prayer. Blood is splattered down his left cheek. His left eye is nothing more than a dark, cavernous void.

Frank raises a hand, his voice firm. 'Penelope, don't come—'

Too late... she's already pushed past him into the room.

The heart stopping wail bounces along the corridor, ricocheting down the staircase and into the dining room.

Guests jolt at the sound, startled from their conversations. A flood of disquiet settles over the room, chairs scraping as a few guests rise, instinctively craning their necks towards the doorway, wondering what's happened.

# 20

Meera places an arm around Penelope Langley's trembling shoulders and gently steers her towards the staircase.

'Let's go downstairs and have a cup of tea,' she murmurs soothingly.

'I don't understand. Did he... do this to himself?'

'I don't know, love. Let Frank and his team do their job. He'll let you know what's happened soon enough.'

Frank, hovering in the doorway, waits until they're out of sight before stepping back into the room. 'Prisha, check your phone. Any reception yet?'

Prisha pulls out her mobile, shaking her head. 'Nope. Still nothing.'

Frank's gaze shifts to Dr Whipple, who has silently joined the scene, then back to Zac. 'Right, Zac. This is a crime scene, and since we can't call in forensics, we'll have to get creative. Necessity's the mother of invention. Go to the kitchen. I need a box of food-handling gloves, as many snap-lock bags as you can find, and a marker pen.'

'And a roll of sticky tape,' Prisha chimes in.

Zac frowns. 'Sticky tape?'

'Yes, Sellotape,' she says. 'A wide roll, if they've got one. It's not ideal, but it'll have to do in place of proper forensic tape.'

Frank nods. 'And we'll need something to cover our feet.'

'Freezer bags?' Zac suggests.

'Aye. Better than nothing. And grab some hair nets, if they've got any.'

Zac spins on his heel towards the door.

'And anything else you think might come in handy,' he calls after him.

Frank gazes at the crime scene.

The undisturbed bed. An open sock drawer. The half-empty scotch bottle discarded on the sheets. The corpse—a crumpled man in body and spirit, utterly defeated.

'Looks like he had another snifter before his demise.' He sighs heavily. 'Alcohol—people think it's their soulmate, but it's not. It's an impostor. A liar. Dance with it occasionally—fine. But propose marriage, and it will waltz you down a long, winding road of misery—straight to the cemetery gates, not the altar.'

Dr Whipple glances at him, as if seeing, and understanding, the real Frank Finnegan for the first time.

'Wise words, indeed, inspector. A chastening perspective,' he murmurs.

———◦———

It's not a good look, by any stretch of the imagination. Frank, Prisha, and Whipple are kitted out in improvised forensic gear.

Freezer bags cover their feet, rubber bands holding the flimsy plastic material tight around their ankles. Blue latex gloves adorn their hands. As for the hair nets, well, what can one say? None were to be found in the kitchen, a point Bennet Whipple has already noted, quoting the Food Safety Act 1990 and the Food Hygiene (England) Regulations 2013. Zac's best efforts to prevent errant hair fibres contaminating the crime scene, is—food-wrap—cling film.

Prisha, and to a lesser degree Frank, have nearly pulled a miracle off.

The cling film, which typically only clings to itself, sits not too badly over their thick hair, twisted into a tight knot at the nape of the neck to hold it in position.

Dr Bennet Whipple is a different matter entirely.

His smooth, bald head now resembles the brown ball on a snooker table—albeit seventy times the size.

'Shall we proceed, Detective Chief Inspector Finnegan?' Whipple prompts in his deep baritone

Frank catches Whipple's reflection in the large mirror on the wall and does a double-take. 'Aye,' he replies, slightly disconcerted by Whipple's absurd appearance. To add to the bizarre scene, Whipple is still wearing the fluffy white dressing gown, which is five sizes too small for him. He obviously picked up his wife's gown by mistake in his hurry to investigate the kerfuffle.

Frank rubs his stubble. 'Right, come on. You examine the body, Bennet, while me and Prisha have a snoop around.'

Whipple's eyes widen. 'Snoop around?' he snorts derisively. 'Do you imply a systematic inquiry? A disciplined and methodical search for pertinent evidence, guided by logic and critical reasoning? Because snooping, inspector, conjures up the image of a nosy neighbour peering over the garden fence.'

Prisha grins. 'You'd be amazed what a bit of snooping around can uncover, doctor.'

'Indeed, I would be amazed, Inspector Kumar, though I suspect my amazement will remain entirely dormant.'

Prisha makes a beeline to the window. 'Look at this, Frank.'

'What?'

'The left curtain is closed.'

'And?'

'The right one,' she says, pointing, 'is half-open. Caught on the edge of the dresser.'

'Ah,' Frank replies. 'As if the window was open at some point, and the wind blew it there.'

'Possibly,' she says, making her way into the bathroom.

Whipple grunts as he lowers himself down to kneel awkwardly beside the body. 'Sweet Jeremiah,' he huffs.

Frank inspects the wardrobes, then drops to his knees, also groaning, and peers under the bed. 'Ah, here's a torch,' he states, stretching underneath with some difficulty before finally retrieving the object. 'Battery's dead, but that doesn't tell us much,' he adds rising.

Whipple focuses intently on the eye cavity. 'The injury is both fascinating and perplexing. The left orbit has been brutally compromised. The ocular tissue obliterated by what must have been a narrow, forceful implement. The trajectory—straight through the eye socket and possibly into the brain—leaves no doubt as to its lethality. One cannot help but note the extraordinary precision of the entry angle, suggesting either a remarkable degree of skill or, more likely, an opportunistic thrust with an instrument of alarming sharpness.' He rigorously examines the hands of the corpse. 'No obvious defensive wounds. No markings to the neck,' he murmurs to himself.

Prisha re-enters the bedroom after searching the en-suite. 'No obvious weapon in the bathroom. What about in here, Frank?'

'Nothing. Can you give us a rough description of the possible weapon, Bennet?'

'Hmm... the implement used to inflict this wound would need to be narrow, yet strong enough to penetrate the orbital cavity and pierce the brain. Something long and tapered. Perhaps six to eight inches in length, with a point sharp enough to minimise resistance. The weapon would have to be of a certain design to account for the maceration of the ocular tissue without fracturing the orbital rim.'

'A small dagger, perhaps?' Frank suggests.

'I think not.'

'What about a meat skewer or screwdriver?'

Whipple frowns. 'Neither a skewer nor screwdriver would have the circumference to have obliterated the eyeball to such an extent.'

Prisha stares down at the wound. 'How about a pastry cone?'

Whipple gazes up at her. 'I am not acquainted with such a utensil.'

'They come in all sizes and lengths. They're cone shaped, and have a sharp point, and some have handles. You wrap pastry around them and bake them in the oven. You can use them to make your own ice cream cones.'

Whipple considers it for a moment. 'It would be an extremely unusual murder weapon, inspector.'

'But possible?'

'In theory, I suppose.'

Frank sighs, scanning the room. 'No sign of a struggle. No defensive wounds. And we can rule out suicide?'

Whipple harrumphs. 'If this man took his own life, inspector, then please enlighten me—where is the weapon? He would have died almost instantaneously, yet here he remains, kneeling, his gluteus maximus settled against his heels. His head lolls forward as if held by a counterweight. None of this suggests a self-inflicted assault.'

'Time of death?' Frank asks.

'The lividity around the jowls and stiffness in the limbs indicates rigor mortis is well underway but not yet reached full rigidity.'

'And?' Frank says, drawing the word out slowly, hoping to illicit a response that may be useful.

Bennet creaks and groans to his feet and glances at the bedside clock. 'The body was discovered at approximately 8:30 am?'

'Aye, thereabouts. And I talked with Virgil last night just after 10 pm.'

'Then my best guess would be he died somewhere after 10 pm but before 4 am.'

'A six-hour window,' Prisha notes thoughtfully.

Frank shakes his head. 'Not much to go one when we have twenty people in the hotel. But the most puzzling conundrum is how did the killer get in and out of a room that was locked and chained?'

Prisha carefully opens the window and stares at the snow covered window ledge. 'Getting in is not the issue. Someone could have followed Virgil in, or already been waiting for him. I dare say the hotel has a master key that will open every room. The real puzzle is, how did they exit the room when the chain was on? The snow on the window ledge has not been disturbed.'

Frank joins her and stares out. 'And that's a hell of a drop to the ground. Even with an extremely long pair of ladders, it would be nigh impossible to get up here, especially considering the conditions last night.' He sticks his head out of the opening and peers up. 'And I think we can rule out the roof as a means of accessing the window, unless, of course, Spiderman is in the vicinity.'

Prisha takes another look around the room, then stares up at the ceiling. 'No adjoining doors. No roof hatch. Didn't Penelope say this used to be their son's room?'

'Aye. The Langleys' main residence is next door, but Virgil and Penelope slept separately.' Frank closes the window and turns to Whipple. 'Anything else you can tell us, Bennet?'

'There is one minor peculiarity,' he says cryptically.

'Oh, aye?'

'There's minor blood release from the victim's eye socket as witnessed by the dried blood on his left cheek, some of which has spilled down onto the collar of his shirt. But you will notice a long damp stain down the left breast of the shirt, which at first, I assumed to be aqueous humour—fluid that lubricates the eyeball. But on closer inspection, I deduced that is in fact—water.'

'And what's the significance of that?' Frank asks, rubbing his neck.

Prisha inspects the stain. 'What's the temperature in here—a pleasant twenty-two degrees?'

'Aye, about that.'

'If Virgil Langley was murdered five to nine hours ago, why is his shirt still damp, and—where did the water come from?'

---

Prisha opens the window and takes another look outside and all around the frame and sill. 'It's possible the murder weapon was thrown from the window, Frank. It would explain why the window was open at some point.'

'But why? If the killer can miraculously escape from a locked room, then why not take the murder weapon with them instead of tossing it outside, where it would undoubtedly be found once the snow melts?'

Whipple rises like a wounded dinosaur, groaning his displeasure, after conducting a secondary examination of the body. Unfortunately, for all concerned, the belt around his micro-dressing gown comes loose, and the gown falls open, revealing his nakedness beneath.

'Oh, for God's sake,' Prisha yelps. 'I can do without looking at that first thing on a morning.'

Frank winces at the sight. 'Christ, Bennet, have you a license for that thing? It's like a blind cobbler's thumb. Cover yourself up, man. We have a lady present.'

Perplexed, Bennet eventually gazes down and blinks, his face flushing an alarming shade of crimson. With an air of affronted dignity, he gathers the sides of his gown together and reties the belt.

'That's put me right off my breakfast,' Prisha says, looking away.

Frank nods in agreement. 'Aye, I think I'll skip the black pudding from now on.'

Still flushing, Whipple replies, 'This incident, I assure you, inspector, is purely the result of substandard tailoring combined with an ill-conceived belt design. I shall lodge a formal complaint with the manufacturer at my earliest convenience.' Turning to Prisha, he inclines his head stiffly. 'My apologies, Inspector Kumar, for this unintended affront to your sensibilities. Rest assured, I shall henceforth take measures to ensure my person remains suitably attired, regardless of the inadequacies of this establishment's laundry provisions.'

'Apology accepted.'

Whipple lumbers towards the door. 'If you've finished with my expertise, I shall leave you to it, inspector. I would like to shower and attend to my victuals. It's been a most calamitous twenty-four hours.'

'Okay. Thanks, Bennet. Right, Prisha, take a video of the room on your phone and photos from every angle. Once you've done that, go outside and search for a murder weapon in the off chance it was tossed from the window.'

'And what are we to do with Mr Langley's body?'

Frank gazes upon the stricken form. 'No other choice. We'll have to put him in a sleeping bag, zip it up and put him with Amy Holland's body in the barn. The storm may have passed, but it must still be about minus ten outside. I'll get Zac to try to lift fingerprints from likely surfaces using

175

the Sellotape.' Pausing, he rubs at his face. 'Hellfire, we're up against it this time. It makes you realise how reliant we are on modern forensics and the latest technology.'

Prisha nods. 'I suppose it's like going back to Victorian times,' she muses.

'All we can do is make the best of a bad job, and what we have at our disposal. Even if we find the killer, I can only imagine what a field day a defence counsel would have with the crime scene investigation. They'd rip it to shreds.'

'Mitigating circumstances, Frank. There is one positive, though.'

'Really? Please enlighten me.'

'The killer was in our midst last night, and I suspect, will be in our midst today. No one's escaping this hotel anytime soon,' she says, gazing out at the vista of white.

'Hmm... you're right. Once we've finished here, it's time to round up all the guests and staff and begin to question them, one by one.'

# 21

The dining room buzzes with murmurs, innuendo, and whispered half-truths. Guests exchange theories like currency, each playing armchair detective in a bid to piece together what has *actually* happened.

Imogen Sato sits by the window, her gaze flitting between the driveway, where cars lie buried under mounds of snow, and the other guests. Across from her, Eve Sinclair cradles a steaming coffee cup.

'What have you heard?' Imogen asks, her tone casual but her eyes sharp.

Eve glances around the room, lowering her voice. 'Not much, really,' she replies, nodding at Frank and Zac, who stand grim faced at the bar, locked in a hushed conference. 'That tall, handsome Scottish detective sergeant knocked on my door and told me I had to be here by 9:30. I was a bit taken aback and asked him on what authority.' She grins slyly. 'He pulled out his warrant card and said—on this authority. Very official. I was half tempted to invite him in for coffee.'

'Hussy.'

'What about you?'

Imogen traces the tip of her tongue over her rouge lipstick. 'Pretty much the same, except I was already here having breakfast.' She throws a surreptitious glance at Frank and Zac. 'The older one is the lead detective, DCI Frank Finnegan. I gather they're here for a Christmas get-together, along with that attractive woman... what's her name? I spoke to her briefly last night.'

'DI Prisha Kumar,' Eve replies.

'That's it—Kumar.' Imogen's voice dips. 'Have you seen the Langleys?'

'No. But something's clearly happened to one or both of them. I hope it's nothing serious. It was bad enough with that young woman dying last night. Do you think it really was an allergic reaction, like the French doctor said, or could it be something more... sinister?'

Imogen arches a brow. 'I don't know what to think. Dr Quint did say she'd been poisoned at first but then seemed to backtrack. All I do know is I've had enough of this place and want to leave.'

Eve stares out at the snowbound vehicles and lets out a wry laugh. 'Good luck with that. We'll be lucky to get out of here before Christmas Day.'

'Oh, God, don't say that.'

Eve sits upright, stirring her coffee thoughtfully. 'Still, this would make a hell of a story. I'm sure one of the dailies would pay handsomely for it.'

Imogen smirks. 'I thought you were an investigative journalist, not a sensationalist hack.'

Eve chuckles, unbothered. 'I am. And when I find out what's really going on, I'll be ready to investigate properly.'

---

At one of the smaller tables, Hugh Foster is in animated discussion with bed-and-breakfast owner Maggie Thornton, while their accountant, Logan Fitch, listens quietly.

'I haven't seen either of them this morning,' Hugh says, lowering his voice as if wary of eavesdroppers.

Maggie takes a sip of her tepid tea, her lips pursed. 'I saw Penelope briefly earlier. She was serving those three detectives their breakfasts. Then, suddenly, all four of them rushed out.'

'Must be Virgil,' Hugh murmurs, his voice tinged with unease. 'You don't think he's...?' He drags a finger across his throat in a slicing motion, emitting a low, rasping "guhhrk" sound like a strangled duck.

Logan Fitch winces. 'That's absurd. I've known Virgil for fifteen years. There's no way he'd take his own life.'

'Not when there's so much whisky still to drink,' Maggie quips, then instantly regrets her tactlessness as Logan shoots her a disapproving look.

Hugh chuckles. 'You have a point, Maggie. But we've all heard the whispers about the Langley's finances since... you know who cooked the books.'

Logan shifts uncomfortably, the memory still raw. 'That's not entirely accurate.'

Maggie narrows her eyes. 'How would you know?' she asks. 'Didn't they give you the boot two years ago when you found the "irregularities"?'

Logan clears his throat, clearly uneasy. 'True, they terminated my services—and, admittedly, it caused a bit of bad blood. But not on my part. I was simply doing what they paid me to do—reconcile their business transactions with their bank statements. Same as I do for you two.'

Maggie waves her hand dismissively. 'Yes, yes, we know the story. But as Hugh pointed out, everyone around here knows the Langley's have been struggling since then. You seemed to suggest otherwise.'

Logan hesitates, then leans forward, lowering his voice. 'I can't go into specifics, of course. But I can tell you this much: the Langley's are in the process of securing a substantial investment. Enough to clear their debts and fund major refurbishments. They have ambitious plans.'

Maggie bristles at the news. Her well-run bed-and-breakfast, though successful, has always been overshadowed by Kindlewood Hall. Resentment flickers behind her eyes, especially towards Penelope Langley, despite Virgil's recent peace initiative.

Hugh, however, is intrigued. 'Substantial investment?' he presses. 'How substantial are we talking, Logan?'

Logan offers a tight smile. 'It wouldn't be appropriate for me to say. But... let's just say it's in excess of seven figures.'

Hugh frowns. 'Which is what, exactly?'

Maggie sighs, exasperated. 'Over a million, Hugh. But less than ten.'

'Blimey!'

'How do you even know this if you're no longer on their payroll?' Maggie asks, her tone sharp.

Logan smiles thinly. 'Virgil and Penelope approached me recently. Cap in hand, so to speak. They paid my outstanding invoice—the one that had been in dispute for two years—and we had a long lunch to discuss their future plans.'

'And who's their mystery investor?'

Logan taps his nose. 'Maggie, you know I can't reveal that. Client confidentiality and all that.'

Hugh looks up as Dr Quint and his elderly mother shuffle into the room, followed closely by Murdoch Langley. Murdoch's face is red, his usual immaculate composure conspicuously absent, his clothing slightly rumpled. He strides over to join Frank and Zac, who are still deep in discussion by the bar.

Hugh smirks, leaning back in his chair. 'I'd wager I know who their investor is,' he says, nodding towards Murdoch Langley. 'He's an investment banker, isn't he? And he's got more brass than sense.'

Dr Pierre Quint steadies his frail mother as she lowers herself carefully into a chair.

'What's all this about, Pierre?' she asks, her voice rasping with age and unease, her distress evident in the tremor of her hands.

'I've told you, maman, I know as much as you do,' he replies gently, the French word for mother slipping effortlessly from his tongue.

'You said the gendarme is here?'

Pierre sighs and rubs the bridge of his nose. 'The police, yes. But they weren't summoned. They're off-duty guests here for a weekend celebration.'

'How do you know this?' she presses.

'Because the tall gentleman over there explained it when he knocked on our door forty minutes ago,' Pierre says, nodding discreetly in Zac's direction.

Edith Quint adjusts the pince-nez perched on her nose, narrowing her eyes as she peers at Zac. 'C'est vraiment un bel homme,' she murmurs with a faint gasp before breaking into a fragile laugh.

Pierre smirks. 'Yes, maman, he is a handsome fellow. But I fear he's a bit young for you—by about fifty years.'

Edith slaps his arm playfully, her humour undimmed. 'I'll have you know I can still satisfy a man!'

'Yes, you can,' Pierre replies with a grin. 'You still make a marvellous orange cake.'

<hr />

Frank breaks away from Zac and Murdoch Langley as Prisha returns from her scouting mission outside.

'How'd you go? Any luck?'

Prisha shivers. 'Nothing. No murder weapon in sight, no footprints. Everything's untouched. Of course, if it kept snowing through the night, the weapon, and prints could've been covered up.'

Frank glances around the room. 'Right, time to break the news. Is everyone here?'

Prisha nods. 'I think so, apart from Meera and Mrs Langley.'

'Meera's still consoling Penelope in the library. I wasn't going to make the recent widow sit through this.'

Prisha scans the room again. 'Oh, the French chef and Lucy from reception are missing.'

'They're probably in the kitchen clearing the breakfast plates. Go fetch them, will you?'

As Prisha enters the kitchen, she walks into the full brunt of a heated argument.

'I didn't put them there!' Chef Antoine snaps, gesturing wildly.

'And neither did I!' Lucy shoots back, angrily.

'Then who did?' Antoine growls.

'I don't bloody know!' Lucy erupts, red-faced. 'Why would I move some decrepit old pots and pans and put them on the dresser? Do you think I'm not run ragged enough? It's all right for you—you've got one job! Run the kitchen. I've got a dozen jobs to do.'

Antoine's hands shoot up in exasperation. 'Sacré bleu! I did not touch them! Madame Penelope would not have, and Monsieur Virgil hasn't even stepped into the kitchen this morning. He's been promising to take them to the recycling for two weeks. But like everything else around here, nothing ever gets done!'

Lucy snatches up the rusty oven tray holding the battered pots and pans.

'Fine! I'll put them away. Where do they live?' she snaps.

Antoine, sensing victory, waves a hand dismissively at a cupboard. 'Monte-plats,' he mumbles.

'What?'

'Stupid waiter—over there!' he bellows pointing.

'Don't be so bloody rude!' Lucy yells. 'And I'm not your waiter—I run front of house.'

Antoine scrunches his face into a tight ball and unleashes a tirade of rapid-fire French, ending with a venomous, 'You crazy woman!'

'Ahem,' Prisha interrupts. 'If you could both stop fighting for a moment, DCI Finnegan has asked for everyone to gather in the dining room. He has an announcement to make.'

Antoine huffs, tosses a tea towel onto the table, and storms out.

Lucy opens the cupboard, throws the pots inside, and slams the door shut.

'Problem?' Prisha asks, her tone soft but curious.

Lucy exhales sharply, her anger still simmering. 'Yes. One of many. Chef Antoine is a twat for a start. This morning, he was happy as Larry—singing, cracking lame jokes. Then he spotted those bloody old pans and exploded. He's a nutter.

A real Jekyll and Hyde.' She softens slightly. 'How's Mr Langley? Is it bad? Is he... dead?'

Prisha nods solemnly. 'Yes, he's dead. Come on, DCI Finnegan will explain everything.'

As they re-enter the dining room, Frank claps his hands to get everyone's attention.

'Ladies and gentlemen, thank you for your patience.' He takes a deep breath, his barrel chest expanding. 'Now, as some of you already know, my name is Frank Finnegan, Detective Chief Inspector with North Yorkshire Police. These are my colleagues, DI Kumar and DS Stoker. We happened to be staying at Kindlewood Hall for the...' He catches himself in time and avoids saying Murder Mystery weekend. 'Ahem... for an end-of-year get-together.'

He pauses briefly. 'Now, I'm afraid I have some bad news. There has been a tragic incident overnight.' The room falls silent, every pair of eyes fixed on him. Murdoch Langley hovers at his side, shifting impatiently. 'Virgil Langley, joint proprietor of this hotel, whom I'm sure you all know, is deceased. At the moment, we are treating his death as suspicious.'

The silence is shattered by gasps and frantic whispers rippling across the room.

Frank raises his hands. 'Please, bear with me and let me finish.'

Murdoch Langley has heard enough and steps forward, his face flushed with anger. 'Let's not beat about the bush, inspector!' he snaps, his voice rising. 'My brother was viciously murdered last night.' His voice trembles with fury as he thrusts out his arm, finger pointing accusingly. Slowly, his hand sweeps the room, pointing accusingly. 'And one of you—is a killer!'

# 22

Murdoch Langley's impromptu and unwelcome accusation sends the room into chaos. Arguments erupt, counterarguments fly, and furious declarations of innocence bounce off the walls.

Frank steps forward, his voice sharp and commanding. 'Ladies and gentlemen, please! May I have your quiet!'

The noise ebbs into uneasy silence, punctuated only by a few murmurs.

'Thank you. Now listen carefully. This is an official police investigation, and as such, I will be asking for—and expecting—your full cooperation. We need to establish facts and timelines as quickly as possible. As you're all aware, we are without mains electricity, and communications are still down. We don't know how long this will last, so we must all show patience. The hotel is well stocked, the kitchen runs on gas, and we have a constant supply of heating thanks to the biomass system.'

Hugh Foster raises a hand, his voice cutting through the air. 'What I'm worried about, inspector, is that there's a killer on the loose.'

Maggie Thornton pipes up before Frank can respond. 'Are we all under arrest, chief inspector?'

Frank shakes his head vehemently. 'No one's under arrest.'

'Then I can leave anytime I want?' Hugh presses. 'I've got two hundred head of prize Aberdeen Angus that'll need feeding today. I was planning to leave right after breakfast.'

'I'd strongly advise against anyone leaving at the moment.'

'But what about my cattle?' Hugh insists.

Frank meets his gaze. 'Where are they now?'

'I brought them into the stockyards yesterday morning.'

'Good. And I assume you employ stock hands?'

'Aye, old Ted's on the farm today.'

'Then I'm sure a wily old stock hand knows exactly what to do.'

Maggie Thornton crosses her arms, her tone sharp. 'But you can't force us to stay. I have guests arriving at my bed-and-breakfast at two o'clock. I need to be there to greet them.'

Frank shakes his head again. 'I can assure you, Maggie, your guests won't be arriving today—if at all. This storm has already ruined a lot of Christmas plans.'

'I need to be back in London by tomorrow,' Imogen Sato announces, her voice curt. 'I have a deadline to meet.'

'And I have plans as well,' Eve Sinclair chimes in, her tone icy.

'I too must return to London, inspector,' Dr Pierre Quint declares. 'My mother and I have an early flight to Paris on Tuesday morning.'

Frank's jaw hardens as he scans the room. Every face is creased with frustration or fear. Keeping this group calm and contained might prove harder than solving the case itself, Frank thinks.

Prisha steps forward, her voice measured, reassuring. 'I don't think any of you fully understand the scale of the storm's havoc. I was outside a moment ago. It took me ten minutes to walk from the front of the hotel to the back. The snow was up to my thighs in places, and that's sticking close to the building where it's less deep.'

'DI Kumar is absolutely right,' Frank adds. 'I know this countryside well. It's surrounded by lakes, ponds, rivers, and becks. Many will be frozen over and buried under snow. The roads won't just be impassable; they'll be invisible. Leaving the safety of this hotel would be pure folly. That's not an idle thought—it's a fact.'

'I'd rather take my chances with the snow than wait around for a madman to strike again,' Imogen Sato declares, to a murmur of agreement from several others.

Prisha raises a single eyebrow but holds her tongue.

Maggie Thornton lifts a hand. 'How did Virgil die, inspector?'

'I'm not at liberty to divulge that information.'

'Where's his body?' Logan Fitch cuts in, his voice tinged with anxiety.

'At the moment, he's in his room. Shortly, we'll move him to the barn.'

Logan is aghast. 'With that poor young woman from last night?'

'Yes.'

'That's barbaric.'

'The temperature in the barn is minus five,' Frank explains. 'It'll preserve the body for a later autopsy. It may seem disrespectful, but it's the only option available. We cannot leave him in the hotel—it would be... unpleasant. I'm sure I don't have to explain what happens to dead bodies once they begin to decompose.'

Eve Sinclair waggles a finger. 'Considering there've been two deaths in twelve hours, do you think they're connected? We can't rule out that the young woman wasn't murdered too.'

Frank massages the tension in his neck, but it does little good. 'Amy Holland's death *is* being treated as suspicious, but not in the same way as Mr Langley's. At this stage, there's no obvious link between the two incidents.'

Zac steps forward, his voice clear and professional. 'What you've got to understand is that most deaths are treated as suspicious by default. That's not because we assume foul play, but because of strict protocols. Unless there's clear evidence of an underlying medical condition, or the circumstances are straightforward—like a terminally ill patient passing away under medical care—any unexpected or unexplained death is referred to the coroner. This ensures every possibility is accounted for, and nothing is overlooked.'

Murdoch Langley's patience frays to snapping point. 'Come, come, inspector. This is wasting time. We need to start interrogating everyone in this room.'

Hugh Foster bristles. 'And does that include you, Murdoch?'

Murdoch turns on him, his face crimson. 'How dare you! Are you suggesting I'm capable of murdering my own brother?'

'Why not?' Hugh challenges. 'We all know you had a volatile relationship with him.'

'That's absurd! It was normal sibling rivalry, nothing more.'

'Where's Penelope Langley?' Maggie Thornton asks.

'She's being consoled by my wife,' Frank replies, but the murmurs and rising tension tell him this meeting is spiralling out of control. He straightens, ready to take charge.

'Will she be interrogated too?' Maggie presses.

Frank's tone sharpens. 'Let me make this perfectly clear.' His voice ricochets off the walls, silencing the room as guests flinch. 'We do not *interrogate* people. This isn't Guantanamo Bay—it's Kindlewood Hall, North Yorkshire. Everyone here will be asked to give a signed witness statement to a pleasant, professional police officer—myself, DI Kumar, or DS Stoker. And yes, that includes every single person in this room, including myself and my officers— and also you, Mr Langley,' he says, pinning Murdoch with a fierce stare. 'And also let me remind you—it will be *my* team, and my team alone, conducting this investigation, not you.'

He turns back to the assembled guests. 'If anyone intends to leave the hotel, we'll need your full name, address, and proof of identity before you go. But heed my warning—you are unlikely to get very far, or worse, you could put your life in serious jeopardy and there will be no one to call to come to your rescue. The conditions outside are deadly.'

'As are the conditions inside,' mutters Hugh Foster.

The room remains still, uneasy murmurs quashed under Frank's commanding tone.

'Now,' he continues, 'my team and I will take thirty minutes, after which we'll begin taking statements individually.' He glances at Lucy. 'Lucy, could you provide refreshments for your guests in the meantime?'

Lucy nods quickly. 'Yes, of course, inspector.'

Frank turns to Zac and Prisha, lowering his voice. 'We'll head to the library and get organised before we begin. Zac, have a rummage behind the reception counter—grab three notepads and pens. Prisha, have a quick word with everyone here and jot down their particulars, then—it's down to business.'

# 23

The library exudes a timeless elegance, its air rich with the leathery scent of old bindings and a faint trace of beeswax polish. Dark oak shelves, lined with worn, hardcover tomes, rise to meet a low, beamed ceiling, while deep armchairs with cracked leather invite touch, their upholstery cool and smooth under the hand. The soft tick of the grandfather clock in the adjoining drawing room blends with the faint crackle of dying embers in the neglected fire, creating a tranquil haven of almost sacred stillness.

The two officers are seated around an antique table, notepads and pens in front of them. Prisha checks her phone, hoping for a message from Adam, while Zac does the same, longing for news from his wife about their son's suspected tonsillitis. Both are met with the same result: no signal, dwindling batteries, and rising frustration.

Frank enters, a steaming cup of tea in hand, breaking their silent torment. The pair hurriedly pocket their phones as he pulls up a chair.

'Right,' he begins, settling into the seat. 'Prisha, you've got a fresh list of everyone who's here—or was here—since yesterday afternoon?'

She spins her notepad around. 'Yes, Frank. Nineteen people, including us. I've already ruled out eight as possible suspects.'

Frank leans in, scanning the names divided by a bold horizontal line. He picks up his pen. 'So, we can scrub myself, you, and Zac off the list,' he says, drawing a line through the names. 'And Meera too.'

Zac leans back in his chair. 'Hang on a sec, Frank. Aren't you being a bit presumptuous?'

Frank looks up sharply. 'Are you serious?'

Zac grins. 'Come on, Frank. I've seen Meera in action. When she loses it, she could stop a rampaging bull elephant with one glare. It's terrifying.'

Frank smirks, crossing off Meera's name. 'Very funny.'

'And the Whipples,' Prisha adds. 'I think we can safely rule them out.'

Zac lowers his voice to a deep baritone. 'Most indubitably, Inspector Kumar.'

Frank chuckles. 'Most indubitably? Sounds like Whipple's rubbing off on you, Zac.'

'Aye, like dogshit on the carpet.'

'Moving on,' Frank says. 'The dead woman—Amy Holland—obviously couldn't have killed Virgil Langley, given she died hours before him. Unless you think the undead are involved.'

Prisha nods at the list. 'And Edith Quint—she can barely manage the stairs. She's hardly a threat.'

Frank agrees, striking the names off the page. 'That leaves...' He counts silently before grimacing. 'Nine ruled out. Ten left. And that,' he says with a wry chuckle, 'brings us to Agatha Christie.'

Prisha grins. 'And Then There Were None?'

'Exactly. A country house, ten people, one killer picking them off until they were all dead.'

Zac frowns, trying to piece it together. 'Wait. Who killed the last person?'

Prisha exchanges a glance with Frank. 'No spoilers. You'll have to read the book,' she teases, gesturing at the shelves. 'It's up there, top left. Might help you fall asleep tonight.'

Zac looks uneasy. 'This isn't some twisted copycat case, is it? Based on a bloody novel?'

Frank suppresses a laugh. 'Relax, Zac. Christie's book had ten victims. There are nineteen of us here—that's a hell of a workload for any killer.'

'That's inflation for you,' Zac mutters.

Frank shakes his head. 'Right, back to work. Any observations during my announcement in the dining room?'

Prisha sits forward. 'A couple of things. Imogen Sato said she'd rather risk the snow than stick around for a "madman" to strike again. Why did she assume the killer was a man?'

Frank sighs. 'Educated guess. Ninety per cent of convicted murderers are men. She's an intelligent woman. Probably playing the odds. What else?'

'When I went to fetch Antoine and Lucy from the kitchen, they were in a heated argument. Something about old pans Virgil was supposed to have taken to recycling. Antoine was adamant Lucy moved them; she denied it. She later told me he's volatile. Flips from charming to nasty in seconds.'

Frank raises an eyebrow. 'Interesting.'

Zac taps his pen on the table. 'Classic small man syndrome—the overcompensating swagger, the endless need to pick fights and assert dominance, as if causing friction was the only way to make up for what he lacks in stature,' he states emphatically. 'Of course, it's all in his own mind.'

'Thank you, Sigmund Freud,' Frank says. 'Anything else, Prisha?'

'Not for now.'

'Zac?'

'A question. Murdoch Langley's outburst earlier—was that genuine shock or an act to imply innocence?'

Frank leans back, considering. 'Hard to say. Could be stress, guilt, or a charade. I told him not to use the word "murder," but he did anyway. And as I mentioned earlier, he was also involved in a heated argument with Virgil last night.' Frank straightens in his chair. 'Now, even though we've ruled out *nine* of the nineteen, we still need witness statements, including our own. So, let's get ours over with. We'll question each other and take notes. Once we're done, I'll interview people in the library. Prisha, you grab a table and two chairs and set up in the swimming pool area, and Zac, you take the billiard room.'

'Are you joking? That room has no natural nor artificial light at the moment. How come you get the nice comfy room, Prisha gets the pool with magnificent views, and I get the black hole?'

'It's the way the dice fell.'

'Pig's arse.'

'You want to know the truth? Shit rolls downhill. You're the junior officer, and you get the shitty end of the stick. Happy?'

Zac pushes back in his chair. 'Happy? No. But thanks for being honest.'

'My pleasure,' Frank replies, winking at Prisha. 'Right, Prisha, you can kick off with the receptionist, Lucy Hargreaves. I'll question Murdoch Langley. And Zac, you take the mouthy farmer, Hugh...' he glances at the list. 'Hugh Foster. We want to know everyone's movements from 10 pm last night to 8:30 am this morning even though we think Virgil died before 4 am. And let's find out as much about the Langley's as we can. What disputes or petty grievances they were involved in? Their financial status. Oh, and from what Penelope said, they have a son. Let's find out about him and where he is. Questions?'

Prisha bites the corner of her lip. 'Who's interviewing Penelope?'

'Hmm...' Frank murmurs, weighing up the options. 'I think it's best you do. You know, a woman's touch.'

'A woman's touch?'

'Yes. Gentler, understanding, empathetic.'

She scowls. 'Sexist.'

'How is that sexist?'

'Why would you presume because I'm a woman I'm more gentle, understanding, and empathetic?'

Zac chuckles. 'Been a while since you sat in on an interview with Prisha, eh, Frank? She's about as empathetic as Heinrich Himmler suffering from haemorrhoids.'

Frank sighs, pinching the bridge of his nose. 'Prisha, you're still doing it—empathetic or not.'

# 24

Prisha sits at the small table, her fingers cradling the warm ceramic of her coffee cup, the faint aroma of roasted beans mingling with the tang of chlorine in the humid air. Across from her, Lucy Hargreaves fidgets with the edge of her jacket sleeve, her brow damp from the faint curls of steam silently rising from the lap pool, mirroring her own rising anxiety. The turquoise coloured water is a warm and stark contrast to the frozen world beyond the glass panels. The countryside, shrouded in dense snow, is featureless, silence broken only by the faint ripple of water and the occasional caw of a distant crow.

Prisha has already gathered the essentials on Lucy's background: how long she's worked for the Langley's, her job description, working hours and whether she enjoys the role. Lucy, usually forthcoming, is decidedly edgy. And who could blame her? Being questioned by the police is stressful enough, but when it involves murder... that's another matter entirely.

'When was the last time you saw Virgil, Lucy?'

She blows air from her mouth, her eyes darting up and to the left. 'I think it was about 9:15, maybe 9:30, last night. I was in the kitchen cleaning up.'

'Did you speak to one another?'

'No. Wait, yes. He thanked me for all my help and said he would pay me time and a half from 6 pm onwards. I asked what time I'd be needed in the morning. And he said 7:30 am. And that was it.'

'Then Virgil left?'

'No. He had a chat with Antoine.'

'Did you hear what about?'

'No. It was obviously confidential. They went over to the far end of the room, near the walk-in freezer.'

'Any inklings what they may have been discussing?'

She shrugs. 'Not sure. I do know Antoine hasn't been paid for two months and there have been one or two flare-ups over it. But Mrs Langley assured him he'd be paid next week. Something about a cash flow problem, which had recently been resolved.'

'Tell me about the rest of your night.'

'I finished up in the kitchen about 9:30 and went to my room. I had a warm shower under candlelight. Got into my PJs and went to bed. I was exhausted. Awoke at 7 am, took another quick shower, got dressed and met Antoine in the kitchen where we began prepping for breakfast.'

Prisha neatly jots down the timelines and makes notes. 'Okay, tell me about this morning. You were in the kitchen with Antoine and Penelope. I think my colleagues and I were one of the first guests to arrive and that was about 8:15.'

'Penelope wasn't in a good mood. I saw her glance at the clock and tut. She was annoyed with Virgil for sleeping in. He's a bit of a drinker, which you may have noticed. She asked me to wake him up and to take the master key to let myself in if I needed to.'

'Master key?'

'Yes. It's a key that can open all the bedroom doors. It's for emergencies in case a guest suffers a medical episode in their room.'

'Go on.'

'I tapped on his door and called his name. No reply. I banged harder and called his name louder. Again, I received no reply. I tried once more, then I used the key and gently pushed the door open. It only got so far before the chain blocked it. That's when I thought... felt that something was not quite right.'

'Was this a usual occurrence, you being sent to wake Mr Langley?'

Lucy meekly shakes her head. 'No. It was the first time.'

'Why didn't Penelope go to wake her husband?'

Another shrug. 'Who knows? Anyway, as you would have seen, I rushed back to the kitchen and told Penelope I couldn't wake Virgil.'

'And where are your living quarters?'

'Normally, it's in the Gatehouse. You'll have passed it on your way in. Just off the main road. About a mile's walk from the hotel.'

'But not last night?'

'No. Penelope knew the storm was going to be bad, although Virgil was blase about it. He said it wouldn't be as bad as predicted. On Friday, Penelope suggested I sleep at the hotel on Saturday night. There are a number of rooms in the private residence.'

'How far is your room from Mr Langley's?'

'Not far. You go to the end of the corridor, turn left, and it's the first room on the right.'

'Far enough away to be private?'

'Yes.'

'And had you stayed over at the hotel before?'

'No. First time. To be honest, I prefer my little Gatehouse. It's completely private and away from all the fuss.'

'Do the Langley's only have the one son?'

Lucy pulls her chin in, surprised at the question. 'Yes, as far as I know. But he's not here.'

'I realise that. What happened to him?'

She briefly gazes through the window and focuses on a Robin Red Breast perched on a spindly branch. 'I'm not sure. I heard rumours. But I've never met him, and the Langley's never talk about him.'

'What rumours?'

Her gaze returns to Prisha. 'I heard he was in charge of the bookkeeping and helped himself.'

'To money?'

'Yes. Quite a substantial amount, apparently. Before my time, though. Mr Fitch, the Langley's accountant, spotted it and brought it to their attention. I think that's when he left.'

'He?'

'Ethan—their son.'

'And he doesn't call or visit?'

'Not that I'm aware of.'

'When you say he helped himself to a substantial sum—what do you call substantial?'

Lucy's shoulders heave. 'I don't know. A lot, I guess.'

'And who told you about this?'

'Mrs Thornton, Maggie. She runs a bed-and-breakfast in the village. Bit of a busybody.'

Prisha notices the necklace around Lucy's neck. 'That's a nice necklace. Is it a Pandora?'

'Yes, it is.' Lucy pulls the chain forward, almost like she forgot she was wearing it.

'A heart, the infinity symbol and... what are the letters?' Prisha asks, leaning forward.

'VH. It's the initials of my best friend—Violet Harper. She bought me it.'

'And where's Violet?'

'In Bali. Working as a tour guide. We met at Uni.'

Prisha smiles sweetly. 'You must miss her.'

Lucy stares at the charms with a wistful air. 'Yes, I do. I wish she was here now.'

Prisha allows a moment's interlude before continuing. 'Were you aware of any issues the Langley's had with any of the present guests, or other people in general?'

Her eyes widen. 'I don't wish to speak badly of my employers, but the truth is they seem to fall out with everyone. Penelope is always having spats with Maggie Thornton. They both sit on the Heritage and Visitor Partnership.'

'What's that?'

'A local committee designed to encourage tourists to the area but in a sustainable and eco-friendly way.'

'I see. And who else have they had spats with?'

Lucy rolls her eyes. 'The farmer, Hugh Foster. Something about drainage from the septic tank flowing onto his land.

And Virgil and Murdoch were always falling out over one thing or another. Petty stuff. The food critic Imogen Sato—they threatened to take her to court for defamation after she, or the paper she works for, published a scathing food review last year. And of course, the accountant, Logan Fitch, who they fell out with when he brought their sons stealing to light.'

'Then why would those people be here for the Murder Mystery Weekend?'

'They'd patched things up, or at least they were trying to.'

'And how was Virgil's and Penelope's relationship? Good, bad, indifferent, volatile?'

'I'd say dysfunctional.'

'In what way?'

'Oh, Virgil is... was, scatterbrained, always going off on a tangent with new ideas and grand schemes. He had this nervous energy about him. But it wasn't directed. He was all over the place. He'd start a project, and it was the be-all and end-all, then within a week or two, he'd drop it and start on something new. Always losing his temper, but not in a violent way. You know, almost like a child throwing tantrums. Everyone became immune to it. That's Virgil, thrown his rattle from the pram again, is a common phrase amongst the staff.'

'And how many staff, including yourself?'

'Erm, there's Chef Antoine, and he normally has three, sometimes four, others in the kitchen with him. Unfortunately, it's a revolving door. They don't last too long, for obvious reasons.'

'The kitchen staff?'

'Yes. They're paid a pittance, and Antoine is horrible to work with. You never know which of his personalities is going to turn up. Then we have a gardener, two cleaners, and an odd-job man. Although, they're not staff—they're contract.'

'Tell me about Penelope?'

'To be honest, I find her a little intimidating. She's a hard taskmaster, but I can see why. She has to be the solid, sensible one to keep Virgil in check. He had another one of his brilliant ideas about six months ago. Said he was going to buy land off Hugh Foster and turn it into a nine-hole golf course. Kept banging on about it and how it would transform Kindlewood Hall and be a big draw card. Anyway, Penelope got sick of hearing about it, so one day she sat behind the counter in reception and spent an afternoon doing research. She estimated it would cost somewhere between three to five million pounds to buy the land, obtain planning permission, construct the course, and add additional facilities. She presented her findings to Virgil.'

'And what happened?'

'They had a blazing row. It was embarrassing, as the hotel was quite full at the time. It doesn't create a very nice atmosphere when the owners are going at it hammer and tong in public. Penelope said the hotel would need to be booked out every night for five years to even recoup the costs. Virgil accused her of always scuppering his plans and said she had no vision. She said she had no intention of being around in five years' time, and they should focus their attention and efforts on improving and maintaining what they already had. So, that was the end of the golf course saga.'

'I see what you mean by dysfunctional.'

Lucy almost laughs. 'Have you ever watched that old sitcom—Fawlty Towers?'

'Yes. My boyfriend watches re-runs on telly sometimes.'

'Well, that's what they were like. Sybil and Basil Fawlty—that's the Langleys.' She pauses and gazes out of the window again, as her eyes narrow. 'Having said all that—Virgil could be kind and considerate. I liked him. He was a bit mad, but he didn't have a bad bone in his body. It won't be the same around here now he's... well, gone.'

Prisha flips her notebook shut. 'Okay, we're all done for the moment. Thank you, Lucy.'

Lucy attempts a smile but fails as she rises. 'Right. I better get back to work.'

Prisha watches on as the young woman walks away, carrying herself with an impressive deportment

'Oh, Lucy,' Prisha calls after her.

She stops and spins on her heels. 'Yes?'

'How was Chef Antoine with the Langleys?'

She ponders for a moment. 'He referred to Virgil as an imbecile, behind his back, of course.'

'And Penelope?'

'They get on very well. In fact, it only seems to be Penelope who can rein in his outbursts.'

# 25

Murdoch Langley carefully lowers himself into the chair, as Frank throws two logs onto the fire and gives it a prod with the poker, before resuming his seat at the table.

'He used to like it in here,' Murdoch reflects ruefully. 'Virgil, I mean. He called it his haven. I'd often find him in here with a cup of coffee, reading a book or scribbling in a notebook.'

'It has a very pleasant and calming ambience,' Frank concurs. 'Libraries usually do. Almost like the knowledge contained within the books imbues the room with wisdom.'

Murdoch smiles in a sad way. 'Yes, I suppose.' He crosses one leg over the other and flicks away imaginary fluff from his thigh. 'Apologies for my outburst earlier, inspector. A bit overly dramatic. It was the shock. The emotion. It's like a dream, or a nightmare, Virgil's death. And killed in such a brutal fashion. Makes me feel sick to my core. And to think the killer is within these walls.'

'We can't be certain of that, Murdoch.'

He pulls a frown. 'You think it could be an outsider? An intruder?'

'I'm not saying that, either. At this stage there are no certainties.' Frank takes the cap off the pen and adjusts his notebook. 'Now, can you tell me about your movements from 10 pm last night until 8:30 this morning, and the last time you saw or spoke with Virgil?'

'As you know, I was in here with him last night discussing various things. I recall the grandfather clock striking ten. Not long after, I retired to my room. Slept all night and awoke this morning around 8:50 when Sergeant Stoker knocked on my door.'

'You didn't leave your room at all?'

'No, of course not.'

Frank deftly makes a few notes in his pad. 'You said you were discussing various things last night in here. From where I was standing, it sounded like you were having an argument?'

Murdoch pushes back in his chair and places his hands on the table, then taps his fingers on the surface.

'It's true what Hugh Foster said earlier in the dining room. Virgil and I did have a volatile relationship, not unlike many siblings. But as quickly as tempers flared, they'd subside just as quickly. We loved each other.'

'That wasn't my question.'

Murdoch shifts uncomfortably. 'Very well. I may as well tell you. You're bound to find out soon enough.' Murdoch puffs his cheeks out, sighs, and drags a hand through his slick, silver locks. 'There's a bit of a backstory. Long winded.'

Frank glances out at the deserted landscape. 'For once, Mr Langley, time is on our side.'

'Virgil and Penelope have a son, an adopted son—Ethan Langley. He was a toddler when they took him on. A bright lad. Excelled at school. Mathematics, languages, music, science. Virgil adored him, as did Penelope at the time. He left school with a clutch of A Levels and went to a good university to study science. After two years, he dropped out. Decided he wanted to become an actor. Virgil and Penelope paid for acting lessons, and Penny, through a friend of a friend, got him an agent. He appeared a couple of times in soap operas. A non-speaking part. I went to watch him in a local play when he returned home one summer. The only other actor who was more wooden than Ethan was a young chap called Pinocchio.'

Frank stifles a laugh, but not a grin. 'Go on.'

'To cut a long story short, Ethan tried his hand at a myriad of careers; musician, rally car driver, the dot.com boom and subsequent bust. All subsidised by Virgil and Penny. In the end, by the time he was in his thirties, Penny convinced Virgil it was time to turn the tap off.'

'You mean stop subsidising him?'

'Exactly. They gave him an ultimatum. Come home and learn the hotelier business, otherwise you're on your own. They said it was all going to be his one day, so he needed to know how it all works. Of course, I was watching all this unfold from the sidelines, biting my tongue. But I knew Ethan was one of life's eternal losers.'

'And?'

'I was wrong. Initially. Ethan returned home and set about learning the business with gusto. He helped in the kitchen, cleaned rooms, worked in the garden and grounds. He seemed happy and inspired. Virgil and Penny were so proud of the turnaround. At that time, Virgil took care of the day-to-day accounts.' He offers Frank a rum smile. 'To be honest, inspector, my brother was hopeless with figures. He didn't have the patience to sit for hours adding and subtracting numbers and reconciling accounts. He paid for Ethan to go on a crash course in hotel management and bookkeeping. It was all going swimmingly. Ethan took to it like a duck to water. He sorted everything out, monetary wise. The hotel was flourishing. Fully booked out for most of the year. Ethan became front of house manager. Took all the bookings. Sorted the accounts. Liaised with the bank and the accountant, Logan Fitch. Virgil and Penelope made Ethan a director of the company, handing over more power.'

He pauses and puckers his lips. 'I always had my doubts about him, even then. But I didn't say anything, as I knew it would inflame Virgil. Anyway, about four years ago, it all came to a head. I still don't know the specifics. You'll have to ask Logan Fitch about it. But in short, Ethan had been embezzling money—a lot of money. By the time Penny twigged—and it was Penny who became suspicious—the business had become financially perilous. They outed Ethan. A furious argument ensued, and he packed up and left. Since then, the hotel has struggled.'

Frank looks up from his untidy scribbles. 'Struggled financially?'

'Yes. A lack of equity. Ready money. The fact is my brother and sister-in-law lost a lot. Somewhere between one to one and a half million. Plus, debts and exorbitant bank fees. They have struggled ever since. As you will have noticed, and I don't wish to sound disparaging, inspector, Kindlewood Hall is—how can I put it—jaded. It needs a facelift. Neither of them are getting any younger.' He halts abruptly. 'Christ, what am I saying? Virgil is dead.'

Frank allows him a moment to reflect. 'You were saying?'

'Sorry, yes. I'm a wealthy man, inspector. An investment banker. I've made my money and know how to look after it. A few months ago, Virgil and Penny took me out for dinner one night and put forth a business proposition. If I'd invest in the hotel, they'd relinquish thirty per cent of the ownership.'

'You'd own nearly a third of the business?' Frank prompts for clarification.

'In essence—yes.'

'And how much were they asking for?'

'One million.'

'And how much is the hotel and grounds worth?'

'In its current state, and dependent on the market, between three and four million.'

Frank nods. 'Seems a fair enough sort of deal.'

'Extremely fair. And of course, Virgil and Penny would still own seventy per cent of the shares. And after the deal, I'd be a silent partner with no say in running the business.'

'So, what was the plan?'

'A makeover inside. Rip out the bathrooms and update them with modern walk-in showers. Then the rest was mainly cosmetic. A lick of paint, some new furnishings, that sort of thing. Give the whole place a modern revamp on the inside without losing its old-world charm. Then the plan was to reopen and run a marketing campaign to ensure full bookings, and a year or so down the line, they intended to put it on the market for hopefully six million plus, and finally retire and live happily ever after. Anyway, I chewed it over for a couple of days and agreed. But I insisted it had to be done right. No short-cuts or half-arsed scrimping. I put a lot of time and effort into creating a business plan and cash flow forecasts. I obtained quotes from three reputable building firms who could handle a job of this magnitude. Obviously, the hotel would have to close for a number of months while the work was carried out. You can't have building work while guests are staying.'

'Obviously.'

'And that's the long and tall and short of it.'

'Not quite: you still haven't answered my original question.'

'Which was?'

'The argument last night—what was it about?'

Murdoch puckers his lips and clasps his hands together. 'A misunderstanding, that's all. An irrelevancy.'

A slight grunt escapes from Frank's throat as he becomes weary of the deliberate prevarication. 'Your brother has been murdered, Murdoch,' he begins forcefully, raising his voice. 'It doesn't get any more serious than this. Any information—whether you consider it relevant or not—could be of the utmost importance. As I said earlier, there are no certainties. But there are likelihoods. And the likelihood of your brother being killed by a random, deranged, psychotic stranger is slim. Which probably means he was killed for a reason, likely by someone he knew.

The top five motives in such cases are domestic disputes, family conflicts, financial gain, revenge, or an argument that spiralled out of control.' Frank places his palms on the table and leans forward, his features hardened, eyes darting back and forth over Murdoch Langley's face. 'Now, are you going to tell me what your argument was about or not?'

Murdoch, unaccustomed to such forceful directness, flinches, and quickly caves. 'Very well. Virgil wasn't happy with the projected cost of the refurbishment.'

'Too high?'

'No. On the contrary. He thought the costs were too low.'

Frank scowls. 'And what led him to that conclusion?'

Murdoch sneers. 'That tuppence a-penny accountant—Logan Fitch. Apparently, Virgil had given Fitch a copy of the business plan last week. It was Fitch who put the idea into Virgil's head about the costs being too low. I mean, what the hell would that backwater bean counter know about building costs?'

Frank leans back, strokes his chin and ponders. 'But surely, that should have simply been a matter of you going over the quotes from the builders in a logical manner with Virgil?'

'Exactly—if he'd been sober. But once my brother hits the bottle, logic and rationality fly out of the window. I knew that after a good night's sleep, and once his hangover had subsided, I'd have been able to explain things to him. Alas, I will never get that opportunity now.'

Frank studies him for a moment. Murdoch Langley appears upset, trying to hide it. But does his story ring true? Possibly—possibly not.

Frank decides to move on. 'What's your relationship like with Penelope?'

'Penelope is a darling. I won't have a bad word said about her.'

'No one is.'

'Yes, well.' He readjusts his position. 'I've always got on famously with Penny. To some, I dare say she may come across as a little severe, but it's just an act to keep people in their places. When you run a business and employ people, you must not be overly friendly. Staff need to know who's the boss. Familiarity breeds contempt.'

'Safe to say you're quite fond of Penelope, then?'

Murdoch leans back violently. 'What are you implying, inspector?'

'I'm not implying anything, Murdoch. I'm merely pointing out you are obviously fond, and maybe a little defensive, of your sister-in-law.'

'Is that a crime?'

'No. But murder is.'

# 26

The billiard room is cloaked in shadows, the faint flicker of candlelight casting jagged shapes on the dark wood-panelled walls. The green baize of the snooker table glows under the wavering light of two candelabras, their bases crudely secured at either end. A torch, propped on a stool, throws a stark beam across the table, illuminating Zac's face in sharp relief. The air smells faintly of polish and chalk, mingling with the musty scent of a room seldom aired. Heavy silence presses in, broken only by the echoing click of boots on the floor as Hugh Foster enters, hesitating at the doorway.

'Hell fire, Sergeant Stoker, this looks like a Nazi interrogation chamber,' he says with a chuckle. 'What's it to be, matchsticks down the fingernails or electrodes to the testicles?'

'Very funny, Mr Foster. Please take a seat,' Zac replies wearily and slightly embarrassed by the setup.

Hugh slumps his large frame down on a chair and stares across the table at Zac. 'Do you play?'

'What?'

'Snooker?'

'Aye, occasionally.'

'What's your highest break?'

'Twenty-seven.'

Hugh laughs again. 'So, you don't play. My highest is sixty-four. Maybe we'll have a game later when all this cloak and dagger nonsense is over.'

'Maybe,' Zac replies without much enthusiasm as he shuffles his notepad and readies his pen. 'Can you tell me your movements last night from around 10 pm until 8:30 this morning?'

'Aye. I was in the drawing room with you and the other guests until about 9:00. Then I went to bed. Woke up around 7:30 this morning. Took a long shower then went to the dining room not long after your gang arrived, about 8:20, I think.'

'You didn't get up during the night?'

'You're right, I didn't. Not sure how you knew, though,' he adds with a snigger.

Zac folds his arms. 'Bit of a joker, are we?'

'You've got to have a laugh, haven't you?'

'This is a murder investigation, Mr Foster.'

'Aye, I know it is. And I'll tell you this for nowt—I didn't kill Virgil Langley, but I know who did?'

Zac's eyes narrow. 'Who?'

'His brother, Murdoch.'

'Where's your proof?'

Hugh points to his face. 'I have eyes in my head, Mr Stoker. I see things others don't.'

Zac's initial optimism at a possible breakthrough is dashed against the rocks. 'Go on, then. Let's hear it.'

'Murdoch's a greedy beggar. Always has been. He's had his eye on this place for some time. It doesn't matter how much money some folks have, it's never enough.'

'So, this hypothesis of yours involves Murdoch killing his brother to get his hands on Kindlewood Hall?'

'Aye, that's right.'

'But he won't, will he—it will all go to Penelope Langley.'

Hugh grins and folds his large meaty arms. 'True.'

'Then your theory is simply that—an unfounded theory.'

'Is it though? Like I said, I see things.'

Zac is already tired of the display. 'Mr Foster, if you have something to get off your chest then say it instead of playing silly word games.'

Hugh glances towards the doorway, checking they're alone, then leans over the table. 'They're having an affair,' he whispers.

'Murdoch and Penelope?'

'Aye. Got it in one. Wouldn't surprise me if she was in on it, too. Bump old Virgil off. Lie low for a year and hey presto, they become an item. Murdoch gets the woman and the hotel he's been coveting for many a year.'

'As fairy tales go, it's a bit cliched.'

'It's no fairy tale, sergeant. I have eyes.'

'Yes, you have pointed out that blatant fact already. What you've failed to point out is any credible evidence. All you've offered is opinion. Did you see either Murdoch or Penelope enter Virgil's room last night or this morning?'

'No.'

'Right, let's move on. How was your relationship with Virgil?'

'All right, I suppose. We'd had an on-again-off-again dispute about his bloody septic tank overflow for about a year, but he said he was getting it fixed in the new year. It runs into my paddock and kills the grass. You see, they're not supposed to use chemicals in the toilets, but they obviously do.'

Zac huffs. 'You've lost me?'

Hugh appears surprised that Zac doesn't understand the rudimentary theory of septic tanks. 'I'll explain how a septic tank works for you, sergeant. It's basically a big underground chamber where all the waste goes. Micro-organisms inside break down the solids—it's their job to eat the, well...

the shite. The system works fine as long as the organisms are alive and healthy. Once they've done their bit, the tank discharges clean water into the overflow system. But if you use chemicals—like bleach or toilet cleaner, for instance—you kill off the micro-organisms. Then nothing gets broken down properly, and the waste builds up or leaks out, including into my paddock. The chemicals also come out in the overflow, and that's what kills the grass. It's basic biology, really.'

Zac sighs. 'Right. Noted. So, this minor dispute was resolved?'

'I never said that. It will be resolved once Virgil gets the plumber in to re-lay the underground discharge pipes in another direction away from my bloody field.'

'I'm not sure that's going to happen, Mr Foster, considering Virgil is in no fit state to call a plumber.'

Hugh winces. 'Hell fire. I never thought of that.'

Zac's patience is not only wearing thin, it's beginning to tear at the seams. 'Anything else of any note?'

'No, not really. Oh, apart from about six months ago, the daft beggar said he wanted to buy some land off me so he could turn it into a nine-hole golf course. I didn't take him seriously. Virgil was like that. Full of big ideas. To be honest sergeant...' he checks the doorway again, 'I think he was a bit—in the head,' he says, tapping at his temple. 'If you get my meaning. You know, a few gherkins short of a pickle jar.'

'Okay, thanks for your time, Mr Foster. And your assumptions about Murdoch and Penelope Langley—keep them to yourself, please.'

Hugh stands and pushes his chair back. 'Suit yourself. You'll see I'm right. Mark my words.'

'And can you tell Chef Antoine I'm ready to see him now?' Zac watches the large farmer retreat, then mutters, 'Dickhead.'

# 27

Frank watches Logan Fitch closely, his inquisitive gaze probing for any telltale signs of unease. So far, his account mirrors his own recollection: after the chaos of the evening, most guests had gathered in the drawing room before quietly retreating to their rooms between 9:30 and 10:00 pm.

'I believe you were the Langleys' accountant for a number of years?' Frank prompts, pen poised over his notebook.

Logan nods. 'Yes, for fifteen years.'

'But that ended a few years ago, correct?'

Logan offers a faint, wry smile. 'Ah, I see Murdoch Langley's already filled you in. Yes, my services were terminated some years ago. However,' he leans back slightly, crossing one leg over the other, 'as of a few weeks ago, I resumed my role as the Langleys' official accountant.'

'Why the sudden change?'

'Virgil and Penelope wanted someone they could trust again. We resolved our old differences, then they told me about Murdoch Langley's proposal.'

'The one-million-pound investment into Kindlewood Hall?'

'Yes. Last week I had lunch with Virgil, and he handed me the business plan drawn up by Murdoch, asking me to go through it thoroughly and confirm it was bona fide.'

'And was it?'

Logan intertwines his fingers and sucks in a sharp breath. 'I didn't get a chance to review it until Friday, and it immediately raised concerns.'

Frank cocks an eyebrow. 'From what Murdoch told me, it seemed like a fair enough deal on the surface: put in one million for a thirty per cent stake in a business worth three to four million pounds on paper.'

Logan tilts his head, his eyes narrowing. 'That's what Murdoch told you?' he asks, the question dripping with scepticism.

'Yes. Is that not the case?'

Logan chuckles softly, casting a glance at the bookshelf behind Frank before refocusing. 'Ah, Murdoch,' he sighs, shaking his head slowly. 'That's the thing with Murdoch Langley, inspector. He has a knack for being... economical with the truth.'

'Care to elaborate?'

Logan leans forward, resting his arms on the table. 'It's partly true—the one million for a thirty per cent stake. But it's what he didn't tell you that's interesting. It wasn't an investment; it was a loan—to be repaid. And I'd say Kindlewood Hall is worth far more than three million—closer to five or six.'

Frank jots down some notes, then fixes Logan with a steady stare. 'You had other concerns about the deal?'

Logan relaxes slightly, leaning back in his chair. 'Yes. I raised them with Virgil in the back office last night during pre-dinner drinks. My main concern was the projected refurbishment costs. In my opinion, they were far too low—comically low, in fact.'

'Do you have expertise in the building industry?'

'No, but let me ask you this, inspector: have you had a new bathroom suite installed recently?'

Frank frowns. 'Not recently—about five years ago, I think. Why?'

'And what did it set you back?'

'It wasn't cheap. About eight thousand pounds, give or take.'

'Exactly,' Logan says, leaning forward slightly. 'I had one fitted six months ago. Cost me ten grand, and that was for a mid-range design.' He lets the weight of the figure linger before continuing. 'Kindlewood Hall has thirty guest bedrooms, not including the private residence quarters. Even if you estimate conservatively, that's three hundred thousand pounds for bathrooms alone. And that's before you factor in repainting the entire interior, upgrading fixtures, furnishings, and replacing all the doors with keyless entry systems.'

Frank's pen pauses mid-note as Logan presses on.

'And there's the schedule,' Logan adds, his voice tightening. 'The job would need to be completed on a tight deadline, meaning the builder would be working seven days a week. That's penalty rates for tradesmen on weekends—an enormous cost multiplier. I told Virgil last night that either Murdoch had wildly underestimated the budget or, more worryingly, deliberately misrepresented it.'

Frank frowns. 'If Murdoch obtained quotes from builders, then they're obligated to complete the job as per the quote.'

'And therein lies the crux of the matter, Inspector Finnegan—they aren't quotes. They're estimates.' Logan leans forward, emphasising the distinction. 'To the layman, they may seem like the same beast, but they're worlds apart. An estimate is little more than an educated guess, subject to change based on countless factors. And in my experience, estimates always rise—they never fall.'

Frank drums his fingers on the desk, his brow furrowed. 'So why would Murdoch put forward such a shaky business plan, especially if he's putting up his own money?'

Logan hesitates, his expression guarded. 'I have my own theory,' he says, his voice abrupt, the reluctance palpable.

'Which is?' Frank presses.

Logan glances at the doorway as if ensuring they're not overheard, then back at Frank, lowering his voice. 'The issue with the costs can be validated easily enough with a little research. But what I'm about to share...' He pauses, his lips tightening. 'It's purely my own speculation—you understand?'

Frank meets his gaze evenly. 'Understood. Go ahead.'

'I think Murdoch has deliberately underestimated the costs on purpose. He wants the refurbishment to fail—to run out of money before the job is complete.'

Frank narrows his eyes, sceptical. 'And what benefit could he possibly gain from that?'

'As the Langley's biggest creditor, he could call in the loan. Then Virgil and Penelope would have two choices: sell up or go into voluntary receivership. If the hotel went on the market in a state of disrepair—halfway through unfinished building works—it would be worth a fraction of its true value. And that's when Murdoch would swoop in, making them a pitiful offer. Essentially, he'd have them over a barrel. Whatever money they managed to scrape from the sale would go straight to their creditors.'

'Including the one million Murdoch loaned them,' Frank says, the wheels turning in his head.

'Exactly. A win-win for Murdoch. He'd finally get his hands on Kindlewood Hall—for an absolute steal.'

Frank leans back, the idea forming. 'If your theory is correct, it would be devilishly cunning. Ruthless.'

Logan smirks knowingly. 'And that, inspector, sums up Murdoch Langley's personality to a tee—cunning and ruthless.'

Frank takes a moment, digesting the information, mindful it's only one man's assumptions.

'Okay, moving on. Tell me about the adopted son—Ethan Langley—and the hotel funds. How much did he steal?'

'We could never be entirely certain, but somewhere between one and two million.'

'That's a lot of money. How did it go unnoticed for so long?'

'Because Ethan Langley was a devious, manipulative fiend.'

Frank wonders if Logan Fitch is the overly suspicious type who sees shadows in broad daylight, forever searching for intrigue where none exists.

'If you were the Langleys' accountant, how come you didn't notice the missing money earlier?'

'Because I only saw what Ethan chose to show me. Accountancy, inspector, operates on a kind of honour system. We trust our clients to be diligent, transparent, and truthful.'

'Did the Langleys ever retrieve the money?'

'No. Ethan insisted he'd gambled it away, although I don't believe that for one minute.'

'Did they call in the police?'

'No. I wanted to, but Virgil and Penelope wouldn't hear of it. They're very conservative inspector. They thought it would cause a storm and sully their reputation—affect the business.'

'I see. If you were the one who confirmed the embezzlement, then why the fallout?'

Logan puckers his lips and runs a hand through his hair. 'I told them a hard truth. Even though the money was technically stolen, it was still income, and we should have informed the Inland Revenue. They'd likely have had to pay tax on it unless it was formally reported to the police as theft. That's what caused the rift. They wanted me to keep quiet. I insisted it was my duty to report it.'

'And did you?'

He sighs heavily, his gaze sliding away. 'To my shame—no, I didn't. The first and only time I've knowingly violated the code of ethics, and the Companies Act in my entire career.'

'I'm intrigued by how Ethan managed to pull the wool over everyone's eyes for so long. In this day and age, with digital banking and cash becoming a relic, how did he do it?'

Logan leans back in his chair, crossing one leg over the other. 'Quite ingenious, really. It all started when Ethan was made a company director. Shortly after, Virgil and Penelope went off on a three-week river cruise in Europe. While they were away, Ethan set up a new business account with a different bank and leased a card reader linked to that account. I said it was ingenious, but it was also stunningly simple.'

'As front of house manager, Ethan handled all the bookings—phone reservations, walk-ins, everything. He would switch out the hotel's card reader for his own, so instead of payments going into the hotel's account, they went straight into his. When Virgil or Penelope were around, he'd hide the fake card reader and use the legitimate one.'

'But surely Penelope or Virgil would have kept an eye on their bank balance?'

'Oh, they did. That's where Ethan's cunning came into play.' Logan leans forward, his voice lowering. 'Unbeknownst to either of them, Ethan had quietly arranged an overdraft with the bank. Not only that, but he increased the limit every six months. So, whenever the Langleys checked their balance online, they saw a healthy bottom line—not realising it was, in fact, the overdraft keeping them afloat.'

Frank frowns. 'And how did it all come to a head?'

'Ethan went on holiday for a week, and during his absence, Penelope received a call from the bank manager. There'd been a technical glitch that temporarily altered the interest rate on their overdraft. He was calling to explain the issue, apologise, and assure her any extra charges would be refunded.' Logan shakes his head. 'Penelope was blindsided. She had no idea what he was talking about. She told him they didn't have an overdraft—never had. That's when it all began to unravel.'

'So, Ethan was sprung once he returned from holiday?'

'Not quite. Penelope told me about it, but not Virgil. In his eyes, Ethan could do no wrong. Penelope and I decided to investigate quietly to figure out the scale of the problem and gather proof. Penny was furious, but I have to hand it to her—she put on a convincing act for a couple of weeks. I conducted a full audit, going back over all the years since Ethan joined the hotel. Thankfully, Penelope kept detailed records of room bookings in her spreadsheets.'

'I started by tallying up the number of guests, the rooms they stayed in, and the time of year. Then I calculated what they would've been charged for their stays. Of course, Ethan wasn't stupid. He filtered enough legitimate payments through to keep the business running and avoid suspicion. But once I'd crunched the numbers, it was obvious money was missing.'

'To leave no room for doubt, I suggested one final step to prove Ethan's guilt conclusively.'

'Go on.'

'I asked my sister and her husband—people Ethan didn't know—to make a booking for a weekend. They stayed Friday through Sunday, racked up a hefty bill on meals and drinks, and paid in full when they checked out. Four hundred and sixty-six pounds. A few days later, I checked the Langleys' account to see if the payment had been recorded. It hadn't. I contacted my brother, who confirmed the money had been deducted from his card. That's when I proved my theory about the second card reader.'

'And that's when you told Virgil?'

'Yes. Penny and I tackled him together while Ethan was out. In typical Virgil fashion, he blew a gasket, accused us of setting Ethan up, and flat-out refused to believe it. That lasted about ten minutes—then he realised the inevitable. Ethan was a crook.'

'What happened next?'

'We confronted Ethan as soon as he got back. We showed him the evidence. It wasn't a civilised conversation. Let's put it that way. A lot of shouting and venom, a lot of threats.

Penny told him to leave and never set foot in the hotel again. Ethan, of course, didn't go quietly. He called them every name under the sun, said he couldn't wait to get out of what he called "this godforsaken backwater dump." Then he packed up his things and left.'

'And that was the last they saw of him?'

'As far as I know, yes. He took off in a lease car registered to the hotel, by the way. Never returned it.'

'And they've had no contact with him since?'

'Not that I'm aware.'

Frank scrutinises Logan Fitch, his pen hovering over the notebook. Something about the man doesn't quite sit right. He taps the pen against the table, the faint sound breaking the silence.

'Thank you, Mr Fitch. That will be all for now.' As Logan rises to leave, Frank's eyes follow him, suspicion gnawing at the edges of his mind.

*How much of his story am I supposed to believe?*

## 28

Prisha knows she must tread carefully. Penelope Langley is not under arrest, not even officially a suspect—yet. But grieving widow or not, she's high on the list simply by proximity. Prisha's task is delicate: gather details about Penelope's movements, tease out any signs of tension in the marriage, and probe for conflicts that might hint at motive. She must walk the tightrope between compassion and professional detachment, aware that grief can manifest in ways that obscure the truth—or reveal it in unexpected ways.

For a moment, neither woman speaks. Prisha lets the silence stretch, a tactic she's found often yields results more than rushed questions.

Penelope sniffs. Her tissue mangled beyond use, the product of restless fingers rather than weeping. Her eyes, faintly rimmed with redness, seem dry now as they fix on some unseen point on the table. She exhales softly, reaches into her handbag, and retrieves a small vanity mirror. The polished silver catches the sunlight creeping along the pool windows. Flipping it open, she inspects her face. Without a word, she dabs at her eyes with the tissue before pulling out a lipstick and reapplying it in a slow, deliberate motion.

Prisha says nothing—but she notices. The action strikes her as odd, not because a grieving woman wouldn't care about her appearance—but because of the calm, almost mechanical way Penelope performs the task. It is too measured, too detached, as if the person in the mirror is someone else entirely.

'Whenever you're ready,' Prisha says softly, her notebook resting in front of her.

Penelope drops the lipstick and compact into the bag and places it on the floor. 'Where would you like me to begin?' she asks at last, her voice level, though there's a frosty edge to her tone that betrays impatience.

'Perhaps you can start with last night,' Prisha replies. 'Where you were, who you saw, anything you noticed out of the ordinary?'

Penelope nods, her gaze drifting momentarily to the glass panels behind Prisha, where a few gentle snowflakes continue their slow, soundless descent.

'Of course,' she replies. 'Anything to help. Such a busy night. After the rather tumultuous dinner, and the sad passing of that young woman, I helped clear up in the kitchen. The other guests, including yourself, had departed into the drawing room to relax. I joined the rather subdued gathering about 9:00 pm. We sang carols for thirty minutes, then I left and went to my bedroom. I awoke this morning at 6:30, showered and arrived in the kitchen about 7:00 to help with the breakfast. There was only me and Antoine there until about 7:30, when Lucy joined us. As the breakfast orders began to trickle in, I noticed the time—about 8:15—I think. I was annoyed Virgil hadn't yet surfaced. I assumed he was suffering from a massive hangover, which I was angry about. He was aware how understaffed we were, and with the storm, the loss of power, lack of communications—well, I thought it downright selfish and unprofessional.' She pauses and reflects, wistful. 'Of course, my anger was ill-founded. How did he die, inspector?'

Prisha leans forward, clasping her hands loosely on the table. 'Unofficially, he appears to have been stabbed in the eye with a sharp instrument. Dr Whipple, who is a Home Office pathologist, suggests the weapon may have pierced the brain. We can't be certain of the exact cause of death until after the autopsy.'

Her head drops in disbelief. 'Sweet mercy,' she whispers. 'And when do you think he was... when do you think he died?'

'Sometime between going to bed, which we think was not long after 10 pm, and maybe 4 am.'

'But how? If the chain was on the door, then how did the killer get into the room?'

Prisha wrestles with her conscience. Penelope is entitled to know the details but furnishing her with too much information could unwittingly backfire, if she's involved.

'We can't answer that at the moment. Later, once we've questioned everyone, I'd like you to show me around your private residence.'

'Yes, of course.'

Prisha hesitates briefly, gauging Penelope's expression, but there is little to read. 'Did your husband usually have a bedroom window open when he went to bed?'

Puzzlement flits across her face. 'No. Maybe in summer, if it was a particularly warm night, he might. But no, not usually. He'd complain about the slightest draft.'

'Did you hear anything unusual last night from your room? A raised voice, footsteps, anything that might have seemed out of place?'

Penelope's gaze flickers, her brow creasing in thought. 'No... nothing. But the storm—' She gestures vaguely towards the windows. 'The wind was howling. It masked everything.'

Prisha makes a note, then leans back slightly. 'What about your relationship with Virgil? How were things between you?'

Penelope stiffens almost imperceptibly. 'Our marriage was... typical,' she says, her words measured. 'We had our ups and downs, like anyone else. But we cared for each other. He was a good man.'

'Did he have any enemies? Anyone who might have wished him harm?'

Penelope's lips press into a thin line. 'Not that I know of. Virgil was respected. Liked. He could be difficult—particular—but that's hardly a reason for murder.' Her voice sharpens briefly before softening again.

Prisha jots down another note, watching Penelope closely. Her answers are tidy, but something feels off. It's not what Penelope is saying—it's what she isn't. There is no anger, no rawness. Her grief seems too polished, too rehearsed. And there's the lipstick, the vanity mirror. Prisha pushes the thought aside, reminding herself not to jump to conclusions.

'Did you hear Virgil come to bed?'

'No. To be honest, inspector, the moment my head hit the pillow, I was out cold. It had been a very long and trying day.'

'I understand you and Virgil have had some minor disputes in the past with some of the attending guests.'

'Who told you that?' she snaps, her demeanour changing.

'It's our job to find things out, Penelope. Is it true?'

She relaxes, as if the fight isn't worth it. 'Yes, it's true. But this weekend was when we put all that behind us. We'd made peace with everyone, and this was our way of starting afresh. And anyway, the disputes were all minor piddly little affairs. Mainly misunderstandings.'

'So, to clarify, you can't think of anyone who would want to harm your husband?'

A shake of the head. 'No. Virgil was irascible, flighty, sometimes harebrained, but he was harmless. Quick to anger but equally quick to calm.' She winces as if in pain. 'Will this take much longer, inspector? I can feel a migraine coming on and would like to lie down.'

Prisha smiles, masking her true feelings. She'd only just started.

'Yes, of course. We can continue later if I have any more questions. I'm truly sorry for your loss, Mrs Langley.'

Penelope rises, offering her a thin smile. Pausing briefly, as though to say something else, she thinks better of it. Instead, she walks towards the door, her heels tapping against the oak timber.

Prisha watches her go, her mind circling back to the small inconsistencies, the moments that didn't quite add up.

Shock can explain a lot, she reminds herself. But it can't explain everything.

# 29

Antoine Galois, in his chef whites, is sitting on a stool with his arms tightly crossed. His face, a picture of restrained annoyance.

'Sergeant Stoker, I am a busy man. I have a Christmas dinner to cook for thirteen guests. I hope this is not going to take too long,' he states as he shuffles on the stool at the side of the snooker table. His manner is terse, offhand, as though the investigation into the murder of his employer is a mere trifle compared to his gastronomic endeavours.

Zac is having none of his flamboyant tactics. 'It will take as long as it takes. Now, tell me your movements last night and this morning.'

He holds his hands up in frustration. 'What is there to say?' he huffs, exasperated. 'I was in the kitchen until 9:30. Lucy left. I followed not long after and went to my room. I showered, went to bed. Awoke at 6:30 am and back into the kitchen to prepare for breakfast. The work of a chef at a hotel is constant. There is only work, sleep, work, sleep. Over, and over, and over.'

Zac ignores his complaints. 'And the last time you saw or spoke with Virgil Langley?'

'I cannot remember,' he replies truculently.

'Then try a little harder,' Zac snaps back, tiring of his melodramatic performance.

He expels air in a frustrated manner. 'I don't know, 9:00, 9:30 perhaps. Mr Langley came to the kitchen.'

'What for?'

'I don't know. You'll have to ask him.'

'Very funny. What did you talk about?'

'Something and nothing. So inconsequential I cannot recall.'

Zac taps a finger on the baize of the table, trying to remain calm. 'How long have you worked here?'

'One year in February.'

'And how has it been since you arrived?'

He snorts derisively. 'Pffft. What can I say? When I arrived, the place was a mess, shambolic. No systems in place. The kitchen was a pigsty. The menu belonged in the 80s. Lack of modern implements. I set to work and turned the place around. A whole new menu. A new dining room. I upgraded the kitchen. My work here saved this place, but for how much longer? I do not know.'

'What do you mean?'

'What I mean is, the kitchen may be the engine room of the hotel, but if you have leaks in your boat, then it doesn't matter how well your engine works. Eventually, you will sink.'

'How did you get on with Virgil?'

His tone softens. 'Virgil was a child. Always wanting to dabble here, dabble there. His interest could not be sustained. He interfered, suggested ridiculous menu items. Do you know what he wanted me to put on the menu?'

'No. Surprise me.'

'Cheese fondue! Can you imagine? Apart from it being another throwback to the 1980s, the hygiene concepts would not be acceptable today. Can you imagine a group of friends sitting around and double-dipping bread into a communal pot? And it's too heavy, too rich. And the cleaning is a nightmare.'

'It's fair to say you didn't see eye to eye?'

'Monsieur, I am not saying that,' he replies, alarmed at the inference. 'We'd chat occasionally about football, politics. But work wise he was like a butterfly, flitting here, there and everywhere doing little of consequence.'

'And what about Penelope?'

His face brightens. 'Ah, Madame Penelope is divine. We get along like, how you say—a house aflame.'

'On fire.'

'Yes, like a house on fire.'

'Is there anyone you know of who would have wished harm on Virgil?'

'Who knows? Their business affairs are there's alone. I am the king of my domain—the kitchen, and that is all.' He checks his watch. 'Now, sergeant, I need to baste my turkey, otherwise it will be dry and inedible. May I?' he asks, indicating towards the doorway.

'One last question.'

'Oui?'

'To say your employer has been murdered, you don't seem very upset?'

His lips downturn in an arrogant, blase manner, as his eyes momentarily flicker shut. 'It is sad, and my heart goes out to Madame Penelope. But to be honest, sergeant, this place now has a chance to thrive under her sole leadership.'

# 30

Zac exits the chaos of the kitchen carrying a tray containing three black coffees. He almost walks headfirst into Dr Whipple.

'Ah, doctor, what's the go?'

Whipple stares at him, bemused. 'The go, Sergeant Stoker?'

'Yes. What are you up to?'

'I am proceeding to the kitchen to see if I can procure a cup of broth for my wife who is lying in bed, prostrate under the initial withering storm of acute viral nasopharyngitis.'

Zac winces. 'Sounds painful. Will it require surgery?'

Whipple closes his eyes in obvious disdain. 'A cold, sergeant, a common cold.'

'Oh dear. They are a nuisance, aren't they?' he replies in an upbeat cheery tone.

'Yes. A mild encumbrance. As pathogens go, they have adapted over time to wreak havoc on the human species for millennia on a regular basis. Unlike the Spanish Flu.'

'The Spanish flu?' Zac instantly regrets asking the question.

'Yes. An excellent example of a pathogen too effective for its own good. The Spanish influenza, you see, was a pathogen of such astonishing virulence that it rather undermined its own longevity. By dispatching its hosts with alarming rapidity, it curtailed the opportunity for sustained propagation. A virus, like any parasitic entity, thrives upon the living—not the dead. A pathogen too efficient in killing invariably condemns itself to extinction. It is not the flamboyant blaze but the steady ember that endures.' He pauses, tilting his head. 'A salutary lesson for all. Don't you agree, Sergeant Stoker?'

'Aye, I suppose I do. I better keep going. A policeman's lot is not a happy one. And if I don't get these coffees to Frank and Prisha, then it will be even unhappier.'

———⋯⊙⋯———

Zac places the tray down on the antique table in the library and dispenses the coffees.

'You're lucky to get these,' he says, handing Prisha and Frank their drinks.

'Why's that?' Frank asks, taking a tentative sip.

'Kitchen is in turmoil. I feel sorry for that young lass, Lucy. That chef is a tyrant.'

'Penelope not surfaced yet?' Prisha asks.

'No. And who could blame her? I bumped into Whipple on the way out. He was hoping to procure a cup of soup for his missus. She's coughing her guts up in her room—I'm paraphrasing there. She has a cold. Then he gave me a brief history of why the Spanish flu died out.'

'He's a walking encyclopaedia, that man,' Frank says with a chuckle.

'He's a walking something,' Zac adds.

Frank places his coffee cup down, becoming serious. 'Okay. We've questioned everyone, yes?'

'Not quite,' Prisha replies. 'Mrs Whipple hasn't been done yet.'

'There's no way I'm going in there. Last thing I need is a bloody cold,' Zac says.

'Hmm...' Frank murmurs. 'Fair point. We'll see how she is tomorrow. Right, Prisha, you're the first cab off the rank. Start with the timelines of the suspects you quizzed then move onto anything of any note.'

Prisha picks up her writing pad. 'Timelines were much of a muchness, Frank. Everyone was in the drawing room after dinner apart from Lucy Hargreaves, Chef Antoine, and Penelope, who didn't join the gathering until around nine. People drifted to their rooms between 9:30 and 10:00, as we did. Long day. A shock death. Big meal. Plenty of alcohol. No power or comms. I guess everyone had the same idea—get tucked up in bed, sleep, and hope tomorrow everything's back to normal.'

Zac takes a sip of his coffee. 'Pretty much the same as what I got on the timelines, Frank.'

'Aye, and me too,' Frank says, grimacing as he scratches his neck.

Prisha flicks over a page. 'In reverse order. I questioned Dr Pierre Quint and his mother Edith. Nothing of note. She seemed a little confused—possibly early-stage dementia. He—the doctor—was polite, understanding, and offered his help if needed. Preceding them was the food critic, Imogen Sato. Again, nothing significant, apart from her mentioning that Virgil Langley was well on his way to being pissed during pre-dinner drinks and was quite rude to her. She thinks he still held a grudge over her negative review of Kindlewood Hall from last year.' She pauses to shuffle her papers, her brow furrowing briefly. 'Ah, yes. Now we get to the interesting one—Penelope Langley. Her behaviour was... odd. Before we started, she pulled out her lipstick and applied it. I'm not judging, but really? She admitted Virgil was a bit offbeat, but not once did she mention love, happiness, or even grief over her husband.'

'Remember the effects of shock,' Frank advises. 'We all process it differently.'

'Yes, I know. I'm just saying.' She glances back at her notes. 'Which brings me to Lucy Hargreaves. At first, she seemed reticent, but once I put her at ease, she painted a picture of barely contained chaos in the hotel—mainly down to Virgil's erratic behaviour. She admitted she's a little intimidated by Mrs Langley but said she's solid and runs a tight ship. As we discussed earlier, Lucy has little time for Chef Antoine.'

Frank turns to Zac. 'And you?'

Zac leans back in his chair, tapping his notes. 'Eve Sinclair is a freelance journalist from London. She's up here for a few days of solitude before the big family Christmas thing. Nothing noteworthy there. Chef Antoine was completely oblivious—or indifferent—to Virgil's death. Acted like it was some minor inconvenience. Didn't think much of Virgil, but they got along if Virgil didn't meddle in the kitchen, which is Antoine's sacred domain. He's very fond of Penelope Langley, though. A touch too fond, maybe.'

He glances at his notes again. 'Then there's Hugh Foster, the farmer. Now, take this with a pinch of salt—he outright claimed to know who killed Virgil.'

'What?' Prisha straightens up.

'Yeah. He accused Murdoch Langley. Said Murdoch's been eyeing up both Penelope and Kindlewood Hall for some time. Even insinuated they're having an affair.'

Frank frowns. 'And did he offer any evidence?'

Zac snorts softly. 'Not a shred. Just said, "I have eyes, I see things." He's full of bluster, but it's clear he doesn't actually know anything.'

'Interesting,' Frank says, glancing at his notes. 'Maggie Thornton had a few run-ins with Penelope. They sit on some committees together, and Maggie accused her of using her position as chairperson to unfairly promote Kindlewood Hall over other local businesses. Petty stuff, really. Typical of small rural communities like this.' He pauses, tapping his pen on the table. 'Then there's Logan Fitch. He was the Langleys' accountant for years and the one who figured out how Ethan Langley was ripping off his parents and bleeding the business dry. The fallout came when Logan insisted they report it to the police and declare the lost income to the Inland Revenue. Safe to say, the Langleys weren't exactly thrilled with those options. But the interesting part is Murdoch Langley is about to invest one million into Kindlewood Hall for much needed interior refurbishments. Logan Fitch had recently patched things up with the Langleys and is acting as their accountant again. Virgil gave him Murdoch's business plan to scrutinise, and Logan didn't like the look of it one little bit. He thinks Murdoch has underestimated the costs. His theory is that during the works, the Langley's will run out of money, and Murdoch would call in the loan and they'd have to sell the business.'

Prisha lifts her cup of coffee to her lips. 'And Murdoch Langley would make a bid for the hotel?'

'Aye. That's the gist of it. Of course, this is all Logan Fitch's supposition—not fact.'

'And what about Murdoch Langley?' Zac asks.

Frank glances at his notes. 'Ah, yes, the high-flying investment banker—Murdoch Langley. According to him, he's the knight in shining armour come to save his brother and sister-in-law. He reckons the hotel is worth three to four million, and he intends to invest one million for a thirty per cent stake—which sounds reasonable. But it contradicts what Logan had to say. He reckons the hotel is worth way more, and that it isn't an investment—it's a loan that needs repaying. One of them is lying. So that's a follow up for you, Prisha—Penelope will know which version is correct.'

'Noted, boss,' she replies, jotting a reminder for herself.

Frank takes a long slurp of coffee. 'So, that's the first round of interviews done. Where does it leave us? Motives, opportunity, means. Why would someone want Virgil dead? Who had the opportunity to get in and out of his room unseen? And how did they do it—what was the weapon, and where the hell is it now?'

Prisha taps the pen against her lips. 'Revenge? Money?'

Frank nods. 'Yes, both top of my list, too. But if there was an argument that escalated out of control, someone should have heard something.'

'The way Virgil was found didn't indicate any kind of struggle,' Zac adds.

Prisha frowns. 'The position of the body was strange. Almost like he'd been made to kneel by his attacker.'

Frank rubs the back of his hand thoughtfully. 'Let's go back to basics. How did the attacker get into the room?'

Prisha cocks her head. 'Remember, the lights were off, but Virgil had a torch. The killer could have shadowed his movements along the corridor—unseen in the dark—and, with the wind howling and Virgil being so inebriated—unheard, too. It wouldn't have been hard to follow him inside.'

'Or,' Zac begins, 'they could've been waiting in the room for him. The open window might have been left as a deliberate distraction.'

Frank nods again, the theories swirling in his mind. 'It's possible. And let's not forget the master key. Who would've known about it, and who had access?'

Prisha scans her list of names. 'Obviously Penelope and Lucy. But I imagine Logan Fitch and Murdoch Langley would've been aware of it too.'

'And Chef Antoine,' Zac adds.

'And what about the son, Ethan Langley,' Frank queries.

Prisha wrinkles her nose. 'I'm not sure he fits into the picture, Frank. He's not here. And there's almost no chance he came to the hotel after dark last night in those conditions.'

'What if he didn't arrive last night?' Frank asks.

Prisha and Zac exchange a glance. 'What are you saying?' Prisha asks.

'What if he arrived a day or two ago? He'd know this place inside out. He could've snuck in and found somewhere to hide. The storm and blackout would've given him perfect cover to strike last night.'

Prisha isn't convinced. 'I told you what the conditions outside are like. If he'd killed Virgil and left, the snow would've been disturbed—it wasn't. Never mind the superhuman effort it'd take to wade through drifts like that.'

'What if he didn't leave?' Frank counters. He leans forward, resting his elbows on his knees. 'Look, whether it's Ethan Langley or some other intruder, we need to rule it out completely. No loose ends. We search every inch of this hotel and the outbuildings. If someone's hiding here, we'll find them.' He straightens up and starts issuing orders. 'Prisha, you take the upstairs rooms. I'll put my boots on and check outside. Zac, you take downstairs, including the cellar.'

Zac's eyes dart between Prisha and Frank. 'What cellar?' he asks warily.

Frank stares at him with mild disapproval. 'It's a Victorian-era building, Zac. Of course it has a cellar. They didn't have refrigerators back in those days—they needed somewhere cool to store food. This place will undoubtedly have a sprawling cellar. Give it a thorough once-over.'

Zac pales, clutching his coffee like a lifeline. 'By myself... after a grisly murder, with the power off? Are you serious, Frank?'

Prisha smirks. 'What's wrong, Zac? Afraid of the dark?'

'The dark, cobwebs, rats, damp... and, oh yeah, murderers who might still be lurking down there,' Zac fires back, his voice dripping with sarcasm.

Frank suppresses a grin. 'Just remember, Zac—no one's ever been killed by a spider web. You'll be fine.' He gives Zac a reassuring pat on the shoulder that feels more like a shove.

Zac mutters under his breath as he stands, his face twisted with distaste. 'Famous last words, boss. Famous last words.'

# 31

Having completed a thorough search of all the rooms, alcoves, and cupboards downstairs, Zac finishes his task in the kitchen, where Chef Antoine and Lucy are preparing the Christmas dinner. The rich aromas of roasted meats, herbs, and spices fill the air, stirring Zac's appetite.

'What time are you serving up?' he asks Lucy.

'Three o'clock,' she replies, peeling a mound of potatoes.

'Bit late for lunch, isn't it?'

'That's the idea. This way, we only have to cook once. Sandwiches will be on offer for supper.'

'Fair enough.' Zac wipes his hands on his trousers. 'Erm... does this place have a cellar? I didn't notice a door leading to one.'

Lucy glances at him, her brow glistening with a fine sheen of sweat as she wipes it with the back of her hand. 'It's outside,' she says. 'Go out the kitchen door, turn right, and you'll come across an old green door. That's the entrance.'

'Oh,' Zac says, less than enthused at the revelation. 'What's down there?'

'Junk, mostly. Virgil was a hoarder. Didn't like to get rid of anything—tables, chairs, old settees, tools, general bric-a-brac.' She pauses for a moment, then adds, 'It's cold and damp down there. Proper creepy.'

Zac frowns. 'Creepy?'

Lucy smirks faintly, her hands busy peeling potatoes. 'You'll see what I mean. It's one of those places that makes the hair on the back of your neck stand up. I don't go down there often, but when I do, it always gives me the heebie-jeebies.'

Zac raises an eyebrow. 'And why's that?'

Lucy hesitates, her knife hovering mid-air. 'Maggie Thornton told me once...' She glances at Antoine, as if gauging whether to continue. 'She reckons the cellar's haunted.'

'Oh, for God's sake,' Zac mutters, his nerves prickling already. 'A haunted cellar. Go on, let's hear it.'

Lucy drops her voice slightly, leaning in as if sharing a forbidden secret. 'Apparently, back in the 1820s, a child was... murdered down there.'

Zac freezes. 'What?'

'It's only a rumour, mind,' Lucy says quickly, waving the knife dismissively in the air. 'That's what Maggie said, though I don't know if it's true. It was long before the Langleys owned the place. The child was supposed to be the daughter of the original owners. No one knows the full story, but some say you can still hear her crying down there at night, calling for her mother.'

Chef Antoine, who has been silent up until now, lets out a theatrical groan. 'Oh, la la, toujours les histoires! It is nonsense, monsieur. A ridiculous tale for scaring children away from the cellar.'

Lucy shrugs but doesn't look entirely convinced herself. 'Maybe. But it's still creepy as hell down there. You'll see.'

Zac feels his stomach sink. 'Right. And... it's not locked?'

'No,' Lucy says, her voice light but matter of fact. 'I don't think it even has a lock. Too much junk to bother stealing.'

Chef Antoine chuckles darkly as he stirs a bubbling pot. 'Bon courage, monsieur. You'll need it.'

Zac mutters under his breath as he turns to leave the kitchen. 'Spiders, rats, damp... murder victims... and now ghosts. Brilliant, just bloody brilliant.'

Exiting the kitchen, Zac steps into the snow, his breath puffing into misty clouds that linger in the icy air. In the distance, he sees Frank disappearing into one of the many dilapidated sheds. Zac glances up, spotting a thin ribbon of blue on the horizon, the only crack in an otherwise leaden sky.

Skirting the rear of the hotel, he reaches the cellar door. Pulling out his torch, he flicks it on and directs the beam at the old green paint, flaked and peeling from years of exposure. He gives the door a push, but it holds fast. After a sharp kick, it groans open, revealing steep, uneven stone steps descending into blackness.

The torchlight cuts through the void but barely penetrates the shadows clinging to the damp walls. A musty, foetid smell rises to greet him, heavy with decay and the scent of the past. He hesitates for a moment, listening to the eerie silence, then starts his descent.

Each step is deliberate, his boots crunching softly on grit and dirt. The noises of the outside world fade away entirely, leaving an oppressive quiet that presses against his ears.

At the foot of the stairs, he casts the beam around the space, revealing the haphazard clutter of the forgotten and discarded. Old furniture looms in the half-light—a broken table missing a leg, a bicycle frame stripped of its wheels, two splintered wooden sledges. Tools lean crookedly against damp whitewashed walls—rusted shovels and rakes, their edges dulled by time. Three tea chests sag under the weight of yellowing linen and moth-eaten bedsheets.

The air is thick, almost claustrophobic, as the light picks out dark corners and shadowy passageways that snake off into a void. Grit shifts beneath his boots as he inches forward, his hand tightening on the torch. The silence feels watchful, alive, and Zac's pulse quickens with every step.

'Christ, it's a bloody labyrinth,' he mutters under his breath.

A shuffle, followed by a dull thump, sends his heart hammering against his ribs.

'Hello?' he calls out, the authority in his voice doing little to mask his rising unease. 'It's the police. Is anyone down here?'

A rustle. A creak.

He freezes, his torch beam darting to the side, picking out an old golf bag leaning against the wall. Without taking his eyes off the shadows, he slides out a putter, gripping it tightly in one hand.

'Hello? If anyone's here, make yourself known. I'm armed and dangerous.'

The sound comes again, closer this time. Too loud to be rats or mice.

His pulse thunders in his ears as he moves deeper into the passageway. The air feels colder here, heavier, like it's trying to suffocate him. Then, faint and warped by the stone walls, muted voices drift to him. Indecipherable. He stops dead, straining to listen, before realising with a shudder of relief—they're coming from above.

He looks up and exhales.

The kitchen.

He's directly beneath it. Somehow, it's a small comfort.

Reassured, he continues down the narrow passageway, the torch beam skittering across flaky whitewashed walls and dead stone glistening with wet. It leads him into another room, stark and empty—except for one thing.

The figure standing against the back wall.

Zac's breathing momentarily ceases.

*'Shit!' he whispers.*

A medieval suit of armour looms in the torchlight, its dull steel surface pitted with rust. It's utterly still, inanimate—but its presence in this cold, forgotten place is so out of place it sends a ripple of unease down his spine.

He notices for the first time that he's sweating, his shirt clinging uncomfortably to his back.

The noise again. But this time, different.

A wail. Mournful. Pitiful. Like a fearful cry for help.

He tries to swallow but can't.

To his eternal shame, his hands shake like he's suffering from the last throes of Parkinson's disease.

*'Get a grip.'*

The high-pitched wail comes again.

This time, he pinpoints it.

Not behind him.

Not to the side.

It's coming from dead ahead.

From the armour.

His throat tightens as he involuntarily performs kegels in rapid succession.

'Hello?' he croaks, his voice barely above a whisper now, any sense of authority long gone.

Step by step, inch by inch, he edges forward, the putter trembling violently in his grip.

He stops directly in front of the armour. Up close, he sees how small it is—built for a man far shorter than himself. The visor stares blankly back at him, its hollow gaze unyielding. It's nothing more than a relic, an elaborate metallic shell.

Then, movement.

Zac's eyes flick upward onto a ledge above him.

Something shifts—but it's too late.

A garbled scream pierces the silence, followed by the deafening crash of steel against stone.

The torch spins wildly across the cold flags, its beam circling in frantic arcs before finally coming to rest, pointing uselessly down the empty corridor.

# 32

Prisha steps into the room, as a wave of melancholia washes over her, a poignant reminder of life's fragility.

*Amy Holland—how old was she? Early thirties, perhaps. Around the same age as me. So much ahead of her. So much to give, to experience. Cut down before she could even fully bloom.*

Shivering at the thought, she's unable to imagine simply... not being here. Life feels like a constant—until it's not.

She wonders if Amy realised she was teetering on the edge of the abyss during those final moments. Poisoned, a fit, a seizure, an allergic reaction—whatever it was, it had been quick. Too quick, surely, for reflection. Death doesn't offer time for navel-gazing or bittersweet goodbyes. It doesn't let you mentally tick off items from a bucket list. It rushes in from the wings, blunt and unyielding.

Death is impatient. It has no room for sentiment.

Even though she'd searched the room only yesterday, Prisha knows if there is an intruder, what better place to hide than in the room of a dead woman? She notices again how unnervingly tidy it is, the sparseness of belongings.

'Some people travel light, I guess. But what happened to her purse? Her bank cards? Her ID?' she murmurs under her breath.

She checks the wardrobe, which is predictably empty, and crouches to look under the bed, finding nothing out of place. Moving to the bathroom, her search turns up the same spartan array of items as before: a solitary toothbrush, a travel-sized micro-tube of toothpaste. No personal toiletries. Only the generic ones provided by the hotel—body wash, shampoo, conditioner.

Re-entering the bedroom, her eyes fall on the interconnecting door. She hesitates, head tilting slightly as muted voices filter through the wood. Slowly, she crosses the room and tries the handle—it's locked.

Pressing her ear to the door, she strains to make out the whispers.

Soft. Indecipherable.

But the contrast is clear: the deeper timbre of a male voice, and the lighter, melodic tone of a woman.

---

Having checked all the other unoccupied rooms, there's one last area of the upstairs to inspect.

She knocks on the door, gently.

'Who is it?'

'It's DI Kumar, Mrs Langley.'

'Come in, inspector.'

Why hasn't she locked the bloody door? Prisha wonders as she pushes down on the handle and enters.

Penelope rises sluggishly from the settee, barefooted, and wobbles towards her.

Prisha perceives a different woman to the one she recently questioned. She's smaller without her shoes. Her commanding persona has evaporated. Stooped slightly. Wrinkles, usually hidden, have returned like unwelcome guests.

When interviewed earlier, she was a woman of authority, an attractive older woman. Now she reminds Prisha of her own mother—a once formidable figure—but now a genial older lady, her spirit somewhat diminished, succumbing to the inevitability of gravity and the relentless attack of life.

'Sorry to disturb you, Penelope. We've undertaken a search of the hotel in case an intruder entered.'

Puzzled, she replies. 'An intruder? That's absurd. Whoever killed my husband is known to one and all and is in this hotel.'

'We need to rule things out. We're simply being thorough. How are you feeling?'

Penelope places a hand on the back of the settee, as if to steady herself. 'I've taken some tablets and have managed to stave off a migraine but I'm feeling washed out, drained.'

'To be expected.'

'This whole thing is a nightmare. I feel trapped, as though this is no longer my home but a macabre prison. Who killed Virgil and why? And when will we regain power and communications?'

'The storm has passed, so the worst is over,' Prisha replies, sidestepping the first question.

'But we're stranded.'

'As I'm sure are many thousands of people, Mrs Langley.'

Penelope sighs and moves towards the kitchenette. 'I'm making a cup of tea. Would you care for one, inspector?'

'No, thank you. I wanted to see the layout of your living quarters. Do you mind if I have a look around?'

'No. Go for it.' Penelope flicks the kettle on and drops a teabag into a cup. 'How are Chef Antoine and Lucy getting on with the Christmas dinner?'

'From the aromas drifting from the kitchen, I'd say they're managing quite well.'

'They're both good workers,' she reflects. 'I'll have my tea then go and help them out. It's not fair they should have to carry the burden themselves.'

Prisha takes in the room. A small open-plan kitchenette that merges with a compact living room. Tastefully decorated, clean, tidy. She pushes open a side door to a bedroom containing a double bed, built in robes. A door slightly ajar leads to the en-suite bathroom.

'Nice and cosy, and easy to maintain,' Prisha remarks.

As steam billows from the kettle Penelope picks it up and pours bubbling water into the cup. 'Yes. It serves a purpose. When you run a hotel, there's not much downtime. Up early, finish late. I basically sleep here. The rest of the time I'm downstairs working.'

Prisha walks to the far wall and places her hand against the plasterboard partition. 'And next door is Virgil's bedroom, right?' she asks.

'That's right. Many years ago, this used to be the deluxe suite for guests. That wall wasn't there, so the area was a lot bigger. About ten years ago we decided to put in a second bedroom. Virgil was a terrible snorer.'

Prisha frowns. 'Why no adjoining door?'

Penelope half-smiles as she dunks the teabag. 'Oh, one of Virgil's faux pas,' she states, wistfully. 'We'd gone away for a fortnight break during the renovation work. Virgil had drawn up detailed plans, for the builder, of what he wanted doing. Unfortunately, he'd forgotten to sketch in the connecting door. When we returned this is how it was. We intended to get the builder back to remedy the situation, but we never did.'

Prisha taps a finger lightly on the wall wondering if now is a good time to press Penelope on a few things she wants to get clear in her mind. She scans the room hoping to see a family photo, but there are none. Not even of Virgil and Penelope together. Obviously not a sentimentalist, Prisha thinks.

'Penelope, what were yours and Virgil's future plans?'

Penelope takes a seat in an armchair opposite a large TV mounted on the wall. 'Another two years max, and we planned to retire.' She takes a sip of tea and wearily leans back in the chair. 'It's been a very difficult few years, inspector.'

Prisha takes a seat in on the couch at the side of her. 'Oh?'

'I'm sure you've heard some of the tittle tattle from the others.'

'I won't lie. Yes, we've heard about your son and the financial struggles you've been under.'

She briefly pouts and stiffens as if she's about to go on the defensive, but like a balloon with a slow leak she deflates just as quickly.

Her bosom heaves as she emits a deep sigh. 'I'm sixty-two, inspector. Virgil was sixty-three. We were married for forty-two years. Managed this hotel for thirty-five years. You'd think at our age things would have become easier, more comfortable. But they haven't. In fact, quite the opposite. What you've heard is probably true. Our son—Ethan, stole a considerable sum of money from us over the space of a few years. It left us financially strapped. We managed to pay our creditors and keep up with the overdraft, but it didn't leave a lot left over. We've always kept up with the maintenance on the exterior of the hotel, but the interior is badly in need of a makeover. Nothing major—new bathrooms, decor, fixture and fittings—that sort of thing. Still, with thirty rooms to update, it amounts to a lot of money.'

'I can imagine.'

'But recently we saw a way out of our predicament.'

'Your brother-in-law, Murdoch Langley?'

Penelope sips her tea and throws Prisha a desultory glance. 'Yes. I suppose he, or Logan Fitch, told you?'

Prisha nods but doesn't specify who.

'Murdoch is to invest in the hotel in return for a percentage of the ownership. We plan to close in February for three months while the renovations take place. Then in a year or so we'll put it on the market.'

'Was that always the plan?'

The question surprises her. 'No, not at all. We assumed Ethan would take over and Virgil and I would slowly wind down. But after what he did, we thought stuff him. We'll sell up and make damn sure we spend his inheritance. We envisaged a modest bungalow on the coast somewhere, and a lot of travel, cruises, luxury resorts, exotic train journeys. And now...' her voice trails off as she stares into the middle-distance.

Prisha allows her a moment of reflection. 'I assume this deal with Murdoch will be handled by your respective solicitors. It wasn't a shake of the hands?'

She blinks rapidly 'Yes. It's all above board. The solicitors said we should be ready to sign in the new year, after the Christmas break.' Her face creases in anguish. 'But that's all changed now. I'm not sure what will happen,' she adds sadly.

'Who else knew of your plans?'

'Me, Virgil, Murdoch, Logan Fitch and obviously the solicitors.'

'Anyone else?'

'No. Oh, hang on, yes, I may have mentioned it to Chef Antoine.'

'May have?'

'Yes. I'm pretty certain I did. He's a top chef, inspector, and doesn't come cheaply. We haven't been able to manage his wages for the last two months. He was threatening to leave which would be a catastrophe for us. I explained about the deal that's imminent, and that Murdoch had provided us with a cash injection to meet our ongoing financial obligations.'

'I see. And when did you inform him of this?'

'Earlier in the week. Monday, possibly Tuesday.'

Prisha rises. 'I've intruded enough. I'll leave you alone.' She pulls at the door. 'Penelope, have you heard from your son recently?'

She shakes her head. 'No. I've washed my hands of him,' she states with a certain amount of venom.

'Oh, one last thing—the money Murdoch is putting up—is it an investment or a loan?'

'It's an interest-free loan. Why?'

'No reason.' Prisha offers a sympathetic smile. 'Penelope, I think it wise, under the circumstances, you keep your door locked when alone. Just in case.'

Baffled by the advice, she says, 'Why? Wait, you don't think for one moment that someone would wish to kill me, do you?'

# 33

Prisha scoots down the stairs and bumps into Frank in the reception area.

'How'd you go?' he asks.

'All clear upstairs. No hidden lurkers. I had another chat with Penelope. Apparently, the investment deal involving Murdoch Langley is due to be signed off in early January—or at least it was. And it's an interest-free loan.'

Frank's bites his lip. 'Is it, indeed? Logan Fitch was right—Murdoch Langley can be frugal with the truth.'

The front door slams shut, jolting them both. A cat streaks down the hallway, tail high, with Zac following close behind, sporting a severe frown. The cat leaps gracefully onto the counter, hops down, and walks serenely into the back office without a trouble in the world... unlike Zac.

'Bastard cat,' he grumbles, trudging towards them.

Frank and Prisha grin at the sight of him. His clothes are smeared with dirt and grime, his hair dishevelled, and his expression one of deep annoyance.

'Had a little accident, have we?' Prisha asks, biting back a laugh.

Frank chuckles. 'You look like you've been dragged through a hedge backwards. How was the cellar?'

Zac glares, brushing at the dirt and whitewash clinging to his jacket. 'The cellar's fine. Thanks for asking. All clear,' he mutters.

'Come on then, what happened?' Prisha prompts.

He appears a little sheepish. 'There was a noise coming from a suit of armour. I went to investigate and as I neared, something caught my peripheral vision. I looked up and that mangy bloody cat leapt from a ledge onto the armour. Startled, I dropped my torch, and fell into the armour, bringing it down on top of me.'

Frank can't help but laugh. 'Sir Zachariah of Whitby, routed in battle by Puss in Boots, the fearsome feline knight of Kindlewood Hall.'

'Ha, ha, very funny—not. I take it you two didn't find anything?'

'Not a jot,' Frank says, becoming serious and checking his watch. 'Nearly time for the Christmas nosh-up. And not a moment too soon. I didn't have a bite of my breakfast. My stomach thinks my throat's been slashed.'

The last thing on Prisha's mind is food, but she knows she'll have to bide her time. 'Frank, after dinner I think we should all gather in the office and go over everything again.'

Frank is slightly distracted as his focus switches to Dr Quint and his mother, Edith, cautiously navigating the staircase, as they converse softly in French.

'Ah, inspector, how is your investigation progressing?' the old woman asks as she descends the final step. 'Have you caught the killer yet?'

'Mother, don't ask such questions,' the doctor hisses, his tone heavy with embarrassment.

Frank smiles. 'That's fine, doctor. As it happens, we are making good headway, Madame Quint.'

Edith leans in, and places a hand on Frank's shoulder, her voice brimming with curiosity. 'How did Virgil Langley die, inspector? A gunshot? A dagger to the heart? Strangulation? Or perhaps... poison?' She pauses, her lips curving faintly, as though relishing the drama of it all.

Prisha glances at the woman's wrinkled hand, a flicker of curiosity crossing her face.

'Mother, enough,' the doctor says, admonishing his mother, his face reddening. He turns to Frank with an apologetic sigh. 'Please excuse my mother, inspector. When people reach a certain age, they think they can say and do whatever they please without regard for propriety.' He offers Edith a firm look. 'Come along, Maman.'

Podger the cat reappears and brushes up against the back of Frank's legs as if announcing his hunger. It glances upwards and arches its back, fur erect, and hisses viciously at the doctor and his mother, then scampers off into the drawing room.

'Bloody queer cat,' Frank says, frowning as the Quints wander off, the doctor holding his mother's arm to steady her as they bicker back and forth in French.

---

The dining room is a feast for the senses, alive with the spirit of Christmas. The golden-brown turkey glistens as Chef Antoine carves the tender, succulent breast, the herb-scented juices pooling on the platter. The sweet tang of cranberry sauce mingles with the buttery aroma of roasted chestnuts and sage stuffing, while bowls of creamy mashed potatoes, flecked with chives, and honey-glazed parsnips send up delicate wisps of steam. The air hums with the soft clink of silverware and the faint crackle of the wood-burning stove, underscored by the gentle pop of a champagne cork—every sound and scent a promise of warmth, indulgence, and festive joy.

And yet, the festive scene feels jarringly inappropriate, a hollow celebration overshadowed by the brutal murder of Virgil Langley, and the untimely, mysterious death of Amy Holland.

Only four people attack the magnificent dinner with any gusto—Frank, Zac, Bennet Whipple, and Hugh Foster. The rest of the guests prod and poke at their food, their movements listless. Murder—and the knowledge that a potential killer possibly sits amongst them—has dulled their appetites.

Conversations bounce across the table, awkward and stilted, like the forced chatter of strangers on a long-haul flight. People try to get to know one another a little better, but their questions are shallow, perfunctory, the kind you'd hear in a job interview.

*Where are you from? What do you do? What are your interests?*

The three officers have deliberately spread themselves around the grand dining table, each positioned strategically, hoping to catch an unguarded word or subtle slip. They listen as forks scrape plates and fragmented conversations ebb and flow, but their expressions remain neutral, betraying none of their intent.

The truth is, they all know the chances of overhearing anything useful are slim to none. Whoever committed this crime didn't just kill—they killed with cunning intent. They've left no sign of entry, no clear means of escape, and no discernible clues in the locked room. A person capable of such subterfuge is unlikely to suddenly blurt out an incriminating morsel over turkey and stuffing.

Still, the officers listen. Because in a house like this, with tensions wound so tight, it doesn't take much for a crack to form.

Prisha is seated between Dr Whipple and Hugh Foster as they wolf their food. Both are extraordinarily large men, and she feels like a toothpick wedged between two sumo wrestlers. To make matters worse, neither are the daintiest of eaters. She's already noticed some by-product of their meal land on her plate. Whether from an overzealous fork or mouth, she can't be certain. It does nothing to bolster her appetite.

She recoils and throws Zac a—get me out of here—look.

Sympathetically, he grins and resumes his conversation with Maggie Thornton and Logan Fitch seated at the end of the table. Directly across from her are Pierre and Edith Quint who are reservedly quiet.

Whipple adjusts his napkin and leans slightly forward. 'I'm curious, Dr Quint. Where did you complete your medical training? One can often glean much about a practitioner from their alma mater.'

Dr Quint smiles, his fork pausing mid-air. But before he has a chance to answer, his mother replies, 'En France, naturellement.'

Whipple chuckles and nods. 'Indeed. I meant specifically, madame.'

Pierre dabs at his lips with a napkin. 'I studied at the Université Lumière in Lyon. A fine institution, highly regarded.'

Whipple's brows knit ever so slightly. 'Lumière, you say?' His tone remains polite, congenial. 'A fascinating and venerated university. Renowned for its contributions to the humanities, if I'm not much mistaken.'

Quint smiles politely. 'Very true. And they have a small but excellent medical faculty. Very specialised.'

Whipple nods slowly, his expression unreadable. 'I must confess, I wasn't aware of that development. Most enlightening.'

Prisha stifles a yawn as Dr Quint picks up his wine glass and takes a sip of red. 'And you, doctor? Where was your seat of learning?'

'Oxford,' Whipple replies without a hint of showmanship, chewing studiously on a buttery parsnip.

'Oxford indeed,' the doctor replies, suitably impressed. 'And your thesis?'

'The pathophysiology of rare ocular mycoses. A study of fungal infections in the posterior chamber of the eye and their systemic implications. A most fascinating subject.'

As a conversation stopper, it doesn't get much better.

Zac is not having a much better time of it, as he labours in polite conversation with Logan Fitch and Maggie Thornton.

'I can't really believe it,' Maggie says as she reluctantly pops a caramelised Brussel sprout into her mouth.

Logan Fitch stabs at a roasted potato, then waivers before lifting it from his plate. 'I know. It seems so surreal, doesn't it? Virgil has been a constant for, well, forever.'

'I feel bad,' Maggie declares.

Logan stares aghast at his plate. 'Good Lord! You don't mean the food, do you?'

Maggie glances sideways. 'No. I feel bad for Penelope. We've never seen eye to eye. That cannot be denied.'

Logan relaxes and laughs. 'You know what they say—two mistresses in the same house spells trouble.'

Maggie glares at him. 'What do you mean by that?' she hisses, clearly embarrassed. 'The rumours about me and Virgil were totally unwarranted and unfounded.'

Logan shrugs apologetically. 'I didn't mean... what I was alluding to, Maggie, is the fact you both run similar ventures in a small village and there's bound to be friction... occasionally.'

'You've always had a loose mouth, Logan,' she sniffs.

Hugh Foster momentarily stops shovelling food into his mouth and glances across the table.

'Logan, fancy a game of snooker after dinner?' he asks, his voice needlessly loud.

Logan hesitates, then smiles. 'Yes, why not? We need to do something to keep occupied.'

Frank is seated between Imogen Sato and Eve Sinclair. 'Your wife not joining us, Mr Finnegan?' Imogen asks.

'Unfortunately, not. She's started with a cold and a slight temperature, same as Mrs Whipple.'

'That's a shame,' she says, checking her phone for the umpteenth time.

'Still no reception?' Eve asks.

'No, this is getting ridiculous. Eighteen hours without power or internet. It's like living in the bloody Dark Ages.'

Eve takes a genteel sip of red wine. 'How long do you think this will go on for, Inspector Finnegan?'

'Hard to say. If the overhead power cables have snapped, it's not an easy fix. And in these conditions, access for repairs will be a nightmare.' He pauses, glancing at the window. 'Although, I was outside earlier, and it feels like it's starting to thaw.'

A loud clatter of cutlery on a plate draws every eye down the table to Murdoch Langley. Sitting alone, shoulders hunched, he stares at his untouched food, his face a tense mask of grief and barely restrained fury. He looks less like a mourning brother and more like the Ghost of Christmas Yet to Come—a silent, foreboding presence casting a shadow over the faux festivity around him. The hum of idle chatter and bursts of forced laughter might as well be nails hammered into his brother's coffin. Rising angrily from his seat, he throws his napkin down onto the table with such force it nearly topples his wine glass.

'I've had enough of this charade!' he bellows, spittle spraying in a cascade of tiny droplets. His angry voice curtails the gentle murmur of conversation, freezing the room into stunned silence. 'Look at you all! Sitting here, stuffing your faces, indulging in your trivial chit-chat!' He points a trembling finger towards the window, eyes blazing. 'My brother's body is decaying in a barn out there, and someone in this hotel murdered him!' His voice cracks, as his anger builds. 'And as far as I can see, none of you give a damn!' He swivels to glare at Frank, the veins in his temple pulsing. 'Why aren't you doing more, inspector?' he roars, his face flushed with rage.

Penelope rushes in from the kitchen, wiping her hands on her pinafore.

'Murdoch, sit down. You're understandably upset, but yelling at everyone won't bring Virgil back. The inspector and his team are doing everything they can.'

'Yes, it damn well looks like it,' he snaps, his voice dripping with scorn, before storming away from the table.

'Murdoch! Where are you going?' Penelope calls after him.

'Outside,' he growls. 'I can't sit around here on my backside while my brother's killer is on the loose—probably sitting at this very table.'

His words cut through the room like a knife, leaving an embarrassed silence in their wake. All eyes lower to plates, napkins, the tablecloth, as though avoiding the accusation hanging in the air. A moment later, the front door slams so violently, the noise shakes the glasses on the table.

Penelope stares blankly her composure threatening to crack. 'I'm so sorry about that,' she mumbles, her voice trembling as she dabs at the corners of her eyes with a tissue.

'No need to apologise, Penelope,' Frank says gently, his tone carrying the weight of unspoken empathy. 'The situation is grim for all of us. But for you and Murdoch, I can only imagine how unbearable it must be.'

Before Penelope can respond, Lucy bursts into the room, her face flushed and her eyes wide with excitement.

'It's on, it's on!' she shouts, practically tripping over herself in her rush. 'The power's back on!'

The mood shifts instantly. Guests exchange looks of astonishment before a collective cheer erupts around the table. The soft radiance of overhead lights stutter to life, as the room seems to breathe again, bathed in the familiar glow of electricity. The faint hum of the refrigerator motor kicks in from the kitchen, a mundane sound that feels almost miraculous.

Penelope clutches the edge of the table, relief flooding her face as the atmosphere lifts, if only temporarily. But as Frank watches the jubilant scene unfold, his eyes flick towards the window and the carpark where Murdoch Langley, shovel in hand, attacks the thick cushion of snow with barely restrained violence.

# 34

Prisha sits in the back office behind reception, hunched over the desk, her pencil moving briskly across the notepad. The faint scratch of lead on paper fills the quiet room as she jots down her scattered thoughts.

*Who killed Virgil?*

*Murder weapon?*

*How did they get into the room? Followed him in? Master key? Definitely not through the window!*

*More importantly—how did they leave when the chain was on? (Doesn't add up.)*

*Who has a motive? Penny Langley? Murdoch Langley? Logan Fitch? Lucy, Chef Antoine? (disgruntled staff)*

*Someone else entirely?*

She underlines *"chain was on"* twice, then taps the pencil against her lips. The question looms, stubborn and unresolved, defying logic.

To her left, a corkboard dominates the wall. Pinned to it are two A3-sized floor plans of Kindlewood Hall. The top plan maps the ground floor—entrance, hallway, reception, office, drawing room, billiard room, library, dining hall, kitchen, pool area. Below it, the top floor layout stares back at her, marked with thirty numbered guest bedrooms, and the Langley's private residence.

She swivels slightly in her chair, the pencil now drumming against the desk, her gaze fixed on the plans. 'No adjoining door. No loft hatch. No obvious way in or out,' she mutters under her breath. Her eyes trace the hallway leading to Virgil's room.

'How do you vanish into thin air?' she whispers, a mix of irritation and intrigue in her voice

Something stirs—an itch at the back of her mind she can't quite reach. She leans closer, the pencil still in her hand, as though waiting to scrawl the answer she hasn't yet found.

'Hmm... interesting,' she murmurs, her curiosity igniting.

She pulls the pins free, takes the two plans down, and lays them side by side on the desk. Grabbing the top floor plan, she carefully aligns it over the ground floor. With a flashlight from the desk drawer, she holds the torch close, illuminating the faint outlines beneath.

Slowly, shapes emerge.

Her lips tighten, her finger following a path on the paper as she ponders. 'The kitchen is directly below the Langley's residence. The rear of the kitchen, exactly beneath Virgil Langley's bedroom.'

The sound of Frank and Zac's banter drifts from the reception area, breaking her concentration. She pins the plans back on the board and drops the torch into the drawer—but not before her gaze catches on something else. A carefully folded piece of newspaper sits in the corner of the drawer, as though purposefully tucked away. She hesitates, then removes it, unfolding it with care. It's a photograph of a man, completely bald, maybe mid-thirties, pictured standing on the entrance steps of the hotel, smiling proudly. The snippet has been expertly cut out, but there is no adjoining article, no context, no explanation.

Her brow furrows as she stares at it, turning it over as if the reverse might reveal some hidden answer. But the back is a disjointed piece about gardening. Folding it into quarters, she slips it into her back pocket, her interest aroused as she steps into the reception to meet Frank and Zac.

'That chef may be a surly sod, but he can certainly cook,' Zac says, patting his stomach.

'He can that. I shouldn't have had two helpings of plum pudding though,' Frank replies, grimacing slightly.

'I've been making some notes,' Prisha interjects, hoping to redirect her colleagues' thoughts back onto the murder investigation. 'I've come across some oddities.'

'Oh, aye. Such as?' Frank asks, hands on hips.

'For starters, Amy...' She pauses abruptly as Logan Fitch and Hugh Foster saunter into the reception.

'How about we make it interesting, Logan?' Hugh asks in his booming, broad Yorkshire accent.

'In what way, Hugh?'

'What about a fiver a game?'

Logan laughs. 'I don't think so. I'm an accountant, not a rich farmer like some.'

'That's the pot calling the kettle. It's you buggers who are the rich ones,' he replies with a raucous guffaw.

Logan nods sagely. 'I tell you what—best of three for a tenner?'

'Okay. You're on,' Hugh replies, spitting on his hand and offering it to Logan.

The three officers watch until the men disappear into the drawing room, turning towards the billiard room.

'You were saying, Prisha?' Frank prompts.

Prisha glances sideways as she spots Lucy heading their way. 'Let's talk in the office, where it's private.'

# 35

Logan places the assorted coloured balls on their allotted spots, while Hugh racks the reds into the triangle.

'So, Logan, who do you think did it?' Hugh asks, voice lowered.

'The murder of Virgil?'

'Who else.'

'Not sure. I can't imagine anyone here wanting to harm Virgil.'

'Really?' Hugh replies with an air of incredulity, as he stares at the gap in the rack of balls. 'What about Murdoch?'

Logan carefully sets the blue ball on the centre mark. 'Why in heaven's name would Murdoch want to kill his brother?'

'Isn't it obvious?' Hugh says, slowly circling the table, checking the pockets for the missing red balls.

'Not to me.'

'You're telling me you've never noticed how he looks at Penelope, and how she looks at him?'

Logan laughs nervously. 'Don't be ridiculous.'

Hugh frowns, pursing his lips. 'Two red balls missing,' he mutters, scanning the room, his eyes lingering on the darker corners where the light doesn't quite reach. 'It would make sense if you think about it.'

Logan double-checks the pockets, becoming irritated at the amateur sleuth. 'What would make sense?'

'Penelope, she's a bonny-looking woman, and this place would be worth a bob or two. With Virgil out of the way, he gets both.'

Logan straightens, spinning the cue ball absentmindedly in his hand. 'The balls definitely aren't here. I'll check at reception. Maybe Lucy's seen them.'

'I'll go,' Hugh replies quickly. 'You chalk the cues and reset the scoreboard.'

Hugh ambles into reception and spots Lucy with her head down behind the counter.

'Ah, Lucy. Two red balls are missing. You haven't seen them, have you?'

She glances up, a nuance of annoyance crossing her face. 'No, I haven't?'

Hugh sucks in air. 'Hmm... You don't think Virgil would have put them in his office for whatever reason, do you?'

'I doubt it, but I'll check,' she replies, hiding her impatience.

As Hugh leans against the reception counter, a shapeless shadow gambols across the drawing room walls, its movement soft and fleeting, like the restless dance of firelight from the open hearth.

Lucy taps on the office door and pokes her head inside, where the three officers are huddled over Prisha's notes.

'Sorry to bother you. I need a quick look in the desk drawers.'

'Go ahead,' Frank says, barely glancing up as Prisha flips her notepad over.

Lucy rifles through the drawers, muttering under her breath, before retreating quietly and shutting the door behind her.

'Sorry, Hugh,' she says as she re-enters reception. 'I can't find them.'

Hugh shrugs and shakes his head as he wanders off. 'Oh, well. We'll have to play with two balls missing.'

Lucy plugs her phone into the charger, watching the faint battery icon flicker weakly on the screen. She taps the network connection, her finger impatient.

'Come on, come on,' she mutters under her breath, willing the stubborn device to work. But the signal stays dead.

Pausing, she cocks her head, catching faint murmurs coming from the office. Her brow creases as she strains to make sense of the muffled voices. Then, a sudden, bellowing shout erupts from the drawing room, cutting through the peace like a jagged, rusty blade.

*'He's dead! He's dead!'*

Lucy jumps to her feet, heart racing, as Hugh sprints into the reception. His face pale, eyes wide with terror.

The office door flies open as the officers rush out. Their expressions sharp with urgency.

'Who's dead?' Frank demands, his voice a thunderclap.

Hugh Foster stumbles forwards, his trembling hand gripping the edge of the counter for balance.

His voice quavers as he gasps, 'Logan... Logan Fitch is dead!'

# 36

The viscous blood flows from an unseen head wound, pooling in a brilliant crimson contrast to the deep green baize covering of the table. The bright overhead snooker lights are reflected in the liquid as it oozes forward, encircling the blue ball before edging towards the centre-left pocket. Logan Fitch is slumped over the table, face down, his torso sprawled across the triangle of reds. A snooker cue lies along the right-hand cushion, and beside it, a black hiking sock with two distinctive bulges.

Frank crouches and places two fingers on Logan's jugular. Straightening, he glances at the small crowd gathering in the doorway.

He shakes his head. 'Dead.'

Gasps burble through the group as Penelope pushes her way forward.

'What's happened?' she cries. Her eyes widen at the sight of Logan's body. Clasping a hand over her mouth, she wobbles, looking ready to faint.

'Zac, get everyone back into the dining room and take a headcount,' Frank orders sharply. 'Not you, Mr Foster. I want a word.'

Zac begins ushering the stunned guests, along with Lucy and Penelope, away from the room. Meanwhile, Prisha steps forward, pulling her phone and a pair of latex gloves from her jacket pocket. Slipping the gloves on, she takes photos of the scene, capturing every detail—the pooling blood, the discarded sock, the snooker balls frozen in their positions.

Frank turns to Hugh, who is visibly shaking. 'So, what happened, Mr Foster?'

'I... I don't know,' he stammers. 'We were setting the balls up and noticed two were missing. I went to the reception and asked Lucy if she'd seen them. She said she hadn't. I suggested they may be in Virgil's office. She checked, and they weren't there. I came back to the billiard room and there he was. I wondered what the hell he was playing at, then I saw the blood.'

'Did you check to see if there was a pulse?'

'No.'

'Did you touch the body at all?'

'No.'

'In the reception, you said he was dead.'

'That's right.'

'But if you didn't check for a pulse, how did you know he was dead?'

'I... well, it's bloody obvious!' he yells, pointing at the body.

After taking photos of the sock from numerous angles, Prisha lifts it up and carefully dislodges the contents—two red snooker balls.

'And here's the murder weapon,' she says, taking more photos.

Frank nods in agreement. 'Looks like it. Mr Foster, wait in the dining room with the other guests, please. Prisha, fetch Dr Whipple.'

---

Whipple adjusts the cling film precariously wrapped around his gleaming bald head, the improvised covering catching the snooker lights. He leans over Logan Fitch's collapsed form with a faint grunt of exertion.

'Chief Inspector Finnegan,' he begins, his voice a soothing rumble, 'though one lacks the customary accoutrements of my esteemed profession, certain observations may yet be made.' He gestures towards Logan's head. 'Firstly, note the profuse cranial trauma. The laceration above the right parietal region is not jagged, but rather exhibits a clean indentation—a hallmark of blunt force impact, likely administered by a dense and rounded object.'

Frank tilts his head to get a better look. 'The snooker balls?'

'Indubitably. And their placement in that sock,' Whipple points delicately with a gloved hand to the black hiking sock and the two red balls lined up alongside, 'would amplify the force exponentially, creating a most devastating instrument of death. One might liken it to the medieval flail in its efficacy and efficiency. A barbaric yet ingeniously effective means of inflicting grievous harm.'

'And the cause of death?' Prisha interjects, her notepad at the ready.

'The fatal blow appears to have ruptured the middle meningeal artery—hence the copious haemorrhaging.' Whipple sweeps a hand towards the blood, slowly congealing on the baize and dripping onto the floor through the centre pockets. 'This would have resulted in a catastrophic intracranial bleed, leading to an almost instantaneous demise. Alas, Mr Fitch's final moments would have been swift, albeit unremittingly unpleasant.'

Frank shifts uncomfortably. 'And his position?'

'Indicative of a sudden collapse. Note the angle of his torso over the table—a loss of motor control coinciding with the injury. He likely fell forward the moment he was struck.

Observe also the blood splatter pattern, inspector, faint as it is. It suggests he was struck from behind, whilst standing in this very spot.'

Frank scratches his chin. 'So, the killer was behind him or slightly to the side as he stood at the table?'

'Unequivocally. A calculated blow requiring proximity, strength, and precision. The weapon, if I may call this ghastly contrivance such, was wielded with deliberate intent and considerable force.'

'And he was struck just the once?' Prisha asks.

'Yes.'

Prisha frowns, gesturing towards the sock and the balls. 'Given the level of force involved, are we looking at someone with significant physical strength?'

Whipple adjusts his gloves, regarding her with his usual air of impatience and superiority. 'Not necessarily, Inspector Kumar. The sock, you see, serves as a rudimentary sling. The mass of the snooker balls within stretches the fabric, creating potential energy upon the upswing, which converts to kinetic energy upon impact. The mechanics are quite efficient, requiring less brute strength than one might assume. Thus, the perpetrator could plausibly be a man—or indeed, a person of the fairer sex.' He carefully removes his gloves and shoots Frank a clouded glance. 'For once, inspector, I assume you do not require me to furnish you with the time of death?'

'Not this time, Bennet,' he says, checking his watch. 'Logan Fitch died approximately ten minutes ago. Can't get much more accurate than that.'

# 37

With another body despatched to the makeshift mortuary in the barn, this time wrapped in three white sheets and tightly bound, Frank, Prisha and Zac reconvene in the hush of the library.

Frank rubs nervously over his stubble. 'Christ, by the end of this, we'll be in the running for the Guinness Book of World Records for festive fatalities.'

Zac smiles. 'I can see the headlines now, Frank—Black Christmas Massacre at Kindlewood Hall.'

Prisha studies her notepad. 'Let's start ruling people out,' she says, pulling the top off her pen. 'Logan Fitch can come off the list as the potential killer of Virgil Langley.' She strikes a line through his name.

Frank gazes around the room. 'Okay, let's step back in time. When we left the dining room, Zac, we were the last ones there apart from Hugh Foster and Logan Fitch.'

'That's right. Penelope and Antoine were in the kitchen, clearing up. Although, when I questioned her a moment ago, she said Chef Antoine did take the bins out and was gone about ten minutes. She said he had a smoke as she could smell it on his breath when he returned to the kitchen.'

'And where are the bins?'

'Out the back, round the corner on the south side.'

Prisha taps her pen on her notepad. 'And Lucy was on reception, so there's no way she could have done it.'

'Hmm... looks that way,' Frank says. 'And Murdoch Langley?'

Zac takes a sharp intake of breath. 'Still outside shovelling snow away in the carpark. Or so he said. No one can specifically remember seeing him there.'

'Come on. Follow me,' Frank commands. He leads the way from the library into the pool area and stands next to the sliding glass doors. Crouching, he rubs a finger on the ground. 'Wet. And I doubt any bugger's been swimming,' he states. 'We have two scenarios. Someone was waiting in the library. Once they saw Hugh Foster head to reception, they snuck into the billiard room and clobbered Logan in the head, then headed back to the library. When the commotion started and people raced to see what was happening, they could have easily mingled in with the crowd. Alternatively, someone could have already been outside and entered through the pool doors and left the same way.'

'Which in theory would put Murdoch Langley and Chef Antoine in the picture,' Zac says. 'They had the opportunity.'

'So did Penelope,' Frank counters.

'How?'

'If Antoine was having a gasper around the corner, she could have sneaked out and come round the back and into the pool area.'

Zac's face doesn't show much belief in the theory. 'Bit of a stretch, Frank.'

'Aye, it is. But let's not rule it out. What about the others?'

'They all said they were in their rooms until they heard shouting.'

Prisha pulls open the doors and steps outside. 'There are footprints leading from both sides, Frank. But we are overlooking the most obvious solution.'

'What?'                                                    '

'Hugh Foster. He could have killed Logan before he even came to reception. Possibly using the missing snooker balls as a tactic to present himself in public.'

'Possible,' Frank muses. 'But where's his motive?'

She shrugs. 'It's highly improbable he killed Virgil over a septic tank dispute, but not impossible. As for Logan—well, he was Foster's accountant. Maybe there were dodgy financial dealings tied to the farm, and Logan was onto him.

And did you notice how loudly Hugh Foster asked Logan for a game of snooker during dinner?'

Frank nods thoughtfully. 'If everyone knew where Logan was going to be, then technically anyone could've done it. It's like he was broadcasting the plan.'

Prisha leans forward, using her pen as a baton. 'And you said they were the last to leave the dining room, right? That means Hugh's little announcement gave anyone enough time to slip away and position themselves in the library before Logan and Foster arrived.'

Frank rubs his chin. 'You think Hugh was signalling? Laying the groundwork to muddy the waters?'

Prisha tilts her head. 'It's possible. If he's our killer, it's clever. By creating a scene where Logan's movements were public knowledge, he ensures suspicion could fall upon anyone else who knew the plan. It's classic misdirection.'

'But it could also mean he's innocent,' Frank counters. 'If he's genuinely planning a snooker game, all this could be pure happenstance.'

'Could be,' she admits, noting he didn't use the word coincidence. 'But it's something to watch. Hugh might be a lot more calculating than he looks.'

Zac interjects. 'And let's not forget how keen he was to point the finger at Murdoch Langley. Just because we don't know his motive at the moment, it doesn't mean he doesn't have one.'

'He has a point, Frank,' Prisha adds. 'Sometimes, as detectives, we can become too hung up on motive. Think of all the thrill kills throughout history—Peter Sutcliffe, Ted Bundy, Dennis Nilsen, even Jack the Ripper. No apparent motive apart from the sheer thrill of killing. If you rule out motive, then all you're left with is opportunity and means.'

Frank emits a low growl. 'True. I did notice something in your random selection of serial killers, Prisha. Probably unwittingly made.'

She raises an eyebrow. 'What?'

'They're all male. And if you're right, that the killer does it for thrills, it opens up a deeply troubling possibility,' he says, his voice dropping.

'I know,' Prisha replies, a chill prickling her spine. 'If there is no motive, then none of us are safe. The next victim could be anyone of us. Which raises another prospect.'

'What?'

'Amy Holland—what if her death wasn't a medical episode? What if she was the killer's first victim?'

Frank's eyes narrow, scanning the horizon and the bleak midwinter setting. 'If correct, it means the killer isn't only unpredictable—they're actively out hunting.'

The weight of his words linger as an icy blast rolls off the hills, the silence punctuated only by the distant howl of the wind—an ill wind that carries no good.

# 38

Prisha pulls the door shut to her bedroom and strolls down the corridor. On the landing, at the top of the stairs, she throws a glance out of the floor-to-ceiling window overlooking the front of the hotel and pauses.

Near the broken entrance gate, Murdoch Langley leans heavily on a shovel. Two thin tramlines, about a car's tyre width, cut through the snow from the hotel to the gate. Opposite him stands Penelope Langley, unmistakable in her long overcoat, scarf, and woolly hat. Her erect, proud frame illuminated by the Victorian gas lamps.

Prisha, intrigued, takes a step nearer to the glass, watching intently.

The two are deep in conversation—too distant to catch their words or expressions, but close enough to read the tension in their body language.

Murdoch faces the hotel, his breath fogging the air, while Penelope has her back to it.

He lets the shovel fall to the ground and rubs his head furiously, then spreads his arms wide, imploring. Penelope seems to reply with something sharp—Murdoch spins away violently, only to circle back and face her again. His demeanour softens, his hands gesturing with what looks like an appeal for understanding—or forgiveness.

Penelope responds with a dismissive motion before abruptly turning on her heels and striding back towards the hotel. Murdoch hesitates, hovering as if stunned, then suddenly rips the woollen hat from his head and hurls it into the snow. His breath bursts out like a geyser in the cold air as he stands there, motionless.

Prisha murmurs to herself, 'What's all that about?'

She positions herself at the top of the stairs, listening intently. When the front door bangs shut, she times her descent perfectly, brushing past Penelope as she enters the reception area.

'Oh, Penelope. Sorry about that. How are you coping?' she asks, feigning a casual tone.

Penelope's expression is resolute. 'I'm fine, inspector.'

She tries to sidestep, but Prisha shifts slightly to block her path. 'I couldn't help but notice your conversation with Murdoch from the landing window. It seemed a little... intense. Do you mind if I ask what it was about?'

Twenty-four hours ago, Penelope Langley would have baulked at such impudence with a sharp rebuke. For a moment, Prisha braces for it. Penelope's face is proud, in control—attractive but hard. But then, unexpectedly, it softens. Her gaze falls, like the wind has been knocked out of her sails.

Slowly, she removes her scarf and hat, sighing. 'We were discussing the deal,' she says reluctantly. 'Murdoch's investment in the hotel.'

Prisha raises an eyebrow, allowing the pause to loiter before asking, 'Oh? What about it?'

Penelope exhales. 'I was thinking earlier. I don't require Murdoch's investment anymore.'

Prisha frowns. 'How come?'

Penelope hesitates, then answers. 'Because Virgil and I both have joint life insurance policies—specifically accidental death insurance, which includes death by murder or manslaughter. It's quite substantial. More than Murdoch was proposing to invest for one-third of the business.'

'And you told Murdoch—thanks, but no thanks?'

'Yes. It makes sense, doesn't it?' Penelope looks at Prisha, almost as if seeking validation.

Prisha pauses, considering her words carefully. 'On the surface, yes. But I'd strongly advise you to consult a lawyer with the right expertise.'

Penelope nods meekly. 'Yes, of course.'

'How did Murdoch react to the news?'

Penelope's cheeks tighten, dimples forming as she suppresses a grimace. 'Less than impressed. But his ego and his plans are secondary to what's best for me now.'

'Was he angry?'

'Yes. Very. But he'll calm down soon enough. He always does.'

Prisha hesitates, her eyes sweeping the empty reception area. She steps closer to Penelope and lowers her voice.

'Mrs Langley, I hate to ask this, but... were you having an affair with Murdoch?'

Penelope's eyes widen briefly before weariness washes over her again. On a different day, Prisha is sure she would have received a fierce tongue-lashing for such a question.

'No. I wasn't,' Penelope replies, then falters. 'But... in the past, there was a slight... dalliance.'

Prisha raises an eyebrow. 'A dalliance?' Her mind races. What constitutes a dalliance—a kiss, a snog, a handjob, a blowjob, or full on recurring sexual intercourse.

'Yes, a dalliance,' Penelope repeats, offering clarification.

'When was this?'

Penelope shrugs. 'A while ago.'

The vagueness frustrates Prisha, but she presses on. 'And who broke it off?'

Penelope straightens, her voice firm but reflective. 'We both did. It was mutual. I could have been happy with Murdoch, but it wasn't meant to be. He's wealthy, handsome, charming, and drinks only in moderation. But... I still loved Virgil.'

Prisha senses something left unsaid. 'Not in the traditional sense, though?'

Penelope sighs, visibly weary. 'No. More like brother and sister. We stopped being intimate years ago.' She flushes slightly, lowering her voice. 'Virgil... wasn't active. Down south.'

Prisha blinks for a moment, thrown, until she deciphers the meaning. 'Ah. I see. You mean in the trouser department?'

'Yes.' Penelope's tone shifts, growing stern. 'But when I make a decision, I stand by it. I married Virgil, and come hell or high water, I was going to see the marriage through to the end.' She lifts her chin. 'As my heroine, Margaret Thatcher, once said: this lady is not for turning.'

Prisha ignores the mention of Thatcher, only vaguely knowing who she is. 'I see.'

Penelope exhales, her voice softer now. 'There are two types of people in this world, inspector: those who act by heart, and those who act by head. I act by head. The liaison with Murdoch was... unfortunate. But I knew it wasn't to be. Scandal would have followed, and I couldn't have broken Virgil's heart or caused a family rift. My head ruled the day and thank God it did. That is not to disparage those who follow their heart. Each to their own.'

Prisha knows she's not going to glean any more information and stands aside.

Penelope gathers herself, her exhaustion clear. 'Now, if you'll excuse me, I'll retire to my room to freshen up. Then I'll return downstairs to mingle with the guests.'

# 39

The guests are scattered between the dining room, where sandwiches, snacks, and drinks from the bar can be ordered, and the drawing room, where the glorious wood fire crinkles and pops, radiating warmth. Gentle carols play in the background, blending with the faint ticking of the grandfather clock.

Prisha is in the dining room, hunched over her notepad, doodling abstract shapes as if deep in thought. But her real focus lies elsewhere. She glances towards the kitchen every few seconds, her eyes narrowing as she tracks the movements behind the swinging door.

'Come on,' she mutters under her breath. 'You must need a pee or smoke at some point.'

Her gaze shifts briefly to the bar, where a handful of guests wait impatiently for service.

———◦———

In the drawing room, Frank is sitting in one of the oversized armchairs, its deep cushions swallowing him whole. Beside him, Penelope Langley mirrors his position, both staring glassy-eyed into the flickering orange and red hues of the fireplace.

Lucy enters, balancing a silver salver in one hand, two drinks carefully placed upon it. The soft clink of glass pulls Frank from his daze, and he glances up as she approaches.

'Here you are, Mr Finnegan. A double whisky on ice,' she says, setting the tumbler down on the small table between the armchairs.

'Thank you, Lucy.'

Lucy turns to Penelope. 'And for you, ma'am, a gin and tonic with ice.' She lifts the second drink from the tray and offers it with a polite smile.

Penelope snaps from her reverie, her head tilting sharply towards Lucy as her expression hardens. 'For heaven's sake, Lucy. Where's the lemon?'

Lucy hesitates and places the drink back down on the tray, her mouth tightening slightly. 'You didn't ask for lemon, ma'am.'

'Didn't ask for lemon?' Penelope's voice rises, her tone laced with disdain. 'How many gin and tonics have you made me? Hundreds? And I always have a slice of lemon with it.'

Frank shifts uncomfortably, his eyes darting between the two women.

Lucy bites her lip, her cheeks flushing. 'Very good, ma'am. I'll get you a slice of lemon.'

Without waiting for a response, she pivots sharply on her heel and marches from the room, the salver trembling, shaking liquid in the glass. Penelope mutters something under her breath, as Frank picks up his drink and takes a gentle nip.

'I always find with my officers that patience and encouragement are better tutors than the iron rod,' he reflects softly.

---

Lucy bangs the tray down behind the bar, a few stray drops of liquid splashing onto the counter. She exhales sharply, brushing her hair back from her face.

Dr Quint leans forward, his tone polite but insistent. 'When you have a moment, Lucy, could I get a dry sherry for Madame Quint and a neat Cognac for myself?'

Lucy nods, her reply crisp but courteous. 'Yes, of course.'

Before she can move, Maggie Thornton steps up to the bar, a cheery grin plastered across her round face. 'And Lucy,' she chirps, 'could I have a snowball? Advocaat and lemonade, please.'

Lucy's smile constricts slightly. 'Yes. I'll be with you as soon as I can.'

The front door slams, the sound rattling the wine glasses hanging above the bar. Hugh Foster strides in, unwinding his scarf as he calls out. 'I'll have a bottle of Carlsberg and a double whisky chaser, Lucy. It's been one of those days.'

Lucy's jaw stiffens, but she forces a polite smile. If you could read faces perfectly, you might detect the sharpness in her expression—daggers hidden behind civility.

'Of course,' she says, her voice light but clipped.

Turning, Lucy pushes through the swinging door into the kitchen, the movement watched from close range by Prisha, who is waiting patiently for her moment.

Inside the kitchen, Chef Antoine is busily assembling an array of sandwiches and snacks. A platter of carefully arranged finger food sits half-finished on the counter, the air thick with the scent of butter and fresh bread.

'I am over this place,' he grumbles, his hands moving briskly as he works. 'I intend to return to France at the earliest opportunity.'

Lucy's head jerks towards him, her voice snapping like a whip. 'Really? Running away from something, are you?' Her gaze darts around the kitchen, wild with frustration. 'Lemons, where are the damn lemons?'

Antoine glances at her, puzzled. 'Un citron?' he asks innocently, his brow arching.

'Yes! A bloody lemon. They're yellow and grow from trees. Sour—like your expression,' she snarls.

Antoine gestures towards a shelf near the back. 'Là, là-bas, le fichu citron, le dernier!'

Lucy spins around, her gaze locking on the lone lemon perched on a shelf. 'Why don't you speak bloody English? It's like playing charades with you!' She storms across the kitchen, snatching the lemon, a knife, and a chopping board. Her movements are sharp, almost violent, as she slices the lemon into rounds, then swiftly cuts them in half.

Antoine wipes his hands on his pinafore, his lip curling in disdain. 'You make me sick,' he spits, pulling a packet of cigarettes from his pocket and storming towards the back door.

Lucy scoops the slices onto a plate and rushes back to the bar, dropping one slice into Penelope's drink with a slight splash.

Maggie Thornton watches her with a raised brow. 'You seem a little flustered, dear,' she notes, her tone tinged with both concern and curiosity.

Lucy straightens, smoothing down her jacket. 'I apologise,' she says tersely. 'But it's been very trying. I'm tired and run off my feet.'

Maggie hums sympathetically but says nothing more.

Through the half-round glass in the kitchen door, Prisha catches sight of Chef Antoine outside, standing under the weak glow of a security light. The faint ember of his cigarette flares briefly before vanishing into the darkness. Prisha takes her chance and silently slips into the kitchen as the clamour at the bar continues. Her gaze sweeps the counters, shelves, and cupboards. She pulls the floorplan from her back pocket.

Back in the bar, the guests reorder their drinks, their idle chatter filling the air. Lucy places a sherry on the counter alongside the gin and tonic.

'Neat cognac, wasn't it, Dr Quint?'

'Oui.'

'Come on, Lucy love. A double whisky and a bottle of Carlsberg when you've got a minute,' Hugh Foster repeats impatiently.

Lucy glowers at him but it goes unnoticed.

Maggie Thornton nudges Hugh aside, 'I was before you. Wait your turn, Hugh.'

Imogen and Eve now enter the fray.

'You see what I mean?' Eve whispers. 'This is typical of the service industry. That poor girl is run ragged. She's supposed to be front of house, that's what her job description says. And today she's prepped food, served at the table, and now she's the barman and waiter all rolled into one. And they don't pay her double time on a Sunday. She gets time and a half after 6:30. It's exploitation.'

'Yes, I see what you mean,' Imogen replies slinking up to the side of Dr Quint.

'I'm going to write a book about my weekend at this place,' Eve adds with a light chuckle. 'What are you having?'

'Oh, a glass of Chardonnay, I think.'

The door is flung open as Murdoch Langley bustles in bringing the cold with him. Wrapped in a thick coat and gloves, his face is red and sweaty from the exertion of shifting snow. He joins Hugh at the bar.

Lucy places the drink on the counter. 'Your cognac, Dr Quint.'

'Merci.'

Maggie Thornton raises a finger in the air. 'Snowball, please,' she reminds Lucy meekly, almost embarrassed.

'Yes, yes. I just need to take Mrs Langley her drink,' she replies scooting from behind the bar.

'I can do that for you if you like?' Dr Quint says. 'Is she in the drawing room?'

'Yes. Thanks. That's very kind of you.'

'Not a problem. My mother is in there awaiting her sherry.'

Imogen rolls her eyes at Eve. 'I tell you what, I'll go find us a nice spot in the library and you bring the drinks through when you've been served.'

'Okay.'

As Lucy pours the Advocaat into a tumbler Dr Quint makes his way into reception carrying the sherry and gin and tonic.

'Merde,' he curses placing the drinks down on a side table. As he turns, he bumps into Imogen. They both share apologies.

'Sorry,' Imogen says gazing up at the tall, handsome Frenchman.

'No, forgive me, madame. It was my fault. I forgot my cognac.'

Imogen flutters her eyelashes. 'Oh, would you like me to take those in for you?' she says pointing at the abandoned drinks on the table.

'Oh, yes. Very kind. The sherry is for my mother, the gin for Madame Penelope.'

Imogen picks the drinks up. 'Maybe you'd care to join me and my friend in the library, later?' she asks, hoping.

Dr Quint offers her warm smile. 'That would be most pleasant.'

---

Prisha paces to the back of the kitchen as if she's reading a pirate map searching for lost treasure. She stares at the cupboard which is different from the others. This one is built into the wall. It sits chest high, the door rising about four feet higher. She yanks it open the and stares inside. Two rusty frying pans, one with a handle missing. A badly chipped Pyrex dish. Two rusty saucepans and four flaky oven dishes. She sticks her head into the confined space and looks up as the back door jars open.

'Crap!'

Closing the cupboard, she spins around as Chef Antoine enters the kitchen muttering angrily to himself in French. He comes to an abrupt halt as he spots Prisha.

'Madame?' he asks suspiciously. 'Can I help you?'

Prisha has no intention of divulging the real reason for her visit so thinks quickly. 'Ah, yes, Antoine, it was you I was looking for, actually,' she says, buying time.

'Oui?' he asks, surprised.

Fumbling in her back pocket she pulls out the folded newspaper clipping she found in Virgil's office.

'Do you recognise this man?' she asks, handing him the black-and-white photo, hoping to divert his attention from her true purpose in the kitchen.

His brow knits together. 'Why, yes. This is my very good friend, Oliver Mcloud.'

Prisha blinks, completely baffled and lost for words.

# 40

Bennet Whipple has joined proceedings in the drawing room. His hulking frame positioned in front of the fire, his hands clasped behind him, blocking all the heat as he warms his cockles. He's facing Frank and Penelope, still ensconced in their armchairs as he waxes lyrical about his precious car—the classic 1963 Jaguar E-Type. His posture is erect and proud, like a preacher preparing to deliver a sermon. His tone is reverent, his words measured and deliberate, each one dripping with admiration for the subject of his adoration. As he speaks, his eyes drift upward, as if gazing into some ethereal realm where only the Jaguar E-Type exists, untarnished by the modern world. Occasionally, he gestures with one hand, palm upward, as if presenting the car itself to an unseen congregation.

'Yes, indeed, the 1963 Jaguar E-Type is an extraordinary creation! The architect of this masterpiece, Malcolm Sayer, was not merely a designer but an artist—a man who brought the principles of aerodynamics from the skies to the roads. Its silhouette—sleek, flowing, perfect. Not a single unnecessary line. It is as though the wind itself sculpted the car. Beautiful and functional, the very embodiment of form meeting purpose.'

'Excuse me, Dr Whipple,' Imogen interjects, interrupting the monologue as she enters with Penelope's long awaited drink. 'I believe this is yours, Penelope,' she says, bending slightly.

'Oh, thank you, Imogen. Doing Lucy's job for her, I see?' she says, taking the glass and placing it on the side table next to Frank's whisky.

Imogen winces slightly. 'She is rather busy and looks exhausted.'

'Nonsense,' Penelope sniffs dismissively. 'She's young, fit and full of energy. When I was her age, I could keep going from dawn until midnight without missing a beat.'

Imogen rolls her eyes at Frank, then wanders off towards the library.

'Where was I?' Whipple says, slightly thrown and irritated by the interruption.

Frank takes a sip of his whisky. 'Beautiful and functional, if I remember correctly.'

'Indeed. The engine is a 3.8-litre inline-six, delivering 265 horsepower—a marvel of engineering for its time. Do you know it could reach 150 miles per hour? In the early sixties!

A machine like that wasn't simply fast; it was revolutionary. And oh, the sound! That glorious growl as the tachometer climbs—it isn't just an engine; it's a symphony. Each gear shift feels like a chord change in a masterpiece.'

'Really,' Frank says, scanning the room for an implement with which he can swiftly end his own life.

Whipple pauses, closing his eyes for a moment, lost in the memory of driving.

'Then there's the handling. A monocoque chassis with a front subframe—brilliantly ahead of its time! Independent suspension on all four wheels, torsion bars up front, coil springs in the rear. The result? It's more than a mere car,' Whipple declares, his voice swelling with awe, 'it's a dancer. The prima ballerina at the grand opera, performing the crescendo of Swan Lake. Every curve, every motion, every gear shift is a step in its choreography, graceful yet deliberate. When it corners, it pirouettes with perfect poise. When it accelerates, it soars akin to Odette in her final flight. And the engine... oh, the engine sings as if Tchaikovsky himself composed it.'

Penelope shoots Frank a sideways glance. Their eyes meet—and although their expressions remain emotionless—their feelings are in sync.

Whipple's voice drops slightly, his tone more wistful now. 'And the interior... leather-trimmed bucket seats that hug you like a mother hugs a newborn babe. Toggle switches on the dashboard, the centrally mounted dials—everything positioned for the driver. Not cluttered, not over-engineered, but a cockpit crafted for...'

Penelope rises wearily. 'Please excuse me, gentlemen, but I've suddenly come over very sleepy.'

'You don't say,' Frank mutters under his breath.

'Oh, leaving us so soon, Mrs Langley?' Whipple asks, bewildered that anyone could not be enthralled by his rhapsody.

'Yes. I think an early night is required. Good evening, gentlemen.'

'Goodnight,' both men reply in unison.

Frank desperately tries to think of an escape plan before Whipple resumes his soliloquy.

'I do believe you can order sandwiches and snacks at the bar, Bennet,' he says.

Whipple considers the proposition and licks his lips. 'I must say, I am feeling rather peckish. A turkey sandwich with cranberry sauce does sound appetising. Maybe there's some left-over plum pudding? Hmm... Can I get you anything, inspector?'

'No, not for me.'

'I shall return,' Whipple says as he rumbles towards the door.

'Aye, take your time, Bennet.'

As Whipple exits, Prisha enters and makes a beeline for Frank.

'Frank, Frank,' she says in an excited whisper, taking a seat next to him.

'Breakthrough?'

'Maybe. Two things,' she replies, scanning the room suspiciously. The only other person is Edith Quint, sitting in an armchair in a corner, apparently dozing.

'Come on then, lass, get it off your chest,' Frank urges.

'The kitchen...'

She breaks off as Dr Quint and Eve Sinclair enter the room chatting away. They're immediately followed by Maggie Thornton.

'Christ,' Frank groans. 'It's like Kings Cross Station in rush hour.'

Prisha notices the glass on the table. 'Whose is that?'

'Penelope's G and T. But she's gone to bed after Whipple sent her into an involuntary coma.' He picks the drink up. 'Here, you may as well have it. No point it going to waste.'

Prisha seems reluctant. 'Has she drunk from it?'

'Not touched a drop.' She takes the glass tentatively and looks around the room again.

Dr Quint is quietly shaking his mother. 'Maman, your sherry,' he says, quietly.

Prisha tilts the glass back but before it touches her lips, it's rudely snatched from her hand. 'What are you doing, Frank?' she snaps.

He sniffs the liquid. 'I thought I smelled almonds,' he says, puzzled.

'Let me smell.' He hands the drink back to her. 'I can't smell almonds,' she says, taking a puzzled sniff.

Frank seizes the drink back again and sticks his bulbous hooter over the rim. 'It definitely smells of almonds.'

'So?'

'It's odd. Isn't there a poison that smells of almonds?'

Prisha shrugs. 'Not sure.'

'Follow me. I'll ask the font of all knowledge—Old Raspberry Whipple.' As they stride into the reception area, Frank glances sideways at the back office. He stops and nods at the open door. 'I tell you what, we'll wait in the office and grab Bennet as he walks past. Best not discuss it in front of the other guests. You know how loud Bennet is.'

'Fine. Who served Penelope the drink?'

'Lucy, originally. She brought it in then had to take it back because it didn't have a slice of lemon in it. Oh, hang on, then Imogen Sato actually delivered it back to her.'

'Hmm... I was near the bar when Lucy was getting the drinks. There were a lot of people clustered around, and she did pop into the kitchen for a moment.'

'With the drink?'

'No. She must have left it on the bar.'

'And who was there?'

'Erm, Dr Quint, Maggie Thornton, Hugh Foster, then Imogen and Eve arrived. I then went into the kitchen and when I came back out, Murdoch Langley was there as well.'

'Bugger me—Old Uncle Tom Cobbley and all. If this is poisoned, then any one of them had the opportunity to do it.'

They make their way into the office and wait, Frank admiring the colourful tropical fish swimming languidly in the tank.

A few seconds pass until heavy, ponderous footsteps catch their attention as Whipple comes into view.

'Psst, Bennet,' Franks hisses in a forced whisper from the office.

Whipple freezes mid-step, clutching a small sherry glass in one hand, his face puzzled.

'Psst, Bennet.'

His eyes dart around the hallway before tilting skyward in extreme confusion.

'Psst... Oi, Bennet, over here.'

Finally, Whipple turns towards the sound, his frown deepening. 'Ah, inspector. I have ordered a sandwich. In the meantime, I endowed myself with a small libation—to wit—a glass of dry sherry.' He sighs heavily, his face a picture of resigned disappointment. 'I fear I may have strayed from the righteous path and am in imminent danger of becoming a hopeless dipsomaniac.'

Frank waves him forward impatiently. 'I'd agree with the maniac bit, but never mind about that now. We need your expert advice.'

Intrigued, Whipple places the sherry down on the reception counter and joins Frank and Prisha in the office. 'What is it, inspector?'

'Is there a poison that smells of almonds?' Frank asks, closing the door.

'Indeed there is, inspector. Hydrogen cyanide stands universally alone in that regard,' Whipple begins, his tone taking on the gravity of a lecture. 'Although, when potassium cyanide comes into contact with moisture, such as water, saliva, or stomach acid— it can release hydrogen cyanide gas, which carries the distinctive odour of bitter almonds. However, only around forty per cent of the population has the genetic capacity to detect it. Why do you ask?'

Frank hands him the glass. 'Here, stick your great big schnozzle over this and tell me what you think?'

Whipple takes the glass delicately and gives it an experimental sniff. 'I detect the faint aroma of gin, a soupçon of tonic water, and the distinctive bitterness of quinine. But as for almonds? That aromatic alludes me.'

'I couldn't smell anything either,' Prisha says with a shrug.

Frank takes the glass and holds it over the fish tank. 'Only one way to find out.'

'I'd advise against that,' Whipple says with a deep seriousness.

Frank ignores his advice and carefully tips a splash of the gin and tonic—no more than a tablespoon—into the fish tank. For a moment, nothing happens. The neon tetras dart about as usual, their iridescent bodies catching the overhead fluorescent light.

'If it is cyanide, how long before it has an effect?'

Whipple harrumphs. 'Hard to be precise. It would depend on the dosage. Even a small amount, one to two grams, diluted in an alcoholic beverage, would be lethal...'

'Yes, but there must forty litres of water in this tank, Frank says, nodding at the fish. 'It will be massively diluted, so I doubt it's enough to harm the fish. Maybe make them a little off-colour, that's all.'

Whipple grimaces. 'You interrupted me, inspector. I was about to say, one to two grams diluted in an alcoholic beverage would be lethal to a fit and healthy human. However, aquatic animals are far more sensitive to environmental toxins than humans. If that drink contains cyanide, the life expectancy of these fish would be... no longer than a minute.'

Frank laughs nervously. 'You are joking, right?'

'The doctor doesn't do jokes. You should know that by now, Frank,' Prisha says, arms crossed.

All three of them lean closer to the tank. For a few moments, the fish swim as normal, their delicate movements steady and untroubled. Frank checks his watch.

'Must be coming up for a minute now,' he mutters. 'Look, they're fine. Maybe it wasn't poison after all—wait a second.' He chuckles as he spots one fish begin to swim madly back and forth. 'Take a look at that little bugger. I think he might be drunk. It's like he's running for the last bus on a Friday night.' His smile fades as the fish careers headlong into the side of the glass, bounces off, and repeats the process at the other end of the tank.

'What's happening, Bennet?' Frank asks, his voice tinged with alarm as the other fish begin to dart around wildly.

Whipple sighs heavily. 'Fish breathe by extracting oxygen from water through their gills. When cyanide is introduced into the water, it is absorbed through the gills into their bloodstream, where it disrupts their ability to utilise oxygen at a cellular level. In short, inspector, they are in a blind panic.'

'Why?'

'Because they're drowning.'

Another fish jerks violently, its movements spasmodic as if trying to escape an unseen predator. It leaps from the water and falls behind the desk. Another goes still, its tiny gills flaring wide before its body begins to float, belly-up. Within seconds, the rest succumb. The tank, once lively with colourful movement, becomes eerily still—its inhabitants reduced to lifeless shapes bobbing about on the surface.

Frank stares at the scene, slack-jawed. 'Bugger.' He glances at Prisha, then at Whipple, and straightens. 'Ahem, I think the less said about this, the better. We'll say there was a malfunction with the aerator when the power came back on.'

Whipple's face darkens. 'You mean lie, inspector?'

Frank nods firmly. 'Aye. That's exactly what I mean, Bennet—lie.'

# 41

Hugh Foster kicks the toe of his boot against the entrance step, shaking off a crust of snow and ice. The floorboards groan beneath his weight as he steps inside, a wave of heat wrapping around him. The smell of wood smoke clings to the air, mingling with the faint drone of conversation drifting down the hallway. Stripping off his hat, scarf, and gloves, he unzips his jacket and enters the dining room and strides towards the bar.

'A double whisky, please, Lucy.'

Maggie Thornton appears at his side. 'Is Murdoch still out there?'

'Yeah,' he replies, a touch of exasperation in his tone. 'The man's possessed. We've cleared a track to the gate, but the drive's nearly a mile long. And who knows if the main road's even passable? I haven't seen a single car headlight all night.'

Maggie nods, her gaze distant. 'He's not himself tonight, is he?'

'We're both going stir crazy. Come hell or high water, I'm getting out of here tomorrow at some point.'

'It must have been a shock earlier,' Maggie presses, her voice softening. 'Finding the body, I mean.'

Lucy places the whisky glass down in front of him, her fingers lingering briefly on the rim.

'Thanks, love,' Hugh mutters to Lucy before turning back to Maggie. 'Aye, I can't lie, Mags. It did rattle me. But, you know, you see a lot of death working a farm.'

Maggie frowns, tilting her head. 'But still, that's animals, not humans.'

Hugh shrugs, taking the glass in hand. 'Death is death, Mags. Happens all the time.' He pauses, swirling the whisky slowly before adding, 'And another thing...'

She leans closer, her brow furrowing, hoping for a snippet of a rumour. 'What?'

Hugh grimaces as the alcohol burns the back of his throat. He sets the glass down with a small thud. 'We'll both have to find a new accountant,' he adds, bursting into a cackle.

His laughter, like the crack of a bullwhip, echoes off the walls

Lucy shakes her head in disgust as Maggie purses her lips, face hardening. 'I find that remark rather callous, I must say.'

Hugh leans back, meeting her glare with a weary shrug. 'Well, it's the truth. Good accountants are hard to come by.

Logan was a good one. He knew how to minimise my tax bill.'

Maggie's glare sharpens. 'You have not an ounce of empathy, nor respect.' Her voice wavers with anger. With a sharp movement, she slams her glass down on the counter. 'I'm going to bed. I've had quite enough for one day... and quite enough of you.'

She storms away, leaving Hugh alone at the bar with his empty glass and an air of self-satisfied indifference.

'Same again, Lucy, love.'

Lucy freezes, then fixes him with an icy glare. 'I'm not your love,' she bites back.

Hugh chuckles, raising his hands in mock surrender. 'Alright, alright. Keep your knickers on... love. Not sure what's wrong with everyone tonight. Has someone died?' He bursts into laughter again at his own sick joke, the sound grating against the solemnity of the room.

Lucy slams the double whisky down in front of him. 'The bar is now closed.'

---

**10 pm**

As Frank and Zac methodically check all doors and windows are locked, they chat casually, their voices low in the quiet house.

'That was a damn close call, Frank. If Penelope had taken even a sip of that drink, we'd have another corpse on our hands. And Prisha—how close was that?' He states, in mild astonishment.

'I know. Tell me about it.'

'And you murdering those fish...'

Frank stops mid-step in the library, spinning around to glare at Zac. 'Keep your voice down,' he hisses.

'Nearly everyone's in bed.'

'Doesn't matter.' Frank glances over his shoulder as if expecting an eavesdropper to emerge from the shadows. 'I didn't murder the fish. Those fish sacrificed their lives to prove a point: the drink was poisoned—intended recipient—Penelope Langley.' His voice drops to a whisper. 'It was a scientific experiment. And with such experiments, sometimes there's... collateral damage,' he adds, sheepishly.

Zac grins, clearly enjoying Frank's misjudgement. 'I'd call it deliberate Poseidonicide.'

Frank fixes him with an unimpressed glare, one eyebrow arching. 'Thank you, Oscar Wilde. Right, come on, let's check the rest of the hotel is secure, then we can go to bed.'

'Steady on, Frank. I think you're coming on a bit strong. And anyway, what would Meera say?'

Frank rolls his eyes. 'Oh, you're on fire tonight. Must have been that two-hour idiot-nap you had earlier.'

---

After checking the swimming pool's sliding doors are securely locked, they turn and head back through the hotel, their footsteps echoing faintly in the silent corridors.

Frank continues explaining Prisha's breakthrough. 'And she figured out how the killer escaped from Virgil Langley's bedroom,' Frank says, his voice hushed but carrying a note of admiration. 'With the door locked and the chain on.'

'Oh, aye?' Zac's curiosity piques, his head tilting slightly.

'I'll show you in the kitchen,' Frank replies, quickening his pace. 'And she also accidentally gleaned some interesting information from Chef Antoine.'

'About?' Zac prods.

Frank glances at him with a knowing look. 'About a certain Oliver McCloud.'

Zac frowns, the name drawing a blank. 'Who the hell's Oliver McCloud when he's at home?'

Frank smirks. 'Exactly.'

---

Zac puffs his cheeks out, then expels air as he closes the cupboard door in the kitchen. 'I think Prisha's on the money,' he says finally. 'It would explain the locked room mystery. A dumbwaiter straight up to Virgil's room. And how did she figure it out?'

'Two things: you may have noticed the floor plans of Kindlewood Hall in Virgil's office?'

'Aye. On the corkboard.'

'She was looking at them and noticed the Langleys' private residence was situated directly above the kitchen. And Penelope told her that years ago their rooms used to be the deluxe suite before they turned it into their living quarters.'

'And the deluxe suite had the luxury of a dumbwaiter—like a fast-tracked room service?'

'Correct. And secondly, remember Prisha saying she walked in on Antoine and Lucy in the kitchen and caught them in the middle of a heated argument yesterday?'

'Aye, that's right. Something about a set of old rusty pans being left out.'

'Yes. During the argument, Lucy picked up the old pans in a fury and asked Antoine where they lived. Antoine pointed vaguely and said—monte-plats. Lucy scowled and shouted she didn't understand. He pointed again, then called her a stupid waiter... or so she thought.'

Zac twigs. 'Ah, I see. Monte-plats must mean dumbwaiter in French, and Antoine tried to translate into English and said stupid waiter instead, and Lucy thought he was referring to her.'

'That's right. Apart from the fact monte-plats actually means—plate-lift. Prisha found a French to English dictionary in the library and looked the words up.'

'Oh, she's clever britches, that one.' Zac pauses and rubs his chin. 'Hang on, why didn't Penelope mention the dumbwaiter?'

'Prisha asked her the same question. She said she'd completely forgotten about it. A mirror, just wide and tall enough, was placed over the hatch a decade ago. I suppose out of sight, out of mind.'

'Sounds a bit suss.'

'You've seen how small the dumbwaiter is. There's no way a woman of Penelope's height could squeeze in there.'

Zac's eyebrows arch. 'No. But an accomplice could.'

'They'd have to be small, and the only three people who fit the bill are Edith Quint, Imogen Sato, and Chef Antoine. And they'd need to be agile, flexible.'

'The first one is impossible; the second one implausible; and the third is very possible. How tall's Antoine? Five three, five four?'

'About that, in his bare feet,' Frank replies.

'And how would Imogen Sato even have known of the dumbwaiter's existence?'

'Don't rule her out. Earlier tonight, when I was speaking with Penelope in the drawing room, she was having a dig about Imogen Sato.'

'About?'

'When Imogen first arrived, she asked Penelope if she could inspect the kitchen at some point. It's something she likes to do for her food reviews. It raised the hackles on Penelope's back considering the impending storm, the lack of staff, and how busy they were, but she reluctantly agreed.'

Zac nods thoughtfully. 'Okay, then we're homing in. We've narrowed it down to two who could have killed Virgil Langley: Imogen Sato or Chef Antoine. Putting aside a thrill kill for a moment, what's their motive?'

Frank scratches at the bristles on his neck. 'Antoine's not the happiest of souls. He's a long way from home, seems to carry a chip on his shoulder, and, according to Lucy, he had little regard for Virgil. Works six days a week. Hasn't been paid in two months. He's isolated—no friends nearby. That's a lot weighing on a man. Depression, maybe? Resentment building up over time? It all adds up.'

'And Imogen?'

'Apart from the Langleys threatening to sue her after the negative food review, nothing I can see.'

'Okay, let's assume for a moment, Antoine killed Virgil. Why kill Logan Fitch?'

Frank stretches his back. 'The—why—is often the hardest to work out. People are complex and we never really know what's going through their mind.' Frank checks the kitchen door to ensure it's locked. 'All good. Let's check the front door, then head upstairs.'

'Smooth talker,' Zac mutters with a grin.

'Oh, shut up. Hey, fancy a swift nightcap before we turn in?' Frank suggests.

'Do Welshmen like sheep?'

———◆———

They clink glasses and down the remaining brandy.

'Nice drop,' Zac notes, setting his glass on the table.

'Aye. Very pleasant,' Frank agrees, wiping his mouth as they both meander out of the dining room towards the hallway.

'Eh, Frank, I've been thinking about it.'

'I was the same at your age, lad. It's a curse we have to bear for being born male. It's never far from the mind.'

'No, I'm being serious.' Zac's tone sharpens. 'The mode of death—it doesn't add up.'

Frank stops by the front door, shooting Zac a sidelong glance. 'Go on.' He slams the top bolt into position with a metallic thunk.

'If Prisha's dumbwaiter theory is correct—and I don't see any other explanation—then it was planned, ingenious. It involved stealth and cunning. Whereas Logan Fitch's death was opportunistic and brutal. And the attempt on Penelope's life was clever as well.' He pauses, brow creased in thought. 'Killers don't usually operate like that. They have a pattern. If something works and they get away with it, they rinse and repeat.'

'Well done, Zac. You got there in the end.'

Zac straightens, scowling. 'And what does that bloody mean?'

'Prisha came to that conclusion a couple of hours ago.'

Zac stiffens, his jaw hardening. 'Did she... did she indeed?' His tone drips with mockery. 'Bloody typical. You know, a person can become a little tired of her smart-arsery. Always one step ahead.'

Frank chuckles as he slides the bottom bolt into place. 'Now, now, Zac, count your blessings. You cannot imagine the amount of the dunderheads I've worked with over the years. Some were so dense, light bent around them.'

Zac sees a saving grace. Puffing his chest out with renewed confidence, he says, 'And did she also come to the conclusion, as I have, that it could be two people working in unison?' His chin juts forward, his expression triumphant as he awaits the accolade he feels is surely deserved.

Frank doesn't miss a beat. 'Aye. That too.' His tone is nonchalant as he turns the key in the door, removes it, and hangs it on a nearby hook.

Zac's chest deflates like a punctured balloon. 'Of course she did,' he mutters under his breath.

Frank glances at him, a wry grin tugging at the corner of his mouth. 'Cheer up, Zac. You're still top of the class. It's just that Prisha's already finished the exam, marked her own paper, and moved onto university.'

Zac shoots him a look, his sulk deepening. 'It's getting harder and harder to enjoy your company, Frank.'

Frank glances out through the side window beside the door, his hand brushing the curtain aside as he surveys the grounds. The security lights bathe the hotel's exterior in sharp relief, while the faux Victorian gaslights cast a soft, magnolia glow over the driveway, their warm halos flickering faintly in the cold night air.

Satisfied, he lets the curtain fall back into place. 'Lights are still on,' he mutters. As they turn to walk away, his expression changes. 'I'll tell you one thing, lad; tomorrow, this is all going to come to a head, one way or another, and we'll have our killer.'

'Or killers,' Zac adds as the faint chime of the grandfather clock drifts through the stillness, marking the half hour.

Frank exhales. 'Right. Time for some shut-eye. We've done all the rounds. Everyone's in bed. Safe and secure.'

Zac throws him a dubious, loaded glance. 'Aye. Apart from the fact we've probably locked the killer in with us.'

As they saunter along the hallway and past the heated cloakroom, neither man hears the slight shuffle from within.

# 42

The night is an unforgiving bombazine black, a heavy funeral petticoat smothering the countryside, interrupted only by the faltering, flicker of Murdoch Langley's dying torch. The weak light casts uneven, jittery beams over the endless expanse of white.

Stumbling, he loses purchase as the icy ground deceives him again, pulling him down. His boots sink into the edge of yet another snowdrift.

'Goddamn it,' he hisses through gritted teeth.

Hauling himself upright onto his knees, his gloves wet and caked with snow, he crouches for a moment, panting. The cold bites through his jacket, sharp, relentless.

*It's not right. It's not fair.*

He knows these grounds like the back of his hand: the driveway, the copse, the lazy paths circling the lake, the bristling beck, the gardens. But now everything feels alien. The snow, deep and unyielding, has transformed the land into a foreign country. The familiar is hidden, landmarks obliterated, his bearings scrambled.

*Which way is north, south, east, west?*

His impulsive decision to walk to the main road—to see if the snowplough had been through—now seems utterly foolish, irresponsible, even. His only choice is to turn around, retrace his footsteps, and hope the torch doesn't give up the ghost completely.

Standing, he grips the flashlight tighter in his numb fingers, squinting at the faint trail ahead. Somewhere in the distance, beyond the trees and snow-laden grounds, lies the hotel.

But Kindlewood Hall feels like a lifetime away, and every step is heavier than the last.

'Just keep walking,' he mutters to himself, his breath misting in the icy air. 'Not far now.'

His body aches with fatigue. Legs, leaden and trembling, protest every weary step. The cold seeps into his bones, gnawing at his resolve. But the physical toll is nothing compared to the storm raging in his head.

He can still hear Penelope's words from earlier in the evening.

'I no longer need you, Murdoch.'

The memory plays on a loop in his mind, the flat, matter-of-fact tone cutting him to the core. She'd stood there so calm, wrapped in her overcoat and scarf, as though dismissing him was merely business, like many of the feckless kitchen staff she'd sacked over the years.

It had hit him like a slap across the cheek.

She no longer needed his money. Not because she'd found another investor. Not because she'd reconsidered the renovations. But because the insurance payout from Virgil's death will solve all her problems. Finally, Virgil had managed to do something right.

'It was foolproof,' he grumbles as his boots crunch through the snow. 'Foolproof.'

He'd thought of everything. Lend Virgil and Penelope the money, interest-free—enough to cover their immediate debts and pay for the refurbishment. Add a clause: repayment within three years. Of course, Virgil wouldn't meet the deadline. He'd bungle everything as he always did and run out of cash halfway through the renovations, the creditors circling like vultures. Bankruptcy would've been inevitable.

Then Murdoch would swoop in, the "kind" brother, buying the hotel for a fraction of its worth. Kindlewood Hall would be his, and he'd sell it for at least twice what he paid for it, maybe more. Once his loan had been repaid, along with the other creditors, there wouldn't be much left. But he'd throw Virgil and Penelope a lifeline—help them buy that cosy little bungalow by the sea. A tidy ending for everyone.

Beautifully simple.

But then Virgil had gone and got himself killed. And now Penelope, clever Penelope, had made his entire plan redundant with her bloody insurance policy.

He hadn't factored that into the bargain.

Sloppy thinking?

And another thing that stings—her ice cold demeanour. Not a jot of emotion. There should have been something, a smouldering ember left burning in the hearth of desire. But no. Somewhere, somehow, that tiny spark had been doused in water.

The thought ignites his anger again, a heat that burns sharper than the cold ache in his lungs.

As he rounds a bend, the twinkling lights of the hotel come into view. The turreted roofline, the grand entrance, the golden glow spilling from the windows—all of it standing proud against the snowy landscape. Relief should come, but it doesn't. Kindlewood Hall mocks him, reminding him of what he's lost—of what could have been.

Passing the broken gate, he steps onto the tramlines he and Hugh cleared earlier. His shoulders sag slightly as the weight of the walk begins to lift.

'A brandy and a good night's sleep,' he murmurs. 'That's all I need. Things will seem better tomorrow. I'll work on Penelope before I leave.'

He staggers up the steps, his gloved hand reaching for the door handle. It doesn't budge.

Locked. Of course it's bloody locked.

He grits his teeth, swiping at the snow clinging to his coat. He pounds on the door with his fist.

'Oi! Someone open the bloody door! It's freezing out here!'

Through the frosted glass panels, he sees a figure approach. Their shadow grows larger, distorted by the icy patterns on the window. The door opens, and the warmth of the hotel spills out, enveloping him like a balm.

'Thank you. I take it everyone else has gone to bed?' he asks, wiping his boots on the foot grill.

'Yes. You're lucky. I came down to make cocoa and heard you banging on the door. Where have you been?'

'I attempted to walk to the main road. The blasted snow was too thick, so I had to turn back.' He shakes his head, rubbing his gloved hands together. 'Didn't even get halfway there.'

'I see.'

Murdoch turns and stares one last time at the muted countryside, taking in the stillness.

'I must admit, though, it's a damn sight warmer now than it was an hour ago. I think the big thaw will come tomorrow, don't you?' he adds, a positive tone in his voice. 'I must admit though, this place is doing my head in—can't wait to leave.'

'Really? Then let me help you leave right now.'

Puzzled, he turns. 'Pardon?'

The heavy object descends swiftly, violently.

The blow strikes Murdoch squarely in the middle of the forehead, the dull crack and metallic ting echoing into the still night. He remains standing for a second, swaying like a sapling in a gentle breeze, eyes wide with shock.

The second blow comes harder, higher, caving in the top of his forehead.

He topples in slow motion, arms outstretched, graceful, like an Olympic diver executing a reverse dive. His head strikes the snow covered steps, the soft powder muffling the impact. Sliding down awkwardly, his body twists, flipping him face down in a crumpled heap at the foot of the steps.

Snow clings to his lifeless form, red blossoming through the white.

The perpetrator descends the steps with chilling calm, delivers one final, fatal blow to the back of the head to ensure the job is done, then tosses the weapon into the snow piled up at the side of the steps.

Without a glance at the body, they re-enter the hotel, lock the door, and slide the scraping bolts into place.

A shaft of moonlight breaks through the clouds, casting a pale glow over Murdoch's inanimate body, and the crimson-streaked snow.

Kindlewood Hall falls silent once more as the lights unexpectedly go out.

# 43

Frank holds the end of the small torch in his mouth, closes the door, and slides the chain across.

'Bloody power's gone again,' he mutters as Meera steps out of the bathroom, a towel wrapped around her, holding a wine bottle with a fluttering candle jammed into its neck.

'Yes, I'd noticed,' she replies, her voice still nasal from her cold. 'I needed a shower—I've been sweating buckets. But I feel a little better now. How's everything going downstairs? Any closer to finding the killer?'

'A few minor breakthroughs,' he replies vaguely, unwilling to worry her with grim details.

'Oh, good,' she murmurs, placing the candle onto the dresser. Her concern deepens. 'I don't know if I'll be able to sleep with a killer on the prowl.'

'Nonsense,' Frank replies, tugging off his jumper and tossing it over the back of a chair. 'Why would the killer come after you? Anyway, you've got your knight in shining armour to protect you.' He unbuttons his shirt, slips it off, and carefully folds it before draping it over the chair.

Meera gazes at her husband, his big baggy Y-fronts drooping alarmingly, as if he's carrying six pounds of spuds in them. 'Knight in shining armour?' she questions doubtfully.

'Aye. That's what I said.'

'What if the killer's a madman? Deranged. What if they kill at random—without rhyme or reason?'

'Two things,' Frank says as he steps out of his trousers. 'Virgil's murder wasn't random or the act of some basket-case. It was planned, meticulously. And secondly, why are you so sure the killer is male?'

Meera shrugs out of the towel and slides a flannelette nightie over her head. 'I don't believe a woman could kill in that way.'

Frank scoffs lightly. 'Trust me, love, women are as capable of atrocities as men are. Not as often, true. But just as capable.'

As he pulls his socks off, an unwelcome realisation surfaces. 'Bugger me backwards,' he exclaims.

Meera spins around, alarmed. 'What?'

'I missed dinner last night. Breakfast this morning. And I meant to grab a sandwich for supper but got so bloody wrapped up in work, I forgot. All I've had since I arrived is Christmas dinner earlier.'

'Oh, is that all? Hardly a tragedy. You're unlikely to fade away overnight, are you?' she says, climbing under the covers.

'That's not the point, Meera. An army marches on its stomach.'

She shoots him a glance. 'With a stomach like yours, you could feed a battalion and still have leftovers.' Curling up on her side, she softens. 'What do you think tomorrow will bring, Frank?'

Frank blows out the candle, switches off the torch, and slides into bed beside her. Draping a thick, muscular arm around her waist, he pulls her close. 'We'll wake to a new day. The snow will be melting. The power and phones will be back on. I'll call for backup and hand this whole bloody mess over to someone else. Then we'll enjoy the rest of our Christmas together. How does that sound?'

'Nice, if implausible. Night, Frank.'

He kisses the nape of her neck and rolls onto his back. 'Night, love. Hope you're feeling better in the morning.'

---

Frank's eyes spring open and stare into blackness. He rolls to the side and glances at the clock on the bedside table—3:07

am. His stomach grumbles incessantly, clearly annoyed at the imposition of missing out on his standard three meals a day—plus snacks. He clicks the torch on, tiptoes to the window, and peels back the edge of a curtain. The courtyard is an impenetrable inky abyss, but at least there's no further snowfall.

He pulls his dressing gown on and fumbles his feet into slippers. Depositing the torch on Meera's bedside table, he strikes a match and relights the candle.

As quietly as he can, he unlatches the door, removes the chain and opens it, feeling for the key in his dressing gown pocket.

The floorboards creak in displeasure as he lumbers along the corridor and down the stairs, the naked flame projecting a grotesque and giant version of his frame onto the ceiling. Apart from the occasional groan from the old hotel, all he can hear is the ticking of the grandfather clock from the drawing room. At the foot of the stairs, he hangs right, passes through the reception area, heads into the dining room—his destination clear—the kitchen.

He abruptly halts.

Noise, muffled, indistinct.

A flit of a shadow dances from behind the glass of the kitchen door.

Swallowing hard, he scans the dining room, searching for a weapon, anything. Nothing springs to mind until his gaze falls upon a cutlass mounted to the side of the wood burner, which is still glowing red.

Carefully, he lifts the cutlass from its mounting. 'This will do,' he murmurs, swinging the weapon back and forth with reckless abandon.

Pausing, he tilts his head to one side and listens. The sound is strange, and eerily sinister. A low bass hum, occasionally followed by indecipherable words, almost like someone speaking in tongues, or proclaiming an evil curse.

'Shit the bed.'

He creeps towards the kitchen, as spectre-like silhouettes cavort and gambol behind the glass of the door.

A soft crack resonates.

More deep bass-like hums.

Then silence.

Shadows melt away.

Frank takes a deep breath, the candle in his hand shaking like a leaf on a tree.

He thrusts open the swing-door and leaps forward, cutlass at the ready.

'Hold it right there! The game's up!'

The two deep rumbling screams are enough to awaken the dead.

# 44

Both men eyeball each other disdainfully, their barrel chests rising and falling in unison due to the intense fright they gave each other.

'Christ, Bennet, what in blue blazes are you doing down here?'

'I could ask you the same question, inspector. Thou art akin to a midnight ghoul haunting me unawares in this benighted chamber! In future, pray, announce thine presence with a clarion call or a sonorous yawn lest I be frightened out of my candle-lit wits!'

'You were the last thing I wanted to stumble across on a night like tonight. I thought you were an overgrown hobgoblin hunched over the table, the candle illuminating your gargantuan, bald noggin.'

'I was merely attending to my vittles. Due to the lamentable tribulations I and Mrs Whipple endured, but days past, my energy reserves are in dire need of replenishment.'

'But not Mrs Whipple's, I note?'

'My wife is still valiantly locked in mortal combat with a rhinoviral foe. While the common cold may seem a trifling adversary to the untrained eye, it has proven itself a stubborn and insidious infiltrator of her respiratory defences. As such, she remains abed, fortifying herself with sleep.'

'You don't say.' Frank spots the crackers on a plate and a tin of something to the side. 'I'm a spot peckish myself. What are you eating?'

Whipple resumes his seat. 'Crackers and a most unusual, but moreish fish pâté. Would you care to join me?'

'Yes, I will. But I need something more substantial than pâté and crackers.' He saunters to the large walk-in cold room and rummages around. 'Ah, just the ticket,' his disembodied voice calls out. He returns with a generous sized pork pie, a bottle of HP sauce, a plate of mince pies, and a bottle of cooking brandy gripped under his armpit.

Holding the brandy aloft, he says, 'Fancy a tipple, Bennet? Calm the nerves.'

He eyes Frank warily. 'You know my stance on alcohol, inspector. I may have erred earlier in the evening with a glass of sherry, but I still conclude the lamentable ingestion of spirits is a blight upon both thine soul and the dignity of humanity itself, leading to nought but ruin and degradation.'

Frank pulls out a chair and plonks himself down. 'Medicinal purposes, that's all. It will aid my digestion and help me sleep. God knows, my nerves are in tatters. Sure I can't tempt you?'

Whipple relents. 'I suppose a modest libation cannot be too ruinous for a man of my formidable constitution.'

'That's the spirit,' he says, reaching for two small glasses from a tray in the middle of the large kitchen table. He decants a generous amount into each glass and hands one to Whipple.

'Here's to your health, doctor, and a merry Christmas... I suppose.'

Whipple takes the drink in his oversized hand and nods in deference. 'And my finest salutations to you too, inspector.'

They clink glasses and take a mouthful of the brandy, each man savouring it in their own unique style.

Frank cuts the pork pie into quarters and offers Bennet a slice. He takes it graciously and devours it in one bite.

'It's a rum one, Bennet,' Frank states, referring to the grisly weekend.

'Indeed. A most vexing and mysterious sequence of events. As to the perpetrator of these atrocities—it alludes me, inspector.' He offers a severe frown. 'I'm as discombobulated as a cat with two tails.'

Tickled, Frank laughs heartily. 'Very good, Bennet. A cat with two tails. I like it.'

Much to Frank's amazement, Whipple emits a deep, resonating chuckle. 'Ha, ha, ha, ha, ha.'

Right on cue, Podger, the hotel cat, saunters in, tail erect, mewing softly.

<hr />

Meera glances up and down the corridor nervously, shining the torch into deathly shadows. She knocks again. 'Zac, wake up. It's me, Meera,' she whispers as loud as she dares.

Grumbling from inside the room is swiftly accompanied by a pained yowl. 'Christ, my bastard toe.' The chain rattles and the door creaks open as Zac's head bobs out. 'Meera, what's the matter?'

'It's Frank. He's gone.'

'What do you mean, gone?'

'Gone. I woke up, and he wasn't there. His dressing gown is missing, and he's taken the candle.'

'Hang on a mo. Let me make myself decent.' The door silently shuts then reopens as he tiptoes out into the corridor dressed in red tartan pyjamas and matching slippers. As they set off on their quest, another room door cracks open and Mrs Whipple emerges in a long chiffon nightdress, which does nothing to hide her nakedness beneath. As Meera shines the torch on her, it illuminates her ample breasts in all their glory.

Zac, being a man, is suitably impressed. 'Sorry, did we wake you?' he says, trying desperately to focus on Mrs Whipple's face.

'Yes, and I'm glad you did. Bennet's missing.'

'Sweet merciful shite. So is Frank,' he accidentally whispers with rising unease. 'What's going on here? Go back inside and lock the door, Mrs Whipple.'

'No, I'm going to search for my husband,' she sniffles, dabbing a tissue under her nose.

Zac relents. 'Very well. Safety in numbers, I guess. But both of you, stay behind me.'

As they descend the creaking stairs, raised voices and bouts of laughter drift to them.

'That sounds like Frank,' Meera says, perplexed.

'And that's definitely Bennet's annoyingly booming voice,' Mrs Whipple concurs.

The missing person's case is instantly answered in Zac's mind as they enter the dining room and stare towards the kitchen and the flickering candlelight emanating from within.

'I think we've found them. I suspect a case of the midnight munchies.'

As they enter the kitchen, Mrs Whipple glowers at her drunken husband and the scraps of food on the table.

'Bennet Whipple! What in Jehovah's name are you playing at?'

Whipple glances up, bemused to see his wife. He smiles and declares, 'Ah, wife, your fiery gaze kindles flames within me! Come, my tempestuous nymph, let us make this kitchen our ballroom of passion!'

'I most certainly will not.' She spies the empty brandy bottle. 'You're drunk, Bennet Whipple. Drunk as the proverbial skunk.'

Bennet chuckles heartily. 'My dearest wife, skunks, being creatures devoid of indulgence in Dionysian excess, cannot, in fact, partake in the inebriated folly to which you allude.'

Her eyes narrow to slits. 'What has got into you? You rarely, if ever, indulge in alcohol.'

Meera sorts derisively. 'Oh, believe me Mrs Whipple, any man who spends time in the company of my husband will soon end up blind drunk. It's his superpower.'

Frank is offended. 'Now hang on a minute, Meera.'

Zac arches his eyebrows. 'She has a point, Frank. You've led me on many an inebriated pub crawl deep into the wee hours.'

Mrs Whipple stomps towards her husband and grabs him aggressively by the arm. 'Stand up, Bennet. You're coming to bed. You're embarrassing yourself and me.' Spotting the empty tin on the table, she picks it up. 'What have you been eating?'

Whipple performs a chef's kiss. 'I've indulged in a tin of delectable pâté. Ambrosia fit for a god.'

Studying the picture on the tin, Mrs Whipple shakes her head in disgust. 'You drunken, clodhopping, dunderhead! That's not pâté. It's cat food!'

His eyes widen to the size of saucers as his jollity evaporates. 'Gadzooks! It is?'

'Yes. Didn't you see the picture of the cat on the tin?'

'In the murky gloaming, I perceived it to be a salmon.'

The cat struts past and rubs his fur against Meera's legs, meowing loudly. 'And I don't think Podger is very impressed, either, doctor,' she says.

Bennet swallows hard. 'Holy Jeremiah's jodhpurs! I've been deceived by a feline feast!' He unwittingly belches and holds his stomach. 'Alas, the cursed tinned repast has laid siege to my constitution, rendering me a mere shadow of my former fortitude. I'm feeling decidedly queasy, wife.'

She drags him by the arm from the kitchen, berating him as she does. 'You never drink? How much have you had?'

Bennet, utterly bewildered, slurs, 'How much, my dear? In truth, the count evades me as thoroughly as my own equilibrium. I fear the bottle has led me on an odyssey beyond mere reckoning.'

As the voices recede, Mecra eyeballs Frank. 'And don't think you're out of the woods, Frank Finnegan. We'll have words about this in the morning.'

Frank stops grinning. 'We will?'

'Yes. We will. Now come to bed.'

# 45

**Monday 23rd December**

Prisha yawns, reaching out instinctively for Adam's warm body, but her hand meets cool empty sheets. Her eyelids flutter open, the fog of sleep slowly clearing. The room feels wrong—the scent, the furniture—it's neither her cosy dormer in Whitby nor Adam's farmhouse.

*Kindlewood Hall.*

She rolls onto her side, squinting at the travel clock—6:18 am. Reaching for her phone, she checks for bars. Nothing.

Her stomach tightens. The battery hovers below halfway, mocking her isolation.

'Great. Power's out again,' she mutters.

Throwing off the sheets, she slips into her dressing gown, grateful for the biomass central heating still holding back the chill. At the window, she tugs the curtains back, revealing a world still buried in white. The snow remains unbroken, save for the faint tramlines left by Murdoch Langley and Hugh Foster the night before.

At least the icicles are melting, rivulets streaking the panes in uneven lines.

'Finally thawing,' she murmurs.

Far in the east, a faint glow struggles against the night, which is reluctant to depart. Dawn is still a long way off. Her mouth is dry, the craving for coffee sharp. She wonders who else might be awake.

Moving quickly, she pulls on thick tights, layers them with snug black leggings, and tugs a heavy wool jumper over her head. Her hair goes into a no-nonsense ponytail, boots laced tight, jacket buttoned briskly.

Whatever's waiting, she won't face it cold.

Opening the door, she peers down the corridor. For a moment, she considers her phone's torch but decides against it. Her eyes adjust to the murky half-light as the old building creaks faintly around her.

She pauses.

*Is that freshly brewed coffee—or my imagination?*

Licking her lips, she starts for the stairs, careful to keep her steps soft.

Halfway down, she freezes.

A muffled shuffling noise drifts through the air, followed by the metallic scrape of a bolt sliding back.

Her pulse quickens.

'The front door?' she murmurs, straining to listen.

Then it comes.

A low, guttural wail, raw and feral, rises through the silence. It climbs, twisting into a piercing scream that slashes the stillness into ribbons.

---

Frank stares at his face in the mirror, the morning ritual as familiar as his own reflection. The wet razor glides down his cheek with a faint, gritty scrrrk—the sound of bristles surrendering to the paper-thin edge of tempered steel. He dips the blade into the sink, swirls it through the water, and taps it gently against the enamel. A man of habit, sixty years of small routines etched into his life, he starts on the right-hand side, adjacent with the bottom of his ear.

Lifting the razor, a few stray droplets slide down his fingers, cold against his skin. Repositioning the cutting edge with expert precision, he lines it up exactly where the last stroke ended. Tilting his head to tauten the skin, he begins the second downward sweep, slow and deliberate.

The bathroom is filled with small, familiar sounds: the gentle splash of water, the rhythmic rasp of the razor, the faint, steady snoring of Meera drifting in from the bedroom. Tranquillity finally visits, superseding the tumult of the past two days.

However... tranquillity is a rare, skittish bird, quick to take wing at the slightest disturbance.

A scream, so raw, so primal it claws at the edges of sanity, tears through the silence like a lightning strike splitting an ancient oak. It pierces the still air, ricocheting through the old walls of Kindlewood Hall, its staccato strains bouncing along corridors and penetrating bedrooms alike.

Frank's hand jerks. The razor slips.

A sharp nick slices his cheek, needle-like pain flashing as a tiny bead of crimson rises to the surface. It swells, then bursts, carving a thin red streak down his face. The droplet gathers on his chin before falling with a stark plip onto the edge of the sink.

'What in seven shades of holy shite has happened now?' he bellows, his voice cracking as the razor clatters into the sink. He snatches a towel, pressing it roughly to his face, smearing the shaving foam with streaks of blood across the white fabric.

He freezes, towel in hand, his ears straining. The scream lingers in his mind like a ghost, chilling and impossible to ignore. His heart pounds. The bathroom suddenly feeling too small, too still.

ELY NORTH

And then it comes again.
And again.
And again.

370

# 46

Prisha's legs move on instinct, carrying her swiftly down the stairs, her senses locked on the scream. As she nears the hallway, a cold draught seeps through the open front door, cutting through the warmth of the hotel. A figure stands hunched in the entrance, illuminated by the weak, shaky beam of a torch.

'What's going on?' she calls out, her voice sharp, commanding.

The figure doesn't respond. Instead, they slope down the stone steps into the snow, vanishing into the dim, pre-dawn gloom.

Above her, hurried footsteps creak across the floorboards—guests startled awake by the commotion.

Prisha reaches the door and peers outside, her torchlight sweeping the area. It lands on Penelope Langley stooped at the bottom of the steps, her face pale and streaked with tears.

'Inspector Kumar,' Penelope gasps, her voice ragged and uneven, 'something terrible has happened!'

Prisha's beam dips lower, slicing through the semi-darkness. It lands on a crumpled body, motionless against the snow.

'Who is it?' Prisha demands, already descending the steps two at a time.

Penelope's voice wavers, breaking into panicked sobs. 'It's Murdoch. He's so cold... freezing!'

Prisha wastes no time. Kneeling beside the body, she shines her torch over Murdoch Langley, who lies face down in the snow. Her gaze immediately lands on the dark stain on the back of his head. Quickly, she pulls on a pair of latex gloves and presses two fingers to his neck, searching for any sign of life.

*Nothing.*

'Mrs Langley, please step back,' Prisha orders, her tone sharp but controlled.

Penelope stumbles backward, clutching herself as she trembles. 'We can't leave him here! We must get him inside—there must be something we can do!' she cries, her voice breaking apart.

Prisha looks up, meeting Penelope's frantic gaze. She softens her tone but keeps it firm. 'I'm sorry, but it's too late.'

Something about the scene gnaws at her. Gripping the torch between her teeth, she leans closer, carefully turning Murdoch's face away from the snow. The beam illuminates a deep, jagged, semi-circular gash across his forehead, its edges brutal and raw. Angry swelling blooms outward, merging into a grotesque halo of purple bruising.

Prisha rises slowly, her eyes scanning the scene. Her torchlight flickers over the snow covered steps. She thinks back to Saturday afternoon when she first arrived—the smooth, well-worn stone, still visible beneath a thin dusting of snow.

'He must have slipped,' Penelope whispers, her voice faltering. She hugs herself tightly, fresh tears spilling down her cheeks.

Prisha's expression hardens as she locks her gaze on the body. She shakes her head.

'No,' she says, her voice low and deliberate. 'This wasn't an accident, Penelope. Your brother-in-law has been murdered.'

---

By the time Frank arrives on the scene, his shirt hastily buttoned, his belt hanging loose, fly undone and blood on his face, the scene has already unfolded in grim clarity. Prisha and Zac are standing next to the body, while a growing cluster of guests huddle near the entrance. All eyes are fixed on the motionless form of Murdoch Langley.

Maggie Thornton, sobbing uncontrollably, clings to Penelope Langley, who holds her tightly in a rare show of solidarity. Their usual barbs and simmering tensions stripped away, dissolved by the sheer horror of the moment. Now they appear more like sisters than adversaries, bound together by the shared trauma of the preceding days.

Frank stops short, at the edge of the group, his breath coming in rapid gasps as he takes in the sight below.

'What happened?' he asks, his voice deep, serious as he steps past the gawping onlookers.

Prisha glances up at him, her expression unreadable. 'Another one, Frank,' she says simply, gesturing at Murdoch's body. 'Looks like his head may have hit the steps when he fell. But there's too much blood for a slip and a fall—in my opinion. And he has contusions to his forehead.'

Frank's sharp eyes scan the scene, taking in the streak of crimson trailing down the steps.

'Who found him, like I need to ask?' he mutters, descending, his brow furrowed as he shoots a glance over his shoulder at Maggie Thornton and Penelope Langley.

Zac follows his gaze. 'Spot on—Penelope,' he whispers. 'That scream woke the dead.'

'Not quite,' Frank says, nodding towards the corpse.

Prisha sticks her hands into her jacket. 'Dead for a while, I'd say, Frank. Cold as ice.'

Behind him, Maggie Thornton lets out another choking sob, burying her face into Penelope's shoulder. Penelope, her face pale and tear-streaked, gently strokes Maggie's back. The tenderness in her movements seems almost alien. Gone is the cold, sharp-edged woman who had sniped and sneered at Maggie for years. In this moment, she is simply human. Her composure cracked like everyone else.

Prisha makes a mental note of the sudden change of demeanour of both women, as does Zac, as they exchange knowing glances.

The onlookers murmur amongst themselves, their voices low and urgent. Words like "murder" and "killed" drift through the air like confetti on a breeze.

Frank gestures for the group to move back inside. 'All right, that's enough. This is a crime scene. I want everyone back inside the hotel, the dining room, to be precise—right now. Zac, take charge of it. And start the questioning. I want to know everyone's movements from 9 pm last night until five minutes ago.'

'Boss.'

Frank spins around searching for his mercurial, yet annoying, pathologist. 'Where the hell's Bennet bloody Whipple when you need him?' he grizzles.

Like the rumble of distant thunder, a voice resonates from the hallway. 'You called, inspector.' Whipple's bulky frame plods into view.

# 47

Whipple rises slowly from his crouched position. With a deliberate tug, he adjusts his gloves and peers down at the body, his expression as inscrutable as ever. Finally, he clears his throat, his voice carrying the weight of grave authority as he addresses Frank and Prisha.

'Hmm... my initial observations, though constrained by the rudimentary tools at hand, paint a picture both grisly and deliberate.' He points to Langley's forehead. 'The victim's ordeal began with a blow to the frontal bone, above the glabella. The impact here was significant—stunning, but not immediately fatal. A strike to disable, rather than to kill.'

He gestures at the bloodied steps. 'A second strike followed, heavier, and delivered to the upper forehead near the scalp line. This blow was decisive, inducing unconsciousness or near-total incapacitation. As the victim fell backward, the occipital bone collided with the edge of the step, fracturing further and leaving this unmistakable blood pattern in the snow.'

Whipple pauses, raising an eyebrow as if daring his audience to follow. 'And yet, inspectors, the killer's work was not yet done. No, they ensured their grim handiwork with a final, devastating blow to the posterior cranium. This obliterated the structural integrity of the skull—cold-blooded and unequivocally fatal.' He straightens, his tone heavy with theatrical gravity. 'Of course, Inspector Finnegan, some conjecture is inherent in my hypothesis.'

Frank folds his arms, his face set. 'What about the murder weapon? What could do that kind of damage?'

Whipple steeples his fingers, considering the question with a flourish of dramatic contemplation. 'The possibilities, though numerous, are easily narrowed. A heavy wooden implement might suffice. A brick, while plausible, lacks the heft for such devastation. No, I lean towards a steel or iron object. Observe the arcs on the forehead—the weapon likely had a circular edge.'

Frank grimaces. 'Like a steel tube or a piece of scaffolding?'

Whipple considers the conjecture, sceptically. 'Perhaps, though I'd expect something larger in circumference than a scaffold pipe.'

Prisha scans the area to the side of the steps and spots an indentation in the snow.

'Wait a moment,' she murmurs, sliding her hand into the hollow. Her fingers close around a cold, solid object, its surface rough with frost. Carefully, she extricates it a red-painted item dulled by ice. She lifts it aloft. 'A fire extinguisher,' she announces grimly.

Whipple tilts his head, his gaze locking onto the weapon. 'Ah,' he intones, his voice tinged with satisfaction. 'A most fitting candidate, Inspector Kumar. Steel, weighted, and devastatingly efficient. This is no impromptu tool of rage—it is the calculated hand of premeditation.'

Frank exhales sharply, his breath clouding in the wintry air. 'Looks like we've found our murder weapon. Time of death, doctor?'

Whipple kneels beside the body again, his gloved hand skimming the air above the exposed skin. 'Estimating time of death in such conditions requires accounting for environmental factors, inspector. The ambient temperature was below freezing, which has significantly slowed physiological changes.'

He gently lifts the victim's arm, testing the resistance. 'Rigor mortis is present but incomplete, which, in these temperatures, suggests death occurred approximately eight to ten hours ago. Lividity is fixed, indicating the body hasn't been moved since shortly after death.'

He gestures towards the snow beneath the body. 'The snow has begun to compact and freeze around the torso, consistent with prolonged contact. Based on these factors, I'd estimate the time of death between 10 pm and midnight. For greater precision, a full post-mortem will be necessary.'

The security lights flicker to life as the mains power returns, flooding the hotel with brilliant, razor-sharp illumination. A crack splits the air, followed by the sharp smash of ice hitting the ground. Shards skitter across the entrance tiles, glittering like splintered glass under the harsh light.

Prisha's gaze drifts upward to the roofline, where a jagged gap breaks the row of icicles. She stares at the shards. Something shifts behind her eyes—a flicker of recognition, like a whisper just out of earshot. Peeling off her gloves, she darts up the steps, an urgency in her movements.

'Where are you going?' Frank calls after her, his frown deepening.

'I've had a thought,' she replies over her shoulder. 'Won't be long.'

Frank exchanges a puzzled glance with Whipple as they stand rooted to the spot, watching as Prisha vanishes into the hotel, leaving only questions in her wake.

# 48

Frank Finnegan is not the sort of man to rattle easily—not during an investigation, nor under pressure. But the murders at Kindlewood Hall are testing his mettle.

'They're taking the bloody piss!' he growls, striding into the back office, with Zac trailing behind. He drops into a chair, the springs groaning beneath him.

'I agree,' Zac replies, folding his arms. 'Shows a certain amount of arrogance, don't you think?'

Frank's jowls harden, his gaze fixed on the middle-distance. 'Not just arrogance. This is hubris. They think they're untouchable—running around, bumping people off with impunity, under our noses. They're making us look like proper Charlies.'

Zac peers into the fish tank and tries to lift the mood. 'Hey, where have all the fish gone, Frank?'

Frank purses his lips, unimpressed. 'Hilarious. Absolutely hilarious. More importantly, where's Prisha buggered off to this time? She's like the Scarlet Pimpernel. Bet she was a nightmare to keep track of as a kid.'

Zac glances at the doorway and spots her descending the stairs, her face set with determined purpose. 'Here she comes now.' He turns back to Frank, his grin widening. 'So, what did you do with the fish?'

'I scooped them out, wrapped them in a bit of newspaper, and chucked them on the fire last night before we locked up.'

'I'm sure they appreciated the warm send-off.'

'Okay, funny man, get your notes out and let's go through everyone's alibis. If it keeps up at this rate, there'll only be us three buggers and the killer left.'

'It'd make it easier to arrest our prime suspect.'

Prisha enters the room. 'Sorry about that.'

'Where've you been?' Frank snaps, swivelling around to face her.

'I went to get this,' she says, pulling a plastic bag from her pocket and holding it up. Inside is a long, glistening shard of ice. 'An icicle I broke off from outside Virgil Langley's window. Sharp, pointed, and conical—exactly as Whipple described the murder weapon. I figure that's why his bedroom window was open. And remember, Whipple noted water on Virgil's shirt. By the time the body was found, the icicle had melted. Pretty ingenious.'

Frank frowns, sceptical. 'Really? I'm not sure an icicle would have the structural integrity to fatally stab someone.'

'That was my first thought,' Prisha admits. 'But I ran it by Whipple upstairs. He said the eyeball is soft tissue, and the orbital pathway provides a direct route to the brain—also soft tissue. He reckons it's unusual, but not impossible. He can't rule it out until the full autopsy.'

Zac shakes his head in mock disgust. 'Like I said last night, Frank—smart-arsery.'

---

For the best part of an hour, the officers huddle together, dissecting every scrap of information: witness statements, alibis, evidence, the murder weapons, and every motive or opportunity among the guests and staff. But the deeper they dig, the murkier the picture becomes. The investigation feels like wading through quicksand—each promising lead slips away, every theory undone by maddening inconsistencies.

Just when they seem close to unmasking the killer—or killers—someone spots a flaw, a loose thread that unravels everything.

Frank leans back in the creaking office chair, his heavy frame testing its structural integrity. Dragging a hand over his face, he exhales, long and heavy.

'Okay,' he says, voice heavy with resignation. 'Let's start again with the certainties. The killer of Virgil Langley used the dumbwaiter in the kitchen to escape from the room. Possibly to gain access as well. Agreed?'

Prisha and Zac nod.

'Good. We suspect the murder weapon may have been an icicle, but that's immaterial for now. What we do know is there are only three people small enough to fit into that lift due to their height: Chef Antoine, Imogen Sato, and Edith Dubois. Realistically, only two of them. Agreed?'

Zac hesitates, wincing. 'What about Lucy Hargreaves or Maggie Thornton? Sure, they're a tad taller, but how do we know they're not... I don't know, contortionists?'

Frank snorts in disbelief. 'Maggie bloody Thornton? Don't talk daft. She's my age and built like a boiled egg. That lift has a weight limit, and Maggie would max it out just breathing near it.'

Zac grins despite himself. 'Okay, fine. Lucy, then?'

Frank exhales through his nose, reluctantly conceding. 'Aye. I suppose if she could fold herself in half, maybe. But for God's sake, Zac, we're trying to narrow this list down, not add names to it.'

Zac bristles. 'Would you rather I ignore the possibilities to make this easier for us?'

Frank's gaze drops to the threadbare carpet, chastened. 'No, lad. No, I wouldn't.' He sighs again, the fight leaving him. 'Fine. Add Lucy back onto the list. But don't forget—we ruled her out earlier because it was impossible for her to have killed Logan Fitch.'

He looks at the other two, his brow furrowed with frustration. 'So... where does that leave us?'

Zac scans the notepad, his frustration breaking through. 'Penelope Langley—maybe working with Chef Antoine or Lucy. Chef Antoine alone or teamed up with Hugh Foster. Imogen Sato, possibly with Eve Sinclair, or even Dr Quint. Or Hugh Foster with Antoine—or Lucy. Or what about Lucy and Eve Sinclair? Or how about...' Losing patience, he flings the notepad onto the desk with disgust. 'This is bloody hopeless. We're clutching at straws. It could be any combination of them.'

Frank exhales heavily, the weight of the case pressing down on him. 'Aye, too many variables. And without forensics, we're bloody hamstrung. No fingerprints, fibres, blood analysis, or DNA to back us up.' He retrieves the discarded notepad, scanning the names with a frown. 'But Murdoch Langley's death ties it together. Virgil—the owner. Murdoch—the incoming partner. Logan—the accountant. It's not a thrill kill, that's for certain. So, who stands to gain the most financially?'

'Penelope, obviously,' Zac replies, leaning back with a groan. 'But she already cashed in after Virgil died—insurance payout and all that. Why bother killing Logan and Murdoch too?'

Frank drags a hand across his jaw, his face set in hard lines of frustration. 'And you're forgetting the attempted poisoning of Penelope.'

'Unless she staged it herself to throw suspicion.'

Frank shakes his head. 'This is a bloody Chinese riddle if ever there was one,' he says wearily.

Zac raises an eyebrow. 'You cannae say that anymore, Frank,' he warns in his soft Scottish brogue.

Frank glances at him, bemused. 'Can't say what?'

'Chinese riddle.'

'And why the bloody hell not?'

'Because it's rooted in stereotypes, boss. Mysterious, inscrutable, and all that nonsense. A Western misinterpretation.'

Frank's face screws into a ball of annoyance. 'Oh, double bollocks with bells on to that.'

Zac holds his hands up in mock surrender. 'Don't shoot the messenger, boss. Just saving you from being cancelled.' He tries shooting Prisha a mischievous wink, but she's oblivious to his wind-up.

Frank snorts. 'Some days, I wish I was bloody cancelled.' He drums his fingers on the desk, frustration written across his face as his attention shifts to Prisha. She's there physically, but mentally miles away, eyes locked on the notes in front of her.

'What's up with you, Mary Poppins?' His voice cuts through the silence, gruff but curious. 'Normally we can't shut you up with your extravagant theories.'

Prisha looks up abruptly, as though dragged from deep waters. 'What? Oh, sorry.' She shoves the folder onto Zac, stands, and strides for the door.

'And where are you off to now?' Frank barks at her.

'The library, then the barn. I need to check something with one of the bodies—it'll only take ten minutes.'

Frank's face contorts as if in pain, eyes wide with disbelief. 'The library?'

'Yes. To refresh my memory about the ending of the book.'

'Which bloody book?'

'Agatha Christie—And Then There Were None. I can't quite recall the ending. Don't worry, I'll skim read.'

Frank throws his hands in the air, incredulous. 'Nay, lass, don't rush it. You go and put your feet up, run a bubble bath, order a bloody cocktail while you're at it. We've only got three murders on our hands.'

'Possibly four. And an attempted murder,' Zac mutters, arms folded.

Prisha grins but ignores them. 'Frank, when I get back, I need you to gather everyone in the dining room for five minutes. Keep them busy—give them an update, whatever.'

'Why?'

'Because after the barn, I need to check someone's bedroom.'

Zac straightens, frowning. 'That's a no-no, Prisha. Without a warrant, anything you find is inadmissible.'

She smirks, her tone light but pointed. 'Exigent circumstances, Zac. Look it up. Rarely used, but legitimate under the right conditions. Oh, and Zac, I want you to be Penelope's shadow. I believe her life is in imminent danger. Don't let her out of your sight.'

Before Zac can retort, his phone buzzes on the desk, then pings relentlessly. His eyes widen as he snatches it up, grinning as messages flood in.

'Yes!' he shouts, punching the air. 'Mobile reception's back!' In a flash, he's on his feet, thumb jabbing at his wife's photo as he lifts the phone to his ear.

Prisha's already gone, the door swinging shut behind her.

Frank watches her leave, then fishes his own phone from his pocket, his expression sharpening into hard determination.

'Right,' he mutters, scrolling through his contacts. 'Time to get some bloody action around here and call in the big guns.' He hits dial on Superintendent Anne Banks' number.

# 49

Prisha descends the stairs briskly, Zac keeping pace at her side.

Frank, standing in reception, ends his call and slips his phone into his pocket. 'All set to go?' he asks.

'Yes, all good,' Prisha replies.

'You definitely explained everything to Penelope, and she's happy to be present?'

'Yes. Twenty minutes ago. Although, I'm not sure she's happy, as such.' She glances towards the dining room, her stomach fluttering with nerves. 'Everyone here?'

Frank nods. 'Yep. Told them I've got three announcements to make. After that, it's all yours. Did you remind Whipple to keep his chemistry lesson brief?'

Prisha lets out a short laugh. 'I did. But what he considers brief is anyone's guess.' She takes a deep breath, steadying herself. 'Right. Let's do it.'

'How are you feeling?'

'Nervous. Don't know why. I feel like Miss Marple in an Agatha Christie play, ready to unmask the killer.' Her gaze shifts between Frank and Zac. 'You two know your parts?'

'Aye, can't wait,' Zac replies, a mischievous grin spreading across his face.

Prisha returns his smile. 'Come on, let's do it.'

Frank leads the way into the dining room, pushing through the double swing doors with an air of deliberate drama. The idle chatter and murmurs inside quickly subside. Nearly everyone is seated in an arc near the bay window, their faces tense with anticipation.

Mrs Whipple and Meera are seated off to the side, both masked and weary from their colds. Penelope Langley sits at one end, hands clasped tightly, her gaze fixed on the floor as though avoiding eye contact at all costs. Dr Whipple is beside her, followed by Lucy Hargreaves, Maggie Thornton, Hugh Foster, and Dr Quint, who is seated alongside his mother, Edith. Imogen Sato and Eve Sinclair round out the lineup. The only person standing is Chef Antoine, positioned near the kitchen entrance, his arms crossed.

Prisha leans towards Zac. 'Don't forget your prop when I give the nod.'

'I won't,' he murmurs.

Frank clears his throat, stepping to the centre of the room. 'Ladies and gentlemen, thank you for your time,' he begins, tugging his belt higher and tucking his shirt further into his trousers. Meera rolls her eyes with mild embarrassment.

'Hopefully, this will be the last time you hear me say those words—touch wood,' he adds, reaching out to tap the bar counter. 'As you all know, about forty minutes ago, mobile reception was restored, and I believe the Cloud thingy is back up and running somewhere,' he adds with a pained expression.

A few relieved murmurs ripple through the room as Prisha and Zac exchange a faint smirk.

'Now,' Frank continues, his voice steady, 'three pieces of news. First, the sobering one. In about thirty minutes, an RAF Chinook helicopter from RAF Leeming will land on the grounds to transport the deceased to the mortuary in Scarborough for post-mortem examinations.'

The room falls silent. A heavy unease settles like a weight over the group.

'Second,' Frank says, his tone lightening slightly, 'some good news. I've recently spoken with the council highways department. The A171 has been cleared, and a snowplough is already working on Kindlewood Lane. They estimate forty to sixty minutes to reach the turnoff. Add another twenty minutes to clear the driveway, and you'll all be able to leave safely.'

A loud cheer erupts, the tension breaking like a snapped wire.

Frank raises a hand. The cheer dies instantly as his expression darkens and his voice drops. 'I say all—but that's not strictly true.'

Puzzled glances dart across the group. The tension creeps back in, sharper this time, like a chill threading through the air.

'Right,' Frank concludes, his gaze sweeping the room, 'I'll hand you over to my colleague, DI Kumar, for the final announcement.'

Frank makes his way to the back of the room and stands with arms folded behind the guests as Prisha steps forward.

'We've all gone through a lot since arriving on Saturday for what was supposed to be a fun and relaxing end of the year theatrical murder mystery weekend. As it turned out, we've all endured a real murder mystery. As most of you will be departing shortly, I thought it only fitting to let you know, for your peace of mind, we have caught the killer—or should I say—killers.'

Lucy shuffles in her seat and shoots a glance over at Chef Antoine, who imperceptibly takes a backward step closer to the kitchen door.

Maggie Thornton drops her head and gazes at Hugh Foster, who returns her look, tight-lipped.

Imogen Sato swivels her eyes onto her new best friend, Eve Sinclair, their eyes visibly widening.

Dr Quint grips his mother's hand and gives it a gentle squeeze.

Penelope Langley remains unmoved, eyes obstinately fixed on the floor.

'It all began with the untimely death of Amy Holland on Saturday night. Naturally, her clothing was searched for identification, but when none was found, I checked her room, hoping for anything—a driver's licence, a credit card—anything to confirm her full name, and possibly an address.' She stares at Lucy Hargreaves, who is now sitting forward, resting her hands under the back of her thighs. 'Lucy, if you recall, you told me Amy arrived on **Friday**. She was making her way from the Midlands, where she owned a fashion boutique, and was heading to Scotland to spend Christmas with her parents.'

'That's correct,' Lucy replies, visibly tensing.

'And she'd stopped off at Kindlewood Hall to enjoy a few days walking before moving on to Scotland?'

'That's what she told me.'

Prisha's gaze drifts around the room from face to face. Even the unflappable Bennet Whipple appears intrigued.

'At the time, I was puzzled. There was no identification on her person or in her room—had someone taken advantage of her death to steal her purse? Possibly. But another oddity struck me. Her clothing.' She pauses, letting the room hang on the point. 'Not much to speak of. Underwear, a blouse, a jumper. No walking boots. No heavy winter coat. Nothing at all to suggest she'd planned a hiking holiday.'

She shifts her attention to Dr Quint, who raises an eyebrow at the sudden focus.

'I didn't have time to dwell on those thoughts,' Prisha continues, 'and after all, it was ruled a natural, albeit unfortunate, death—as you confirmed, Dr Quint.'

Dr Quint inclines his head with a small shrug. 'C'est correct. In my opinion,' he replies smoothly, slipping between French and English with ease.

Prisha nods, her voice hardening slightly. 'Later, Lucy also told me that not long after Amy Holland arrived, she had an altercation with the hotel cat, Podger.'

A low mutter escapes Penelope Langley, drawing a few nervous glances from the others.

'Podger scratched Amy on her left arm, all the way down to the back of her hand. Had she died from an infection caused by that scratch? It niggled at me, I'll admit, but the thought was soon eclipsed by the discovery of Virgil Langley's body.'

The room seems to contract around Prisha's words.

'Murdered in cold blood,' she continues, her voice measured. 'A classic locked room mystery. We may not know for certain how the killer entered the room, but we do know how they escaped—even with the door locked and chained.'

She pauses to gather her words. 'Fifteen years ago, Virgil Langley's bedroom was part of a larger deluxe suite, and as such, it had its own dumbwaiter so guests could order food and have it delivered via the mini-lift. Hidden behind a mirror in that room is the original hatch to access the dumbwaiter. It connects directly to the kitchen below. The confines are tight, but someone small, short, and flexible could squeeze into it.'

All eyes shift to Imogen Sato.

Imogen squirms in her seat, her face flushing a deep red as the scrutiny lands squarely on her.

Prisha lets the moment hang, then turns smoothly away, moving to the bar. She picks up a glass, pours herself some water, and takes a sip before engaging with her audience again.

'It's true—we discounted any connection between Amy Holland's death and Virgil Langley's murder, for obvious reasons. At the time, our focus was motive. Who would benefit most from Virgil Langley's death? It's fair to say many of you were prime suspects—particularly Penelope and Murdoch Langley, and to a lesser extent, Logan Fitch.'

Prisha pauses, her gaze scanning the room. 'But then Logan Fitch was killed. And shortly after that, there was the attempted murder of Penelope Langley—her drink poisoned. That changed our thinking.'

'What if there was no clear motive? What if this wasn't about money, revenge, or business disputes? What if someone was killing for the thrill of it? What if Amy Holland hadn't died of natural causes at all? What if she too, had been deliberately poisoned?'

She lets the possibility hang for a moment before turning her attention back to Penelope.

'Or perhaps, Penelope, you orchestrated the poisoning of your own drink to throw us off the scent? After all, when that drink finally arrived—with a slice of lemon—you suddenly retired to bed without touching a drop. Curious, isn't it?'

Penelope stiffens, but Prisha presses on.

'But then again, the poison was real. Would you have been so callous as to leave it there, untouched? A deadly cocktail which, I might add, I myself almost drank.'

Prisha shifts her gaze, sweeping the rest of the room. 'And what of that drink? It was prepared and delivered by Lucy, but then sent back by Penelope to have a slice of lemon added. Lucy, rushed off her feet, was dealing with the growing chaos at the bar: Dr Quint, Maggie Thornton,

Hugh Foster, Imogen, Eve, and Murdoch Langley were all in attendance.'

'Any one of you had the opportunity to drop a few grams of poison into that glass. And you, Dr Quint, you kindly offered to take the glass through to Penelope in the drawing room, since Lucy was so busy. But then, conveniently, you stopped in reception, placed the glass on a table, and claimed you'd forgotten your cognac.'

'And who should you bump into there, but Imogen Sato, who offered to deliver the glass to Penelope, herself. As you can see, it was a very tangled web.'

'The murder of Logan Fitch raised even more questions. The timeframe for his death was no more than a couple of minutes—barely a sliver of opportunity. Did the killer simply seize the moment, acting on impulse? Or was Logan Fitch already dead before Hugh Foster even left the billiard room?'

Hugh leaps to his feet, his chair scraping loudly against the floor. 'That insinuation is ridiculous! I know what you're implying, inspector—that I killed Logan. I'll bloody well sue you for this!' His voice booms as he points an accusing finger at her, his ruddy jowls quivering with rage.

'Take a seat, Mr Foster,' Frank says calmly, his tone cutting through the outburst.

Hugh reluctantly slides back into his chair, casting angry, hurt glances around the room.

Prisha fixes her eyes on Maggie Thornton. 'And you, Maggie—I couldn't help but notice your interaction with Penelope this morning, after Murdoch's body was discovered. Two women who can barely stand the sight of each other, locked in petty disputes for years, suddenly embracing like sisters.'

'That is an outrageous slander!' Maggie shrieks, her face flushed crimson.

Prisha remains composed, but slightly puzzled. 'I don't think I said anything slanderous.'

Maggie surges forward, her voice trembling with indignation. 'This weekend has been horrific! It put everything into perspective for me. When I saw Murdoch's body, I realised that nothing else matters—nothing but life itself. We should all try to be more forgiving, more understanding. Love, not hate.' She glares around the room, her tone defensive. 'Clearly, Penelope felt the same way.'

Prisha raises her hands, palms outward, as if to ward off the rising chaos. 'Calm down, Maggie. Calm down, Hugh.' Her voice is firm but steady, cutting through the tension. 'I can state categorically—neither of you are the killers.'

# 50

The febrile atmosphere hangs like a sliver of ice, brittle and ready to crack under the slightest weight. Guilty or innocent, everyone is on edge. It wouldn't be the first time the police had fallen prey to their own infallibility—blinkered to the point of detriment, to both the investigation and the innocent. A single-minded focus that bends evidence to fit preconceptions instead of the truth. A square block hammered into a round hole. History is littered with such cases. No doubt—the future too.

But Finnegan, Kumar, and Stoker aren't those kinds of officers. They don't plod through their tasks, chasing quotas, deflecting press scrutiny, or pandering to career-hungry superiors. They don't watch the clock for knock-off time, and they don't resent cancelling holidays when a case reaches its critical juncture.

And they never, ever cherry-pick the facts—what to believe, what to discard. To them, all evidence is born equal.

What they share is simpler, deeper, and unspoken—a commitment to justice.

They get the job done.

They capture the guilty.

And above all... they speak for those who can no longer speak for themselves.

Prisha continues, her voice steady.

'Another anomaly presented itself. The murder of Virgil Langley was meticulously planned—perfect timing, every detail considered. It was designed to baffle everyone, including the police. But the deaths of Logan Fitch and Murdoch Langley were entirely different. Logan was struck with a powerful blow to the head using two snooker balls stuffed inside a sock. Murdoch was bludgeoned repeatedly with the base of a fire extinguisher. These attacks were crude, opportunistic, and relied on sheer luck. No sign of careful planning.'

Letting the silence linger, her gaze drifts across the room.

'It left us wondering: were there two killers? Perhaps acting independently, unaware of each other... or working together?'

Prisha pauses. 'Then we found a vital clue. I was working in the back office, where Virgil Langley spent a lot of time. I opened a drawer and found something unexpected:

a newspaper clipping, carefully folded into quarters—a photograph of a man, but no article.'

She turns to Chef Antoine, whose pallor deepens.

'Chef Antoine, I showed you the photograph. You recognised the man, didn't you?'

'Oui, inspector,' he says, his voice barely above a whisper.

'Who was it?'

'It was une photographie of my good friend, Oliver McCloud.'

Prisha's expression doesn't shift. 'You met him in London a couple of years ago. You became friends, kept in touch, shared long emails about Kindlewood Hall—even private matters Penelope Langley confided in you. Is that not true?'

Antoine's shoulders slump as he stares at the floor. 'Oui, inspector.'

'Look around the room, Antoine. Do you see your good friend Oliver McCloud?'

Antoine hesitates, then shakes his head. 'No, madame. Of course not.'

Prisha turns to the group. 'Anyone here know or heard of an Oliver McCloud?'

A few murmured "no's" are accompanied by the faint shuffle of feet.

'I thought not.' Prisha's voice is calm but firm. Her gaze returns to Antoine. 'Because the man in the newspaper clipping is not Oliver McCloud.'

Antoine swallows hard, his jaw tightening.

'Tell me, Antoine,' she says, her tone almost conversational, 'I couldn't help but notice you wear Cuban-heeled boots.'

Antoine shifts, his face reddening. 'Oui, madame.'

'Unusual footwear for kitchen work, wouldn't you say? After all, professional kitchens require footwear that's practical—non-slip soles, water-resistant, cushioned for support.'

He mutters something inaudible.

'Do you mind taking them off for a moment?'

'Really?' His voice rises.

'Yes. Really.'

Reluctantly, Antoine removes the boots, his movements stiff.

'How tall are you, Antoine?'

'One hundred and sixty-two.'

'Centimetres?'

'Oui.'

'Which is roughly five feet four inches?'

He shrugs. 'I only know metric. You English are obsessed with imperial.' He pulls his boots back on, his chin lifting defensively.

Imogen speaks up, breaking the silence. 'Inspector, are you saying Chef Antoine is small enough to climb inside the dumbwaiter?'

Prisha turns to her. 'Yes, he's small enough, but then again... so are you.' Her gaze lingers for a moment.

'I'm sure some of you are fans of police dramas—books, TV, films. And I'm equally sure most of you have some idea of what powers the police do and don't have. We can't simply walk into someone's home or room and search it. To do that, we must convince a magistrate we have good reason. We're bound by strict guidelines. However, there's a caveat. Under exceptional circumstances, police can bypass the need for a warrant. Legally, this is known as exercising powers of entry without a warrant. For example, if we believe someone's life is in danger... or that crucial evidence may be destroyed.'

The room is deathly silent.

'Which brings me to earlier today and a search I conducted.' She reaches into her pocket and holds up a clear snap-lock bag. Inside is a black Explorer sock.

A murmur ripples across the group.

'An orphaned sock. The same brand as the one used in the murder Logan Fitch.'

She lets the image settle for a beat, then pulls out a second bag. This one contains a small glass vial.

'And this.'

Prisha turns slightly, her attention shifting. 'Over to you, Dr Whipple.'

Whipple rises unsteadily, towering over the group. Clearing his throat with the gravity of an actor about to deliver Hamlet's soliloquy, he begins.

'Whilst at Oxford, I had the distinct privilege of completing a Master's in Forensic Toxicology and Analytical Chemistry alongside my medical studies. The field of forensic toxicology, as some of you may be unaware, is the meticulous study of poisons and their effects—a cornerstone of pathology and criminal investigations.'

He pauses dramatically, casting a stern gaze across the audience.

'Though deprived of a proper laboratory, I have determined, with a confidence exceeding reasonable doubt, that the substance in question, contained within the vial, is potassium cyanide. My conclusion, though not laboratory-verified, was reached using a rudimentary yet effective field test—one even a moderately competent student of chemistry could perform.'

He raises a hand for emphasis. 'The test began with ferrous sulphate, conveniently sourced from my wife's iron supplement tablet—ferrous gluconate, to be precise. The tablet was crushed into a powder. A small amount of the suspected cyanide was dissolved in water in a Pyrex dish. To this solution, I added the ferrous sulphate and a few drops of malt vinegar.'

'The concoction was gently heated over a candle, yielding a distinctive dark blue precipitate—Prussian blue, the hallmark of cyanide's interaction with iron. Thus, while lacking full laboratory verification, I am thoroughly satisfied with the results.'

He sweeps the room with his gaze, clearly enjoying his moment.

'Potassium cyanide, when ingested, acts with lethal rapidity. A mere three grams—less than a teaspoon—can kill within minutes, suffocating the body from the inside. Victims experience dizziness, seizures, and a burning sensation in the chest before cardiac arrest.'

He glances at Frank. 'Inspector, you noted an almond-like odour in Mrs Langley's gin and tonic last night, did you not?'

'I did.'

'Curious,' Whipple muses. 'Only forty per cent of humans can detect the smell. A cruel irony of nature, wouldn't you say? Of course, I didn't immediately suspect cyanide. Many things can mimic an almond scent. It was only after Inspector Finnegan poured a drop into the—'

Frank coughs loudly, lurching forward. 'No need for every detail, Bennet. Let's not over-egg the pudding. We've established it's cyanide. If you'd care to resume your seat.'

Whipple scowls, his moment cut short.

'Hmm,' he growls, sinking back into his chair with exaggerated indignation.

Prisha offers a faint smile. 'Thank you, doctor.'

She re-focuses on the group, her tone sharpening. 'It was this discovery that made all the other pieces of the puzzle fall into place. There was one last thing we needed to do—inspect the barn, specifically the body of Amy Holland. Zac, if you would?'

All eyes follow Zac as he steps behind the bar, bending down. A moment later, he straightens, holding something aloft.

The room erupts in a collective gasp, louder than any that came before.

'A mannequin,' Zac announces, his tone flat but the words landing like a bomb. 'A shop dummy,' he continues, 'about five foot four.'

Hugh Foster, who's been silent since his outburst, finally finds his voice.

'You've bloody lost me, Inspector Kumar. What are you saying? What happened to Amy Holland's body? Don't tell me we've got a body-snatcher on the loose, as well as multiple murderers?'

'No, Hugh, we don't,' Prisha replies, her voice calm but firm. 'You see, Amy Holland—if that's even her real name—didn't die on Saturday night. In fact, she didn't die at all.'

'What?' Hugh sputters. 'I saw it with my own eyes. I even saw Inspector Finnegan, Dr Quint, and Sergeant Stoker carry the body to the barn.'

'That's true. They did,' Prisha acknowledges. 'But what they carried, wrapped in that sleeping bag, wasn't a dead body. Amy Holland was very much alive—playing dead. My guess is that as soon as they left the barn, she slipped out of the sleeping bag and replaced herself with the mannequin, which she must have hidden nearby beforehand. Maybe during a walk earlier that day.'

Hugh's not buying it. 'And where the hell did she get her hands on a bloody shop dummy?'

'It wouldn't have been too hard—she said she ran a fashion boutique.'

Hugh folds his arms, placated as Prisha continues.

'After she substituted the mannequin, I believe she sneaked back into the hotel and hid in a different room—one she wasn't booked under.'

Prisha strolls towards Imogen Sato and Eve Sinclair, her gaze fixed on them like a hawk sizing up its prey.

The room holds its breath.

'I said there were two killers,' she says softly.

Eve's eyes dart nervously, her voice trembling. 'This is ridiculous, inspector. You can't possibly accuse us of the murders!'

Imogen's face drains of colour, her hands fluttering like trapped birds. 'Inspector, I don't understand... We've done nothing wrong,' she implores.

Prisha tilts her head, her silence heavy with accusation. 'There are only three people in this room who could fit into the confines of the dumbwaiter—you, Miss Sato, Chef Antoine, and Madame Quint.' Her gaze briefly flickers down to the wizened old woman seated next to her son. 'And I hardly think Madame Quint, at her age or level of agility, could contort herself into such a tight space.'

Imogen stiffens, her jaw tightening. 'What are you saying?'

Prisha's voice is calm, deliberate. 'You mentioned you make your own jewellery?'

Imogen narrows her eyes, her tone defensive. 'What of it?'

'Potassium cyanide, although difficult to obtain these days, is accessible if you have the right contacts. And as you're no doubt aware, cyanide is often used in jewellery making—for cleaning metal, or in the gold plating process.'

Imogen's hand flies to Eve's arm, gripping it tightly. Her voice rises in panic. 'You're making a big mistake, inspector... a big mistake!'

The room buzzes with murmurs, tension rippling through the air like an electric current.

Prisha's lips curve into the faintest trace of a smile. 'You're right. I would be—if I were actually accusing you and Eve of the murders.'

Imogen's head jerks back, her breathing rapid, but before she can respond, Prisha suddenly spins on her heels.

Her eyes lock onto Edith Quint, whose frail form shrinks further into her chair as Prisha leans over. With a single, sharp motion, she snatches the pince-nez glasses from the old woman's nose.

'Mon dieu! What is the meaning of this, inspector?' she cries, her voice shrill with indignation.

Prisha half-smiles. 'You can drop the French accent, Amy,' she says, tugging off the chignon wig to reveal sleek, deep black hair pulled into a short, tight ponytail.

Gripping Amy's left arm firmly, Prisha licks her fingertip and rubs vigorously over the back of Amy's hand. The beige foundation smears away, revealing a long red scratch.

'Podger's handiwork, I assume?'

Dr Quint makes to move, but Frank's heavy hand clamps down on his shoulder.

'Not so fast, sunshine,' Frank growls, yanking the grey, slicked-back wig from Quint's head to reveal a shiny bald scalp beneath.

Chef Antoine leaps to his feet, pointing an accusatory finger. 'Oliver! Oliver McCloud—no, it cannot be!'

'You're correct, Antoine—it cannot be,' Prisha replies coldly.

Hugh Foster bolts upright, the pieces snapping into place. 'Ethan bloody Langley. It was you all along, you slippery, evil, conniving bastard!'

For the first time, Penelope speaks, her voice trembling with a mix of shock and fury. 'How could you, Ethan? After all, we did for you! We took you in, cherished you, gave you everything you ever wanted. And how did you repay us? By nearly ruining us financially, and concocting this grisly, evil plan in the hope you'd get it all. Your greed consumed you and turned your heart black.'

'Mother, you must believe me,' Ethan pleads desperately. 'It wasn't my idea. It was Amy's. She manipulated me.'

'You lying bastard!' Amy screams, leaping to her feet, pummelling Ethan with her fists. 'It was you who manipulated me, you liar!'

Prisha seizes Amy, restraining her, as Frank steps in, snapping handcuffs onto Ethan's wrists.

'Ethan Langley,' Frank says grimly, 'I am arresting you on suspicion of murdering Virgil Langley, Logan Fitch, and Murdoch Langley, and the attempted murder of Penelope Langley. You do not have to say anything, but it may harm your defence if you do not mention when questioned something which you later rely on in court. Anything you do say may be given in evidence.'

He glances at Prisha with a wry smile. 'I'll let you do the honours with Amy Holland.'

'My pleasure,' Prisha replies crisply. 'Amy Holland, I am arresting you on suspicion of murder...'

# 51

As the bunny-suited forensic team swarms the hotel, Frank, Prisha, and Zac watch on as Ethan Langley and Amy Holland are escorted towards the blue flashing lights of two marked police cars, their hands cuffed behind their backs.

Meera's voice calls out from the top of the stairs. 'Frank, can you help me with my suitcase, please?'

A flicker of resignation darts across his face, though he knows the moment was inevitable.

'Coming, my love,' he replies, raising his eyes to the heavens with a long-suffering sigh. 'No rest for the wicked,' he mutters as he walks off.

Zac frowns. 'Hang on, Prisha—you never did explain how you suspected Amy Holland faked her own death.'

Prisha's gaze drifts, as if her thoughts are miles away. 'It was the book—And Then There Were None. I mentioned it to you yesterday in the library.'

'Aye.'

'I couldn't sleep last night. My mind kept circling back to the story, but for the life of me, I couldn't remember who the killer was.' She pauses, her voice calm but deliberate. 'Then earlier today, it hit me—or at least, I thought it had. The killer faked their own death. Because if you're dead, you're no longer a suspect, are you? You're free to kill at will, because no one's looking your way.'

Zac raises an eyebrow, intrigued.

'But I wasn't completely sure,' Prisha admits. 'That's why I had to check the book earlier. I needed to know I was right. Also, during pre-dinner drinks on Saturday, I had a quick chat with Amy, and she mentioned her boutique and her homemade jewellery.'

'Hence the access to a mannequin and cyanide.'

'Correct.'

'And when did you realise Edith Quint was none other than Amy Holland in disguise?'

'I was never certain, but yesterday before we went into the dining room for Christmas dinner, Edith asked Frank how Virgil Langley had died.'

Zac nods. 'That's right.'

'She placed her hand on Frank's shoulder, and I noticed a long beige line on the back of her hand. At first, I thought it was skin discolouration that comes with age. Then, during dinner, I overheard a conversation between Dr Quint and

Whipple. Quint said he studied for his medical degree at Université Lumière Lyon. Whipple appeared puzzled, and remarked he was under the impression it specialised in arts and the humanities, not medicine. It would be very unlikely for Whipple to be wrong. Also, Penelope briefly mentioned Ethan was a smart lad at school and one of the things he excelled in was languages. And he also spent a number of years trying to break into acting. Hence the elaborate get-up and French accent.'

Zac frowns. 'No one likes a smarty pants, Prisha.'

She chuckles. 'Believe me, this was no Poirot like flash of brilliance, I had plenty of other theories, and suspects. All the clues were locked away in the back of my mind, but eventually they emerged into the light the more I prodded and poked at them.'

A beep-beep interrupts the conversation as a taxi pulls up outside. Dr Whipple and his wife approach.

'Inspector. Sergeant,' he says with a polite nod of acknowledgement. 'It has been a lamentable few days, but at last our vehicular transit has arrived to carry us back to the comfort of our abode.'

Prisha has been curious about Mrs Whipple's first name since they met. Despite numerous attempts to coax it out of Bennet, she's failed miserably every time. And since no one else seems to have the faintest idea what it is, the mystery continues to gnaw at her. Deciding to give it one last shot, she offers a warm smile towards Mrs Whipple.

'It's been nice to meet you...'

She leaves the pause hanging.

But there's only so long one can hesitate before finishing a sentence.

'... Mrs Whipple,' she says finally, defeated again.

'Likewise,' Mrs Whipple replies, sniffling into a tissue. 'Let's hope next time it's under more pleasant circumstances.'

'Come, wife,' Whipple says, gesturing towards the waiting taxi. 'Let us depart this place of harrowing misdeeds and make haste.'

Prisha and Zac watch them amble off, then turn to each other.

'Nice try,' Zac says with a grin.

'I'm going to make it my mission to find out her bloody first name.'

'Why didn't you just ask her?'

'That's rude. Anyway, that's not the point, is it? Any rational, reasonable person would introduce themselves fully.'

'You're talking about Bennet Whipple. He was hardly likely to attract a rational or reasonable person, was he? A pair of oddballs together.'

Frank huffs and puffs as he bumps the oversized suitcase down the stairs. 'I swear this thing's got heavier, Meera. You haven't pinched anything from the room, have you—like the bar fridge?'

'Oh, stop griping, old man. Did you start the car engine?'

'Yes. Should be nice and warm inside.'

'I hope you're feeling better soon, Meera,' Prisha says.

'Thanks, love. I'm over the worst. At least all the cooking's done and the larder's well stocked, so we can both relax for the next few days.'

Frank pulls the suitcase past them, heading to the door. 'Oh, by the way, if you haven't any plans for Boxing Day, why don't you pop in for a bite to eat in the afternoon? Maybe we can saunter down to the White House for a few drinks, then back to ours for nibbles. Partners included, of course.'

Prisha and Zac glance at each other.

'Aye, why not,' Zac says.

'That would be nice,' Prisha replies.

'Right, a Merry Christmas to you both.' Frank hesitates and lowers his voice. 'Hardly seems appropriate, does it, considering the carnage?'

Zac shrugs. 'No, it doesn't. But I guess life goes on—for the rest of us.'

Frank nods thoughtfully. 'Aye. I guess it does.' He turns to leave, then stops and throws them one last glance. 'Well done, by the way. Good teamwork. Oh, and next Christmas, no surprise end-of-year get-togethers, eh? Just let me enjoy my Christmas in peace. My perfect day is to lie on the couch watching The Dirty Dozen and chomping on pork pie and fruit cake.'

'The Dirty Dozen?' Prisha queries.

'Yes, it's... Never mind. Not sure it's your cup of tea. Right, I'll see you Boxing Day. Come along, Meera. The Shipping Forecast is about to start. Don't want to miss it.'

She shakes her head in annoyance. 'The things I have to put up with,' she mutters.

Prisha and Zac watch in mild amusement as Frank and Meera descend the stone steps of the entrance, bickering gently all the way to the car.

———— ◦◦◦ ————

Prisha has one last word with the lead forensic officer before joining Zac in the car park as he throws his bag into the boot of the car.

'I guess our Christmas leave has been cut short?' Zac says.

Prisha shakes her head. 'Not for you. I'll take the next two days off, then go into the station on Thursday and start writing up my report. No need for you to. You take the week off as planned. We won't get any results from forensics for weeks.'

'You're sure?' he replies, his mood lifting.

'Positive. You need time with Kelly and your boys. Adam will be busy on the farm, so I may as well make good use of my time.'

Zac jumps into his car and fires the engine, the window rolling down as he leans out. 'Right, I'll catch you later. We must do this again more often,' he shouts with a cheery cackle and a wave.

Prisha watches on as the car spins around and trundles away.

Thrusting her hands deeper into her overcoat pockets, she gazes up at the imposing Kindlewood Hall, the day prematurely dark as heavy clouds creep over the desolate countryside.

A few fluttering flakes of snow pirouette down, a deathly hush hanging in the air.

She notices Penelope Langley gazing out from the upstairs landing, her pale figure framed against the frosted windowpane as she fiddles with her pearl necklace. For a brief moment, their eyes meet, and in Penelope's weary expression, Prisha catches the unmistakable shadows of heartache and loneliness. The case is closed, the culprits arrested, and the mysteries solved—but for Penelope, the resolution has brought no peace. While the others will soon be surrounded by festive cheer—nibbles, laughter, warmth, and loved ones—Penelope seems destined to remain here, in this vast, echoing house, a prisoner of its memories and horrors.

Prisha lifts her hand as if to wave, but Penelope has already turned away, disappearing into the shadows of the Victorian manor.

For a moment, Prisha lingers, her chest tightening with a mix of pity and relief. There's nothing left for her here, nothing more to do. Kindlewood Hall, with all its secrets laid bare, feels like a chapter finally closed. But as she exhales into the chilly air, she can't help but feel the weight of what remains: a woman bereft, left behind, bound to this house and its ghosts.

She shakes off the thought and steps into her car. The engine hums to life, and as the vehicle crunches over the frozen gravel, Kindlewood Hall shrinks behind her, fading into the mist and the encroaching dark.

The strains of Fairytale of New York rumble from the car radio—bittersweet, full of hope and regret. Prisha grips the wheel a little tighter and drives on, the hotel disappearing in her rearview mirror.

# A Word From The Author

Thank you for reading **Murder Mystery,** book 9 in the DCI Finnegan series. A few things before you go. Book 10 in the series, **Wicker Girl,** is available on pre-order. Here's the link for e-readers. QR code below for paperback readers.

Book 10 – Wicker Girl: Everyone Knows... Smoking Kills Pre-order now

⸻ ◆ ⸻

Why not sign up to my entertaining newsletter where I write about all things crime—fact and fiction. It's packed with news, reviews, and my top ten Unsolved Mysteries, as well as new releases, and any discounts or promotions I'm running. I'll also send you a free copy of the prequel novella, **Aquaphobia – The Body In The River.** Here's the link.

### Sign up to Ely North Newsletter

Alternatively, you can follow me below on Facebook, Amazon or Bookbub to keep up to date with new releases. Links below.

 facebook.com/elynorthcrimefictionUK

 amazon.co.uk/Ely-North/e/B0B6F4JMFV

 bookbub.com/profile/ely-north?list=about

---

And lastly, if you enjoyed this book then a review (or rating) on Amazon, Goodreads, or a share on Facebook would be appreciated. Or even better, why not tell someone you know about the book? Word of mouth is still the best recommendation.

I thank you for giving me your time, a very precious and finite commodity.

All the best,

**Ely North**

Printed in Great Britain
by Amazon

56353998R00243